By the same author

Corrigan's Revenge
The Fourth of July
Showdown at Medicine Creek
The Sheriff of Fletcher County
Coyote Winter
Judgement at Red Rock
The Man Who Tamed Mallory
Ghost Town
The Smiling Gunman
The Marshal from Hell
The Legend of Injun Joe Brady
The Wolf River Outfit

A Hero of the West

A Hero of the West

J.D. KINCAID

ROBERT HALE · LONDON

First published in Great Britain 1999

ISBN 0 7090 6342 3

Robert Hale Limited
Clerkenwell House
Clerkenwell Green
London EC1R 0HT

Photoset in North Wales by
Derek Doyle & Associates, Mold, Flintshire.
Printed and bound in Great Britain by
WBC Book Manufacturers Limited, Bridgend.

One

The first warm winds of Spring were blowing through the State of Colorado. It was April 1880 and the news that Wild Willie Jamieson was dying had already spread like wildfire throughout the Old West.

Lieutenant General William George Jamieson was just forty-three years old, but looked a good ten to twenty years older. A man of medium height and build, with thinning, grey-flecked hair and a grey moustache, Jamieson was undoubtedly a very sick man. He was rarely without pain and it showed in his pale, sombre features. However, his jaw remained strong and his mouth firm. He bore himself well and faced the world with courage and with dignity. He did not complain, and a hint of humour still lurked in the depths of his wise grey eyes. Since he was now a deal thinner than once he had been, Jamieson's uniform fitted him none too well. Nevertheless, he wore it with the same zealous pride that had helped raise him to his present, exalted rank.

He reflected that he was no longer the Wild Willie Jamieson of his younger years. He was now at the top of his profession, a staid, respectable member of the establishment. Upon reaching the rank of lieutenant general, Jamieson had been assigned a desk at Army Headquarters in Washington, and it was there that, two years earlier, he had suffered his first heart attack. A severe form of heart disease had been diagnosed, but he had insisted on remaining in post. There had been four more attacks, each weakening him further. The last had occurred three months ago, when he was told that the next was likely to prove fatal. By this time he was too ill and too weak to perform his duties. Consequently, he came to a decision.

Jamieson decided to return to his home town to die. And, so, when eventually, after several weeks' recuperation, he was considered fit to travel, he had made the long journey westward to the State of Colorado, reaching the small cattle town of Harrison Creek, in Larch County, just as the snows began to melt off the mountains of the Front Range. Indeed, from the window of his room, he could observe the snow-covered top of Pike's Peak, the highest mountain in the range. He wondered bleakly whether he would live long enough to see summer come and all but the very pinnacle of Pike's Peak be freed from its white blanket.

The general had arrived back in his home town late on the previous afternoon and had taken a room in Sarah Yeates' rooming-house, at the quiet end of Main Street, well away from the saloons, livery stables and stage line depot. He had spent a reasonably comfortable night and, after washing and dressing, had partaken of a little breakfast, fetched to his room by his hostess. She had left him with the local newspaper, the *Larch County Recorder.* He was thumbing idly through its pages when there came a knock upon his door. He promptly removed the spectacles from his nose, slipped them into the breast pocket of his uniform jacket and cried out, 'Enter!'

Sarah Yeates popped her head round the door. She was anxious to please the general, for she hoped that he would stay. As a young widow with a twelve-year-old daughter to support, she needed as many paying guests as the house had room for. At present, she had six, though there was room for a further four.

Sarah was thirty-four years old, blackhaired, petite and very pretty, with rosy cheeks and large, innocent blue eyes. Dressed in a neat blue cotton dress, she presented a charming picture. And, until twelve months earlier, she had led a charming life. She had been married to the local schoolmaster and blessed with a lovely young daughter, Sally. But then tragedy had struck. Her husband had been killed in a freak riding accident, and she had been left to fend for both herself and Sally. With the help of a bank loan, she had purchased her present abode and turned it into a rooming-house. And, so far, she was just about managing to make ends meet.

'Yes, my dear?' enquired Jamieson.

'You have a visitor, General,' replied Sarah nervously.

'A visitor?'

'Yes; Doc Wharton. If you don't want to be disturbed ...?'

'No, that's OK. Do show him in, Mrs Yeates.'

'Yessir. This way, Doc.'

'Thank you.'

Doc Wharton strode confidently into the room. He was a rotund, redfaced, bespectacled man of about fifty and he sported a brown, city-style, three-piece suit. When he removed his Derby hat, it was to reveal a bald pate fringed by a semi-circle of short-cut grey hair. He smiled cheerfully at the general.

'I received a telegraph message this mornin',' he explained. 'From the Surgeon-General in Washington, no less. He asked that I attend upon you, General.'

'You are, I take it, the only doctor in town?' said Jamieson.

'Yessir, that I am. Doctor Nicholas Wharton at yore service.'

Doc Wharton extended his arm and the two men shook hands.

'The Surgeon-General explained my situation, I suppose?' enquired Jamieson.

'He didn't have to,' replied Doc Wharton. 'Hell, General, yo're a legend! News that you are dyin' has spread right across the entire West, believe me.'

'So, why should I need a doctor?' asked Jamieson, adding drily, 'A mortician, mebbe, but . . . .'

'Yo're in some pain?'

'Some.'

'Wa'al, perhaps I can ease it a little. I should certainly like to try.'

The general shrugged his shoulders. He realized that, as he deteriorated, he was going to need medical attention.

'OK, Doc,' he said.

Doc Wharton smiled and turned to Sarah.

'If you will excuse us, Mrs Yeates?' he said. 'I should like to examine the general.'

'Of course,' said Sarah, and she immediately withdrew, closing the door behind her.

Doc Wharton then asked Jamieson to remove his jacket and proceeded to give him a very thorough examination indeed. At its completion, while he was buttoning up the uniform, the general concluded that Wharton knew his business, that he was in good hands. Not that that would save him from his fate, though, he mused wryly.

'Wa'al, Doc, what's yore opinion?' he asked.

Doc Wharton grimaced.

'I'm sorry to say, General,' he sighed, 'that I concur with my colleagues in Washington. Yore next heart attack is almost certain to be yore last.'

'Can you tell me when I'm likely to suffer it?' asked Jamieson.

'No, I cannot. It could be in a few days, or in a few weeks, or even in a few months from now.'

'What would be yore prediction?'

'A few weeks, I guess. But I cain't be sure.'

'I see.'

'So, regardin' the pain . . . ?'

'I can handle it.'

'But, General, a little morphine might help dull it.'

'It would also dull me, Doc.'

'I suppose. However . . . .'

'When I find the pain too much, I'll let you know.'

'As you wish. If you need me at any time, jest send for me.'

'I will. Thanks, Doc.'

'I'll look in from time to time, though, if that's OK?'

'Yes, that's OK, Doc.'

'Good mornin', then, General.'

'Good mornin'.'

As the door closed behind Doc Wharton, Jamieson smiled. He did not doubt that the doctor meant well, but he rather suspected that Wharton's concern for his well-being was not entirely free from self-interest. Should the good doctor wish in the near future to exchange his present practice for a rather more lucrative one in either San Francisco or some East Coast city, then having been general practitioner to the legendary Wild Willie Jamieson would certainly do his chances no harm whatever.

While these thoughts were still flitting through the general's mind, there was yet another tap upon the door. Again Jamieson shouted the word, 'Enter', and Sarah reappeared in the doorway.

Smiling nervously, she asked, 'Is there anythin' I can git you, General?'

Jamieson shook his head.

'No, my dear, I don't think so,' he said.

'I hope that you are quite comfortable here?'

'Perfectly, thank you.'

'I am sure that you are used to rather grander accommodation than I can offer. But if ... if at any time you feel you'd like to escape the confines of this room, you are more than welcome to ... to come to my sitting-room.'

'That's very kind of you, Mrs Yeates, and I may well take advantage of yore offer. For the sake of a li'l company, an' for no other reason.'

'You don't miss yore quarters back in Washington?'

'Not a bit. This here is clean an' comfortable ... an' real peaceful. That's enough for me, Mrs Yeates. If I'd wanted some place swanky an' expensive, I guess I'd have chosen to stay at the Prince Albert Hotel.'

'Wa'al, it's sure got a fine reputation, an' it's owned by the mayor. But I'm glad you have chosen to stay here,' said Sarah. 'An' not just for the money,' she added quickly.

'You need the money, though?' said Jamieson.

'Yes.'

'Tell me about yoreself, how it is you come to be runnin' a roomin'-house here in Harrison Creek?'

Sarah entered the room and slowly, rather hesitantly, began to tell the general her story. It was quite comforting, she found, to relate her tale to this grey-haired, fatherly-looking stranger, this man in whom initially she had stood in such awe. As she spoke, she almost forgot that he was not only a high-ranking officer in the US Army, but also arguably the most famous Indian-fighter in the West.

Sarah had barely completed her sad narrative when her young daughter pushed open the half-closed door and dashed into the room. Sally, black-haired and wide-eyed, a tiny version of her mother, cried excitedly, 'Mommy! Mommy! The mayor has come to visit the general!'

'My! My!' smiled Jamieson. 'This certainly is a mornin' for visitors! An' me only jest arrived in town!'

As he spoke, the mayor stepped briskly into the room.

Jim Bannon was a year younger than the general, although an impartial observer would have maintained that there was, at the very least, a decade between the two men. Tall and darkly handsome, with strong, regular features, intelligent brown eyes and a flashing smile, Bannon exuded wealth and power. A snappy and expensive dresser, he wore a black Derby hat, knee-length black coat, light grey trousers and highly polished black boots. Beneath the coat, he had a bootlace tie, a fresh white linen shirt and green brocade vest. And he carried a long-barrelled, .30 calibre Colt revolver in a shoulder-rig, hidden beneath the coat. This gun was there in case of an emergency, although Bannon, who was no gunman, hoped never to have to use it. He employed others to do the shooting for him. His own special weapons were his keen wits, his air of affability and general bonhomie, and an extremely astute business brain.

'I hope I don't intrude, General?' he cried, as the two men shook hands.

'Not at all, Mr … er …?' said Jamieson politely.

'Bannon. Jim Bannon. Jest callin' to pay my respects.'

'That's most civil of you.'

'The least I could do. Holy cow, yo're, without question, the most famous son Harrison Creek has ever produced!'

'Wa'al, the town hasn't been in existence all that long!'

'Long enough, General. Long enough.' Bannon

gave the old soldier the full benefit of his flashing smile and continued, 'It is with a real feelin' of pride an' gratitude that the good folks of Harrison Creek welcome you home, sir!'

'Indeed?'

'Yessir. We're mighty proud that you were born here, an' grateful that you thought fit to return to us, in order to spend yore final days back in the place where you grew up an' where you belong.'

'Thank you, Mr Bannon.'

'No, thank you, General! It's men like you who have been responsible for pushin' back the frontiers an' bringin' civilisation to the West, an' for defendin' us white settlers from the murderous onslaughts of those infernal red savages, the Plains Injuns.'

Jamieson reflected that he had once thought of the Indians in exactly those terms. But no more.

'I did my duty,' he replied quietly.

'You did more 'n yore duty,' said Bannon. 'An' I can tell yuh that a grateful nation will mourn yore passin'. Nor will it go unremarked here in Harrison Creek. This town, an' indeed Larch County, is gonna have the biggest, most impressive funeral ever. Why, the governor will be here, an' Senator McBain, an' . . . .'

Jamieson raised a weary hand.

'Enough, Mr Bannon,' he said. 'I don't think I particularly want to hear about the funeral arrangements.'

'I apologize, General. I'll say no more on the subject. Tactless of me,' said Bannon.

'It ain't the prospect of death that bothers me,' remarked the old soldier. 'It's all this goddam fuss. I jest want a little peace an' quiet to think back on my life. That's why you won't find Harrison Creek besieged with newspapermen. I asked the editors back East to hold fire until after I died, an' they promised me they would do that. So, y'see, there's unlikely to be much action around here for a while at least.'

'That's fine by me, General,' declared Bannon. 'An' you may depend upon it that I, as mayor of Harrison Creek, will do my darnedest to ensure that you are in no way disturbed during yore remainin' days back here in yore home town. I hope, though, that I may call upon you from time to time, jest to chew the fat?'

'Certainly, Mr Bannon. I can always use a li'l company.' Jamieson smiled and continued, 'I left Harrison Creek at seventeen to join the Army, an' I don't suppose there are many folks left who I knew in my childhood. You, for example, are not a native of this town.'

'No, General, I arrived here 'bout five years ago.'

'Indeed? Then you have done well to become mayor in so short a period.'

'I guess so. I've always been somethin' of a gamblin' man, an' I won me enough at poker to buy the Prince Albert Hotel. That was jest the beginnin'. Over my five years here I've acquired several other properties an' businesses, which has made me a pretty influential figure both in the town an' in the county. Which is how I got elected mayor.' Bannon beamed at the general. His story, as far as it went, was true. But he had omitted to state that the gambling winnings alone would not have bought him the hotel. These had needs been supplemented by a large mortgage. 'An' that, General, is the long an' the short of it,' he concluded.

'You have done well,' repeated Jamieson.

'An' now I think you should leave us, Mr Bannon,' interjected Sarah.

The mayor turned in surprise to face the young woman.

'I beg yore pardon?'

'The General looks rather tired. He has had a long, wearisome journey to git here an', as you know, he is a sick man. I would suggest, therefore, that you curtail your visit. You can always call again in a few days' time, when he has had time to recover.'

'Yes; Mrs Yeates is quite right, Mr Bannon, I am indeed a mite weary,' confessed Jamieson.

Bannon shrugged his shoulders, flashed his much practised smile, and said, 'In that case, I shall go an' let you rest. But, should you require anythin', anythin' at all, be sure to let me know. Good mornin', then, General; Mrs Yeates.'

He bowed politely to Sarah and, skirting young Sally, who remained standing in the doorway, he left the general's room. As the mayor disappeared from view, Jamieson sank back in the armchair near the window and slowly closed his eyes. Sarah put a finger to her lips and silently led Sally outside. Then she closed the door ever so gently behind her.

Jim Bannon, meantime, was marching briskly down Main Street in the direction of the Foaming Jug, one of the two saloons he owned. Besides these and the Prince Albert Hotel, he had acquired, in the space of a mere five years, the town's livery stables and two of its four stores. And elsewhere in Larch County he had procured several other properties. The mayor of Harrison Creek was by now a very rich man indeed.

It was late morning and, consequently, there were few customers in the Foaming Jug. Bannon pushed his way through the batwing doors and signalled to the five men seated at a corner table playing poker, to follow him into his private office at the rear of the saloon. They promptly laid down their cards, rose and set off after him. These five were his enforcers, men employed by Bannon to extract tribute from ranchers, farmers, homesteaders, hoteliers, saloon-keepers and storekeepers across the length and breadth of Larch County.

Bannon sat down behind his large mahogany desk and lit up a cigar. Then, once all five had joined him and the last of the party had closed the office door behind him, he glanced up. He liked what he saw. He reckoned he had chosen his enforcers well.

His first recruit had been Painless Peachum, a tough, teak-hard, cold-eyed, hatchet-faced man in his mid-thirties. A livid white scar, received in a knife-fight, decorated his face from immediately beneath his right eye to the corner of his jaw, adding to the gunslinger's menacing aspect. Peachum sported a grey shirt, black leather vest, black pants and grey Stetson, and he carried a Remington revolver tied down on his right thigh. He was a one-time dentist for whom the nickname, 'Painless', was not particularly apt. Several years earlier, Peachum had killed a man in Utah, during the course of a quarrel over a woman. Unfortunately, he had also badly wounded a peace officer and, so, had been forced to flee the state. Since then he had ceased to practise as a dentist and, instead, had acted as a hired gun in various states across the West.

Three years ago, Bannon had been struggling to meet his mortgage commitments and had hit upon the idea of extracting tribute from those in the county who could afford to pay. He had, therefore, recruited Peachum and asked him to put together a band of gunslingers who would be prepared to do his, Bannon's bidding. Peachum had recruited the other four gunmen and Bannon had sent them out to visit a few selected victims. These visits had proved most successful and the list of victims had subsequently been increased. Now there was not one successful businessman in Larch County who did not hand over a good percentage of his profits to the mayor of Harrison Creek. Bannon had long since paid off his mortgage and by now had no money worries whatsoever. He no longer needed to practise extortion, yet could not stop. He had become addicted to both the power and the riches which this activity engendered.

As the leader of the enforcers, Painless Peachum was ideal, for he actually enjoyed frightening people. He was quite ruthless, and there was no doubting that he would, if need be, happily carry out his threats. The others consisted of the Dixon brothers, their cousin, Butch Mabey, and a lone gunslinger known only as Raven.

Ike and Arnie Dixon and their cousin were wanted in several states for armed robbery and murder. The brothers, who were in their mid-twenties, had turned outlaw in their late teens and Butch Mabey, who was a mere nineteen-years-old, had joined them at sixteen. Both Dixons were of medium height, thickset and blond-haired, while Mabey was a rather podgy, pimply-faced youth with cruel, close-set eyes. All three were dressed in check shirts, brown vests, levis and brown leather boots. But, where the brothers wore brown Stetsons, their cousin favoured a grey one. They, each of them, carried a Colt Peacemaker.

The fifth of Bannon's enforcers, Raven, was a tall, rake-thin man of some thirty summers. He invariably wore a deadpan expression, his pale blue eyes were as cold and hard as chips of ice, his thin-lipped mouth resembled a rat-trap, and he dressed entirely in black: shirt, vest, pants, boots and low-crowned, wide-brimmed Stetson. His choice of weapon was a pearl-handled, forty-five calibre British Tranter, and he carried a pair.

Raven rarely spoke. He was a psychopath who gained real pleasure from killing people. So far, he had accounted for a score or more victims. Even Peachum and his fellow enforcers regarded the man in black with a degree of trepidation.

Jim Bannon smiled affably at the gunslingers and asked Peachum for his latest report.

'Wa'al, boss,' said Peachum, 'we made our usual monthly calls on all three ranches.'

'An'?' said Bannon.

'Dan Walters of the Big Mesquite an' Curly Johnson of the Lazy J both paid up.' Peachum tossed two fat wads of ten-dollar bills onto the mahogany desk. 'In full,' he added, with a wicked grin.

'What about Ned Brown?' enquired the mayor.

'He refused to pay.'

'What?'

'Said he wasn't gonna hand over no more tribute.'

Bannon frowned. Ned Brown, who owned the Double B spread, had proved difficult from the start.

However, the fatal shooting of his top hand and the loss of several head of cattle had eventually persuaded him that he needed Bannon's 'protection'. Up until now, he had paid up regularly, albeit reluctantly. Bannon hoped that the rancher was not going to be obstinate.

'Jerry Pine didn't pay up either,' added Ike Dixon.

'No?'

'No, boss. Said his business hadn't been doin' so good lately, an' he needed more time,' explained Peachum.

Bannon swore.

'We cain't have this,' he rasped. 'Two of the bastards refusin' to pay!'

'Jerry didn't exactly refuse. He jest . . . .' began Peachum.

'Didn't pay.' Bannon smiled thinly. 'I cain't accept no excuses.'

'No, boss?'

'No, Painless. If I let Jerry have extra time to pay, others'll expect the same. It'll be taken as a sign of weakness.'

'So, what do we do, boss?'

'You an' Raven had best call again. Make sure there ain't no witnesses an' then rough him up a li'l. But hit him in the belly an' the ribs. Don't mark his face. I don't want no bruises showin'.'

'OK, boss.'

'An' don't leave until he does pay.' Bannon turned

to the pimply-faced Butch Mabey and snapped, 'You go visit Sheriff Lloyd an' warn him to keep well away from Jerry's store. We don't want him blunderin' in there, now do we, boys?'

The others laughed. Sheriff Dave Lloyd was paid by Bannon to turn a blind eye. He did not, himself, take part in any nefarious activities. He simply chose to pretend that they did not happen. And, so, Jerry Pine's complaints, if he were foolish enough to make any, would receive short shrift from the sheriff.

'What about Ned Brown?' enquired Arnie Dixon.

'Yeah. That sonofabitch could cause us a whole heap of trouble,' snarled Peachum. 'Jest give the word an' me an' the boys'll take out both him an' his men.'

Again Bannon frowned. It was true that the rancher's hands would be no match for his enforcers in a gun-battle. Yet he did not want it to come to that. It might be necessary to eliminate Ned Brown. However, this would need to be done discreetly, for, while Bannon might own the local sheriff, he did not own the US marshals in Denver. And Ned Brown was one of Colorado's most prominent citizens.

'I'll give the matter some thought,' he said. 'Now, you fellers go settle with Jerry Pine.'

'Sure thing, boss.'

Painless Peachum turned and, followed by the other four, promptly left the mayor's office. Then, while the Dixon brothers returned to the corner table, Peachum and Raven headed for Jerry Pine's general store and Butch Mabey set off towards the law office.

Jim Bannon, meantime, fetched a glass and a bottle of bourbon from the cabinet behind him. Not for the mayor the red eye which he sold over the counter at the Foaming Jug. Bannon poured himself a generous measure of the whiskey and settled down to consider the problem of the recalcitrant rancher, Ned Brown.

TWO

Lieutenant General Jamieson sat quietly with his eyes closed. But he did not fall asleep. Instead, he reflected upon times past, going back fifteen years to 1865 and the incident which had earned him the nickname, 'Wild Willie'.

It had been the same time of year as the present, namely late Spring. He was then a twenty-eight-year-old Army captain, newly married and on his way to Fort Anderson in the State of Montana.

The weather was excellent. There was a clear blue sky, warm sunshine and a light breeze, and Jamieson was in the best of spirits. He was accompanied by two women: the wife of the fort's second-in-command, Major Dunn, and his, Jamieson's young wife, Louise. The latter had asked for and received permission from the commander, Colonel Proudfoot, to come and reside with her husband at Fort Anderson. The Colonel's wife had Mrs Dunn for company and Proudfoot was keen that his twenty-year-old daughter, Julie, should also enjoy some female company, but of her own age.

Louise was, in fact, two years Julie's senior, a tall, slender, dark-eyed and black-haired girl of considerable beauty. In contrast, Hannah Dunn was short, plump, ginger-haired, fortyish and rather plain. She was returning from a visit to her sister at Denton, some one hundred and fifty miles to the north.

The two ladies were travelling in a carriage driven by Corporal Harry Eales, a big, gangling, blond-haired twenty-one-year-old, with frank, boyish good looks and a perpetual smile. Riding ahead were Jamieson and two others, while bringing up the rear was an escort of half-a-dozen troopers.

Jamieson's two companions were Jack Stone and Fletcher McBain.

Stone was a tall, broadshouldered, rawboned Kentuckian who was intending to take up the post of Army scout at the fort. He was six-foot two-inches in his stocking feet and nigh on two hundred pounds of muscle and bone. A cheroot protruded from between his lips, and he wore a red kerchief round his strong, thick neck. A grey shirt, faded denim pants over unspurred boots, a knee-length buckskin jacket and a grey Stetson completed his apparel. He rode a bay gelding, carried a Winchester in his saddleboot and a Frontier Model Colt tied down on his right thigh. Although only twenty years of age, he had known more than his fair share of tragedy and suffering, and his tough-looking, square-cut face had lost its youthful bloom. His pale blue eyes glinted as he scanned the distant horizon.

Fletcher McBain was a quite different kettle of fish, a man on his way up in the world. A thirty-five-year-old lawyer, McBain was en route from the prairie town of Lewistown to Billings, where he hoped to catch an eastbound train. His ultimate destination was Washington, there to take up a position in one of the capital's leading law practices. A smart, ambitious man, he was keen to rub shoulders with the country's power-brokers, for he intended, in due time, to move from the law to a career in politics.

Intelligent grey eyes peered out from a rather sharp-featured face, softened a little by the lawyer's black drooping moustache and goatee. McBain, a lean man of medium height, rode a small black mare and sported an expensive grey city-style three-piece suit and Derby hat. The suit and the hat and McBain's soft black leather shoes were, however, somewhat dusty by this stage in the journey. And, since he was unaccustomed to such a long ride, his buttocks were very sore indeed.

'How much further 'fore we stop?' he enquired wearily.

It was by now late afternoon and the plan was to break their journey at Beaver Wells, a staging-post about thirty miles north of Fort Anderson and fifty miles north of Billings.

'We should reach Beaver Wells any time now,' replied Jamieson.

'Wa'al, I sure hope we do, for I confess I'm bone-weary,' groaned McBain.

The young captain smiled. 'Civilians!' he thought contemptuously. Aloud, he said, 'I reckon we've only about another coupla miles to ride an' we'll be there. Ain't that right, Mr Stone?'

'That's right,' affirmed the taciturn Kentuckian.

The trail ahead wound its way through some low-crowned hills and shortly afterwards, upon rounding a bend, they found themselves riding down into a pleasant grassy hollow, at the rear of which was a small wood. Huddled together in front of the wood were stables, a log cabin and a corral. And, standing before the open door of the cabin, was a stagecoach and four horses. Smoke curled up lazily into the sky from the cabin's single chimney. A welcome sight.

With Jamieson leading, the party cantered down into the hollow and drew up next to the stagecoach. However, nobody appeared at the cabin door to greet them.

'Hullo, anyone at home?' cried the young captain.

There was no response. Jamieson glanced anxiously at the Army scout.

'Strange!' he commented.

'Yeah,' said Jack Stone, and he slowly dismounted.

The Kentuckian drew his revolver, cocked it and cautiously approached the cabin. Then he dived quickly inside, dropped into a crouch and swept the cabin with his gun. The room into which Stone had stepped was a simple bar-room, with a fireplace and four tables at its far end. And, with the exception of Stone, there was not a living soul inside. But there were several dead people, seven men altogether, all of whom had been scalped.

Stone gasped and straightened up. Then, as he turned, intending to go and tell the others of his awful discovery, a series of bloodcurdling screams rent the air. He hurried out of the cabin to see a band of thirty or so Crow Indians swooping down from the hills.

They were hostiles, braves who had sworn to drive the white man from their native lands. They had refused to recognize the ignominious peace treaty signed by their elders. Freedom to roam the ancestral hunting-grounds, not confinement to some reservation, was what they craved. And they were prepared to fight to the death to attain this freedom.

At their head rode Red Lynx, a twenty-one-year-old buck whose natural courage and ferocity in battle had marked him out as their leader. He was a small, sturdy Crow, mounted upon a coal-black racing pony. Fierce black eyes flashed furiously; and these, together with a large hooked nose, grim-set jaw and mouth and black war-paint, combined to give the Indian's dark face an almost Satanic look. Long black hair hung down from beneath a head-dress of eagle's feathers, and he wore buckskins decorated with tiny bells that jangled as he rode. He was well-armed, carrying a Winchester rifle, a tomahawk and a knife designed for stabbing.

Indeed, the entire war-party was well-armed, for most, like Red Lynx, had Winchesters, only a handful of the Crows having to rely upon bows and arrows for fire-power. And several Indians carried either tomahawks or lances. Whooping and hollering, they charged down towards Captain Jamieson and his small company.

Jamieson and the half-dozen troopers made a valiant effort to hold off their attackers, while Jack Stone and Corporal Harry Eales helped the two women clamber down from the carriage. Fletcher McBain, for his part, neither went to the aid of the ladies, nor joined the captain and his men. Instead, he fled towards the safety of the cabin and hastily dived inside.

Outside the cabin, the bullets flew thick and fast. Of the six troopers, three were swiftly shot dead and another two wounded, one in the chest and one in the shoulder. Two Indians were toppled from their horses and Louise Jamieson was hit in the back as she approached the cabin door. Jamieson, Eales, Stone and the sixth trooper, John Vincey, returned fire, bringing down a further couple of hostiles. Then, without further ado, the survivors made a run for the cabin. Hannah Dun was the first through the door, closely followed by the Kentuckian bearing the stricken Louise in his arms. Next came the captain and the corporal. They helped the two wounded troopers stagger inside, with Vincey bringing up the rear.

Vincey slammed the door shut behind him, while his two wounded comrades were gently, carefully, lowered to the floor. Stone laid Louise Jamieson down beside them and, leaving all three to Hannah Dunn's ministrations, joined Eales and Vincey at the windows on either side of the door. From there he and the two soldiers proceeded to blast away at their attackers.

The Indians had, by now, reached the cabin and were circling it, still whooping and hollering wildly and firing fusillade after fusillade in through the front windows. There was also one rear window, but Fletcher McBain had already closed the shutters, thereby denying the redskins access at that point. He did not go to the support of the others, though. Instead, he crouched down behind the bar. And there he remained, ashen-faced, shivering with fear and clutching his two-barrelled Derringer in a shaking hand.

Three more Indians bit the dust and the defenders' sustained gunfire forced the rest of the band to retreat back up into the hills, where they paused to review the situation and re-group. It was as the Crows turned and galloped off that an anguished cry suddenly rent the air, causing Stone and his companions to whirl round in alarm. They observed that Captain Jamieson was sprawled weeping across the prostrate body of his wife.

A tearful and distraught Hannah Dunn explained.

'Mrs Jamieson is dead!' she cried. 'Oh, sweet Jesus!'

As she dissolved into tears and the three men stood dumbfounded, not knowing what to do or say, Jamieson leapt to his feet. His eyes blazed out of a face drained of all colour. It was for all the world like some death's head. In three strides he was at the door. Hurling it open, he drew his sword and rushed outside. Then, with the sword in one hand and his Army Colt revolver in the other, Jamieson set off at a run towards the Indians.

Red Lynx gave the command and the Crows galloped back down the hill, the entire band bearing down on the solitary officer. But, this time, their whoops and cries were matched by those spewing forth from Jamieson's mouth. Screaming like some whirling Dervish, he ran to meet them. Bullets and arrows whistled past his head, yet he paid no more attention to them than if they had been a flight of gnats. An overwhelming desire for revenge had expunged all fear. Jamieson was within a mere fifteen yards of the charging Indians before he opened fire. But when he did, he made each shot count. Four times the Army Colt barked and four braves were blasted off their steeds. A fifth rode up to the officer and attempted to hack him down with his tomahawk. Jamieson was too quick for him, however, and blocked the blow with his sword. The blade snapped and, in the same instant, Jamieson dragged the brave from his horse and slammed him into the turf. Then, wresting the tomahawk from the winded warrior's grasp, he proceeded to smash in his skull with a series of violent blows.

In the meantime, leaving Trooper John Vincey still firing from one of the cabin windows, Jack Stone and Corporal Harry Eales set off in hot pursuit of their courageous young commander. Stone grabbed his Winchester from its saddleboot, as he passed his bay gelding on his way up the hill. Between them, he and the corporal succeeded in bringing down four more braves with shots from their revolvers. Then, finding that he had emptied his Frontier Model Colt, Stone began blazing away with the Winchester. He was joined by Jamieson, who had grabbed hold of a rifle dropped by one of the fallen Crows. Between the pair of them, they accounted for no fewer than another five of Red Lynx's band. Since the commencement of the attack, the Crow war-party had lost nineteen of their number. Thoroughly demoralised, the survivors turned and fled back up into the hills.

Red Lynx alone remained, still prepared to fight. He attempted to rally his braves, but to no avail.

Then, all at once, he found himself confronted by the vengeful Army captain. Grasping the by now empty Winchester by the barrel and swinging it like a club, Jamieson aimed a furious blow at the Crow's head. Red Lynx hastily blocked this with his tomahawk, then wheeled round his racing pony and set off at a gallop after his fast-vanishing braves.

The three white men were now joined by John Vincey, and he, Stone and Eales all continued to blaze away at the retreating war-party. But their efforts proved unsuccessful. Red Lynx and the remainder of his renegade band escaped into the hills without further loss.

As soon as he realized that the Crow Indians were gone and unlikely to return, Captain Jamieson, still half-crazy with grief, turned upon his heel and, without as much as a word to his fellow combatants, rushed off back towards the cabin.

'Holy cow!' exclaimed Stone. 'I reckon, if 'n' them redskins had stood their ground, the Cap'n would've accounted for each an' every one of 'em single-handed. Darned if he wouldn't!'

'Yo're right there, Mr Stone,' said the corporal. 'I ain't never seen the like!'

'Me neither,' cried Trooper Vincey. 'He didn't act like no officer I've ever known. He was ... wa'al, jest plain wild! Wild as some goddam hoppin' mad grizzly!'

'An' about as dangerous,' commented Eales.

'Sure was,' said Stone.

As Stone spoke, the door of the cabin was suddenly thrown open and an ashen-faced Fletcher McBain emerged. He attempted a smile and, accosting the approaching officer, said nervously, 'I … er … I was jest comin' to yore aid. However, I see that. . . .'

The lawyer got no further, for Jamieson pushed him roughly aside and plunged on into the cabin.

The young captain found Hannah Dunn on her knees, attending to the two wounded troopers. She looked up as he came into the cabin.

'Oh, William!' she gasped. 'What … what can I say?'

Jamieson spared Hannah scarcely a glance, far less a word. He rushed past her, and then, throwing himself across the body of his late wife, he burst into a bout of uncontrollable weeping.

Three

William George Jamieson found that he was quietly crying. Even after fifteen years, thoughts of his beloved Louise could still, at certain times, reduce him to tears. The fact that he had never re-married bore witness to his continued love for, and devotion towards, his late lamented wife. During the course of his subsequent extremely successful career, he could have had his choice of several eligible beauties, but none held any interest for him. Like the wild swan, Jamieson had mated for life.

Sitting there in the tranquillity of his bedroom, on that still Spring morning, he reflected upon his career and how that terrible day at Beaver Wells had affected it.

His actions that day had earned him his nickname, 'Wild Willie', and his further daring exploits against the Indians had ensured that it stuck.

From that day forward, he had borne all Indians an implacable hatred. Whenever the Army had required an officer to lead a foray against either a renegade band or a troublesome tribe, Jamieson had volunteered. And, since he was a natural leader and a brilliant soldier, he had invariably been successful. So successful, in fact, that the name, Wild Willie Jamieson, had struck terror throughout the tribes of the Plains Indians. Arapaho, Blackfoot, Cheyenne, Crow, Fox, Pawnee and Sioux all feared Wild Willie, probably the most famous, and certainly the most ruthless, Indian-fighter of his time.

Jamieson had sought to trap and destroy each and every tribe and band he had come up against. And always he had hoped that, one day, he might again come face to face with Red Lynx, the Indian he considered responsible for his wife's death. On his arrival at Fort Anderson, following the incident at Beaver Wells, he had described to the fort commander, Colonel Proudfoot, what had happened. And it was from the colonel that Jamieson had learned the identity of the Crow. Red Lynx's renegade band had, it seemed, been a thorn in the army's side for some considerable time. But Jamieson's desire to meet up with and kill Red Lynx had not been gratified. Although he had pursued and harried the Plains Indians, almost without remit, for many years, he had never again encountered his mortal enemy.

His enthusiasm, his utter fearlessness and his many successes had ensured that Jamieson progressed swiftly through the ranks until, at the age of forty, he was finally promoted to lieutenant general. It was within a few months of this promotion, however, that he had suffered the first of his heart attacks. And it was while recuperating at the Army hospital in Washington that he had met the Reverend Joseph Henry.

Jamieson thought back to that meeting and how, in a quite different way from the confrontation at Beaver Wells, it had changed both his outlook and his subsequent conduct.

The Reverend Joseph Henry was a newly appointed Army chaplain, fresh from theological college. A tall, handsome, well-built young man, Henry was imbued with a fine Christian zeal and fervour. Sincerity shone out of his intelligent brown eyes, and he possessed a kind, compassionate heart.

The lieutenant general had a private room at the hospital, and it was into this that, late one sunny summer afternoon, the young chaplain strode. He introduced himself and then drew up a chair beside Jamieson's bed.

'I hope that I don't intrude, General,' he said amiably, 'but it is one of my duties to visit the sick.'

'An' the dyin',' replied Jamieson, with a wry smile.

'Er ... yes ... of course, the dying. But you aren't dying, surely, General? You've merely had a heart attack . . . .'

'Which the doctors tell me could have proved fatal.'

'Yet it didn't.'

'No, Reverend, it didn't.'

'The doctors said more?'

'Yes; it seems I have a heart condition that is certain to get worse. I can expect to suffer further heart attacks, one of which will undoubtedly prove fatal. So, you see, Reverend, I shan't make old bones.'

'Yet you have lived a most active life. You had no earlier sign of illness?'

'No. Odd, isn't it? The doctors cain't explain why I have been so suddenly struck down. They can only tell me that the heart disease is such that, sooner or later, it will kill me. At most, they give me two or three years.'

'I see. I am so sorry, General.'

Jamieson shrugged his shoulders resignedly.

'It's OK, Reverend. I have never been afraid to face death.'

'No, I guess not. You have a reputation for fearlessness. Wild Willie Jamieson is what folks call you, General; the most renowned Indian-fighter of them all.'

Jamieson laughed.

'I am not so wild these days,' he confessed.

'Only because you are a sick man.'

'True.'

'Fit and well, you would still ride out against the red men?'

'I s'pose.'

'Why?'

The general glanced sharply at the preacher.

'Whaddya mean, why?' he demanded.

'I mean, why are you so all-fired keen to kill Indians?' enquired Henry.

'You don't know?'

'No, General.'

'You haven't heard of what happened at Beaver Wells?'

'No: when was this?'

'Twelve years ago. I've hated those stinkin' redskins ever since.'

'A long time to nurse such hatred.'

'Perhaps.'

'Would you care to tell me what happened?'

'Why not?' Jamieson sank back onto his pillows and proceeded to recount the events of that tragic afternoon in the Spring of 1865. Then, when he had finished, he asked, 'Don't you reckon I've got good reason to hate the red man?'

The Reverend Joseph Henry pondered this question for some moments before replying gently, 'Wa'al, as I said, twelve years is a long time to nurse a grudge. And surely you cain't blame an entire race for the misdeeds of one renegade band? You have gone to war against several different Indian nations. Can you really hold the Cheyenne, or the Pawnees, or the Sioux responsible for the action of some crazy Crow?'

'They're all the same,' retorted Jamieson. 'Goddam savages, all of 'em!'

'They didn't all kill your wife,' remarked the preacher. 'And how many Indian wives and children have you killed since?'

'Me, personally?'

'No, General; you and your men between you.'

'I have no idea. But I didn't make war against women an' children. Never.' Jamieson's eyes flashed angrily and he continued. 'If a few got themselves killed, that's too bad. It wasn't my intention to kill 'em. It was the braves I was after. However, in any war, there are bound to be some non-combatants killed.'

'Just like your Louise?'

'You cain't compare some stinkin' Indian squaw with my Louise!' cried the general.

'They're both God's children,' commented the preacher.

'Now, look here . . . .'

'No, you look here, General. This isn't easy for me to say, but I'll say it anyway. It's one thing for you to have done your duty as a soldier, yet quite another for you to have sought out and killed the Plains Indians simply in order to satisfy your detestation of them.'

'You lecturin' me, Reverend?' rasped Jamieson angrily.

'Maybe I am.' Joseph Henry smiled sadly and asked, 'I take it that your wife, Louise, was a good

Christian woman?'

'She was.'

'And would you consider yourself a good Christian man?'

'Pretty good, I guess.'

'So, you believe that, when eventually you die, you will be reunited with Louise in Heaven?'

'That is my earnest hope; yes.'

'In that case, you must try to forgive, even if you cannot forget, for both your own and Louise's sake.'

'Forgive whom? That red savage who murdered her?'

'Yes, although which red savage are you referring to? It seems, from your own account, that you have no idea who fired the fatal shot.'

'That's true. But I hold the leader of that war-party responsible.'

'The brave called Red Lynx.'

'Yes. I've sought him ever since, but I've never found the murderin' sonofabitch!'

'Wa'al, it is Red Lynx whom you must forgive.'

'Never!'

'Jesus forgives all of us miserable sinners who repent our sins. Indeed, did He not redeem us by dying for us on the cross?'

'I ... I guess so.'

'Then, if you desire salvation and truly want your soul to go to Heaven, you have absolutely no choice. You must forgive Red Lynx.'

'I cannot. I will not.'

'But, General . . . .'

'Leave me, preacher. I will hear no more of this.'

'General . . . .'

'Leave me. That is an order.'

The Reverend Joseph Henry slowly rose. He crossed the room and threw open the door. Then he paused on the threshold.

'I shall pray for you,' he said quietly, whereupon he departed, gently closing the door behind him.

The preacher left, assuming he had failed and that his words had fallen on deaf ears. However, he was quite wrong in this assumption. He had, in fact, given Jamieson much food for thought.

For a tough, seasoned and stubborn old soldier, it was no easy matter to admit, even to himself, that he had been wrong to harbour such bitter hatred against the red man. Although it had been his duty to mount punitive expeditions, to search out and destroy renegade bands of hostile Indians, this was a duty he had sought, had volunteered for. He had taken positive pleasure in executing such duties.

Now he was being forced to reconsider his motives and his actions. Jamieson knew that he was likely to meet his Maker in the very near future, and he wanted desperately to be reunited with his beloved Louise. It was not Hell that he feared, it was the possibility that his soul and Louise's should remain apart for all eternity. He had not been a particularly devout Christian, yet he did possess a simple and unshakeable faith. And so it was that, in the weeks that followed, Jamieson eventually came to accept that his hatred had been irrational and unfair. He finally began to see matters from the Indians' point of view, and he even lost his urge to kill Red Lynx.

His perceptions having changed, Jamieson now regretted a great many of his actions. Yet what was done was done. He could not change that. But he could repent and, in the short time left to him, do his best to make amends. Consequently, Jamieson had taken it upon himself to ensure the Indians were fairly treated. During his last two years in service he had naturally enough, considering the state of his health, been confined to administrative duties. He had, therefore, used his influence over this period to see that treaties were strictly adhered to, reservations properly managed and corrupt Indian agents rooted out. All of this he had done quietly, yet effectively, behind the scenes. Indeed, the Plains Indians, had they known, would have been amazed to find that their foremost persecutor had now become their greatest defender.

Jamieson smiled to himself. He had truly repented and he had done his best to make amends. Surely, therefore, his most fervent wish would be granted, and he and Louise would be reunited in Heaven?

He sighed and stretched. The long journey home

to Harrison Creek had taken its toll. In his present weakened state, not even a good night's sleep had been sufficient to revitalize him. Perhaps a short stroll and a breath of fresh air might help? He rose and put on his hat. He had, in any event, run out of cigars. He would walk as far as the general store and purchase some.

As Jamieson left the room, he encountered Sarah Yeates in the hall.

'Oh, hullo, General! Going out?' she enquired shyly.

'Er … yes, my dear. I thought I'd walk as far as Horace Day's general store an' purchase some cigars.'

'Horace Day doesn't own the general store any more.'

'No?'

'No; he retired a coupla years back. The present proprietor is Jerry Pine.'

'Indeed? Wa'al, it's quite some years since I was last in Larch County. I guess a good number of the folks I knew will either have moved out or died by now.'

'I s'pose so, General.'

'Tell me, Mrs Yeates, does Tom Brown still run the Double B? His son, Ned, and I were particular pals when we were boys together.'

Sarah shook her head.

'No; I'm afraid Mr Brown died four or five years

ago. But yore pal is still around. Ned Brown runs the ranch these days.'

The general brightened at this piece of news.

'I must look him up,' he said.

'Oh, I'm certain he will call on you, once he knows yo're back here!' said Sarah.

'Wa'al, that would surely save me the trouble of ridin' out to his ranch,' admitted Jamieson.

'Quite so. You still look very pale and very tired, General,' remarked Sarah. 'Are you positive you want to bother to walk to Jerry Pine's store? I can easily fetch those cigars for you.'

'No, thank you, Mrs Yeates. The walk'll do me good. I could do with a li'l gentle exercise.'

'If you are sure?'

'Quite sure.'

'Enjoy your walk, then, General.'

'Thank you.'

Jamieson left the rooming-house and proceeded to walk very slowly along the sidewalk. He could see the general store once owned by Horace Day, a mere fifty yards away, on the opposite side of Main Street.

Jerry Pine was a man in his mid-fifties. He had taken over a thriving business and managed it well. Therefore, like his predecessor, he, too, had prospered. But he needed to, for he had married late in life and had a wife and six young children to support.

Small, balding and bespectacled, Pine sported a

thick, grey moustache, and his thin, scrawny figure was clad in a fresh white shirt and grey trousers, the latter held up by red suspenders. The trousers, though, were mostly covered by a dark green apron, while the bow tie, which he wore, was of the same colour as the suspenders.

There had been several customers in the store earlier in the morning, but now it was fast approaching noon. Lunch-time. Consequently, it was empty, and Jerry Pine was taking advantage of the fact to tidy and re-stack his shelves. He was quite alone when Painless Peachum and Raven sauntered in through the open doorway.

Pine was standing on a pair of step-ladders, attending to his top shelves, when the two gunslingers approached. He paled at the sight of them and hastily descended the ladder.

'Er ... what ... what can I do for you two gen'lmen?' he enquired nervously.

'We ain't come to buy nuthin',' rasped Peachum.

'No?'

'Nope. Jest called for a li'l chat.'

'Oh, yeah?'

'Yeah, Jerry. We gotta message for yuh. From Mr Bannon.'

'Oh, an' what ... what does he have to say?'

'He ain't a happy man.' Peachum spoke softly, yet there was no doubting the menace in his voice. 'He ain't a happy man 'cause you ain't paid him no tribute this month.'

'I ... I explained. I will pay. It's jest that business has been kinda slow this last month,' said the storekeeper.

'I don't think so. A reg'lar gold-mine, this.'

'I ... I gotta large family to support.'

'That's yore problem, not Mr Bannon's.'

'But . . . .'

'Mr Bannon wants his money. Now! Not tomorrow, or next week. Now!'

'I ... I don't see why I should have to pay Jim Bannon anythin'!' protested Pine, his temper suddenly getting the better of his all too natural caution.

'No? Then, let me explain,' hissed Peachum. 'Mr Bannon provides you with protection. He guarantees that nobody won't smash up nor set fire to yore store. Wa'al, that kinda guarantee don't come cheap, which is why yuh gotta pay. Is that clear, Jerry?'

Jerry Pine swallowed hard. The only people likely to smash up or set fire to his general store were the no-account ruffians employed by Bannon. The mayor's enforcers had no interest in protecting his property. All they were concerned with was extorting money from him.

'You ... you'll have to wait,' he gasped.

'No, we won't,' rasped Peachum, and he promptly stepped forward and hit the storekeeper hard in the belly with a vicious right hook.

Jerry Pine gasped and fell to his knees, whereupon Peachum kicked him sharply in the ribs. He toppled over sideways and Peachum again lashed out with his boot. The gunslinger's toe caught Pine in the small of the back and the storekeeper let out a cry of pain. Bending down, Peachum grabbed Pine by the collar of his shirt and dragged him to his feet. He stared the frightened and painwracked storekeeper straight in the eye and snarled, 'That's jest a small taste of what I can dish out. You want some more?'

Pine shook his head and muttered groggily, 'No, no; please don't hit me no more.'

'Then, I guess you'll pay up?' said Peachum.

'Yes … yes, I'll pay up.'

'Now!' This was not a question, rather a statement.

'Y … yes. Right away.'

Jerry Pine staggered across towards the counter on top of which stood his till. He proceeded to open the till and take out the amount of cash that Peachum had earlier that day demanded. He paid it out slowly, some in notes and the rest in coin. Peachum grinned and pocketed the money.

'There, y'see, that wasn't too difficult, Jerry,' he sneered, adding, with an evil grin, 'An' you could've saved yerself a whole heap of pain. So, next time, pay up promptly. That's my advice.'

'Yeah. OK, I … I'll do that,' replied Pine sourly, clutching his aching ribs.

'Y'see, Mr Bannon don't like to be kept waitin' for

his money,' continued Peachum. 'An, if 'n' you do it again, it might not be me yuh have to deal with. It could be Raven here.'

The tall, rake-thin man in black smiled, but there was no humour in his eyes. His hands hovered above the two pearl-handled butts of his British Tranters. The inference was plain. Jerry Pine shuddered.

'I ... I don't figure Mr Bannon would want me killed. Surely he wouldn't go that far?'

'Not as long as yuh pay up,' retorted Peachum. 'Otherwise . . . .'

The mayor's chief enforcer left the rest of the sentence unsaid. He smiled broadly at his victim. He had enjoyed inflicting pain upon the little man and would happily have hurt him even more, had he not been afraid of actually incapacitating him. That would have been to exceed Jim Bannon's orders, not something Peachum was anxious to do.

The gunslinger turned on his heel and, followed by his black-clad companion, strolled nonchalantly out of the store and back into Main Street.

As the two men left the premises, they almost collided with Wild Willie Jamieson, who had just that minute completed his gentle stroll from Sarah Yeates' rooming-house. The gunmen had heard of Jamieson's arrival in Harrison Creek and immediately recognized him from his lieutenant general's uniform. They stepped nimbly aside and doffed their Stetsons, for they knew that Bannon would want them to show the soldier respect. Jamieson, for his part, acknowledged the pair with a quiet smile and a brief nod, then walked on into the store.

He found Jerry Pine still behind the counter.

'Mornin', Mr Pine,' said Jamieson. 'Can I trouble you for a dozen cigars?'

'Certainly, General,' replied the storekeeper, viewing Jamieson with a curious eye, for, like everyone else in town, he was interested to see Harrison Creek's most famous son.

As Pine went to fetch the cigars, he suddenly paused, clutched his ribs and winced.

'You in some pain, Mr Pine?' enquired Jamieson observantly.

'Er … yes. I … er … I fell off a ladder. Hurt my ribs.'

'You seen the doc?'

'No, but I shan't bother. They're jest bruised a li'l; that's all.'

Pine forced a smile and, hastily changing the subject, asked the general where he was staying in town. Then, while Jamieson settled up for the cigars, the storekeeper sang Sarah Yeates' praises and said he hoped the general would be comfortable at her rooming-house. Jamieson replied that he was perfectly comfortable. Whereupon, having secured his cigars, he left the store and slowly made his way back to the house.

Once again he encountered Sarah in the hall.

'Got yore cigars, General?' enquired Sarah, with a smile.

'Yes, thank you, Mrs Yeates,' said Jamieson, adding quietly, 'Yore Mr Pine seems to have had an accident.'

'Oh, really?'

'Yes. Says he fell off a ladder an' hurt his ribs.'

'Indeed?'

'Yes. Hurt 'em quite badly, I'd say.'

'Hmm; that's not like Jerry. A most careful kinda man usually. Not the sort I'd expect to fall off a ladder.'

'Accidents do happen, though, even to careful folks,' commented Jamieson.

'I s'pose.'

'He had a coupla customers jest 'fore I went in. Rather rough-lookin' fellers. One was a scar-faced son-of-a-gun, an' the other tall an' thin an' dressed all in black. Know who they might be, Mrs Yeates?'

Sarah pulled a wry face.

'The first is Painless Peachum an' the other calls hisself Raven. They both work for Jim Bannon.'

'The mayor?'

'Yes.'

'Why in tarnation would he want to employ a coupla fellers like them?' demanded Jamieson.

'Mr Bannon owns two saloons here in Harrison Creek an' several others elsewhere in Larch County. Guess he needs Peachum an' his kind to help keep the peace. 'Specially when the cowpokes ride into town, lookin' for a good time.'

'Haven't you got a county sheriff to do that?'

'Yes. Sheriff Dave Lloyd. But he cain't be everywhere at once.'

'No, I reckon not,' conceded Jamieson.

The general smiled wearily and retired to his room. Then he removed his hat, unbuttoned his uniform jacket and sat down in the armchair beside the window. He did not like to admit it, but the short walk had tired him considerably. He lit a cigar and, leaning back in the armchair, picked up the local newspaper which he had discarded earlier.

Four

The Wells Fargo staging-post at Standing Rocks was situated plumb on the Arizona–Utah border. There were seven horses, standing hitched to the rail outside, when Fancy Brookes drove up in her gig, pulled by a single grey mare. Fancy was a plump and pretty blonde in her mid-thirties, smartly attired in a low-cut, dark-red velvet dress and matching bonnet. She was both dusty and tired, for she had driven hard and covered the ten miles between Cactusville and the staging-post in near record time. She reined in the grey mare and jumped down. Then she straightened her bonnet, smoothed down her dress and marched boldly into the log cabin that, together with some stables and a small corral, was all that Standing Rocks had to offer the weary traveller.

Inside was a bar-room, with half-a-dozen tables scattered across the sawdust-laden floor and a high copper-topped bar at the far end. Behind the bar, a thin, elderly, cadaverous-looking man stood idly polishing glasses. Lon Bentley ran the staging-post singlehanded. He had once been married, but his wife had run off with an itinerant medicine-man. This experience had soured him and, although he performed his duties satisfactorily, he did so without any real enthusiasm. Lank black hair hung down almost to his shoulders, and he wore an extremely grubby white apron over a frayed white shirt and faded denims.

It was high noon and there were seven customers in the bar-room when Fancy burst in. All of them were male.

Four sat round a table in the centre of the bar-room playing poker and drinking whiskey. They comprised of Bart Redmond, a professional gambler, Sam Newton, a whiskey salesman, and two horse-traders, Nick Smith and Johnnie Hart. Redmond was a slim, thin-faced man who sported a pencil-thin moustache and wore an expensive black three-piece suit and Derby hat. Newton, too, wore city-style clothes, though in beige, and he evidently sampled his wares, for he was extremely redfaced and corpulent. The horse-traders were both tough-looking, stocky men, dressed in Stetsons, check shirts, brown leather vests and levis. All four looked up as Fanny entered.

The two saddle-tramps standing at the bar also leered lustfully at the blonde. Seth Hornby and Joe Keith were similarly attired to the two horse-traders, though their clothes were considerably more travel-stained and were badly worn. And neither man seemed to have shaved for several days.

The seventh fellow sat at a table in the right-hand corner. He was quietly drinking a glass of beer and, unlike the others, barely seemed to notice Fancy Brookes' arrival. He looked to be a pretty rough, tough character, probably in his mid-thirties, whose craggy, weatherbeaten features were not improved by his broken nose. A grey Stetson topped thick, grey-flecked brown hair, and his huge frame was contained in a knee-length buck-skin jacket. Pale blue eyes stared frostily ahead of him at nothing and nobody in particular. Not a man to lightly cross, decided Lon Bentley, as he observed the big man from his position behind the bar-counter.

Fancy wended her way between the tables and approached the Wells Fargo man.

'Am I in time to catch the stage bound for Phoenix?' she enquired anxiously.

'Yes, ma'am,' replied Bentley. 'It's expected within the hour.'

'Thank Heavens!' sighed the blonde. 'For I've driven all the way over from Cactusville in order to catch it.'

'You'll be a mite thirsty then. That's one helluva hot, dusty ride.'

'It sure is.'

''Can I git yuh a drink, then, ma'am?'

'A beer'll do fine.'

Lon Bentley blinked. He had expected the blonde to ask for a coffee. But she was evidently no stranger to saloons. So, just what had she been doing in Cactusville? The same question crossed the mind of the gambler, Bart Redmond.

He watched as the girl sipped the beer, all the while glancing nervously towards the door of the cabin. He smiled to himself, then, at the completion of that particular hand of cards, he called out.

'Excuse me, ma'am,' he cried, 'but would yuh care to join us?'

His fellow poker players nodded enthusiastically.

'Yeah, please do,' said Sam Newton, his fat, florid face wreathed in a wide smile.

'You'll be most welcome,' added Nick Smith, while Johnnie Hart simply grunted his approval.

Fancy hesitated. 'I ... I don't know?' she began.

'You do play poker?' said Redmond.

'Er ... yes ... yes, I do.'

The gambler had guessed as much. He continued to smile.

'Wa'al, then, join us for a coupla hands. It'll help pass the time till the stage turns up,' he argued.

Fancy considered the gambler's offer. It would, as he had pointed out, make the time pass quicker. It would also take her mind off her worries. She shrugged her shoulders.

'Why not?' she said. 'Thanks for the invitation, gen'lmen.'

Redmond quickly rose and, pulling up a chair from another table, placed it between his own and that of the whiskey salesman. Fancy smiled and sat down. Then Nick Smith, whose deal it was, began dispensing the cards.

The Phoenix-bound stagecoach did not, as Lon Bentley had predicted, arrive within the hour. It was a little over the hour and five hands of poker later when it eventually rumbled to a halt outside the cabin. By this stage, Bart Redmond was regretting having invited Fancy to play, for the blonde had had a splendid run of luck and had won all five hands. She smiled brightly at her fellow-players and, gathering up her winnings, began to stuff them into her reticule. They, for their part, looked less than pleased. It was the professional gambler who spoke for all four of them.

'You ain't thinkin' of quittin', are yuh, ma'am?' he enquired.

'Of course, for I intend boardin' the stage,' replied Fancy.

As she spoke, the driver, the guard and the stagecoach's three passengers, a railroad man, a schoolteacher and a lawyer, entered the cabin.

'While me an' Bob see to the change of hosses, y'all have got 'bout half-an-hour to git yoreselves somethin' to eat an' drink,' announced the driver.

'What about you two? Ain't yuh gonna have a beer 'fore yuh see to the hosses?' enquired Bentley.

'You bet yore sweet life we are, Lon, for we're 'bout as dry as can be,' replied the driver.

'Sure are,' agreed the guard, bashing his Stetson against his thigh and sending up a great cloud of dust.

'I have driven here from Cactusville to pick up the stage,' interjected Fancy. 'I s'pose there is a spare seat available?' she added anxiously.

'If 'n' you got the fare, we got the room,' said the driver.

It was at this point that Bart Redmond intervened.

'You can't jest up an' leave,' he rasped.

'No?' said Fancy.

'Hell, no! You've won five goddam hands on the trot! Therefore, it's only fair that yuh give us a chance to win some of our money back,' said the gambler.

'That's right!' cried Nick Smith, while his partner, Johnnie Hart, grunted his agreement.

'Yeah; you cain't quit now,' growled Sam Newton, the whiskey salesman.

'But I must catch the stage,' protested Fancy.

'I don't think so,' said Redmond.

'I told you from the beginnin' I was aimin' to catch it.'

'You hadn't won our money then.'

'But there … there ain't another due till this time

next week.'

'So, go back to Cactusville meantime.'

'No; I will not!'

'Mebbe you cain't?' Bart Redmond had earlier observed the blonde's nervous glances towards the door of the cabin and had guessed that she was in fear of pursuit. For what reason and from whom he had no idea. Yet he was convinced that this lay behind her anxiety to catch the stage. 'Wa'al?' he growled.

Fancy Brookes had no intention of telling the gambler her secrets, although, in fact, he was quite right. She could not return to Cactusville. She had been there for four years, running the Golden Nugget Saloon in partnership with her lover, Ben Early. Then, a month ago, Early had dropped her for a twenty-year-old redhead. He had subsequently offered her a paltry sum for her share of the partnership, which she had reluctantly promised to consider. He had told her that she could either take it or leave it; he would give her until April the nineteenth to get out of town, with or without this sum. Today was the nineteenth and, in the small hours of the morning, Fancy had crept into the saloon, slipped into Early's office and opened the safe, using the combination known only to Early and herself. That he had not troubled to change this combination said much about the man's egotism and rank over-confidence. In the event, Fancy had emptied the safe, reckoning that the takings were nearer what he owed than the derisory amount he had offered. But now she was anxious to put as many miles as possible between herself and Cactusville, before Ben Early discovered his loss and set out in pursuit. She turned to face the gambler, who had risen to bar her way.

'I ain't sayin',' she said quietly. 'But I am goin'.'

'Oh, no, you ain't!' snarled Redmond. 'You ain't goin' nowhere till you've played some more poker.'

'Unless you jest refund us what we've lost?' suggested Nick Smith, adding rapaciously, 'With a li'l interest.'

'Now that's an idea!' remarked the other horse-trader.

'No, it is not!' exclaimed Fancy angrily. 'I won those hands fair 'n' square, an', like I said, y'all knew from the start I was plannin' to leave on the stage.'

'An', *like I said*, you hadn't won our money then,' rasped Redmond.

Fancy responded by trying to sidestep the gambler, but, as she did so, the other three players rose and together the four formed a formidable barrier between the blonde and the doorway. Realizing that she was not going to be able to pass them, she turned and appealed to Lon Bentley.

'Are you gonna let them lunkheads prevent me from leavin'?' she cried.

The Wells Fargo man shrugged his shoulders. He

certainly had no wish to take on the four poker players.

'I ... er ... I don't reckon on interferin',' he mumbled sheepishly.

'What about you folks?' she demanded, eyeing the driver, the guard and their three passengers.

The passengers all shook their heads. They were no keener than Lon Bentley to challenge Bart Redmond and his pals. Both the driver and the guard were more inclined to help, but they had a job to do.

'Come on, fellers, let the li'l lady pass,' protested the driver.

'You gonna make us?' enquired Redmond. 'An', before yuh decide, jest think 'bout the odds: four to two.'

The driver lowered his gaze.

'Sorry, ma'am,' he muttered. 'But me an' Bob, our first responsibility is to Wells Fargo. We cain't afford to git involved in fights that don't concern us.'

'That's right. Sorry, ma'am,' added the guard.

Fancy's gaze shifted to the two saddle-tramps at the bar. But Seth Hornby and Joe Keith had no inclination to get involved either. They were thoroughly enjoying the drama enfolding in front of them and were determined to remain merely interested spectators.

The blonde gazed round in mounting alarm. Then, out of sheer desperation, she attempted to push her way between Redmond and the whiskey salesman. Each man grabbed an arm and held her, Redmond digging his fingers so hard into her flesh that she screamed with pain.

It was at that moment the big tough-looking man in the buckskin jacket rose from his corner table. He slowly pushed open the buckskin jacket to reveal a Frontier Model Colt tied down on his right thigh.

'I suggest you fellers let go of the li'l lady,' he growled.

Redmond and the others turned their gaze upon the big man. They had scarcely noticed him earlier.

'You gonna make us?' sneered the gambler.

This was the same question he had posed to the stagecoach driver, but, this time, he got quite a different answer.

'You can bet on that,' snarled the big man.

Sam Newton gulped. The odds might be four to one, yet, despite that, he sensed the four were likely to lose.

'I ... er ... I guess I ... I'll jest step aside,' he stammered. 'Far as I'm concerned, the lady can keep her winnin's.'

So saying, the whiskey salesman let go of Fancy Brookes' arm and hurried across to join the others at the bar. As he did so, Fancy, taking advantage of the temporarily distracted Bart Redmond, abruptly tore herself free from his grasp and dashed to one side. This left the three remaining poker-players facing the big man from a distance of approximately thirty feet.

'Wa'al, gents, you gonna follow yore pal's example?' he enquired softly.

By way of response, Bart Redmond made a sudden grab for his gun. He was carrying a Colt Peacemaker, while Nick Smith and Johnnie Hart both sported Remingtons. A split second after Redmond, the horse-traders, too, went for their revolvers. But they were none of them quick enough.

For a big man, the buckskin-clad stranger was surprisingly fast. He dropped into a crouch, and drew, aimed and fired his Frontier Model Colt before any of the trio had even cleared leather. Once, twice, thrice, the Colt barked. The first shot hit Bart Redmond in the centre of the chest and knocked him backwards six feet or more. The second pierced Nick Smith's heart and sent him crashing to the floor. The third struck Johnnie Hart in the belly, ripping open a huge hole through which a mixture of blood and guts spewed forth.

While Redmond struggled to sit up and Holt clamped both hands over the hole in his belly, in a vain attempt to hold back his intestines, their protagonist coolly and deliberately despatched them with his fourth and fifth shots. The first slug struck Bart Redmond plumb between the eyes and blasted his brains out through the back of his skull. The second smashed through Johnnie Holt's left cheekbone and lodged in his brain, killing him instantly. And, as for Nick Smith, he lay spreadeagled across the floor, with his life's blood slowly oozing away.

The spectators stood in a stunned silence as the reek of cordite permeated the air. The gunfight had lasted no more than a few seconds, yet, in that short space of time, three men had died.

The stagecoach driver was the first to speak.

'Don't reckon you folks are gonna want much to eat?' he commented, surveying the pale, frightened faces of his three passengers.

'I surely am not,' declared the lawyer.

'Nor me,' said the schoolteacher.

'Me neither,' croaked the railroad man.

'OK. Then me 'n' Bob'll change the hosses as quick as we can, an' we'll be on our way.' The driver turned to Lon Bentley and added, 'However, 'fore we do that, we'll both have a glass each of yore red-eye.'

The three passengers had certainly lost their appetite, but they, too, were quick to order, and then down, large measures of Bentley's rot-gut whiskey. The two saddle-tramps, meantime, had their glasses refilled and, slouching across the bar-counter, wisely kept their heads down. They had no wish to draw the big man's attention, for he scared the living daylights out of them.

Lon Bentley helped himself to a whiskey, although from a bottle he kept beneath the counter for his personal consumption. He hastily threw back the amber liquid and, then, fixing his eye upon the three corpses, asked of nobody in particular, 'What ... what in tarnation am I s'posed to do with them thar bodies?'

The big man, who had returned to his corner table, where he sat smoking a cheroot and drinking his beer, looked up and scowled darkly at the Wells Fargo man.

'Bury 'em,' he snarled.

Bentley blanched.

'Y ... yessir. I ... I'll do jest that,' he stuttered.

The only person in the bar-room who did not fear the big man was Fancy Brookes. She had no cause to, for had he not come to her rescue? She walked across to the corner table and extended her hand.

'Fancy Brookes,' she said, as her protector took her small, slender hand in his huge mitt.

'Jack Stone,' replied the big man.

'Wa'al, thank you, Mr Stone. I am mighty indebted to you.'

'Not at all,' said Stone and, glancing at the corpses with a contemptuous eye, he added, 'It was a pleasure.'

The blonde eyed him curiously.

'Jack Stone,' she said thoughtfully. 'Yore name is kinda familiar, yet ... Holy cow, it's jest come to me! You're the famous Kentuckian gunfighter, the man who tamed Mallery, the feller who helped Bat Masterson bring law an' order to Dodge City, the . . . .'

'You got me,' Stone interrupted her. 'But, these days, I'm lookin' for a quiet life.'

'Oh, yeah? So, how come you stepped in an' took on them three sonsofbitches?' she enquired, indicating his three victims.

'I couldn't jest stand by an' do nuthin'. It's agin' my nature,' said Stone.

This was true. In his thirty-odd years, the Kentuckian had experienced more than his fair share of tragedy, and witnessed and participated in more than his fair share of violence, yet he had always stood on the side of the angels. If he retained nothing else, Stone retained a strong sense of justice. He simply could not abide evildoers.

'You don't wear a badge no more?' said the blonde.

'Nope. I gave up bein' a lawman some years back. These days I jest wander around doin' whatever takes my fancy: mebbe a li'l huntin', or trappin', or wranglin', or ridin' herd.' Stone smiled and asked, 'What about you, Miss Brookes? Was ...?'

'Jest call me Fancy,' the blonde interrupted him.

'Wa'al, Fancy, was that feller right when he surmised that you cain't return to Cactusville?' enquired Stone.

Fancy returned his smile.

'Yup.'

'You gonna tell me why?'

The girl shrugged her shoulders.

'Why not?' she said, and she proceeded to tell Stone about her partnership with Ben Early, and how she had taken what she figured he owed her from the safe in the Golden Nugget Saloon.

'Yore friend Early ain't gonna be none too pleased when he finds out,' commented Stone.

'He sure ain't. Which is why I aim to put as many miles 'tween me an' Cactusville as I can,' explained Fancy.

'Wa'al, the stage'll git yuh to Phoenix, but won't Early follow you there? He's sure to come lookin' for you, an' it won't take him long to find out that you took the stage,' said the Kentuckian.

'But I ain't plannin' on stayin' in Phoenix. I'm gonna catch me an eastbound train an' head for one of the East Coast cities, New York mebbe, or Boston.'

'Yeah?'

'Yeah. Ben won't wanta chase me that far. If he don't catch me in Phoenix, I reckon he'll give up an' head on back to Cactusville. After all, he's got a business to run.'

'Seems likely. But, what about you; what're yuh gonna do in Boston or wherever?'

The blonde laughed.

'Oh, I grabbed a tidy sum from that safe! Enough, at least, to start up a li'l business. What I've got in mind is a dress shop or . . . .' Fancy paused and, fixing Stone with a speculative eye, asked silkily, 'Wanta come along?'

Stone grinned.

'Thanks, Fancy, but life in an East Coast city jest wouldn't suit me at all.'

'Wa'al, then, come with me as far as Phoenix. We could have ourselves a real good time. Spend a coupla days . . . .' Again Fancy paused, before adding, with a saucy smile, 'an' nights together.'

Stone was sorely tempted.

'What about Early?' he said.

'Aw, I reckon I can afford a coupla days' delay,' replied Fancy blithely. 'Ben ain't gonna trace me that quick. An', even if he does, I figure you could take care of him without too much trouble.'

Stone smiled wryly. The blonde was right. He did not doubt that he could easily deal with her ex-lover and business partner. And the prospect of bedding Fancy certainly appealed. He glanced longingly at the plump white breasts almost bursting out of the low-cut bodice of her dark-red velvet dress. Then he reluctantly shook his head.

'I'm sorry, Fancy, but I jest cain't afford the time,' he said.

'Oh!' the blonde pouted, disappointed.

'I'm headin' north-east for Colorado,' explained Stone. 'A friend of mine there is dyin', an' I wanta see him 'fore he makes that last journey.'

'Life is for the livin', not for the dyin',' said Fancy.

'Mebbe so. But this feller an' me, we go back a long way.'

'Wa'al, for you to refuse my offer on his account, I guess he must be real special!' exclaimed the blonde.

'Oh, he is, Fancy! Name of Wild Willie Jamieson.'

Fancy's bright blue eyes widened in surprise.

'Yo're a friend of Wild Willie Jamieson?' she cried. 'Whew! He ... he's a hero of the West an' no mistake!'

'Yup.'

'But ... but you made yore reputation as a lawman, not as an Injun-fighter. So, how come ...?'

'I was once an Army scout.'

'You ... you weren't with him at Beaver Wells, was you?' gasped Fancy, her eyes widening still further.

'I was.'

'Gee!' Fancy had read various exaggerated reports of the famous incident. 'Didn't Wild Willie kill more'n a hundred of them red savages single-handed?' she asked.

'Somethin' like that,' replied Stone with a grin. Then, finishing his beer, he took the blonde by the arm. 'I do b'lieve the stage is ready to go. So, let me help yuh climb aboard,' he said.

When they stepped outside the cabin, they found that the change of horses had been completed, the three passengers were already inside the stagecoach and the driver and his shotgun guard were in position on the box. Stone helped Fancy remove her portmanteau from her hired gig and then handed it up to the guard, who carefully loaded it onto the roof. This accomplished, the Kentuckian held out his hand to the blonde.

'Goodbye, Fancy, an' good luck!' he growled.

Fancy ignored the outstretched hand and, hurling herself into his arms and clasping her own round his neck, stretched up onto her toes and kissed him. Stone responded, savouring to the full the sweet taste of her lips and relishing the feel of her soft, voluptuous body pressed against his. Indeed, he was sorry when, eventually, Fancy released him from her embrace and stood back. He regretted even more his inability to accept her tantalising offer. Yet he dared not delay, for, if he did, his arrival in Larch County, Colorado, could well be too late.

''Bye, Jack. Take good care of yoreself,' whispered Fancy.

'An' you,' Stone replied.

He helped the blonde climb into the stagecoach and, as he closed the door, so the driver flicked his reins and set the horses in motion. The stage rattled off, and the last Stone saw of Fancy Brookes was her waving a tiny lace handkerchief from the coach's open window. He raised a hand in reply and then stepped across to the hitching-rail and untethered his bay gelding.

As the Kentuckian swung himself into the saddle, Lon Bentley appeared in the doorway of the cabin. The Wells Fargo man looked none too happy.

'Don't s'pose yuh'd be prepared to help me bury them fellers yuh killed?' he enquired in a thin, whining voice.

'Yo're quite right; I wouldn't,' retorted Stone. 'I aim to give you the same kinda help that you gave Miss Brookes. None.'

So saying, Stone turned the gelding's head and set off at a canter, across the border and into Utah.

Five

Jessica Eales drove the buckboard along the trail towards the town of Elgin. It was early afternoon and the sun shone down out of an azure-blue sky. Nevada was enjoying a particularly fine Spring. Jessica smiled to herself. All was well with her world, she had no cares and, indeed, was completely relaxed and very happy as she drove into town to pick up supplies.

A forty-year-old brunette, Jessica appeared younger than her years. She was handsome rather than beautiful, a sturdy, big-breasted woman who looked, and was, both warm-hearted and competent. She was a regular customer at Joe Harman's general store. Reining in the horses, she climbed down from the buckboard and stepped inside the emporium.

Jessica found it deserted, except for its large, bald-headed proprietor, who was sitting on a chair, with his feet on the counter, reading the latest edition of *The Elgin Enquirer.* He did not observe her enter the store and consequently, when she spoke, he was thrown into some confusion.

'Some interestin' news in the paper?' she said quietly.

'Er ... yes ... yes, Mrs Eales, there is, as a matter of fact,' Joe Harman replied, hastily removing his feet from the counter, and rising and smoothing down his white apron.

'Wa'al, are yuh gonna tell me what it is?' enquired Jessica.

'Sure thing, ma'am,' he said. 'I was jest readin' 'bout how Wild Willie Jamieson is dyin' an' has gone back home to Harrison Creek in Larch County, Colorado, to die. You ... you've heard of Wild Willie, Mrs Eales?'

'Oh, yes, Mr Harman, I've heard of him!' said Jessica.

'A sad business. One of our finest generals an' probably the best goddam Injun-fighter of 'em all!'

'Yes.'

'He'd never have got his troops massacred like Custer did at Little Bighorn.'

'No.' Jessica stretched out her hand. 'May I read that report?' she asked.

''Course. Here y'are.'

Joe Harman handed the newspaper to the brunette, and Jessica slowly and carefully perused the article. This detailed Lieutenant General William George Jamieson's illustrious career, described his illness and commented upon his decision to return to his home town to die. When she had finished, Jessica returned the newspaper to the proprietor. But she made no remark concerning what she had just read. Instead, she immediately began to order the supplies she required.

Harman, with the aid of his young assistant, Lennie, carried the goods outside and loaded them onto the buckboard. All the while, the storekeeper prattled on about the general and his forays against the Plains Indians. That Harman considered Wild Willie to be a hero of the West was in no doubt whatsoever. Jessica, for her part, contented herself with a few monosyllabic replies, enough to satisfy Harman, who was, in any event, more of a talker than a listener. Then, once all the supplies had been loaded onto the buckboard and firmly secured, Jessica paid her dues and, without further ado, commenced her return journey. Normally, she would have had a look round Elgin's other shops, the dry goods store for instance, but the article in the *Enquirer* had given her a great deal to think about. Consequently, her interest in shopping had, for the moment, faded.

As she drove the buckboard back along the trail, her mind went back three years. Her husband, Tom Younger, had died suddenly, leaving her to manage their horse-ranch and, at the same time, bring up their two sons, then fourteen and twelve years old respectively. It was proving quite a struggle when, six months after her husband's demise, Harry Eales had come along. He was four years her junior and newly retired from the US Army as a Master Sergeant. A tall, broadshouldered, blondhaired man, with smiling eyes and a frank, open countenance, Eales was in receipt of a small Army pension, but this was not sufficient to keep him. Therefore, he was looking for a job. Desperate for help in running the ranch, Jessica had taken him on.

This had proved to be a shrewd move on her part, for Eales was a darned good wrangler. Also, her two young sons took a liking to him straight away. A friendly, easy-going man and a first-rate worker, Harry Eales was the answer to her prayers.

They each found the other physically attractive from the start. But both were hesitant and, as a result, their relationship developed slowly, though surely. Eventually, however, Eales mustered the courage to declare his love for her, and to ask her to marry him. And so it was that, twelve months earlier, she had become Mrs Jessica Eales.

The marriage had been, and indeed still was, a resounding success. The boys had acquired a good and kindly stepfather, the horse-ranch was being run by an excellent manager, and she had found herself a gentle, loving husband. The question was: should she give him the news about Wild Willie Jamieson? He had told her that he was at Beaver Wells when the general first earned the soubriquet, 'Wild Willie'. It was almost certain, therefore, that he would want to go see the general and pay his respects before the old soldier died. And, since Wild Willie was in Colorado and Harry Eales in Nevada, this would entail a lengthy journey and an absence of several days, perhaps even several weeks.

She cogitated on the matter as she drove home. Unwilling to spend so long apart from him, Jessica was sorely tempted to keep the news to herself. Yet, in her innermost heart, she knew that she could not do this. She would rather be parted from him for a few weeks than have him discover later that she had deliberately withheld this information. It was not as if she and the boys could not manage the ranch for a while without him. They would miss him certainly, but they could, and would, manage. It was on a personal level that she would miss him most. She loved her gentle giant of a husband dearly and would feel his absence terribly. Nevertheless, she realized that she had to tell him of Wild Willie's impending death. Then it would be up to him to decide whether or not to make the long journey to Harrison Creek.

Jessica smiled wryly, pleased to have resolved her dilemma. She urged the horses into an even faster canter and, half an hour later, reached the horse-ranch, where she was greeted by Harry Eales and her two bright-eyed sons, Joey and Kevin.

Eales had altered little in the fifteen years since he had stood with Wild Willie Jamieson at Beaver Wells and helped beat off Red Lynx and his band of Crow braves. Eales' hair remained as blond as ever and his countenance had retained its frank youthfulness, although he had filled out and now was a couple of stones heavier. The boys, well on their way to becoming young men, were, by now, both taller than their mother.

They and their stepfather quickly unloaded the buckboard and tended to the horses while Jessica hurried into the ranch-house. By the time they had completed these tasks, Jessica had brewed some coffee, and they all sat down together at the large, well-scrubbed table in the kitchen. Jessica dished out flapjack for all, coffee for herself and Harry Eales, and buttermilk for Joey and Kevin.

It was as they were munching the flapjack and washing it down with either coffee or buttermilk that she broke the news to her husband about Wild Willie Jamieson.

At the conclusion of her narrative, she asked anxiously, 'So, what d'yuh intend doin', Harry? Do you wanta go pay yore last respects?'

Harry Eales scratched his head.

'Guess,' he said. 'We go back a long way. An', sides, the general, he was, an' … er … still is, a true hero. I oughta make the effort.'

'It's a long journey from here to Harrison Creek, Colorado. 'Bout five hundred miles.'

'Yeah.'

'The general might die 'fore you even git there.'

''S'pose so. That's a chance I gotta take.'

'So, you intend goin', Harry?'

'Yes, Jessica, I gotta go.' Eales smiled reassuringly at his wife. 'Don't worry, I won't be gone long. You'll manage OK. You got Joey an' Kevin to help yuh.'

The two boys grinned.

'That's right, Mom,' said Joey. 'We'll take good care of you while Harry's away.'

'You can rely on us,' promised Kevin.

Jessica smiled warmly at them.

'Thanks, boys. I know I can,' she said, and then, turning to her husband, she asked, 'Is there anyone else likely to make the journey to Harrison Creek, d'yuh think?'

'Guess quite a few folks will.'

'Yore companions at Beaver Wells, for instance?'

'Some of 'em at least,' Eales replied. 'Jack Stone, an' Fletcher McBain, an' Mrs Dunn survived the encounter, as did three of the troopers.'

'So, you may meet up with all of them?'

'One of the troopers, John Vincey, was killed with Custer at Little Bighorn.'

'Ah!'

'An', assumin' Major Dunn an' the two survivin' troopers are still servin' in the Army, their duties are almost sure to prevent 'em makin' such a journey.'

'Mrs Dunn ain't likely to travel there on her own?'

'No, I don't reckon so, Jessica.'

'Which leaves Jack Stone an' Fletcher McBain.'

'Yeah. Jack, he's somethin' of a legend hisself.'

'The celebrated gunfighter an' lawman?' said Jessica.

'That's the feller, though I heard he'd retired as a peace officer an' was takin' things kinda easy these days.'

'In which case, Harry, if he has no commitments, he may well head for Harrison Creek.'

'Guess he might at that.' Eales reflected thoughtfully and continued, 'But I ain't so sure 'bout Fletcher McBain, for he didn't exactly cover hisself with glory at Beaver Wells.'

'Isn't he a US senator now?' enquired Jessica.

'So, I b'lieve.'

'He'll go then. With the elections comin' up in the Fall, he will be keen to make what political capital he can outa his connection with the dyin' hero.'

'Yo're a cynic, Jessica,' grinned Eales.

'Wa'al, you wait an' see.'

'Even if 'n' he an' Stone do pay a visit to Harrison Creek, there ain't no certainty that their visits an' mine will coincide.'

'No, but it's quite likely, partickerly if they decide to stay on till the general dies.'

'In order to attend his funeral, y'mean?'

'Yes. What about you, Harry? Will you wait on in Harrison Creek until the end?'

Harry Eales shrugged his brawny shoulders and

looked grave.

'I dunno,' he said quietly. 'The newspaper report said Wild Willie was dyin', right? But it didn't say how long he was expected to last.'

'No.'

'It could be days. Or weeks. Or months.'

'The report implied that he hadn't very long to live. A few weeks at most, I'd guess,' said Jessica.

'Wa'al, I reckon I'll have to make up my mind on that score when I've been an' seen the general.'

'Right.'

'I can promise yuh one thing, though, Jessica. I won't stay away more'n one calendar month at most,' declared Eales.

He meant this. He had no wish to leave, but felt it was his duty to do so. It was a point of honour with him that he should pay his last respects to the man whom he regarded as the bravest soldier he had ever met. Nevertheless, he also owed a debt of duty to his wife. He had no intention, therefore, of abandoning her for any longer than was strictly necessary.

With this promise, Jessica had, perforce, to be content. Harry Eales, for his part, went about making certain that everything pertaining to the horse-ranch was in good order. And he gave Jessica and the two boys strict instructions on how to manage matters while he was away. Finally, he and Jessica made love with an intensity unmatched since the early days of their marriage.

At first light, Eales said farewell to a tearful Jessica, asked Joey and Kevin to take good care of their mother, and then mounted his sorrel and set forth eastwards, towards the border with Utah. Although sad to be leaving his wife and stepsons, Eales nonetheless felt a certain exhilaration. It reminded him of the feeling he had had when, as a soldier, he had ridden out to do battle.

Six

Spring in Montana was not so far advanced as it was in the states further south. The Sapphire Mountains remained covered in snow and, indeed, the forests and foothills that lay in their shadow were similarly bedecked. A few miles south of the mountains lay the small township of Darby, on the edge of which stood Hugh Fraser's trading-post. It was towards this that the two trappers were heading that morning.

They dropped down out of the mountains, riding a couple of run-down pintos and trailing mules laden with a variety of traps and pelts. But the winter had not been any too kind to them, for the loads of pelts were undeniably small, much smaller than usual in fact. Consequently, both men were somewhat dispirited as they slowly wended their way down through the foothills.

Gus Boyd was in his early forties, a small, weasel-faced man with a scruffy ginger beard and whiskers. He wore thick, foul-smelling furs, a racoon-skin hat and moccasins, and he carried both a skinning and a stabbing knife in sheaths attached to his belt. He sported neither pistol nor revolver, but had a Winchester rifle in his saddleboot.

His companion was equally unprepossessing. Pete Flynn was a few years younger than Boyd, with an ugly, pockmarked face, close-set black eyes and a rat-trap for a mouth. He was similarly clad and carried the same weapons as his fellow-trapper. However, in addition to these, he possessed a Colt Peacemaker, in a holster on his right thigh, tied down.

Disgruntled, dissatisfied and in the foulest of tempers, the two trappers were debating whether to stop for a rest, or press on and hope to reach Hugh Fraser's trading-post before dark. As they did so, they suddenly emerged from the trees into a small glade. At the far side of this a camp-fire was burning, and sitting beside the fire, picking the bones of a roasted buck rabbit, was an Indian wrapped in a buffalo robe. The two white men assumed he was either an Arapaho or a Crow. As they approached the Indian across the glade, they studied him with mounting interest.

He was small and sturdy, with fierce black eyes, a large hooked nose and a grim-looking visage. His long, thick black hair was streaked with grey and hung down almost to his shoulders. It was held in place by a beaded headband, out of which protruded a couple of eagle feathers. He tossed the well-picked carcass of the rabbit onto the fire and withdrew his hands and arms inside the folds of the buffalo robe. All that was revealed of him were his head and his feet, the latter clad in moccasins of the finest buckskin. He seemed to be of an indeterminate age. His looks were such that he could have been anywhere between thirty and fifty years of age.

The trappers continued to study the Indian carefully. They observed that he had a cayuse and a mule hobbled nearby. A large load of pelts was strapped onto the back of the mule. Flynn calculated that the Indian had more pelts in that one load than he and Boyd had managed to collect between them. And both he and Boyd noted that the Indian's Winchester was tied across the top of the bundle of pelts, several yards away from where he was sitting.

As they rode up to within a few yards of the Indian, Flynn commented, in a voice loud enough for the redskin to hear, 'That's a fine collection of pelts the Injun's got.'

'Sure is,' agreed Boyd.

The Indian made no comment, but continued to stare stonily into the fire.

Pete Flynn grinned wickedly.

'Don't reckon the goddam savage understands no English,' he growled.

'No?' Gus Boyd addressed the Indian. 'You have many pelts, yes?' he said in a stentorian voice, as though speaking to someone who was rather deaf.

The Indian looked up, but again said nothing. Then he reverted his gaze to the fire, in the embers of which the rabbit carcass was burning brightly. The two trappers glanced at each other.

Both had the same thought. They intended selling their pelts to Hugh Fraser and then spending the proceeds on whiskey, women and gambling. The shortage of pelts, though, meant that these pleasures were sure to be curtailed. This year it would be an early return to the mountains. Not a prospect either man relished.

'I said, you have many pelts, yes?' Gus Boyd repeated, staring hard at the Indian.

Again the Indian looked up. His face remained as impassive as ever and still he made no response.

'I told yuh the Injun don't understand no English,' whispered Pete Flynn out of the corner of his mouth.

'Hmm. Reckon yo're right,' muttered his companion.

'So, whaddya think?'

''Bout what?'

''Bout takin' the Injun's pelts. Don't tell me that thought ain't crossed yore mind?'

'Sure it has.' Boyd glanced at the Indian still sitting steadfast and silent beside the fire. 'But what about him?' he asked.

'Wa'al, he ain't gonna sit tight an' let us take 'em,' said Flynn.

'So, whaddya propose?'

'We'll have to kill him.'

'But, Pete, that ... that's murder!'

'No, it ain't, Gus. He ain't no white man. He's jest a goddam redskin, an' redskins don't count.'

'But . . . .'

'Hell, there's folks is accounted heroes for killin' Injuns! There's Buffalo Bill Cody, an' George Custer, an' Wild Willie Jamieson, an' . . .'

'Didn't that woodcutter feller we encountered a day or two back say he'd heard Wild Willie was a-dyin'?'

'Yeah. That's right. More's the pity! The West needs men like him.' Flynn grinned and added, 'You could say we're gonna kill this here Injun as a tribute to Wild Willie.'

'Wa'al . . . .'

'We need them pelts, Gus.'

Boyd reflected for a moment or two and then returned the other's grin.

'OK,' he said. 'Why not? After all, as you say, he is only a no-account savage.'

Flynn's grin widened and he drew the Colt Peacemaker from its holster. As he did so, Boyd reached back and pulled his rifle out of the saddle-boot. But they had underestimated their supposedly unsuspecting victim. Before either man could bring his gun to bear, the Indian threw open the buffalo robe, whipped out an Army Colt revolver and fired.

The first shot struck Pete Flynn in the centre of the forehead and killed him instantly. The second hit Gus Boyd in the chest and knocked the trapper clean out of the saddle.

Boyd sprawled helpless in the snow, the blood seeping from the huge hole in his chest. His Winchester had escaped his grasp and flown through the air to land several yards away. Desperately, he tried to crawl towards it, but a kick in the ribs turned him again onto his back. He stared up in terror at the small, sturdy figure of the Indian.

'You ... you understood everythin' we said,' he gasped.

The Indian nodded solemnly.

'You ... you gotta help me,' pleaded the trapper.

'No,' said the Indian.

'I ... I'll make it worth yore while. Them ... them pelts of mine . . . .'

'Are now mine,' stated the Indian, and he finished off the trapper with a bullet in the brain.

It was shortly before dusk on that same day when the Indian reached Hugh Fraser's trading-post on the outskirts of Darby. In addition to his own pelts, he now had Boyd's and Flynn's pelts and their two mules for sale. Their pintos he had set free. He had decided not to try to sell them in case they were recognised. The mules and the extra pelts he regarded as legitimate spoils of war.

Hugh Fraser was a hardheaded, forty-year-old Scot, a lean man with slicked-back black hair, cool blue eyes and a stern, unsmiling countenance. He wore an unbuttoned black vest over a white shirt and black trousers and highly-polished black shoes; and he invariably held a fat cigar clenched between his teeth. Fraser was renowned for striking a hard bargain. But he never allowed prejudice to interfere with his trade. He would do business with anyone.

Indeed, he had done business with the Indian for several years, and knew all about him. A one-time renegade, the Crow was called Red Lynx and still had a price on his head. Fraser was not tempted to turn him in, however, for Red Lynx was an excellent trapper and Fraser had no wish to end their business relationship. It was much too profitable. Besides, Fraser held a sneaking admiration for the Crow.

In exchange for Red Lynx's pelts, Fraser provided him with supplies of food and clothing, to be despatched to the nearby Crow reservation. This he had been doing from the start of their trading some years earlier. Fraser recalled the first occasion the two had met. Red Lynx had then made it clear that Fraser must personally ensure the supplies were handed over to the Crow chief. In the event of there being any double-dealing, Red Lynx had intimated that he would kill him. Fraser smiled wryly. He was by nature an honest man and would have kept his side of the bargain without his being threatened. Nevertheless, he could well understand Red Lynx's concern. Many of those administering the Plains Indians' reservations were extremely corrupt and bent only on feathering their own nests.

'Weel, Red Lynx,' he said, once the bargaining had been completed and the deal struck, 'I'll see tae it your chief gets the supplies. I take it that's a'?'

'No.'

'No?'

'No. I need information.'

'Och, aye? And what kinda information dae ye need?'

'About Wild Willie Jamieson. I am told he is dying.'

Hugh Fraser eyed the Indian closely. He was both surprised and intrigued by Red Lynx's request. He produced a newspaper from behind the counter and handed it to the Indian. Red Lynx frowned, shook his head and brushed the paper aside.

'I do not read,' he said. 'You tell me.'

'Tell ye what it says in the newspaper?'

'Yes.'

'Very weel.'

Fraser took hold of the newspaper, opened it and read aloud the article concerning Wild Willie Jamieson's return to Harrison Creek in Larch County, Colorado, and the reason behind his return. When he had finished, Red Lynx stared him straight in the eye and asked, 'How many days' ride to Harrison Creek?'

'Weel, it's several hundred miles frae here. If anyone was intending tae visit Wild Willie afore he dies, I'd advise him tae tak a train,' said Fraser.

'A train?'

'What you ca' the iron horse.'

'Ah!'

'You planning tae mak that journey?'

'I am.'

'May I ask why?'

'No.' The Crow glowered at Fraser and demanded, 'Where do I find this iron horse?'

'Weel, not here in Darby. But, if ye were tae ride ower tae either Butte or Helena, ye could catch a trai … iron horse that'd tak ye tae Denver.' Fraser smiled and explained, 'Denver is only aboot a day's ride frae Harrison Creek.'

'I shall need how many dollars?'

'Tae pay for your journey on the iron horse?'

'Yes.'

'Weel, I'm no' altogether sure. I suppose it'd cost aboot ten or twelve dollars for the return journey tae Denver. Ye are planning tae come back?'

'I am.' The Crow thought for some moments. 'I shall want twenty dollars,' he said finally.

'OK, but we'll need tae renegotiate. I'll have tae reduce your supplies tae tak intae account . . . .'

'No. The supplies are agreed.'

'Ye expect me tae pay ye twenty dollars in addition tae the supplies?' exclaimed Fraser.

'I do.'

There was a note of finality in Red Lynx's voice. Fraser stared at him. He wanted to protest, but the menacing look in the Indian's eyes warned him against doing so. He reflected that, over the years, he had concluded a number of highly profitable deals with Red Lynx. He could, therefore, easily afford to part with the twenty dollars. What, though, was Red Lynx intending? A confrontation with the famous Indian-fighter, perhaps? But, if so, for what purpose? To assassinate him? That would be pointless, surely? To gloat? This was more likely, yet scarcely a worthwhile reason to make such a journey. Fraser shrugged his bony shoulders.

'Very weel,' he said, 'I'll gie ye the twenty dollars. But be carefu'. The folks in Harrison Creek are liable tae view the arrival o' a redskin wi' some degree o' suspicion, bearin' in mind Wild Willie Jamieson's reputation as an Indian-fighter.'

'It is OK,' replied Red Lynx. 'I do not seek trouble.'

'No; but it may come seeking you,' thought Fraser. Aloud, he said, 'Weel, I maun wish ye a safe journey.'

'Thank you.'

Red Lynx accepted the twenty dollars and then asked Fraser to take care of his mule until his return. He had already sold Boyd's and Flynn's mules along with their pelts.

Fraser watched the Indian ride off eastward in the direction of the township of Butte. If he rode through the night, he would probably arrive in time to catch the mid-morning train bound for Denver.

The trader remained anxious to know what lay behind Red Lynx's decision to travel to Harrison Creek. He wondered whether he should telegraph the authorities in Denver and warn them. But Red Lynx had said that he did not seek trouble, and, strangely enough, Hugh Fraser believed him. If the Crow found it and, as a result, got himself killed, then so be it. Fraser prayed sincerely, however, that this would not happen, and not simply because he looked forward to further highly profitable dealings with the Crow. No; over the years he had actually grown to like and respect the Indian.

Seven

Senator Fletcher McBain had recently celebrated his fiftieth birthday. He was elegantly clad in a dark-grey three-piece city-style suit, light-grey Derby hat and his highly-polished black shoes. Greyhaired and extremely distinguished-looking, McBain had come a long way since that day at Beaver Wells when, as an up-and-coming young lawyer, he had found himself caught up in Red Lynx's raid upon the staging-post. In the years since, he had made a great deal of political capital out of the incident. He had always pretended that modesty forbade him relating his part in the proceedings. Nevertheless, he had invariably managed to convey the impression that it had been truly heroic.

McBain clambered out of the noon-day stage and waited while the driver handed down his portmanteau and various valises. Behind him, in the doorway of the Prince Albert Hotel, stood its proprietor, Jim Bannon.

'Welcome to Harrison Creek, Senator,' said Bannon, grasping the politician warmly by the hand.

'Afternoon, Jim. Good to see you again,' replied McBain.

Bannon smiled and instructed the hotel porter to take the senator's bags up to his room. Then he escorted McBain through to the bar-room. This bore little or no resemblance to most Western bar-rooms. It was more like one to be found in London or Paris. There were crystal chandeliers, superbly engraved glass mirrors, a gleaming mahogany bar-counter and plush red velvet chairs and settees. Bannon led McBain across to a corner table and ordered the waiter to bring a bottle of whisky and two glasses. When it came, the whisky was not the usual red-eye, but a five-year-old blended Scotch.

'I think you'll like yore room, Senator,' said Bannon, as he filled the glasses. 'It's the best in the hotel.'

'Good! For I may be stayin' a li'l while.'

'Any prizes for guessin' why yo're here?' enquired Bannon, with a sly grin. 'You come to pay yore last respects to the general?'

'Wa'al, I was at Beaver Wells, where he earned the soubriquet, "Wild Willie",' said Bannon.

'So, you'll be callin' on him?'

'He's still alive, then?'

'Yeah.'

'But sinkin' fast?'

'I dunno for sure.'

'I cain't hang about here too long. I got the impression the general was likely to last days rather than weeks.'

'Mebbe? Mebbe not?' Bannon shrugged his shoulders.

'Reckon I'll have a word with his doctor.' McBain frowned. His socialite wife would be letting those who mattered know where he was, and making much of the fact that he had been with Wild Willie at Beaver Wells. Nevertheless, there was business in the Senate that required his attention. It was awkward. There was no doubt that he would reap a rich reward by remaining in Harrison Creek and being seen as a principal mourner at the general's funeral. Indeed, he intended to milk the situation for all it was worth. It could, after all, prove crucial in his forthcoming campaign for re-election in the Fall. Yet he could not afford to be away from Washington for too long. 'I hope the general ain't gonna linger on indefinitely,' he muttered.

'You could always return to Washington an' then . . . .'

'Like I said, I'll have a word with his doctor. If it's only gonna be a matter of a few days, I'll stay put. Otherwise . . . .' McBain left the rest of the sentence unsaid.

'An' will yuh be payin' a call on the general?' enquired Bannon curiously, for it had not passed his notice that McBain had earlier evaded this question.

'I ... I ain't made up my mind,' said McBain. 'Hell, I don't wanta disturb him! I b'lieve he's asked for peace an' quiet.'

'That's very considerate of you, Senator. However, as an old comrade-in-arms, I'm sure you'd be welcome to drop in.'

'Yeah. Wa'al, 'course I wanta talk over old times with him, but I ... I figure on waitin' till after I've spoken to his doctor. I ... er ... I b'lieve the newspapers are respectin' the general's request that he's not to be disturbed. I feel, therefore, that I must do the same.'

'So, when d'yuh reckon on speakin' to Doc Wharton?'

'Sometime tomorrow, I guess.' McBain smiled, but it was a forced smile. He had no doubt that, should he call, Wild Willie would give him a dusty reception, and, if news of that leaked out .... The senator prayed that either the general expired within the next few hours or Doc Wharton forbade him any visitors. After all, he had come to Harrison Creek to attend the old soldier's funeral, to rub shoulders with the Governor, and Colonel Cathcart from nearby Fort Benwell, and the various other dignitaries who would be there. Paying a call upon the hero of Beaver Wells was not included in his plans. 'Guess the representatives of the Press'll come flockin' into town once they git news of Wild Willie's death,' he remarked.

'They sure will,' agreed Bannon. 'I reckon the local fellers will make a packet selling their stories, reports an' photos to the big syndicated newspapers back East.'

'Don't seem right folks makin' money outa the death of one of our national heroes,' commented McBain virtuously.

'That's the way of the world, Senator,' replied the mayor, adding, with a sly grin, 'Not everyone is as disinterested as yoreself, only here to pay yore last respects to an old comrade.'

'Quite so.'

''Course, with the elections comin' up in the Fall, bein' seen at Wild Willie's funeral won't do you no harm.'

'That ain't why I'm here, Jim.'

'I know that, 'course I do. You ain't the kinda feller who'd deliberately make political capital outa this extremely sad an' sorrowful situation.'

'I sure ain't.' McBain eyed the other suspiciously. He rather suspected that Bannon meant exactly the opposite of what he said, yet the senator could not be certain, for there was no trace of irony in the mayor's voice. 'My motives for bein' here are beyond reproach,' he protested.

'I'm sure they are, Senator,' said Bannon soothingly. 'However, talkin' 'bout those forthcomin' elections, I hear that old Andy Elliott is retirin'.'

'That's true.'

'So, the Party'll be lookin' for a new candidate to fight Elliot's old seat?'

'Yes.'

'You got anyone in mind?'

'There are one or two possibilities, I b'lieve.'

'You'll need to be careful. There are those who, while they might be pretty darned good local politicians, would be way outa their depth in Washington.'

'I realize that, Jim. It takes a special kinda feller to make a good Congressman.'

'Wa'al, I figure I'm that kinda feller, Senator.'

Fletcher McBain smiled. There was no false modesty about Jim Bannon. The man knew what he wanted, and he went for it head on.

'You want me to propose you?' said McBain.

'Yup. If 'n' you do that, an' then go on an' give my nomination yore full support, I figure I'll git the candidature. Hell, you got considerable influence within the Party, Senator! Everyone knows that,' declared Bannon.

'S'pose so,' smiled McBain smugly.

'I helped you win yore seat in the Senate last time, an' I'll help again. 'Deed, I can guarantee Larch County's vote both for you an', if I'm nominated, for me.'

Fletcher McBain nodded. He knew that Bannon had Larch County well and truly stitched up.

'OK, I'll see what I can do,' he promised.

'Thank you, Senator.'

'But you'll need to be careful, Jim.'

'Whaddya mean?'

'I mean, there are rumours 'bout you extractin' tribute from some of the folks round here. An' there have been two kinda suspicious deaths within the last year. It's said both men had refused to pay you tribute.'

'Is someone accusin' me of their murder?'

'Like I said, there are rumours.'

'Put about by my rivals. Fellers who are jealous of my success.'

'Mebbe.'

'I'm a respectable businessman. Sure, I drive a hard bargain, but I don't extract tribute an' I ain't responsible for the murder of anyone.'

'So, why do you employ Painless Peachum and his gang?'

'For the protection of my various properties.'

'Ain't Sheriff Lloyd supposed to uphold law an' order round here?'

'Sure. An' Dave does a good job. But he's got one helluva large territory to cover an' cain't be everywhere at once. Which is why I need Painless an' the others.'

'I see.' McBain had to concede that the mayor's explanation was plausible. Nevertheless, he did not believe him. 'OK, Jim,' he said, 'jest make certain there ain't no trouble 'tween now an' election time, for, if there is, the Party'll disown yuh.'

'There won't be no need for them to do that.'

'I hope not. But, remember, as soon as Wild Willie dies, the newshounds are gonna pour into Larch County.'

'Yeah; I said as much earlier.'

'Wa'al, I trust that all their stories are gonna relate to the general an' his doin's. I don't wanta read 'bout you in the papers. Any scandal an' . . . .'

'You can sleep easy on that score, Senator,' declared Bannon confidently. 'I won't figure in no stories.'

'Good!' McBain smiled and then, yawning, he remarked, 'Gee, that goddam journey's taken its toll! Guess I'll go lie down for an hour or so.'

''Course. Take the Scotch with yuh. It's on the house.'

'That's very civil of you, Jim.'

'Not at all. We're friends, ain't we?' said Bannon, adding silkily, 'Naturally, there won't be no charge for yore stay here at the Prince Albert Hotel. An' tomorrow, if 'n' yo're agreeable, I propose to arrange a li'l luncheon party an' invite along a few local dignatories to meet you.'

'That's fine by me,' replied McBain. Thereupon, he picked up the bottle of five-year-old blended Scotch whisky and a glass, and slowly rose from the table.

While Fletcher McBain retired to his room for a rest, Jim Bannon left the hotel and headed down Main Street towards the Foaming Jug. He was feeling very pleased with himself. The senator's support would assuredly gain him the Party's nomination. And, once nominated, he felt certain he would go on to win the election. Congressman James Bannon. He liked the sound of that.

Pushing his way through the batwing doors, the mayor marched boldly into the saloon. There was the usual mid-day crowd, though none of his enforcers was present, for Painless Peachum and the others were out and about collecting tribute from various homesteaders. Bannon caught the eye of Sheriff Dave Lloyd, who was standing at the bar drinking whiskey, and beckoned him through into his private office.

Lloyd was a big, red-faced man in his mid-forties. His hair was grey and curly, while, surprisingly, his whiskers remained as black as pitch. He wore a low-crowned grey Stetson, white cambric shirt, bootlace tie, knee-length black jacket, grey trousers and black leather boots. In a holster, on his right thigh, he carried a Colt Peacemaker.

The sheriff pulled forward a chair and sat down opposite the mayor, who had taken his usual place behind the large mahogany desk and was in the process of lighting up a cigar.

'Wa'al, Mr Bannon,' said the sheriff, 'what can I do for you?'

'Jest wanted to talk over a few things,' replied Bannon. 'Did yuh know Senator Fletcher McBain is in town?'

'Yup. I saw him git off the stage.'

'We had a most constructive chat.'

'Oh, yeah?'

'Yes, Dave, we did.' Bannon smiled and continued, 'I got me some ambitions which I don't want thwarted.'

'What kinda ambitions, Mr Bannon?'

'Wa'al, for one thing, I aim to be yore next Congressman.'

'Gee!'

'So, I cain't afford no scandals.'

'Whaddya mean?'

'I mean, Dave, I don't want folks spoutin' off 'bout me collectin' tribute from 'em.'

'Who in tarnation are they gonna spout off to?' enquired a puzzled Sheriff Lloyd.

'Newspapermen are liable to descend on us in hordes when Wild Willie finally drops dead. Which could be any day now.'

'I guess.'

'So, how do we keep folks from talkin' to them?'

'Ah, yes!' Lloyd thought hard upon the matter for some minutes, and then eventually commented, 'A newspaper story would do you no good at all.'

'No. That sure ain't the kinda publicity I want.'

'You could send Painless an' the others round to

warn folks to keep their mouths shut … or else!'

'Yeah. An', regardin' most folks in Larch County, I reckon that oughta suffice. But what about Ned Brown? How do we keep that sonofabitch quiet?'

Dave Lloyd frowned. The rancher was refusing to pay for Bannon's 'protection'. Indeed, there was always the fear that he might persuade Dan Walters of the Big Mesquite and Curly Johnson of the Lazy J to join him in his protest. If all three ranchers stood out against Bannon, the mayor could find himself in deep trouble.

'You don't think sendin' Painless or Raven out to the Double B would do the trick? Surely they could scare Ned Brown enough to guarantee his silence?'

'They ain't scared him into payin' this month's tribute.'

'That's true.'

'I'm afraid, therefore, that we gotta take rather more drastic measures. We need to shut him up permanently!'

'Now, wait a minute, I ain't . . . .'

'Shut up, Dave, an' listen.'

'But . . . .'

'You can have yore say when I've finished.'

'Aw, OK, Mr Bannon! Go ahead.'

'Thank you.' Bannon withdrew the cigar from between his lips and began, 'I want Ned Brown dead, but it's vital that no suspicion should fall on me. An' that means Painless an' his pals will need water-tight alibis for the time of Ned Brown's death.'

'An' jest when are yuh plannin' on killin' him?' enquired Lloyd nervously.

'Tomorrow's Friday, the day Ned comes into town to pick up supplies an' collect the week's wages for his hands. He invariably hits town late mornin' an', havin' accomplished his business, leaves again shortly after noon. Wa'al, I'm holdin' a luncheon party at the Prince Albert in honour of Senator McBain. I reckon on invitin' the town's most influential citizens along: Henry Potterton, who manages the Cattleman's Bank, Doc Wharton, Clarence Joab the mortician, an' several of our storekeepers. Painless, the Dixon brothers an' Butch Mabey will also attend.'

'Er ... what about Raven?'

'He'll be with you.'

'With me?'

'That's right, Dave. There's a rumour that some renegade Arapahos have been spotted over on the south side of Larch County. Have you investigated that rumour yet?'

'They ain't attacked nobody as far as I know. So, I ain't bothered.'

'Wa'al, you'll bother tomorrow, an' you'll take Raven with you. In fact, to make it all nice 'n' legal, you'd best deputize him. You'll leave town midmornin' when there's plenty of folks around to witness yore departure, an' you'll return either late afternoon or early evenin'. An', if an' when questions are asked, you'll confirm that Raven never left yore side all day. Got that?'

'Got it, Mr Bannon.'

'But you won't ride south.'

'We won't?'

'No; you'll head north through the hills as far as Copperhead Gulch. Ned Brown's gotta pass through that gulch on his way to an' from town. You'll ambush him there as he returns to the Double B.' Bannon smiled grimly and continued, 'Once you've killed him, you'll take the men's wages so as to make it look as though he's been bushwhacked by some bandit. That way, it'll be assumed he was murdered for the money, an' for no other reason.'

Lloyd shook his head.

'No,' he said. 'I'm prepared to turn a blind eye to what Painless an' his gang git up to, but I ain't gonna be directly involved in no murder. Hell, I'm supposed to be Larch County's principal peace officer!'

Bannon shrugged his shoulders.

'OK, Dave, so you got some scruples. Then, let's compromise. You do as I said, except that you don't take any part in the ambush. You wait a coupla miles back, in the lee of Windy Mountain, while Raven does the killin'. How does that suit yuh?'

The sheriff was none too happy at the prospect, but he was afraid to refuse. Should he do so, he knew that his tenure as county sheriff would be short-lived. Bannon would have no compunction whatsoever in arranging for him to have a fatal accident.

'All right, Mr Bannon,' he said reluctantly. 'So long as I ain't expected to do no actual killin'.'

'Good man! Oh, an' Dave, I know yo're headin' north, but yo're s'posed to be ridin' south in search of them Arapahos. Therefore, be sure to leave town in a southerly direction an', when you an' Raven return, circle Harrison Creek an' approach it from the south.'

'Yessir.' Sheriff Lloyd was no less anxious than Jim Bannon that he and Raven should remain clear of all suspicion. Consequently, he intended to follow Bannon's instructions to the letter. Then, all at once, a thought struck him. 'Hey!' he cried. 'S'pose Ned Brown's body ain't discovered till sometime the followin' day? Where does that leave our alibis?'

'That ain't likely,' retorted the mayor. 'When he don't return to the Double B by early evenin', someone's bound to go lookin' for him. An' it won't be difficult to calculate the time of his death; now, will it?'

'Guess not.'

''Course it won't. An' that time will coincide exactly with my li'l luncheon party an' yore peregrinations in the south of the county. So, we'll be in the clear.'

Lloyd nodded, although he continued to look

rather apprehensive. He had committed himself, but most reluctantly.

'C'mon,' said Bannon. 'I'll buy you a drink. An' not that goddam red-eye yo're drinkin'. Some genuine Scotch whisky. I gotta bottle behind the counter.

He rose and clapped the lawman on the shoulder. Lloyd smiled weakly, and, the matter now settled, they returned to the bar-room.

Eight

Sally Yeates had ridden further than she intended on the pony that, three months earlier, her mother had bought her for her twelfth birthday. She loved to ride and, at every opportunity, would mount the pony and head out into the surrounding hills. She had set out mid-morning and now it was mid-afternoon.

Having ridden up into the hills, Sally was skirting the rim of Copperhead Gulch when she decided that both she and the pony needed a short rest. This was as far as she proposed to venture. Once she and the pony had rested awhile, Sally intended to ride back to Harrison Creek.

The girl dismounted and, leaving the pony to munch the sparse, spiky grasses, she walked across to the rim of the gulch and sat down. It was a warm, sunny afternoon, and a pair of hawks wheeled lazily in the sky above Copperhead Gulch. Sally watched them, fascinated to observe how the two huge birds used the thermals to help them glide so effortlessly between the steep walls of the gulch.

She was still watching the hawks when, from the floor of the gulch, there came the sound of wheels clattering and hooves pounding. Sally glanced down and saw, trotting round the bend immediately beneath her, a buckboard drawn by two grey mares. It was being driven by a stocky figure in a brown Stetson, brown jacket, check shirt, levis and unspurred brown boots. Sally recognized him at once as the owner of the Double B ranch, Ned Brown. The buckboard was loaded with supplies, and Sally guessed that the rancher was returning from his regular trip to town.

As the girl watched, a black-clad figure suddenly rode out from a tumble of boulders, where he had evidently been hiding. He blocked the trail and forced New Brown to rein in the mares. The buckboard came to a juddering halt and the rancher shouted something at the rider in black. What it was he shouted, Sally failed to hear. But she saw only too clearly what happened next. The lone rider swiftly drew a pair of pistols and cold-bloodedly emptied them into the rancher's body. Ned Brown cried out and toppled backwards amongst the supplies. He twitched once or twice and then lay quite still.

Sally gazed down into the gulch in shocked disbelief. She watched as the rancher's killer dismounted and carefully examined the body of his victim. Then he coolly removed from Ned Brown's person a wallet full of ten-dollar bills and a small leather bag containing several silver dollars. He placed both of these items in one of his saddlebags, mounted his horse and promptly rode off. Sally remained transfixed on the gulch's rim, her mind in a turmoil of conflicting emotions: horror, fear, anger, outrage. Tears ran down her cheeks, cheeks from which the colour had completely drained. She could scarcely credit what she had seen. And she was the more shocked because Ned Brown's killer had not been some outlaw stranger, but rather someone she recognized, indeed saw almost every day walking the streets of Harrison Creek. There was no doubt in her young mind that the killer was Raven, a man who was in the employment of Mayor Jim Bannon.

It was some minutes before Sally was able to stir herself, so shaken was she at having witnessed Ned Brown's brutal murder. Once on her feet, however, the girl quickly mounted her pony. Now her only purpose was to return to town, as fast as she was able, and report what she had seen to her mother.

Sally took the shortest route back to Harrison Creek. She rode as though pursued by the Devil himself, pushing the pony to the very limits of its endurance.

Upon reaching it, she found the township slumbering in the afternoon sunshine. There were few people about and several businesses had 'Closed' notices up, for their proprietors were still in the

Prince Albert Hotel, attending the luncheon given in honour of Senator Fletcher McBain. It had already lasted several hours and, while Jim Bannon kept the drink flowing, was set to continue on into the evening.

Sally leapt from the pony, hastily hitched it to the fence outside her mother's rooming-house and hurried inside. As she slammed the front door shut behind her, she began crying, 'Mommy! Mommy! Where are you? Somethin' terrible's happened!'

Immediately, her mother replied, 'I'm in here, Sally. In the general's room.'

Sally quickly turned in the hallway and, without bothering even to knock, threw open the door of Wild Willie's room and burst in.

'Whatever is the matter?' gasped Sarah, eyeing her young daughter's tear-stained face with alarm.

'Oh, Mommy, I ... I . . . .' Sally began and then broke off, as she observed the two big, tough-looking strangers sitting on either side of the general's bed.

'It's all right,' Sarah reassured her. 'These gen'l-men are friends of the general. Mr Jack Stone an' Mr Harry Eales. They fought with him at Beaver Wells an' are come to pay their respects. By sheer coincidence, they arrived within a couple of hours of each other.'

Wild Willie nodded. He lay fully dressed upon the bed. He had been taking a short nap when they arrived.

'Do, please, tell us what's the trouble,' he said quietly.

Sally glanced apprehensively at the two big men. Shaken as she was from the incident in Copperhead Gulch, the girl had, naturally enough, been rather taken aback at finding two complete strangers in the general's room. However, if they were the general's friends . . . .

'It ... it's Mr Brown!' she cried.

'Ned Brown from the Double B?' enquired Sarah.

'Yes. He ... he's dead!'

'Dead?'

'Oh, yes, Mommy!' Sally dissolved into tears and threw herself into her mother's arms, while the others looked on, nonplussed. 'It ... it was terrible!' she cried.

'What was terrible, Sally?' asked Sarah. 'Jest ... jest take yore time an' tell us what happened.'

It was some moments before Sally could stop crying. Then, held tightly in her mother's arms, she described in a low voice exactly what she had seen from the rim of Copperhead Gulch.

When she had finished, it was Stone who spoke first.

'Wa'al, General,' he growled, 'I reckon we better send for the sheriff.'

'Before we do, let's be sure of our facts,' said Sarah.

'Whaddya mean, ma'am?' demanded the

Kentuckian.

'I wanta be sure it was the man called Raven that Sally saw,' said Sarah.

'It was him! I swear it was him!' exclaimed Sally.

'You were up on the rim. The murder was committed at the bottom of the gulch. You ... you are absolutely certain you ain't mistaken?'

'No, Mommy, I ain't!'

'OK!' sighed Sarah. 'We'd best git the sheriff.'

'Why the hesitation, Mrs Yeates?' probed Stone, eyeing the widow keenly.

'Because the man, Raven, works for Jim Bannon,' said Sarah.

'Our mayor,' explained Wild Willie.

'Yo're frightened of him?' said Stone perceptively.

'Yes, I am.' Sarah lowered her eyes and asked softly, 'Will either you or Mr Eales go fetch the sheriff, please?'

'I'll fetch him,' volunteered Harry Eales.

The ex-soldier hurried from the room and, while the others awaited his return and the arrival of Sheriff Dave Lloyd, Sarah comforted Sally as best she could. Stone and the general, meanwhile, sat silently smoking and reflecting upon what the little girl had told them.

Eventually, Eales returned. He brought with him, not only the peace officer, but also the mayor of Harrison Creek.

'What in tarnation's all this 'bout young Sally

witnessin' a murder?' demanded Bannon, as he entered the room.

'Yes. You'd best tell us everythin' you saw,' added the sheriff.

Both mother and daughter gazed apprehensively at Jim Bannon. Neither had anticipated his turning up. However, the presence of Wild Willie and his two tough-looking friends helped reassure them, and, with a little prompting from Sarah, the girl repeated her story.

When she had finished, Sheriff Lloyd and the mayor exchanged glances. Bannon remained his usual urbane self, but the lawman looked distinctly worried. It took a nudge in the ribs from Bannon to start him off.

'I ... I ... er ... I reckon yore eyesight was ... er ... playin' yuh false, girl,' he stammered.

'No, Sheriff, it wasn't. That's exactly what I saw,' replied Sally firmly.

'I don't doubt you witnessed a murder,' said Lloyd. 'But I think you mistook the killer. It ... it couldn't have been Raven.'

'But it was, I tell you!'

'Nope. It couldn't have been.'

'Why not Sheriff?' enquired Jamieson quietly.

'Because, General, Raven was with me from mid-mornin' till we rode back into town 'bout half-an-hour ago,' declared Lloyd.

'I can confirm that,' added Bannon. 'I saw 'em

ride out together. They was headin' south to investigate the rumour that some renegade Arapahos have been spotted out near the Southland Hills.'

'An' did yuh find any Arapahos?' asked Stone.

'Nope. Not a trace of 'em.'

'But you swear Raven was with you all day?'

'Sure was.' Lloyd was beginning to gain in confidence. It was, after all, his word against that of a twelve-year-old girl. The fact, that the murder had been witnessed, had initially unnerved him. Now, however, he felt that her identification of the murderer could easily be challenged and discredited. She had been some distance from the murder spot, and children were not always the most reliable of witnesses. 'I'm afraid, Sally, you simply mistook Mr Raven for somebody else,' he said.

'No; I am sure . . . .' began Sally.

'Now, Sally, don't keep on. Raven couldn't've been murderin' Ned Brown in Copperhead Gulch an', at the same time, scourin' the Southland Hills for Injuns, could he?' said Bannon.

'But, I tell you . . . .'

'What we gotta do now,' continued Bannon, ignoring the girl's protest, 'is to head on out to Copperhead Gulch an' check to see if Ned Brown really is dead. I mean, he may only have been wounded. Dave, are you gonna take a posse out there?'

'No, Mr Bannon. Don't reckon I'll need no posse. I'll jest take Deppity Truelove along.'

'Good man!' Bannon smiled broadly and turned to Sally. 'Don't you worry none, Sally,' he said in a kindly voice. 'We'll git to the bottom of this; an', believe me, it ain't yore fault you mistook Raven for the killer. It's the kinda mistake anyone could make. Why . . . .'

But here the mayor was interrupted by loud cries emanating from the street outside. All the men except Wild Willie rushed across to the window and peered out. What they saw temporarily silenced them. The buckboard, with Ned Brown lying spread-eagled stiff and cold on top of the supplies, was being led into town by a couple of homesteaders. They had come across it, only moments after Sally had left the scene, while on their way into town. They halted fifty yards further on, opposite the law office.

'Wa'al,' observed Stone drily, 'at least Sally wasn't mistaken 'bout the murder. That there feller's dead as a doornail.'

'That there feller was a boyhood pal,' said the general.

'I'm sorry,' growled Stone.

'Me, too, General,' said Bannon. 'To think that such a thing could happen in Larch County!'

'But why would anyone wanta murder Mr Brown?' enquired the Kentuckian.

'Aw, the motive's clear enough!' said Lloyd. 'Robbery.'

'Robbery?'

'That's right,' said Bannon. 'Everyone knows Ned picks up the wages for his hands on a Friday.'

'So, you reckon the killer's a local man?' said Eales.

'Not necessarily. Someone passin' on through could've picked up that information. Hell, it sure ain't no secret!'

'Wa'al, guess I'd best check to see if Ned still has those wages on his person,' said Lloyd. 'If he hasn't, then . . .'

The sheriff left the sentence unfinished, but everyone in the room got his drift. As he departed, Bannon turned to face the others.

'I'd best leave, too,' he said. 'Senator McBain'll wanta know what's goin' on. I left him at the Prince Albert.'

'Oh, yeah?' said Jamieson.

'Yeah. I've been hostin' a li'l luncheon party in his honour. I invited along some of the town's more prominent citizens an' also a few chosen employees.'

'An' ... er ... which employees would they be?' enquired Sarah.

'Painless Peachum, the Dixon brothers an' Butch Mabey. Good, reliable men, all of 'em.'

'I see.'

'Yes, wa'al, let's hope we catch the miscreant who committed this foul crime.' Bannon smiled amiably at Sally and commented, 'From yore description at least we know he dresses all in black, jest like Raven.

That should be a help. I … I'll let you know, General, of any developments.'

'What about the widow?' enquired Jamieson. 'For I believe Ned was married?'

'Yes; yes, he was. I'll git Deppity Truelove to ride out to the Double B an' break the sad news,' said Bannon.

Thereupon, the mayor hurried from the room.

The door had barely closed behind him when Sally, who was still being held in her mother's embrace, raised her head and said quietly, 'That man in black *was* Mr Raven. I know it was.'

'But the sheriff . . .' began Wild Willie.

'Is in Jim Bannon's pocket,' said Sarah. 'He will say an' do anythin' Bannon tells him to.'

'But why should the mayor …?'

'A day or two back, you asked me why Jim Bannon employed men like Painless Peachum an' Raven. I said it was to help keep the peace, to protect his saloons an' other properties. I told you that 'cause yo're an ill man.'

'A dyin' man,' Wild Willie gently corrected her.

'Yes. Wa'al, I didn't see no point in involvin' you in what's happenin' here in Larch County. I thought it best to leave you in ignorance, to let you die in peace.'

'An' now?'

'Ned Brown was yore friend, right?'

'That's correct, Mrs Yeates.'

'Then, I reckon you gotta right to know what's goin' on.'

'An' jest exactly what *is* goin' on, Mrs Yeates?'

'Jim Bannon is milkin' Larch County dry. He uses Painless Peachum an' his gang of hired guns to extort tribute from every rancher, homesteader, storekeeper an' businessman who can afford to pay. Last year, two refused an' both died in suspicious circumstances. This year, Ned Brown refused.'

'An' what about you?'

'I don't earn enough, General. I jest about make ends meet. That's all. Jim Bannon ain't interested in mere dimes an' cents. 'Course, as my business increases . . . .' Sarah smiled wryly and then continued, 'It's one helluva coincidence, don't yuh think, that, on the very day Mr Brown is murdered, Peachum an' his pals should all be lunchin' with Senator McBain at the Prince Albert Hotel, an', so, provided with a water-tight alibi? An' that, on this same day, Bannon's other hired gun, Raven, should be on the opposite side of the county, in the company of Sheriff Lloyd, supposedly searchin' for renegade Injuns?'

'Coincidence, my ass!' rasped Stone.

'You don't buy it, Jack?' enquired Jamieson.

'No, General, I don't.'

'None of us buys it,' said Eales.

'Jim Bannon is the uncrowned king of Larch County!' cried Sarah. 'An' his reign is nuthin' less than a reign of terror. I tell you, the man's a liar, an extortionist an' a murderer!'

'Yeah,' said Stone. 'From what you've told us, I reckon I wouldn't trust him no more than I would . . . .'

'A Crow Indian?' suggested a voice from behind the Kentuckian.

All five immediately turned their eyes towards the doorway. And there stood the short, stocky figure of an Indian, wrapped in a buffalo robe. Despite the passage of years, Lieutenant General William George Jamieson recognized him at once. He was none other than Wild Willie's mortal enemy, the Crow brave, Red Lynx.

Nine

There was a short silence, then Jamieson spoke.

'Whaddya doin' here, Red Lynx?' he demanded. 'Come to gloat over me as I slowly die, or come to finish me off?'

The Crow smiled and shook his head.

'No,' he said quietly. 'I was in Montana when I was told you were dying. I have come to pay my respects. From one warrior to another.'

Jamieson returned the Indian's smile.

'You have come to bury the hatchet?' he said.

'Yes,' replied Red Lynx. 'The old days are over. I know that now. The white man has finally conquered this country. The Crow are doomed to remain forever on their reservation. There is nothing left to fight for.'

'But you don't live on that reservation, do you?'

'No, I am free like the wind. I roam the Sapphire Mountains with the bear and the wildcat.'

'An' is there still a price on yore head?'

'Yes.'

'Yet, despite that, you took the risk of comin' down here to visit me!' exclaimed the general.

'I wanted to see you, Wild Willie, to explain I do not make war on women and children. It was not my intention that your wife should die at Beaver Wells.'

'I believe yuh. It was simply an accident of war.' Jamieson frowned. 'I did not always regard it as such. For many years I have waged war on yore red brothers, an' prayed nightly that I might catch up with you an' kill you.'

'And do you still wish to kill me?'

'No, Red Lynx, I do not. I am weary of killin' redskins.'

'It would seem, then, that we are both changed men, Wild Willie.'

'Yes, Red Lynx; that we are.'

Harry Eales stared in astonishment, from the general to the Crow, and back again. He could scarcely believe that these two men, who, for a dozen or more years, had been mortal enemies, should finally meet in friendship. He watched warily as the Indian crossed the room towards Wild Willie's bed, and his hand dropped surreptitiously onto the butt of his Remington revolver. However, he had no need to draw the gun, for Red Lynx extended only an empty hand to the old soldier. The two shook hands and Eales breathed a sigh of relief, as did Jack Stone. The Kentuckian had also been prepared, if need be, to draw and fire his revolver.

'I'm surprised you were permitted to approach this building,' remarked Stone. 'Considerin' the General's reputation as an Injun-fighter, I should've thought yore comin' to Harrison Creek would've been regarded as plumb suspicious.'

Red Lynx grinned.

'There was much excitement in the town,' he explained. 'Everyone was too concerned with the arrival of a dead man on a buckboard to notice me.'

'Even so. How did you happen to know the general was residin' in this here house?' asked Sarah.

'Two men came out of the house. The second asked the crowd round the buckboard to be quiet. He said that he did not want them to disturb Wild Willie.'

'I see.'

'So, I came straight across and entered the house,' said Red Lynx.

'An' nobody saw yuh?' said Stone.

'No; they were all looking at the dead man.'

'I wonder what folks'll make of Ned Brown's death?' sighed Sarah.

'They surely won't believe that he was the victim of some unknown bandit,' said Stone.

'Wa'al, four of Bannon's enforcers are outa the frame,' stated Sarah.

'The four who attended the luncheon given in

honour of Senator McBain?' said the Kentuckian.

'Yes.'

'Which leaves the man called Raven.'

'Folks may well conclude that he, rather than a stranger murdered Ned Brown, yet there's no proof that he did,' commented Eales.

'But, I ... I saw him!' cried Sally.

'We believe yuh, honey,' said her mother. 'However, it's yore word against Sheriff Lloyd's.'

'The sheriff is lyin'.'

'Mebbe so, Sally, but there's no way of provin' that. No judge would sanction a trial in these circumstances. How could he?'

'Because I'm tellin' the truth, Mommy!'

'Yore mother's right, though,' said Jamieson darkly. 'We've got conflictin' evidence here, an' any judge is sure to favour the evidence given by an experienced peace officer over that of a twelve-year-old girl.'

'That's not fair!'

'No, Sally, it ain't,' growled Eales.

'So, what are we gonna do about it?' demanded Sarah angrily. 'Do we jest let Bannon an' his hired gun git away with this murder?'

'You don't think the citizens of Larch County will protest?' asked Jamieson.

'No; they're too darned scared. An' Ned Brown's death is gonna make 'em even more frightened. They'll simply button their lips an' do nuthin'.'

'You could try writin' to the US marshal's office in Denver,' suggested Eales.

'There ain't no point,' said Stone. 'The law won't act on Sally's unsubstantiated evidence.'

'Wa'al, Jack, as an ex-lawman, I guess you oughta know,' said Eales.

'So, what do we do?' repeated Sarah.

'Y'know, when we were young, Ned an' I rode, an' swam, an' larked about together. Hell, we were practically inseparable!' said Jamieson. 'Consequently I figure on makin' that sonofabitch of a mayor pay for Ned's murder. I consider it's high time there was a day of reckonin'.' He smiled grimly and added, 'For Jim Bannon an' all his gang.'

Stone studied the prostrate old soldier, lying gaunt-faced upon the bed. That he was dying and had only a little time to live was painfully obvious.

'You proposin' to take 'em on, General?' Stone asked, with a crooked grin.

'I am,' declared Wild Willie.

Stone's jaw dropped.

'Y'are?' he gasped.

'Yup.'

'But, General . . . .' began Eales.

'I have only got days or, at the most, a few weeks to live, so I may as well go out in style,' said Jamieson.

'But these fellers yo're proposin' to take on, they're professional gunslingers, shootists! You won't stand a goddam chance,' protested Stone.

'That's for sure,' agreed Eales.

Jamieson considered this for a moment or two.

'OK, so I don't take on Raven or Peachum, but challenge only Bannon. If 'n' I kill him, reckon the game's over.'

'But, General, Peachum an' them others won't let yuh kill Bannon. They won't let you git nowheres near him,' said Eales.

'You wanna bet?'

'Mr Eales is right,' said Sarah. 'You try an' draw on Jim Bannon, an' Raven, or one of the others will gun you down 'fore you can even clear leather.'

'That's a risk I must take, for somebody's gotta rid Larch County of that connivin', murderin' bastard.'

Red Lynx's black eyes blazed fire.

'You are a great warrior, Wild Willie. And I, too, am a great warrior. We shall go together,' he stated.

The others gazed in amazement at the Crow Indian. He, who for so long had defied the US government, was offering his support to its most famous and successful Indian-fighter. They could scarcely believe what they were hearing.

'Yo're proposin' to stand with the General against Bannon an' his gang?' said Stone.

'I am.'

'It ain't yore fight, Red Lynx,' said Jamieson.

'We have fought against each other, you and I. Now I should like to fight with you.' Red Lynx grinned, his eyes suddenly twinkled and he added humorously, 'After all, it is only good-for-nothing white men I shall be killing.'

Jamieson laughed.

'You red sonofabitch!' he exclaimed.

Red Lynx joined in his laughter and, while these two best of enemies struggled to contain their mirth, Jack Stone and Harry Eales exchanged long, meaningful glances. Red Lynx had put them on the spot.

'Guess I'll come along, too. Ain't got nuthin' else to do,' drawled the Kentuckian.

Harry Eales faced a dilemma. Should he join the general's crusade against Jim Bannon and his hired guns, he would be putting his life on the line. And, unlike the others, he had everything to lose, for he loved his wife and step-sons dearly. Yet how could he refuse? He knew that, if he did so, he would regret it for the rest of his life. He had been too long a soldier not to feel loyalty towards his old commanding officer.

'Count me in, General,' he said.

William George Jamieson studied the three men: the short, stocky, stone-faced Crow brave, the big, tough-looking Kentuckian gunfighter and the tall, blond ex-soldier. They formed a pretty formidable bunch. He reckoned that Jim Bannon and his gang of killers were in for a nasty surprise.

'So, how do we handle this?' he asked.

'Wa'al, firstly, we gotta seek out Bannon an' the others,' said Stone. 'Where are they likely to be hangin' out?'

'Bannon said somethin' 'bout returnin' to the Prince Albert to inform Senator McBain what's goin' on,' said Eales.

'Yes. He could be there. Or he could've spoken to the senator an' then gone on to the Foamin' Jug,' remarked Sarah.

'An' hows about his hired guns?' enquired Stone.

'Wa'al,' said Sarah, 'if by now, Ned Brown's body has been removed to the funeral parlour, they will probably have adjourned to the Foamin' Jug. That's where Peachum and his gang usually hang out. It's a saloon owned by Jim Bannon,' she explained.

'I can easily find out if they're all there,' volunteered Sally.

'I'm not havin' you settin' a foot inside that saloon!' protested her mother.

'No. Tommy Trimble, he'll go an' look, if I ask him,' said the girl.

Tommy was an eleven-year-old boy living next door, and he was sweet on Sally. Consequently, she was forever getting him to help with chores and run errands.

'All right, Sally,' said Sarah. 'You can ask young Tommy to go take a look.'

'But tell him not to draw attention to himself,' warned Jamieson.

'Yessir.'

The girl hurried from the room and, while she was gone, the others discussed how they should tackle

Bannon and his men, supposing they all were to be found in the Foaming Jug.

'If we exclude the sheriff,' said Sarah, 'you will be four against six.'

'Who are the six?' enquired Stone.

'Bannon hisself an' his enforcers: Painless Peachum, he's their leader; then there's the man in black they call Raven; then the brothers, Ike an' Arnie Dixon; an' finally the brothers' cousin, Butch Mabey.'

'Hmm, wa'al, I wanta be the one who plugs Bannon,' declared the general. He turned to the Kentuckian. 'You've been a lawman in yore time, Jack, an' you've roamed most of the West. So, have you ever heard of any of 'em?' he asked.

'Painless Peachum is a one-time dentist turned hired gun. He's reckoned to be pretty darned quick on the draw an' not a feller to tangle with. That's the story, though I ain't never met him. As for Raven, I hear he's a psychopath, who jest loves killin' folks. You don't even have to pay him. He'll do it for fun.' Stone paused, before adding, 'I know nuthin' 'bout the other three.'

'So, Peachum an' Raven, as the most notorious of the gang, are probably also the most dangerous?'

'Guess so, General.'

'Then, we'd best have a plan of campaign.'

'Whaddya suggest?'

'I suggest, Jack, that, while I tackle Bannon, you, as

the seasoned gunfighter amongst us, take on either Peachum or Raven. You cain't mistake Raven, for he's the one dressed all in black. An' Peachum is a big, hatchet-faced feller, with a livid white scar disfigurin' the right-hand side of his ugly mug.'

'I'll take Raven,' said Stone.

'And I shall kill the one you call Painless Peachum,' said Red Lynx.

'Which leaves you to choose whichever of the other three you fancy,' said Jamieson to Harry Eales.

'But ... what about the other two?' asked Eales.

'We'll have to take them out with our second shots,' said Jamieson.

'But ... but they're professional killers an' they outnumber you! You'll all be killed!' exclaimed Sarah.

'I don't think so,' replied Wild Willie, 'though, of course, there's a fair chance some of us won't survive the encounter,' he admitted.

'Then don't do it!' cried Sarah. She dearly wanted Larch County rid of Jim Bannon and his hired guns, but not at the cost of the lives of the general and his friends.

'Somebody's gotta stand up against Bannon an' his gang, Mrs Yeates,' said the general quietly. Then, turning to face the others, he asked, 'You fellers sure you wanta git involved in this?'

'Yup,' said Stone.

The Crow nodded silently.

'Guess so,' said Eales, 'but, s'posin' I don't make it, I'd sure 'preciate if 'n' you'd see to it my body's transported back to Nevada. As I told yuh, I have a wife an' step-sons on a hoss-ranch there, a few miles south of Elgin.'

'Wa'al, I hope it won't come to that, but, if it does, you have my word yore wishes will be respected,' said Jamieson. He glanced at the Kentuckian. 'What about you, Jack? You got any similar request to make?'

'Nope,' said Stone.

'An' you, Red Lynx? Do you want yore body taken back to Montana, to yore people at ...?'

'No.' Red Lynx's eyes flashed angrily. 'I do not wish to be buried on any reservation. I was born free and I shall die free.' He looked out of the window towards the distant mountains of the Front Range. 'You can bury me out there, in the mountains,' he said.

Jamieson followed the Indian's gaze and smiled.

'I like yore choice,' he said.

Sarah glanced questioningly at him. There was something in his tone of voice that gave her pause for thought.

''Course, yore funeral will be here in Harrison Creek, General,' she said.

'Will it?'

'Yes. Everythin's arranged. The Governor's gonna come. 'Deed, Senator McBain's already here. Why, it'll be the biggest darned . . . .'

'No,' said Jamieson. 'It won't. Whenever I die, whether today or in a few days' time, I, too, wanta be buried out there, in the mountains.'

'But, General . . . !' protested Sarah.

'It jest this minute came to me, Mrs Yeates,' he declared. 'I no longer have any wish to be buried here in Larch County. With one or two exceptions, the men-folk hereabouts have acted shamefully. They should've stood together against Bannon an' his gang. But they didn't, the yeller-bellied cowards! Wa'al, when I die, they sure as Hell ain't gonna bask in my reflected glory!'

'I see.'

'This is no reflection on you, Mrs Yeates. An' I hope that, once it's rid of Jim Bannon, Larch County will return to bein' the decent, quiet, law-abidin' place it used to be.'

'Yes, of course.'

'Anyways, now it's time for me to git ready,' said Jamieson.

So saying, he climbed slowly, and with evident difficulty, off the bed and began to fasten his uniform. He strapped on his gun-belt and holster and checked his Army Colt revolver. Then, he put on his hat.

The others, meantime, also prepared for the encounter to come. Stone and Eales donned their Stetsons. And Harry Eales checked his Remington, whilst the Kentuckian examined his much-used

Frontier Model Colt. As for Red Lynx, he thrust aside the buffalo robe and practised drawing the Army Colt from its holster. Jamieson eyed the Crow's revolver and wondered curiously who had been its deceased owner, for he did not doubt that the gun was a trophy of war.

And so it was that, by the time Sally and her friend, Tommy, returned to the rooming-house, the four men were ready for action.

'Wa'al, Sally,' said the girl's mother, 'what did you find out?'

'They're all there,' said Sally.

'In the Foamin' Jug?'

'Yes. Mr Bannon an' Sheriff Lloyd were jest enterin' as we arrived,' Sally smiled shyly and went on, 'Tommy snuck in after them, didn't yuh, Tommy?'

'Sure did,' said the eleven-year-old.

'They didn't spot you, did they?' enquired the general anxiously.

'No, sir, they didn't. I was in an' out 'fore you could shake a leg.'

'An' they were all of 'em there? Is that right?'

'It is. Painless Peachum an' the rest of his gang were already standin' up at the bar. Mr Bannon an' the sheriff crossed the bar-room an' joined 'em,' said Tommy.

'Good boy! That's all we need to know,' said Jamieson.

Taking slow, yet determined steps, he made his way across the room. Stone held open the door and the general went out, closely followed by Harry Eales and the Indian. Then the Kentuckian gave Sarah Yeates a final, reassuring grin before striding off after the others.

'Good luck!' she cried, as they left the house and began the long, unhurried walk along Main Street in the direction of the saloon. It lay two hundred yards away, and, watching the pale-faced, frail figure of Wild Willie Jackson proceed with deliberate, laborious steps, she wondered whether he would manage the distance. It seemed incredible to her that someone so ill and so near death should still have sufficient strength of purpose and raw courage to go up against Jim Bannon and his five gunslingers.

Ned Brown's body had been lifted off the buckboard and taken into the funeral parlour under the direction of Clarence Joab, the town mortician. There were still, however, various groups of townsfolk on the street, anxiously discussing the murder. The sudden, unexpected appearance of Harrison Creek's most famous son caused them to turn and stare. It also provoked a multiplicity of comments.

'Holy cow, ain't that Wild Willie?'

'Don't he look ill?'

'Yeah. Looks as though he could drop dead any moment!'

'Where in tarnation is he headin'?'

'An' who're those fellers with him?'

'Gee, I've seen it all now! Wild Willie in company with an' Injun, for God's sake!'

'Ain't that Jack Stone, the famous Kentuckian gunfighter?'

'The man who tamed Mallory?'

'The same.'

'Could be.'

'But what's the general doin' marchin' along with a gunfighter an' an Injun? an' who in Hell's the fourth feller?'

'Dunno; let's follow on an' see.'

And so it was that the various groups broke off their discussions and began to follow the four men's leisurely progress along Main Street. And, as group after group joined the march, a large crowd formed, all of whom were eager to discover the reason for Wild Willie's unanticipated emergence from Sarah Yeates' rooming-house.

The four marched in line abreast, Lieutenant General William George Jamieson and Red Lynx shoulder to shoulder in the centre, with the tall figures of Harry Eales, on the general's left, and Jack Stone, on the Indian's right, flanking them. The one-time Master Sergeant and the Kentuckian gunfighter had difficulty reducing their pace to match that of the general. Indeed, the further they marched, the slower and more deliberate became Jamieson's steps. Stone glanced anxiously round the Crow at the general. His breathing was shallow and uneven, and his pale features had turned a sickly shade of grey. But he gritted his teeth and pressed on relentlessly.

Finally, the quartet reached the Foaming Jug. Red Lynx and Harry Eales made to help the general up the short flight of wooden steps from the street to the stoop. However, he shrugged them off.

'I'll do this on my own, gen'lmen; thank you,' he said.

As Jamieson and his three companions climbed the steps, the crowd behind them halted, their curiosity roused to fever-pitch by now. In fact, so anxious were they to discover the reason for the general's visit, that the foremost of them followed the four men up the steps, across the stoop and into the saloon.

The appearance of Wild Willie and his friends caused a minor sensation inside the bar-room. And, sensing that some kind of showdown was imminent, the customers nearest the bar edged nervously away, leaving the mayor, the sheriff and Painless Peachum and his men isolated there. The two bartenders, no less perceptive than their customers, unobtrusively removed themselves to the far end of the bar-counter. Jim Bannon, meantime, placed his Scotch whisky on the bar-top and turned to face the newcomers.

'Afternoon, General,' he said affably. 'I sure didn't expect to see you in here.'

'No?'

'No, General. But let me git you a drink.' He raised his glass. 'This ain't no red-eye. This here's genuine Scotch whisky. You'll have a glass?'

'No, thanks.'

'Oh!' Bannon replaced the glass on the bar. 'Wa'al if 'n' you ain't drinkin', what exactly are yuh doin' here?' he asked.

'I'm here to kill you,' replied Jamieson softly.

Bannon's air of nonchalance for once abandoned him. He gazed thunderstruck at the frail figure of the old soldier. Then, he laughed, but there was no humour or gaiety in his laughter.

'Yo're gonna kill me! But why in . . . .'

'You know why, Bannon. You arranged Ned Brown's murder. Wa'al, Ned was a boyhood pal of mine, an' I aim to have my revenge.'

'This ... this is crazy!'

'I s'pose it's also crazy to suggest that yo're exactin' tribute from practically anyone who's anyone in Larch County?'

'Of course it is! I'm jest a businessman, a plain, respectable businessman.'

'Liar!'

'Now, I'll wager you ain't got no actual proof, General?'

'No.'

'Rumours. Malicious rumours.'

'That's right, General. There ain't no truth in any

of 'em,' declared Sheriff Dave Lloyd. 'An', as for Mr Bannon arrangin' the murder of Ned Brown, why that's darned ridiculous.'

'Is it?'

'Yessir. Jest who d'yuh suppose he ordered to do this killin'? Painless, the Dixon boys an' Butch were all attendin' a luncheon at the Prince Albert this afternoon, an' they got witnesses in plenty. As for Raven, wa'al, I already told yuh, he was with me, searchin' for some renegade Arapahos. An' we was nowhere near the spot where Ned Brown was murdered. We was at the opposite side of Larch County, in fact.'

'How convenient.'

'It's the truth.'

'I don't think so.'

'Are you callin' me a liar?'

'Yes, Sheriff. That is exactly what I'm calling yuh.'

'Goddammit! How dare you?'

'Sally Yeates witnessed the murder. She is adamant that Ned Brown's killer was yore friend, Raven.'

'She must've been mistaken.'

'No; I don't believe so.'

'Yo're takin' a twelve-year-old girl's word against mine?'

'She had no reason to lie.'

'Yo're sayin' I have?'

'Jim Bannon has bought you, Sheriff. That's well-known.'

'You cain't prove that.'

'Nope. Jest as I cain't prove Raven killed Ned Brown.'

'So, what are yuh gonna do? Shoot Mr Bannon? You try, General, an' I'll arrest yuh. Now, I don't wanta have to do that, you bein' a national hero, an' a sick man an' all, but if you . . . .'

'Shuddup, Sheriff. You ain't gonna arrest nobody.'

'I am the law round here.'

'The law's defunct.'

'That's right,' added Stone. He smiled grimly. He observed that all seven had been drinking liquor, whereas he and his companions were stone-cold sober. That, he reflected, should give them quite an edge in any ensuing gun-fight. 'This ain't no court of law,' he growled, 'so, we don't need no proof. We know yo're guilty, an' we aim to act as judge, jury an' executioner.'

'But . . . .'

'No buts, Sheriff,' said Jamieson. 'As far as I'm aware, you haven't actually killed anyone yet. Therefore, if yuh wanta step aside, yo're free to do so.'

Lloyd scowled. He had no wish to get involved in a shoot-out with Wild Willie and his friends. The general might be no shootist, but he recognized Stone, and he rather suspected that the big, blond-haired man and the stony-faced Indian would prove no mean gunfighters. He glanced anxiously at Bannon.

The mayor smiled thinly.

'Yo're either with us or against us, Dave,' he hissed.

The sheriff's heart sank and the colour began to drain from his fat, florid cheeks. He knew that, should he withdraw, Bannon would regard him as a traitor. Without him, the odds were still six to four in Bannon's favour, and Bannon's men were all professional gunmen. The general and his friends, on the other hand, were something of an unknown quality. He might hope to survive the gun-battle with them. He could not hope to escape retribution, however, should he defect and the mayor and his enforcers win the shoot-out, as Lloyd assumed they would.

'OK, Mr Bannon,' he croaked finally. 'I ... er ... I'm with you.'

Bannon grinned broadly at the general.

'Odds of seven to four against. They ain't too good,' he sneered.

'I've known worse,' retorted Wild Willie.

The four promptly lined up against the seven. From a distance of approximately thirty feet the two groups faced each other. It was at this point that the sheriff made one last desperate attempt to avert the inevitable.

'General!' he cried. 'You an' yore men are takin' the law into yore own hands. That ... that ain't very sensible. Why . . . .'

'Shuddup!' snarled Raven. 'If 'n' these fellers

wanta die, then let's oblige 'em.'

'Yeah, let's do jest that,' agreed Painless Peachum gleefully, for he had no doubt that he and his fellow hired guns would easily out-shoot the frail-looking general and his friends.

The other three gunslingers were a little less sure, and Jim Bannon and Dave Lloyd were downright apprehensive. However, there was no room for further argument. The die was cast.

'I'll give yuh up to the count of three, General,' rasped the mayor. 'If 'n' you an' yore friends don't back off by then, we start shootin'.'

'OK,' said Jamieson.

'Right! One ... two . . . .'

Neither Raven nor Painless Peachum waited for Bannon to complete his count. Both went for their guns immediately he reached the count of two. But they were by no means quick enough. It may be that the whiskey they had consumed slowed them down a fraction. At any rate, before either gunman could aim and discharge his revolver, Jack Stone and Red Lynx fired off their first shots.

Stone drew, aimed and fired his Frontier Model Colt in one smooth, lightning-fast movement. The .45 calibre slug struck Raven in the chest and hurled him back against the bar-counter. The black-clad gunslinger thudded into and slowly slid down it until finally he found himself in a sitting position on the floor. Stone's shot had ripped a huge hole straight through Raven's body, causing blood to seep out back and front. A wide smear of it ran down the bar-counter, while his shirt-front was soon soaked in the fast-spreading gore. Raven vainly attempted to staunch the flow with his bare hands, his mouth fell open, his eyes glazed over and he toppled sideways, to lie motionless on the floor.

Painless Peachum fared no better. The Crow drew and fired his Army Colt with a speed to match the Kentuckian's. And he was equally as accurate. His shot drilled a neat hole in the centre of Peachum's forehead and exploded out of the back of his skull, sending splinters of bone and a mixture of blood and brains splattering against the highly polished, engraved mirror that ran the length of the wall behind the bar. The scar-faced gunman was dead before he hit the floorboards.

As for Jim Bannon, he had never claimed to be much of a shootist. He hastily attempted to pull the long-barrelled .30 calibre Colt from the shoulder-rig beneath his coat, but the gun caught in the coat. Before he could release it, Wild Willie Jamieson had drawn his service issue revolver. The general smiled coolly and aimed and fired. Once, twice, thrice, the slugs thudded into Bannon's body, hitting him in the shoulder, the chest and the belly. He, too, crashed into the bar-counter, then bounced off it and collapsed in a heap, his blood and guts spilling out across the floor. The second of Jamieson's three shots had smashed through his rib-cage and literally ripped his heart in two. Bannon's reign of terror was ended. Forever.

The sheriff and Harry Eales had, by chance, lined up against each other. They fired simultaneously. However, while Lloyd hurried his shot and missed, Eales, who had out-drawn the sheriff, took careful aim and made no mistake. His shot blasted an enormous hole in the sheriff's chest, knocking Lloyd backwards. Using the bar as a prop, Lloyd somehow or other managed to remain on his feet. He attempted to raise his revolver for another shot at the horse-rancher, but he was too late. Eales' second shot struck him in the right eye and ricocheted upwards into his brain.

Of the remaining three of Bannon's hired guns, only Butch Mabey succeeded in loosing off a shot. However, like Sheriff Lloyd, he rushed it, and the bullet whizzed harmlessly a good foot above Red Lynx's head. At the same moment, Jack Stone blasted the Dixon brothers with his second and third shots. One slug hit Arnie Dixon in the throat, demolishing his Adam's apple, while the other ploughed into Ike Dixon's chest. A split second later, shots from Red Lynx also ripped into the brothers' chests, and Stone's fourth bullet struck Butch Mabey in the shoulder. Then, Jamieson fired a second time, and Eales a third, to finish off Mabey.

As the gunsmoke slowly cleared and the acrid reek

of cordite permeated the air, the crowd inside the bar-room, and those peering in through the windows and over the top of the batwing doors, gazed in a stunned silence at the heap of bodies spreadeagled across the floor immediately in front of the bar-counter. Jim Bannon, the sheriff and Bannon's five enforcers had all been cut down in less time than it takes to consume a glass of red-eye. Wild Willie Jamieson and his three friends, meantime, remained standing, all of them seemingly unhurt.

The general smiled, slowly replaced his pistol in its holster, then suddenly appeared to stumble. He staggered forward a couple of steps and, before either Harry Eales or Red Lynx could grab him, pitched face-downwards onto the floor.

Ten

Between them, Stone and Eales turned the general over onto his back and carefully examined him. He was completely unscathed, yet he was stone-dead. His faulty heart had finally given out.

The Kentuckian glanced up at Red Lynx and said quietly, 'I guess this is how he would've wanted to die. With his boots on.'

The Crow nodded.

Stone thereupon closed Wild Willie's eyes, and then he and Eales examined the other seven bodies. None was breathing. All were quite dead.

By the time they had finished, the crowd inside the saloon had swollen considerably, and everybody was discussing the drama they had just witnessed, although in rather subdued tones. Outside, the news had quickly spread throughout the town. As a result, Senator Fletcher McBain and the mortician, Clarence Joab, soon arrived upon the scene. While Joab promptly went to work, measuring the various corpses, the senator confronted Stone and his two companions and demanded an explanation.

'It's been a long time, Senator,' said the Kentuckian, ignoring, for the moment, the other's demands.

'Whaddya mean?' enquired McBain.

'I mean, since we last met.' Stone smiled grimly. Earlier mention of the senator had pricked his memory. He recalled only too clearly the inglorious part the lawyer, Fletcher McBain, had played during the battle at Beaver Wells. The man had prospered since then, that was evident. And the years had been kind to him. Yet he would always remain, in Stone's view, a stinking, lousy coward. 'Yo're a man of some importance these days,' remarked the Kentuckian.

'Yes, wa'al, I guess I have risen a li'l in the world,' replied McBain smugly.

'But that don't cut no ice with me,' growled Stone.

'Nor with me,' added Harry Eales, eyeing the senator coldly.

'We ... we ain't talkin' 'bout me,' said McBain hastily, for he had no wish that either man should reveal in public his part in the events that had earned the general his famous soubriquet.

'No?' said Stone.

'No. I asked you for an explanation as to what's happened here? An' why? Goddammit, we've got the mayor an' the sheriff both shot dead, an' Harrison Creek's favourite son an' national hero, General

William G. Jamieson, also dead on this bar-room floor! As a representative of the US Government, I must demand an explanation. Indeed, it is my duty to do so.'

Stone nodded. He had no particular wish to converse with McBain, yet he recognized the other's legitimate claim to an explanation.

'OK,' he said, 'it's like this . . . .' The Kentuckian thereupon related the details of Ned Brown's murder and how Sally Yeates had chanced to witness it. He then told McBain what Sarah Yeates had revealed and how the general had determined to end Jim Bannon's reign of terror. 'An', as you can see, Senator,' he concluded, 'the general achieved what he set out to do.'

McBain eyed the seven corpses, then glanced at the body of the famous Indian-fighter.

'At the cost of his own life,' he remarked.

'His heart finally gave out,' explained Stone.

'Yes, wa'al, while I obviously cannot condone the general takin' the law into his own hands, I can nevertheless understand an' sympathize with his havin' done so.' McBain smiled wryly and added, 'That still leaves you fellers in a difficult position.'

'It was a fair fight. Anyone here'll tell yuh that,' drawled Stone.

'Even so, a peace officer was killed.'

'A dirty, low-down skunk who connived at murder.'

'That may be the case, but, if 'n' you three remain

here in Larch County, then Deppity Truelove, when he returns from his visit to the Double B, will be duty-bound to try to arrest you.'

'I don't see why?'

'It'll take a trial to determine yore guilt or innocence. Sure, you may well step free at the end of it, but . . . .'

'I do not submit to any white man's trial,' declared Red Lynx.

'Nor me. I cain't hang around here for days on end, while the law takes its course. I got me a hoss-ranch to run,' said Eales.

'Quite so.' Again McBain smiled. Then he continued, 'Now, we don't want no confrontation with Deppity Truelove, do we?'

'Guess not,' said Stone.

'Then, take my advice an' skedaddle. Once yo're gone, I'll explain things to the Governor an', on account of the general bein' involved, I figure he'll sure as Hell want the matter dropped. The general will have his grand funeral, Jim Bannon an' the others will be quietly laid to rest, an' the whole incident will be forgotten. Leastways, it will outside Larch County.'

The three exchanged glances. What the senator said made good sense. Colorado's governor would not want its favourite son's reputation tarnished in any way. He would be only too happy to let matters rest. And, since none of them had any thought of returning to Larch County . . . .

'OK,' said Stone. 'We'll lam outa here pronto.'

'Good thinkin'!' said McBain. 'It's a pity you fellers won't be able to attend the general's funeral, but, you may depend upon it, I shall make certain he has a fine send-off. Indeed, I'll personally contact the Governor an' all interested parties. I'll go telegraph 'em straight away.'

So saying, the senator turned and, pushing his way through the crowd that still thronged round the scene of the gun-fight, he headed for the door.

Once outside, Fletcher McBain breathed a sigh of relief and grinned to himself. The forthcoming funeral was going to be the biggest event of its kind in Colorado for as far back as he could remember. And he was proposing to make the most of it. He felt certain he could extract sufficient political capital out of the situation to virtually ensure his re-election to the Senate in the Fall.

First of all, he must volunteer himself as one of the pallbearers. Then, in the aftermath of the funeral ceremony, he would naturally find himself besieged by newshounds eager for a story, any story, concerning the late lamented Lieutenant General 'Wild Willie' Jamieson. This would give him the opportunity to promote himself as one of the heroes of Beaver Wells. As he had done hitherto, he would play the part of the modest hero, saying very little, yet inferring that he had fought shoulder to shoulder with Wild Willie. Then, regarding the gun-fight in the Foaming Jug saloon, he would regale the newspapermen with the story Jack Stone had just told him. And he would go on to state that he had become aware that all was not well in Larch County, and that he had been preparing to launch an investigation when Wild Willie had suddenly made his move.

This, McBain told himself, would establish him, in the eyes of the public, as a hero in the mould of Wild Willie and as a politician eager and willing to stamp out wrong-doing. With Stone and his two companions long gone from Larch County, there would be nobody to contradict McBain's version of the incident at Beaver Wells, and, as for his claim that he had intended to investigate Jim Bannon, who could disprove it? Not a soul. Indeed, should anyone make a reference to his stay at Bannon's hotel and the luncheon-party thrown in his honour, he need only say that his suspicions had not been aroused until some time after his arrival in Harrison Creek, and that he had attended the luncheon simply in order to lull Bannon into a false sense of security.

It was in a state of supreme optimism, therefore, that Fletcher McBain returned to the Prince Albert Hotel, where he promptly demanded a bottle of the mayor's five-year-old Scotch whisky.

Meantime, back at the Foaming Jug, Clarence Joab was superintending the removal of the eight bodies to his funeral parlour. As he emerged through the batwing doors of the saloon, he found himself confronted by Jack Stone, Harry Eales and Red Lynx.

'I … I thought you fellers were gonna leave town pronto?' said Joab.

'We are,' said Stone, 'but, first, we'd like a word with you.'

'Indeed? Wa'al … er … wh … what can I do for yuh?' stammered the mortician.

'A coupla favours.'

Joab stared nervously at the three tough-looking strangers. He had just finished observing the carnage they had created. They were not, he decided, men he would wish to cross.

'Anythin' I can do to oblige,' he muttered.

'OK. First of all, how many rooms d'yuh have in yore funeral parlour?' enquired Stone.

'Two,' said Joab. 'One at the front, an' a somewhat larger room at the back.'

'Then, place the general's body in the front room an' the others in the rear.'

'But . . . .'

'No buts. I don't want them stinkin', murderin' sonsofbitches in the same room as Wild Willie.'

'Ah!'

'You'll arrange it that way?'

'Yes … yes, I'll see to it. You … you have my word.'

'Good! Now my second request. Do yuh lock the door to the funeral parlour?'

'Nope.' Joab laughed. 'There ain't no need. Them corpses ain't goin' nowhere.'

'Fine. So, tonight, leave a lantern lit in that first room.'

'But, why should ...?'

'Me an' my friends gotta quit town in a hurry,' explained Stone. 'However, we'd like to pay our last respects to the general. So, we plan on returnin' during the night when folks is asleep.'

'I see.'

'We'll be gone long 'fore first light.'

'Yessir.'

Stone fixed the mortician with his cool, pale-blue eyes.

'If 'n' we should run into Deppity Truelove an' a reception committee, yo're a dead man,' he said softly.

Clarence Joab shuddered. The menace in the Kentuckian's voice was unmistakable.

'Don't worry,' he said. 'I'll keep my trap shut.'

The church clock struck twelve. It was the midnight hour as Jack Stone, Harry Eales and Red Lynx crossed the town limits and cantered down Main Street towards the funeral parlour. Before they had left Harrison Creek, they had purchased a black mare, a saddle and a couple of shovels. Stone led the mare, who was ready saddled, by her bridle, while

Eales and the Crow each carried one of the shovels, strapped to his saddleboot.

Eventually, the three riders reached the funeral parlour and dismounted. They tied the four horses to the hitching-rail outside, climbed the short flight of wooden steps onto the stoop and then tried the door. It was unlocked, and they stepped quickly inside.

A lantern was burning, as promised by Clarence Joab, and, directly beneath it, Lieutenant General William George Jamieson was laid out on a marble slab. He was in full military uniform.

The two white men removed their Stetsons and all three stood for a few moments, in silence and with bowed heads. Then Stone replaced his hat on his head, stooped over the general and lifted him off the slab. Preceded by Harry Eales and followed by Red Lynx, the Kentuckian carried the body of Wild Willie across the room and out onto the stoop.

They clattered down the steps and then proceeded to hoist the general into the saddle, on the back of the black mare. Using whipcord, Stone secured him to the saddle.

'This ain't very dignified,' muttered Harry Eales.

'Nope,' said Stone.

'A travois . . . .' began the Crow.

'Would leave a trail,' said Stone.

'Yes.'

'So, this is the only way, dignified or not.'

The others nodded and then all three mounted and, with Stone again leading the black mare, they headed out of town and off towards the distant mountains of the Front Range.

They journeyed throughout the night and then, following a brief halt for breakfast, pressed on once more. Stone grinned to himself as he imagined the furore created back in Harrison Creek when the general's body was discovered missing. Doubtless search parties had been sent out to scour the countryside. However, there was little or no chance that any of these parties would pick up their trail. Stone and his companions had forded rivers and streams, cantered across rocks and scree, through woods and gulches, and over hills and high ridges. It would have taken an extremely experienced Indian scout to follow their tracks, and, as far as Stone was aware, no such person was likely to be found anywhere in Larch County.

It was late afternoon, a full seventeen hours after they had ridden out of Harrison Creek, when eventually they reached their destination. They chose to stop at an isolated spot in the foothills, directly beneath the towering, snow-capped eminence of Pike's Peak. Here they dismounted and, while Jack Stone and Harry Eales proceeded to dig a grave, Red Lynx collected together a pile of small rocks.

Once the hole was large enough to satisfy the Kentuckian, he and Eales climbed out. Then Stone unfastened the cords binding Wild Willie to the saddle and lifted him down from the black mare's back. He and Eales, thereupon, carried the general across to the grave and laid him gently to rest.

When they had heaped the dirt back into the hole, they took the rocks, which Red Lynx had gathered, and built a small cairn at the head of the grave. This done, Harry Eales said a few words culled from various Army funerals he had attended. Afterwards, the three stood for a few moments in silent prayer, Harry Eales and Jack Stone praying to their God and Red Lynx to his.

'Wa'al,' said Stone finally, 'guess we've done what the general wanted us to do. So, may he rest in peace.'

'Amen to that,' concurred Eales. Then he asked, 'Where are you aimin' for now, Jack?'

'I ain't rightly made up my mind,' said Stone, 'though I s'pose you'll be headin' for Nevada?'

'Yup.'

'Mebbe I'll ride along for a li'l way?'

'Fine.'

'What about you, Red Lynx? enquired the Kentuckian.

'I go north,' said the Crow.

Stone nodded, and the two white men thereupon shook hands with Red Lynx. Then all three remounted their horses and rode off, Jack Stone and Harry Eales heading westward, while Red Lynx began his long journey north to Montana and the faraway Sapphire Mountains.

CURRICULUM AND INSTRUC

CURRICULUM AND INSTRUCTION

An Introduction to Methods of Teaching

R. Nacino-Brown
Festus E. Oke
Desmond P. Brown

First published 1982 by
MACMILLAN EDUCATION LTD
London and Oxford
Companies and representatives throughout the world

ISBN 0–333–32181–2 (pbk.)

11 10 9 8 7
06 05

This book is printed on paper suitable for recycling and made from fully managed and sustained forest sources.

Printed in Malaysia

Contents

Preface

This book has been written specifically for students in Advanced Teachers Colleges, Colleges of Education and for first-year students studying education in Nigerian universities. Practising teachers and those involved in in-service courses should also find the book useful, as well as students doing NCE by correspondence.

It follows the syllabus in Curriculum and Instruction drawn up in Zaria in 1980 by representatives of the Faculty and Institute of Education, ABU, Zaria, assisted by representatives of numerous Advanced Teachers Colleges and Colleges of Education.

Every effort has been made to cover all aspects of the new syllabus in the manner suggested by representatives at the Zaria meeting. If some topics are briefly or extensively treated, it is because the syllabus seemed to demand that kind of treatment.

Education students in Nigeria should find the book very useful in that it has been written by people who have a combined experience of over thirty years in Nigerian education and are familiar with most, if not all, of the current problems and needs.

Further reading is advised and lists of readings that are considered essential and supplementary are included at the end of each chapter.

R.N.-B.
F.E.O.
D.P.B.

Acknowledgements

The authors wish to thank their colleagues, past and present, and former students in the Department of Education, ABU, Zaria from whom they derived the inspiration to write this book. Many have moved, or are about to move on to assume positions of greater responsibility in different higher institutions of learning throughout Nigeria. Others are Principals, Vice-Principals, Senior Masters in Secondary Schools or Grade II Colleges or are teachers performing equally valuable work in the classroom.

In particular we would like to thank Professor Adamu Baikie, our former head of department who brought us all to Zaria, and who is such an excellent teacher himself.

Zaria, Nigeria
March 1982

MRS R. NACINO-BROWN
FESTUS E. OKE
DESMOND P. BROWN

1

The Teaching Profession

INTRODUCTION

This book is about teaching, planning teaching strategies and learning techniques to improve teaching. It is intended for students who plan to become secondary school or Grade II college teachers but it should also prove useful even to those who never take up the teaching profession, because in most other professions and in domestic life everyone is involved to some extent in teaching those around him.

In this introductory chapter the meaning of teaching is discussed with reference to learning, education, content and method. The reasons why teaching is regarded as a profession are explained and the factors that contribute to effective teaching are introduced.

WHAT IS TEACHING?

People can preserve the achievement of their generation by passing on to their children the experience they have gained and thus enable the young to begin where they (the old) left off. Without this 'passing on' of wisdom, each generation would be compelled to begin the life of man all over again; there would be no continuity and growth from one generation to the next. Moreover, human society functions by its members performing certain roles in the community. The skills needed to perform these functions or roles do not come naturally but have to bc taught and acquired through learning.

In traditional society, the task of directing the formal education of the young was the responsibility of the elders.

Social heritage, traditions and cultural values were transmitted to the young through symbolic ceremonial activities, examples and stories, which were told over and over again.

As technological and industrial developments began to influence and change the nature and values of rural and urban communities the role of teaching was passed on to professional teachers. In present day society such teachers work in schools and colleges which are the predominant teaching agencies.

Teaching and learning

What does the word *teaching* really mean and how is it related to learning? The word has often been used loosely to give the impression of a single unitary process to which a general theory could be applied. In fact teaching embraces many kinds of process, behaviour and activities that no single theory can explain adequately.

Teaching has been defined as an attempt to help someone acquire, or change, some skill, attitude, knowledge, ideal or appreciation. In other words the teacher's task is to create or influence desirable changes in behaviour, or in tendencies toward behaviour, in his students. John Dewey maintains that in order to say one has taught, some changes in student behaviour should have taken place, when he says: a person might as well say he has sold when no one has bought as say he has taught and no one has learned. This statement is probably too harsh, but it does introduce an important point: the goal of teaching is to bring about the desired learning in the students. Therefore the only valid criterion of success in teaching is the degree to which the teacher has been able to achieve this learning in his students.

Whilst it is necessary to have a learner in order to teach, it is not necessary to have a teacher in order to learn. People can and often do learn many things on their own without the aid of a teacher. In chapter five, where newer approaches to teaching are discussed, teachers are encouraged to use discovery and inquiry modes of teaching in which students learn largely through their own efforts and experiences. The teacher is still needed to organise and direct the students in those learning experiences, but they are more responsible for their own learning. The main aim of teaching as we have already said, is learning, and the teacher has to use his imagination, experience and intuition to choose suitable content and the most effective teaching method.

Content, method and technique

Content can be described as the subject matter, ideas, skills or substance of what is taught. It is a very important part of the curriculum. Method is the manner in which the content is presented to the students. Content and method are factors closely related to teaching and are an integral part of the teaching process. In choosing a particular method a teacher might make use of special techniques to ensure more effective learning. Hence technique is a part of teaching. In chapter three the curriculum is discussed in more detail and you should find it helpful in understanding how the content of what is taught in Nigerian schools is selected. Chapters seven and eight on organising instruction and behavioural objectives will help you understand how you can plan and structure the content that is to be learned. Chapters four and five deal with methods of teaching, and chapter six with teaching techniques.

Research evidence concerning the best method of teaching has been ambiguous. There are many studies which compare one general teaching method to another, but the results are so difficult to interpret that the evidence to date gives little or no encouragement to hope that there is a single, reliable, multi-purpose approach which can be regarded as the best. Instead of searching for a single right way, we should therefore focus on the possibility of combining a variety of teaching methods to improve learning. There is at present no known single approach that can succeed with all kinds of students or achieve all instructional goals. Teaching has to be approached in variety of ways that facilitate learning or development.

Education and teaching

People's understanding of the meaning of education has changed over the past few hundred years. At one end of the scale is the older view which refers to just any process of bringing up or rearing. What is lacking in this concept is the development of understanding and of modes of thought in the learner which are desirable. Being initiated into family or cultural traditions which involve no thinking, only memorising or copying, cannot be called education. In the same way, learning practices that are not generally considered desirable in society, like stealing or acting violently, also cannot be considered as education. The more recent and more specific concept links educative processes with the development of states of a person that involve knowledge and understanding in depth and breadth, and also suggests that they are desirable.

Education, as far as we are concerned in this book, will be considered as initiation into activities and modes of thought that are worthwhile. Education implies that a person has achieved or will eventually achieve a state of mind characterised by a mastery of and a care for worthwhile things viewed in some kind of cognitive perspective.

A trained or skilled man is not necessarily educated. Trained suggests the development of a competence in a limited skill or mode of thought, whereas educated suggests a linkage with a wider system of beliefs. In the same way teaching is not necessarily educating, because teaching and training are used synonymously. Teaching someone to type, ride a bicycle, weld metal or kick a football, with purely vocational or economic ends in view, is not educating. To educate implies giving people a wider cognitive perspective so that they develop breadth and depth in knowledge and understanding. The teaching of skills can be done in such a way as to be called educating if such skills are seen as part of a broader picture and their historical perspective, social significance and aesthetic merit are understood.

People can become educated through vicarious experiences apart from formal teaching or training. Private reading or study, travel or social contacts can be very educative. In a philosophy of education course the concept of education and its connection with teaching and training will be treated in more depth than is possible here.

Whether a person is a teacher or an educator really depends on his aims or goals. If a teacher approaches a subject from a narrow viewpoint without seeing it from a wider perspective in relation to other subjects and life itself, he could be said to be teaching or training and not educating. For the benefit of our students we should attempt to do more than teach or train – we should educate.

TEACHING AS A PROFESSION

A profession is generally considered to have certain characteristics:

1. It deals with a special field of knowledge or information.
2. Its practitioners must have had special training in the field and have demonstrated their ability by some sort of examination that tested their qualifications to serve the public in the profession and hence work for the improvement of society.
3. Its members belong to an organisation that makes provision for the licensing and certification of its members and sets up machinery for their professional growth by organising regular courses and seminars and by publishing journals.

Doctors, dentists, lawyers and engineers, to mention but a few, are considered professionals by most people. The question arises as to whether teaching is also a profession. Under (1) above teachers do specialise in particular subject areas and also study education itself in some depth. They have special training in the field, in the form of teaching practice, as required by (2) and they have to pass examinations in order to qualify as trained teachers.

In many countries there are national or state bodies to which all teachers belong. In Nigeria there exist professional organisations like the Nigerian Union of Teachers (NUT), the Science Teachers Association of Nigeria (STAN) and the Mathematics Teachers Association of Nigeria (MAN), and most of these organisations publish regular journals as required by (3) above. In countries where private colleges and universities exist in addition to state universities, as in the USA, Canada and the Philippines, teachers must be certified or licensed to teach in addition to possessing a degree in education. In Nigeria and the UK, since all universities and colleges of education are financed and run mainly by the respective governments or government agencies, the granting of educational qualifications by any university is considered to be certification in itself and no additional licensing is required. In-service training courses in Nigeria are arranged for teachers by State and Federal Ministries of Education and hence it would seem that teaching can also qualify as a profession under (3) above.

Why then is it that in Nigeria teachers are not universally regarded as professionals in the real sense of the word? Some of the reasons for this may be:

(a) The employment of untrained teachers in schools and colleges, to counter the current shortage of qualified teachers.
(b) The lack of respect and low status accorded teachers in present day society.
(c) Some teachers failing to regard themselves as professionals and as a result not taking sufficient pride in their work.
(d) Teachers rarely get disciplined or dismissed and hence some tend to become casual and neglect their work.

It is unlikely that the shortage of qualified teachers will become less acute in the next few years, as the number of schools is increasing and teachers are leaving the teaching profession to take up jobs which are more financially rewarding. If those remaining in teaching are going to improve their status and professional image they will have to concentrate on being more dedicated and disciplined, in other words behave more like professionals, and see to it that members who discredit the teaching profession are appropriately dealt with.

FACTORS CONTRIBUTING TO EFFECTIVE TEACHING

Teacher characteristics

As Douglas has pointed out, the greatest single factor in the teaching process is the teacher. No technique, no method, no device, no gadget can guarantee success – only the teacher can do this. The greatest motivating device yet discovered is the highly motivated teacher.

The characteristics of a successful teacher can be conveniently grouped under two main headings: personal and professional.

Personal characteristics

Researchers generally believe that students are the best judges of the personal characteristics of teachers. Studies indicate that in the opinion of students the most highly ranked personal characteristics are: sympathy and kindness, helpfulness, patience, a pleasing personal appearance and manner, emotional stability and self control. Lower ranked, but still considered important, were such characteristics as fairness and impartiality, a sense of humour, honesty, enthusiasm, creativeness and resourcefulness. It is impossible to be dogmatic about the way a teacher should behave towards his students in terms of the characteristics, except to say that the best teachers probably possess most of these to a fairly high degree. There are possibly as many different types of successful teachers as there are methods of teaching. As you gain in experience you will develop your own style of dealing with students inside and outside of the classroom, and it would be advisable to incorporate the above characteristics in your approach as best you can.

Possibly one of the main failings of some Nigerian teachers is a certain lack of dedication to teaching which often results in lessons not being properly prepared and planned, and teachers being absent from their classes. The rather low salaries teachers receive forces some to engage in small businesses on the side to help supplement their income. Such businesses should not result in the teachers neglecting their duties to their students. If a teacher finds that he is spending so much time on his own private enterprises that he does not have sufficient time to attend properly to his lessons and his students, it would be better for him to leave the teaching profession altogether.

A dedicated and hardworking teacher will find the job quite rewarding and can derive satisfaction from seeing former students succeed in life. Students never forget the teachers who really helped them in school and years after they will talk about them with affection and gratitude, even imitating their mannerisms. If you take up teaching you will find it a difficult profession to practise. It can be extremely taxing and exhausting at times. Some people cannot take the life for very long and eventually give it up but not without some slight feelings of regret. D. H. Lawrence once said: 'I was, but am no more, thank God – a schoolteacher – I dreamed last night I was teaching again – that's the only bad dream that ever afflicts my sturdy existence' (*The Macmillan Treasury of Relevant Quotations*, 1980 p. 552).

Professional characteristics

No matter how kind, amiable and well meaning a teacher is he cannot possibly succeed unless he has a thorough knowledge of the subject he is teaching and a good general knowledge. On the other hand a very knowledgeable person completely lacking in sensitivity or human emotions is not likely to be successful either, especially if he behaves like an army sergeant on the parade ground. In Nigeria there are certain professional characteristics which when combined with the personal characteristics we have mentioned should help a person succeed in the teaching profession. We will merely list them here as they are dealt with in more depth in other parts of the book.

A professional teacher should have the following qualities:

(a) A mastery of the subject to be taught.
(b) An understanding of the basic principles of children's growth and development.
(c) A good general knowledge.
(d) A knowledge of methods and techniques.
(e) A positive attitude to the work.
(f) A willingness to adapt his or her teaching to local needs taking into account the materials available.
(g) Courage to struggle for better standards and conditions in the school.

ACTIVITIES RELATED TO TEACHING

Understanding students

A theoretical knowledge of students' growth and development must be translated into a real and active effort to understand individual students who are being taught. In order to guide learning effectively the teacher should know how much the students are capable of grasping at their various levels of maturity, and their interests and previous experiences, so that he will be in a better position to motivate them. It is also important that a teacher actually likes most, if not all, of the students. Those he or she finds it difficult to like will require an extra effort. Students are very perceptive and if they note a certain positive attitude or warmth in a teacher they are likely to respond. However, if they sense that the teacher does not really care whether they succeed or not they will become discouraged and may even cause a discipline problem for the teacher concerned. Whatever your physical appearance, big or small, fat or thin, good looking or plain, whatever your personality, introvert or extrovert, quiet or talkative, if the students sense that you care about their passing their exams and succeeding generally you are unlikely to experience any serious discipline problems.

Planning: organising learning experiences

Teacher planning, which involves formulating objectives and organising learning experiences, are treated more extensively in chapters seven and eight. We will briefly introduce them here.

In every facet of life it is important to plan ahead. If you are a student in a university or an advanced teachers' college, and if you are sensible, you plan your study hours, your expenditure, your leisure and your vacations. We all have personal short and long term plans about what we want to do and where we want to go. In the business world planning, cost accounting, profit projections and future expansion all have to be planned meticulously. The same is true of teaching: a teacher has to plan ahead regarding what, when, and how he is going to teach if he wants his students to succeed. Selecting *what* to teach implies selecting objectives and content. Deciding *when* to teach topics or subject matter involves structuring a course in a logical sequence. Choosing *how* a particular lesson or unit should be taught involves the selection of appropriate methods and instructional materials.

Apart from planning your teaching in order to help the

students you should also plan to help yourself. If you enter a class with only a vague idea of what and how you are going to conduct the lesson, you will probably leave it having caused a certain amount of confusion among the students and lost their respect in the process.

Selecting and utilising instructional materials

If a teacher wants to teach effectively, he or she is bound to make use of a variety of instructional materials. The chalkboard, textbooks, student guides, pictures, handouts, laboratory and other forms of equipment, radios and cassette recorders are examples of instructional materials that can and should be used. Their selection, utilisation and evaluation requires professional skill which can only be acquired through training and practice. In chapter ten the use of instructional materials in teaching and learning is discussed more extensively. Suffice it to say at this point that by making use of such materials a teacher has a chance to teach well, but without them he will almost certainly not teach at all.

Management and discipline of students

When you begin teaching in a secondary school or teacher training college for the first time you will almost certainly be a bit nervous and on edge, and unless you are superhuman you are bound to make a lot of mistakes. Be prepared to listen to the advice of older teachers if the advice seems reasonable and is likely to prove effective. You will meet very good teachers in your school and others who are unfortunately somewhat ineffective. An older and very experienced teacher was once overheard when he advised a young graduate about to meet his first class. He firmly told the teacher not to smile for the first two years in front of his students. Clearly this is too severe but young teachers so often have problems because they are too familiar with those they teach. You will find classroom management and discipline treated in more depth in chapter nine. It is an area of increased concern in this decade when students are becoming more and more rebellious. It requires a skilled teacher to manage and ensure a certain amount of discipline in the students in his class. Too much severity will cause a rebellion, while an over casual attitude will result in academic chaos.

Choosing and implementing appropriate teaching strategies

How often have we heard it said of a teacher that he knows his subject but cannot put it across to his students? Such a teacher is poor in methodology. He will be trying to teach decimals to students who cannot add, political theory to students who do not know the meaning of the word politics, and chemical equations to students who do not know what an atom is. Surely you have met such people in your years as a student? You might meet some in your years at university or advanced teachers' college.

In this book we have treated teaching strategies extensively in chapters four and five and teaching techniques in chapter six. Also in chapter twelve you will find some hints on innovative practices in teaching. The way one teaches is so important. With the right methods and techniques students can grasp concepts and ideas that they never believed possible. Poor methodology resulting in bad teaching not only frustrates students but minimises their chances of success in the future.

Evaluating students' progress

The evaluation of students' performances in attaining predetermined goals or objectives is another factor which contributes to effective teaching. From the students' point of view it helps to motivate them, a good grade rewarding those who have worked hard and achieved success while a poor grade can be a warning to do better in future to those who have been somewhat lazy or careless. With the ever-increasing competition in Nigeria for admission to higher institutions of learning, students like to be realistically evaluated so that they are better able to judge how they will fare at the WAEC examinations. Teachers who give assignments and fail to mark them or who give terminal or end of year exams which are unreasonably easy, or difficult, do not gain the respect or admiration of their students. In fact they will only discourage them and possibly make them opt for other subjects in which the teachers are better assessors.

Evaluation is treated more extensively in chapter eleven. Readers are encouraged to refer to it as it is another factor contributing to effective teaching.

CONCLUSION

In this chapter we have briefly discussed the nature of teaching, what is involved in teaching as a profession and the factors that contribute to effective teaching. We have tried to point out that the life of a teacher is not an easy one but that there are some long term intrinsic rewards even if the extrinsic rewards are fairly minimal. To be a successful teacher requires certain personal and professional characteristics as well as the ability to understand students, plan the curriculum effectively, and make good use of instructional materials, teaching strategies, and evaluation techniques.

As Sidney Hook once pointed out: everyone who remembers his own educational experience remembers teachers, not methods and techniques. The teacher is the kingpin of the educational situation. He makes or breaks programmes.

EXERCISES

1. Briefly discuss what teaching is and its relationship to (a) learning, (b) content, method and technique, (c) education.
2. Is teaching a profession? Why are teachers not regarded by everyone as professionals?
3. Discuss the personal and professional characteristics that are likely to make a teacher effective.
4. Discuss activities related to teaching which are essential for effective instruction.

ESSENTIAL READING

Highet, G. (1963) *The Art of Teaching*, Methuen, London.

Moulay, George, J. (1970) *Psychology of Effective Teaching*, Holt, Rinehart & Winston, New York.

Risks, Thomas M. (1958) *Principles and Practice in Secondary Schools*, American Book Company, New York.
Shipley, Morton C. *et al.* (1964) *A Synthesis of Teaching Methods*, McGraw-Hill, New York.

SUPPLEMENTARY READING

Hirst, P. H. and Peters, R. S. (1970) *The Logic of Education*, Routledge & Kegan Paul, London.
Peters, R. S. (1966) *Ethics and Education*, Allen & Unwin, London.

2

The Theory and Practice of Communication

INTRODUCTION

A good number of our waking hours is spent communicating in various ways, through various means and at various levels. Often we talk to our friends about things that interest us, listen to the radio broadcast for the weather forecast; watch television for the late night news; attend conferences or lectures; read books, magazines and newspapers; write and often read what we write. In other words we continually interact with people, with ourselves and with our physical environment, and the basis of this interaction is communication.

In teaching, the teacher engages in communication when he gives a lecture; leads a discussion; explains the content of a chapter in a book; demonstrates a laboratory procedure; explains visual materials; elaborates his own point of view of an issue; and many others. In fact the teacher is constantly communicating everytime he is with his students and his colleagues. It is for this reason that we deemed it necessary for every teacher, especially the new ones, to have an understanding of the process involved in communication. This chapter deals with the elements which make communication occur as well as factors that will affect its effectiveness. Barriers to successful communication and possible ways of overcoming them with special reference to teaching are also discussed.

WHAT IS COMMUNICATION?

Communication has been defined in many different ways.

Like 'education' it is a concept which has no single, correct or best definition. In fact there are as many different meanings as there are people who might attempt to define it. Basically communication means the transfer, transmission, or exchange of ideas, knowledge, beliefs or attitudes from one person to another. Probably one of the most comprehensive definitions, and the one we will base our discussion on, is that given by Warren Weaver and Claude Shannon (1949) in their classic work *The Mathematical Theory of Communication*. They defined communication thus: 'The word communication will be used in a broad sense to include all the procedures whereby one mind may affect another. This involves not only written and oral speech but also music, the historical arts, the theatre, ballet, in fact all human behaviour.' This definition implies the existence of people who have something significant to share with each other and that this sharing affects the way they behave. This also implies that there are many different media through which people communicate and language is just one of them. This chapter however, considers only human communication with special reference to teaching.

THE COMMUNICATION PROCESS

'Process' has been defined as 'any phenomenon which shows a continuous change in time' or 'any continuous operation or treatment'. On the basis of this we can say that communication is in fact a process. It is an activity that is on-going, dynamic and not static but continually moving. It has no fixed sequence of events in that it is impossible to talk about the beginning and the end of communication. Furthermore, the elements which make communication possible are fluid; they interact with each other and each affects all the others.

Three fundamental elements have long been identified as necessary for any form of communication to occur. These are the communicator, the message and the receiver. However, Berlo (1960) forwarded a more complete picture of the process by identifying the following elements: (a) source, (b) encoder, (c) message, (d) channel, (e) decoder, and (f) receiver.

Any form of human communication has a *source.* This source could be a person or a group of persons with a purpose or an intent to communicate. This purpose is expressed by the source in the form of a *message.* The message is then translated into a code of a systematic set of symbols, which may be verbal, gestural, written, graphics, or any other form available. This process of translation is referred to as *encoding.* The encoder is responsible for taking the purpose and expressing it in a message. In human communication encoding is performed by a person's vocal mechanisms which produce the sounds and by the muscle systems which produce bodily movements such as hand gestures, facial expressions, and posture. The message is then transmitted or carried via a certain *channel.* A channel can be thought of as a medium, a carrier, or a message vehicle. In short, it is the means through which the message is transmitted to the *receiver.* The receiver is the person at the end of the channel for whom the message is intended. He then re-translates or decodes the message into a form that is useful to him. *Decoding* is done by the receiver's motor skills and senses; he listens, reads, thinks, evaluates, and so on. As soon as he understands the message, he reacts or responds to it in his own unique way. This response the source gets from the receiver is what we call *feedback* which is an additional necessary element of the communication process. In human communication the encoding and the decoding of the message are performed by the source and the receiver respectively, thus the source and encoder are treated as one and the receiver and the decoder as one as well. Figure 2.1 is a diagrammatic representation of the process of communication showing the different elements as discussed.

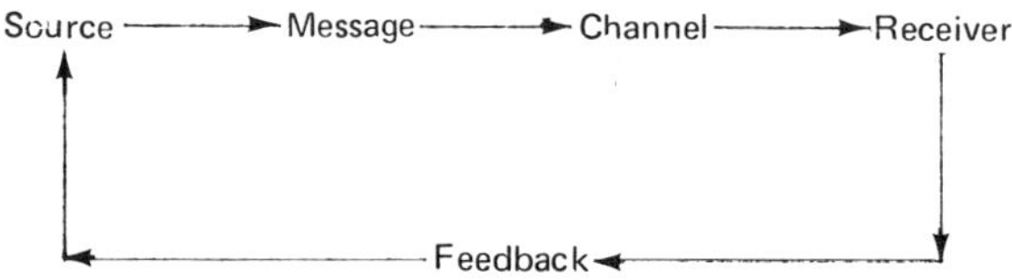

Figure 2.1 *The communication process*

Let us translate figure 2.1 into the communication process that takes place in a classroom between teacher and students.

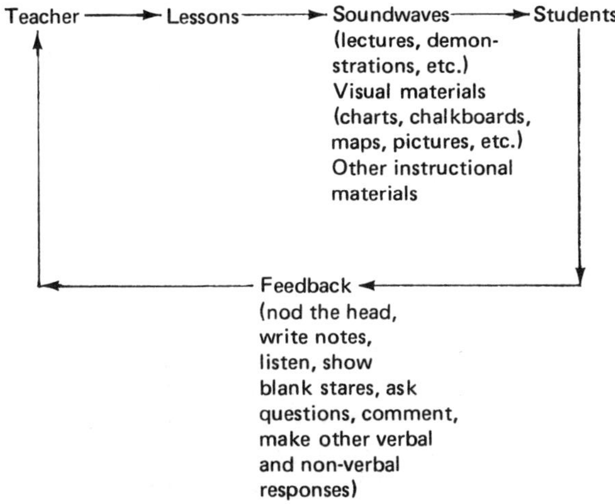

Figure 2.2 *Communication process in a teaching–learning situation*

In a teaching--learning process the teacher is almost always the source who initiates communication. Given a purpose which may be teaching students the operations involved in solving problems concerning fractions, the teacher through his vocal mechanisms and other muscle systems, translates his intentions in the form of a forty-five-minute lesson plan. He carries out this plan through the use of language, oral and written, and other visual and auditory materials or aids to convey his ideas, knowledge and others. The students who are the receivers in this case, listen, interpret, evaluate and assimilate the message in a form that they can understand. These functions they perform through the use of their sensory skills. As soon as they receive the message they react or respond to it. They may write notes; copy something from the board; listen intently; frown, which may signify bewilderment or confusion; or even ask questions. These responses which we call feedback are an important element in the process because they enable the teacher (source) to adjust or re-construct his message to suit the existing situation. For instance, if the teacher gets feedback that indicates boredom, hostility, or confusion, she can stop and try another avenue for clarifying that part of the message which elicited the said responses. She can therefore, regulate the rate of her speech, change her choice of vocabulary, or change the structure of the message. If a teacher is not observant and resourceful, she may not be sensitive to consider what feedback she is getting from her students and therefore, may not respond to it. In this case, the teacher is not communicating, merely transmitting, which is not the true essence of effective communication.

A story was once related to me by a colleague concerning a new member of the staff who was teaching mathematics. As soon as the new teacher entered the room, he greeted the students with 'Good Morning!' and a big grin. Then he took out his chalk and eraser and after briefly stating the lesson for the day, proceeded to write on the board. He started from one end of the board and finished right down the bottom of the other board with a bold circle around the final answer. While writing, he kept on trying to explain to the students (more likely to the board) what he was doing. At the end of his exposition, he said, 'Did you understand?', to which one courageous student answered, 'No Sir!'. The teacher then asked, 'Which part of the lesson did you not understand?' and the student replied, 'Sir, that part after you said, "Good Morning" '.

BARRIERS TO EFFECTIVE COMMUNICATION

Have you ever found it difficult to get other people to understand what you mean or do what you want them to do? Often we wonder why some teachers have discipline problems in class. Even you get a shock everytime you read your students' examination booklets and find answers which are contrary to what you thought you said. Preachers and priests are concerned with the apparent indifference exhibited by members of their congregations to their sermons. Parents' advice about honesty, respect, industriousness and the like, seems to fall on deaf ears. Evidence around us and our personal experiences suggest that successful communication is difficult to achieve. There are certain barriers which, when not adequately considered, might cause communication to breakdown somewhere along the process. Some of the more important ones are discussed below.

(1) *Inadequate verbal communication skills.* The most essential verbal communication skills necessary for human communication (face-to-face, interpersonal) are speaking, writing, listening and reading. Although the first two may be regarded as more relevant to the source, and the last two to the receiver, at some point in the communication process the roles of the source and the receiver may be reversed. This is the reason why the above mentioned skills are necessary to both communicator and receiver.

Adequacy in all four verbal skills means sufficient vocabulary and knowledge of the structure of the code (language) being used. Speaking needs additional skills such as correct pronunciation, appropriate voice inflection, good diction and enunciation as well as an accurate interpretation of feedback (verbal or non-verbal) from the receiver. Writing needs additional skills such as the ability to spell words correctly and the ability to use punctuation marks in their proper places. Listening is probably more critical than reading in the sense that there is no way to verify what is heard or said because the sound quickly disappears. Besides, listening is not just a matter of hearing sounds but it involves catching the patterns of thought and giving meanings to the words or phrases. It implies therefore, that listening involves comprehension or understanding.

If the source is inadequate in verbal communication skills, then he is limited in his ability to translate his thoughts, ideas, or intentions into a message that would elicit the response he desires. Likewise, certain deficiencies in the receiver's verbal skills will affect the way he gives meaning and consequently the way he reacts or responds to it. When the receiver fails to understand the message or some portion of it, then communication breakdown results.

(2) *The problem of meanings.* When communicating it is important to recognize that the same word has different meanings to different people depending on their experience and background, their patterns of thought, and their verbal communication skill level. The words themselves have little or no intrinsic meanings. Their meanings lie with the people who act on them. They also depend on the context in which they are used. For instance the word 'silly', which a European or Asian would take to mean 'be serious', can on occasions

be very offensive to a Nigerian. In other words, meanings cannot be transmitted, because they are not in the message but in the receiver.

Serious communication breakdown then can be attributed to the false assumption that people have the same or similar meanings for identical things. What is suggested here is that no two people can ever have the same meaning for anything. They can have similar meanings only to the extent that they have had similar experiences or are expecting to have similar experiences. Thus a man who has taken part in a battle will give a different meaning to the concept of war than somebody who has never seen a gun fired.

(3) *Contradicting verbal and non-verbal messages.* Verbal communication is often accompanied by non-verbal behaviours such as facial expressions, hand gestures and posture changes, which in themselves give out certain messages. When verbal and non-verbal messages contradict each other a feeling of unease or confusion is aroused. You may be saying, 'I like your dress', but your facial expression shows a look of distaste or aversion. Somebody may be explaining her side of the issue, but her facial expression and other gesticulations may give away the fact that even she does not believe in what she is saying. Sometimes it is difficult to recognise the meanings of non-verbal messages, although we recognise that they are there. It has been found that misunderstandings between races have resulted from basic cultural differences in non-verbal habits. For instance, Europeans generally seek for more eye contact when talking to others than do Africans. White people might assume that the averted gaze of Africans is a sign of insecurity and shiftiness while for them it is a learned and accepted habit showing a sign of respect. Likewise, black people can assume the white man's stare is aggressive and domineering.

(4) *Noise.* Miscommunication sometimes results because of some kind of interference in the reception of the message. This may be caused by noises such as shouts and laughter of children playing in a nearby playground, or hooting of horns of cars passing by, or even the buzzing of a bee. A man may be trying to listen to somebody talking, but because there are other groups of people engaged in conversation in the same room, he may miss the message or some portion of it. In the

classroom, students may create unnecessary noises by shifting their feet too often, dragging their chairs, coughing or tapping their desks with their pencils. In any case, noise will distract receivers from listening and will disrupt the source's train of thought causing him to falter in his speech or to stop because he has forgotten what he was saying.

IMPROVING CLASSROOM COMMUNICATION

Effective teaching implies effective communication. Hence there can be no separation of the goal to improve teaching and the goal to improve communication. The following are suggestions that may be useful to teachers in their effort to achieve successful communication with their students. Some points may seem obvious but it is our experience that it is often the more obvious things that seem to be most neglected.

(1) *Make an effort to improve on your speaking ability or skill.* Learn to speak in a direct, confident, friendly and conversational fashion. Make your words alive by accompanying them with appropriate gestures of the body, head and arms. Vary the tone of your voice and the rate of your speech to obtain desirable effects. It is generally believed that the overall effects of heightened feeling on utterances is that the voice becomes high pitched, loud and rapid. In contrast, depressed states will result in a low pitched, weak voice, and slow rate of speech. Thus, a teacher's voice will reveal whether he is inspired and enthusiastic about his subject matter, or whether he is bored, tired, irritated or indifferent about what he is saying.

When speaking, pronounce every word distinctly and loud enough to be heard by everyone without yelling or without using too much energy.

(2) *Plan and organise your message* (in this case your subject matter) in a logical, and easy to understand manner. You may be able to use with effect Aristotle's suggestions in the art of persuasion. He advocated that a discourse should be divided into three clear sections: (a) Introduction: Tell them what you are going to tell them; (b) The Argument: Tell them; and (c) The Recapitulation: Tell them what you have just told them. The ability to recapitulate could be very

useful, even necessary, because no matter how keenly your audience (students) attend to what you are saying, their attention may wander due to physical or mental fatigue or some kind of noise.

(3) *Assess the needs, abilities, and possible interests of your students.* Adjust your choice of words, concepts and examples to suit them. Do not take it for granted that because something is interesting to you, it will equally be interesting to your listeners.

(4) *Be a good listener.* Listen attentively to students' questions, answers or comments. They become more interested and satisfied if they know that you too consider what they say.

(5) *Beware of students faking attention.* This is a common habit among students. They try to appear to be listening when their minds are somewhere else.

(6) *Try to avoid technical and difficult materials.* If they cannot be avoided, explain them thoroughly in terms that the students understand. Many students are alert and enthusiastic at the beginning of the class, yet tune out when the teacher begins to give the meat of the lesson.

(7) *Try to eliminate possible noises that might distract students from listening.* If they can not be avoided, try and overpower them by speaking louder than normal, or better still by engaging the class with other activities that do not involve listening.

(8) *Encourage students not to get over-stimulated about things that they hear.* Often because of their eagerness they jump at an idea, make a quick decision without listening and consequently often come to the wrong conclusion.

EXERCISES

1. Identify some factors that affect the effectiveness of the communication process. How does each factor contribute to successful communication?
2. What are the essential elements in the communication process? Discuss each briefly.
3. What are some of the causes of communication breakdown? Explain each briefly by giving examples.

4. Discuss why effective teaching implies effective communication.
5. Make a plan that one could follow to help improve one's speaking skills.

ESSENTIAL READING

Berlo, D. K. (1960) *The Process of Communication*, Holt, Rinehart & Winston, New York.

SUPPLEMENTARY READING

Cherry, Colin (1957) *On Human Communication*, The Technology Press, Massachusetts Institute of Technology, Cambridge, Mass.

Shannon, C. and Weaver, W. (1949) *The Mathematical Theory of Communication*, University of Illinois Press, New York.

Tanner, B. (ed.) (1976) *Language and Communication in General Practice*, Hodder & Stoughton, London.

3

Curriculum Studies: An Introduction

THE MEANING AND SCOPE OF CURRICULUM

The term curriculum has been defined in many different ways. It has been used to describe (Oliver, 1960):

(a) All the experiences a child has under the guidance of a school.
(b) All the courses or subjects which the school offers.
(c) The systematic arrangement of subject matter and activities within a course offered by a school (Integrated Science or Social Studies, for example).

The most complete and generally accepted definition of curriculum and the one we prefer to adopt in this book is under (a) above. What is described under (b) could be a collection of syllabi and (c) could be a scheme of work drawn up by a teacher. Curriculum is a broad term meant to include the complete experience of the student while under the guidance and direction of the school. It includes activities which are academic and non-academic, vocational, emotional and recreational.

A complete description of curriculum has at least three components:

1. *What* is studied: the 'content' or 'subject matter' of instruction.
2. *How* the study and teaching are done: the 'method' of instruction.
3. *When* the various subjects are presented: the order of instruction.

We accept this definition of curriculum because the author goes on to describe 'content' in a broad way to include academic subjects like Mathematics, Science, Language, Social Studies, vocational subjects like Creative Arts and Business Education, and recreational activities like drama and sports as well as other 'in school' activities.

In every country throughout the world the school has a role to play in training and educating the young. That complete *plan of action*, whether written down or simply in the minds of those involved in the instructional process, is the curriculum. It includes everything that is currently the *input* to the system of education, involving what is planned to take place both inside and outside of the classroom, under the direction of the school.

It is relatively easy to define or describe what a curriculum is, but it is much more difficult to plan and organise one. In the next section we will review some of the models of curriculum organisation that have been used in different parts of the world with a view to seeing Nigerian curricula from a better perspective.

PATTERNS OF CURRICULUM ORGANISATION

Introduction

The first, and possibly one of the most important decisions concerning the curriculum occurs when a country decides on its national aims or goals of education. These aims, if realistically and intelligently formulated, can set the stage for the remaining work in curriculum organisation. The problem is that national policies on education tend to be rather vague, possibly deliberately, and it is then up to the curriculum designers to work out how best the goals can be achieved.

The second major decision concerning the curriculum involves *what* is to be taught. Is it subject matter, concepts, intellectual powers, practical skills, or attitudes, or all of these? This is no small task, as you can imagine. As we will see later in this chapter, decisions as to what is to be learned are based on national policies, the demands of the society, the nature of the learners, the learners' stage of development and their interests.

As decisions are being made as to *what* is to be learned in an educational institution, thought has to be given to how this learning will be organised. In Nigeria schools have been used to *subject organisation*, but even this has been modified over the past fifteen years, being influenced by other forms of curriculum organisation such as the Broad Fields Curriculum. In 1965 few schools had heard of Social Studies, Integrated Science, Creative Arts or Language Arts, but now these are incorporated in many curricula from primary school to university. In addition, other activities like sports, school plays or cultural shows, which were before regarded as extra-curricular (outside of the curriculum) are now incorporated as Physical and Health Education and Drama and are considered an integral part of the school curriculum. These changes may have been brought about as a result of the philosophy behind the Social Processes and Life Functions form of curriculum organisation.

Science subjects which were taught from a largely theoretical point of view are now being taught experimentally and experientially, influenced by the Activity or Experience form of curriculum organisation.

It would seem appropriate at this point to examine in more detail the main patterns of curriculum organisation as identified by Hilda Taba and other writers on curriculum. Whatever pattern of organisation educational planners decide to adopt, they need to decide on the *scope* of what is to be learned and on the *centres of organisation* around which they will build learning units or experiences. Taba (1962) points out that there are different emphases in each of the different patterns of organisation and inherent strengths and weaknesses in each.

> Few curriculum designs give equal weight to scope of content covered and scope in intellectual powers, habits of mind, skills and attitudes to be acquired by the students. A broad scope of content may be accompanied by a narrow range of intellectual skills. And in reverse it is conceivably possible to develop a wide range of behaviours by studying content of a relatively narrow scope.

Subject organisation

This is the oldest and probably still the most widely used form of curriculum organisation. The content and skills to be mastered are divided up into distinct areas called subjects. Each subject has its own logical order, and teaching and learning takes place according to a definite sequence decided on by the content specialist.

In the last fifty years or so, as the boundaries of knowledge rapidly expanded so the number of subjects to be studied increased. Even within a subject, sub-divisions appeared and the result was excessive compartmentalisation and atomisation of knowledge. Chemistry was divided up into Physical Chemistry, Organic and Inorganic Chemistry, Biochemistry and Radiochemistry. English was fragmented into Language and Literature, Phonetics, Grammar, Syntax and Linguistics. While these sub-divisions might be justified at university level, at the secondary level they are likely to confuse and hinder rather than assist students in their attempts to learn.

Life problems, it has often been said, do not respect subject boundaries, and most value judgements cut across what we would call school subjects. For example a doctor who is trying to restore one of his patients to health will in some cases need to have an understanding not only of the medical (biological, chemical, physiological) problems involved but also of the psychological and emotional background of his patient.

Arguments that (a) specific subjects cover the important areas of social heritage and that mastery of them takes care of the full scope of education, and (b) that rigorous training in academic disciplines detached from social reality develops the abilities and skills most needed in meeting the demands of life problems, are clearly exaggerated and as such are highly suspect. A final argument against the traditional subject organisation of the curriculum is based on manpower studies which suggest that considerations other than high academic performance, such as values, motives and skills in social perception, are important factors which among equally able people differentiate those who succeed in life from those who do not.

The current form of curriculum organisation in Nigeria is

predominantly subject oriented but differs to some extent from what we have called the *traditional subject-oriented curriculum* and hence some of the arguments against the subject form of organisation do not apply to it. Whatever is studied does have to have a name or title. What is important is what is put under the umbrella of that title. Those who wish to do away with subjects have to suggest viable alternatives that will make learning in secondary schools more useful and relevant.

The Broad Fields Curriculum

This curriculum is essentially designed to overcome the compartmentalisation and atomisation of the curriculum by combining specific subject areas into larger fields. Under this form of organisation History, Geography, Civics, Government and Economics are combined into Social Studies, and Biology, Chemistry, Physics, Agriculture and Astronomy are combined into Integrated Science. Other fields which resulted from an integration of subjects are Language Arts and Creative Arts.

The unification of knowledge which it was believed would result from the Broad Fields Curriculum has not completely materialised. One of the reasons is that teachers, trained under the university system or in colleges of education, tended to specialise in a particular subject (Geography for example) and hence found it difficult to teach an integrated curriculum. Also the universities retained their subject oriented curriculum, and when candidates were considered for admission they were expected to have specialised in their later years in secondary school in particular subjects. Examining bodies like the WAEC were slow in drawing up examinations in Integrated Studies. The result has been the adoption of integrated studies in the first three years of secondary school, followed by two or three years of a subject oriented curriculum.

The wide coverage advocated by supporters of the Broad Field Curriculum also has its dangers. Students are in danger of acquiring a rather superficial knowledge of many topics and no deep understanding of anything. It has made apparent the weaknesses of the subject curriculum but before it is universally adopted more study needs to be carried out as to how the essential ideas of a field can be taught, provision being made for depth as well as breadth of understanding.

The curriculum based on social processes and life functions

This represents an attempt to provide a patterned relationship between the content of the curriculum and life. The curriculum is organised around the types of activities which constitute the common features of life in any culture. It is an attempt to overcome the disadvantages of the subject curriculum in which some of the academic disciplines were felt to be divorced from reality and hence of little use in solving everyday life problems.

The State of Virginia in the USA was one of the first to attempt to organise its curriculum around the processes of life. The nine areas of life that were used were the following:

1. Protecting life and health.
2. Getting a living.
3. Making a home.
4. Expressing religious impulses.
5. Satisfying the desire for beauty.
6. Securing education.
7. Co-operating in social and civil action.
8. Engaging in recreation.
9. Improving material conditions.

Some of the advantages of this curriculum as outlined by Marshall and Goetz were believed to be these:

1. It makes learning meaningful and relevant.
2. The students can draw on their own personal experiences and learn from each other.
3. It gives students an overview of social living of all times, places and cultures.

As Taba pointed out, several difficulties appeared in using the Social Process/Life Functions approach. It was difficult to link content meaningfully to the life function it was supposed to clarify. For example, how does one link Developing and Using Electricity to Earning a Living? This difficulty of finding one's way back to adequate content is common to all organised schemes which depart markedly from the conventional subject organisation.

The activity or experience curriculum

This type of curriculum organisation was specifically designed to counteract the passivity and sterility of learning and the isolation from the needs and interests of children of the conventional curriculum that existed in the first few decades of the twentieth century. The rationale behind this curriculum was that *people only learn what they experience*. In order to think logically children needed not only to absorb logical arguments or master logically-arranged material but actually to construct logical arguments themselves. Initially children were allowed a considerable amount of freedom to follow their interests, impulses and whims in investigating and experimenting. This was soon found to be unsatisfactory, however, as the children, though very active, learned little or nothing of value. There was at that time considerable confusion about how experience was related to organised learning. As the complexity of learning experiences increased it became more and more difficult to channel direct experience into intellectually organised knowledge. More recent modifications and adaptations of the experience and activity curriculum have taken the view that direct experience and spontaneous interests are an aid to learning but should not necessarily be used as organising centres for the development of units of learning.

There is no doubt that the activity or experience curriculum has had a profound effect on curriculum developments in recent years. Taba identifies two such effects:

> Experimentation with the activity or experience design has made perhaps two lasting contributions to the curriculum. One is the recognition of the role of active learning through manipulation, experience, construction and dramatisation . . . The second is the impetus it has given to studying child development, the principles and sequences of growth, and an effort to consider these sequences in the planning of the curriculum sequences.

Methods of teaching have also undergone considerable changes since the inception of the activity or experience curriculum and these are discussed at some length in the next two chapters.

The core curriculum

The advocates of this type of curriculum design saw in it a culmination of all the other designs mentioned in this chapter. The core curriculum was meant to develop integration of knowledge, to serve the needs of students, to promote active learning and a significant relationship between life and learning.

Possibly the choice of the word 'core' was unfortunate because it was interpreted in different ways almost from the beginning. There are several different types of core programmes, some of which are mentioned here;

(1) The core consists of broad problems, units of work, or unifying themes which are chosen because they afford the means of teaching effectively the basic content of certain subjects or fields of knowledge. These subjects or fields retain their identity, but the content is selected and taught with special reference to the unit, theme or problem.

(2) The core consists of broad pre-planned problem areas, from which are selected learning experiences in terms of the psychological and social needs, problems and interests of students.

(3) The core consists of broad units of work, or activities, planned by the teacher and the students in terms of needs perceived by the group. No basic curriculum structure is set up.

(4) The core consists of a number of subjects or fields of knowledge which are unified or fused. Usually one subject or field (English or Mathematics) serves as the unifying centre.

Core also came to mean those parts of the curriculum required of all the students as opposed to those which were elective. In a great many cases the core programme was not actually a design but one way of scheduling classes in large blocks of time and with more than one teacher assigned.

Where the core curriculum was adopted criticism centred on two main points:

1. The core curriculum failed to offer significant and systematic knowledge.
2. Teachers trained in specific disciplines found it extremely difficult to engage in integrated thinking about life problems since they lacked the broad competence required.

The core curriculum as described here might not appear suitable for adoption in Nigeria, except in the lower classes of the primary school, because of the series of state and government examinations that the students have to take and the competition to obtain entrance to higher institutions of learning. In countries where everyone is guaranteed a place in secondary school and where entrance to university is the rule rather than the exception for those who wish to, the core curriculum form of organisation might be successfully adopted. Nevertheless in Nigeria some of the ideas which the core and other types of curriculum organisation have put forward have been adopted to good effect. In drawing up syllabi there has been greater attention to relevance, student interest, integration of knowledge and active learning. Teachers are also being trained with a broader competence and in methods which allow for greater student participation in the planning and learning process.

WHO DECIDES WHAT THE CURRICULUM SHOULD BE?

The curriculum, as we said earlier in this chapter, comprises all the experiences a child has under the guidance of the school. It is the function of educational planners to draw up aims, goals, objectives and policies, as well as syllabi for examinations, that will give direction to those experiences that the child has while in school. In Nigeria, as in many other countries throughout the world, there are many bodies that influence the type of curriculum organisation that is adopted and what is eventually included in the school curriculum.

The role of national organisations

In Nigeria national bodies like the Federal Ministry of Education, the Nigeria Education Research Council, the Joint

Consultative Committee, the Interim Joint Matriculation Board in consultation with the West African Examinations Council and university and State Ministry of Education representatives help to draw up national policies on education, syllabi and examinations, for use within the country. Most examinations in Nigeria are of a federal nature except for certain papers within the Grade II certificate which are more regional. This type of arrangement ensures a certain uniformity of standards throughout the country. Universities and advanced teachers' colleges enjoy more autonomy and set their own syllabi and examinations subject to moderation by other university personnel. In the USA each state enjoys the freedom to experiment with its own curriculum and examinations, and even within a state each school district can pursue its own programmes within certain limits set down by the state Board of Education. Schools are still responsible for preparing their students for college and university, as well as for the College Aptitude Test, but the teachers seem to prefer to be able to design their own courses without being told what to teach by an official organisation.

In the United Kingdom there are numerous examining bodies, similar to the West African Examinations Council in Nigeria. Each of these bodies draws up its own syllabus and course objectives for those students who choose to take their examinations. Usually a school district or county will select which board of examiners is to be used in their area. Private schools are free to choose whichever board of examiners they prefer. Students in Nigeria used to take exams with the London GCE board and the WAEC was at one time connected with the Cambridge Board. Each of the examining boards has its own way of examining but the standards do not vary very much between them.

The system in Nigeria for setting syllabi should take into account the views of the teachers in the various subjects. The WAEC does get some feedback when examinations are marked each year by teachers. Ministry officials also conduct surveys in which teachers are asked to identify parts of the syllabus that they are having difficulty with. However the point still remains that if one examination syllabus in each subject is going to be used throughout the country, teachers must have voice in the setting of that syllabus.

The role of State Ministries of Education

In Nigeria, State Ministries of Education have to be aware of the needs of their own particular states, and of the different areas within those states, in translating what the Federal or National Organisations have stipulated as desirable of attainment. Subject syllabi are fairly uniform throughout Nigeria, but the number of lessons per week per subject may differ from state to state. Out of class activities can vary widely throughout the country and will be governed by environmental and climatic conditions. For example, swimming may be one of the important sports in one area but almost non-existent in another.

The Ministries of Education throughout Nigeria are responsible for ensuring that there are adequate facilities for learning. These facilities will include things like classrooms, laboratories, playing areas, a school auditorium/theatre, dining rooms and hostels for boarding students. In addition, materials like textbooks, exercise books, and sports and other recreational equipment are needed if the curriculum is going to become a reality. The most ambitious syllabi, aims and objectives may be drawn up for schools but without adequate facilities and materials they are just like so much hot air. Adequate funding is also necessary for feeding students, especially in boarding schools where school food is the only food available. Hungry or ill-fed students are not likely to learn effectively or participate in curricular activities to any great extent. Finally the teachers employed by the ministries should be satisfactorily and regularly paid. Contented teachers are very necessary for the successful implementation of the curriculum.

The role of the local community

There are not currently as many community schools in Nigeria as there were when private schools and voluntary agency institutions were in operation. However, with the recent emphasis on day secondary schools it is likely that the local community will be asked to play a more important role in curriculum decisions. When parents or guardians live close to their children's school, they tend to take a more active interest in the day-to-day affairs of the school. Fund raising activities can be organised to help buy needed equipment or to put up an extra classroom. Contractors and businessmen can help the school by supplying materials at cost price, which they are quite likely to do if they know that their children are going to benefit. Parents who work nearby at factories, co-operative farms, water-pumping and purification plants and such like can help to arrange field trips for students. School sports teams are likely to have greater support in local and state competitions when parents do not have to travel far to see their children participate. When the local community participates in any of the ways outlined above they are in fact participating in and contributing to the curriculum. Professional people from the community can be invited to talk to the students about their work and traditional leaders can be asked to give a detailed history of the area of their jurisdiction.

In most cases it will be up to the school authorities and the teachers to involve the local community in the running of the school. This will mean developing a good relationship with the people of the area, and gaining their co-operation and respect. How the local community can contribute to the school curriculum will vary and will depend on the school's immediate needs, but there is no doubt that it can in many ways make a very valuable contribution.

The teacher's role in the curriculum

The teacher's role in the curriculum can be described in this way:

> [The curriculum is not so much what is found in the printed guide (syllabus or scheme of work) as what the teacher makes of it in the classroom. It is his adaptation of it to meaningful learning experiences that really counts. The teacher should use the guide as a framework and must feel free to express his teaching methods in the way that can best help make him a success in the classroom.]

From this statement it is obvious that the curriculum can be a great success or a dismal failure, depending on the teachers. They are the key persons who alone can make the curriculum design achieve what it was designed to achieve. If they are dedicated, hardworking and imaginative they can enliven what would otherwise be dull and lifeless.

It will require a lot of imagination and inventiveness on the part of all teachers to make the syllabus vital and stimulating in the classroom. In addition the teachers' efforts as a team will to a very large extent determine whether the students' total experience in school will later be pleasantly remembered or best forgotten.

Outside the classroom the teacher also has an important part to play in the curriculum. Her informal contacts with students in the dining-room or the sports field will give her valuable information about the characters and personalities of her students. The students for their part will also be making value judgements about the teacher. To some extent the teacher *teaches what she is in herself*; long after students have forgotten the content of the subjects they were taught they will remember their teachers as caring, kind, lazy or even indifferent.

Of all the personnel involved in curriculum implementation and design, the teacher is almost certainly the most important. She is the one who implements the ideas and aspirations of the designers.

The teacher also has a role to play in curriculum design as a source of feedback to the school authorities and ministry representatives. If certain recommended practices or elements of the syllabus are not satisfactory, the teacher should endeavour to see that they are changed or eradicated. Educational administrators sometimes lose touch with what is happening in actual classrooms and need this important element of feedback from the teachers to keep them informed.

The learner and the curriculum

When it comes to the curriculum, the learner is the centre of attention, being both the subject and object, without whom the curriculum does not exist.

A *curriculum design* incorporates aims and objectives which it is hoped will be realised when the curriculum is implemented. It goes without saying that without the active and wholehearted co-operation of the students such aims can never be achieved. The curriculum is a joint venture which, though defined in terms of students' experiences while under the guidance of the school, requires that students and teachers work harmoniously together.

In some countries like the USA university and high school students participate in the curriculum design to the extent that they actually plan with their lecturers and teachers what they are going to study, at least in outline form. In order for this mutual co-operation to succeed a certain maturity and seriousness is required in the students, and for this reason is not suitable for younger people. When such joint planning had taken place, what was studied tended to be more relevant and interesting and since the students helped select the subject matter they felt more responsible for what they learned.

In Nigeria the school syllabi are determined by the West African Examinations Council. However, within a particular subject area there are still some choices about: (i) the order in which topics are to be treated, and (ii) which topics should be treated in depth or virtually ignored. A WAEC syllabus is extensive and it is not possible to cover all of it with every class. If the teacher feels the students in a particular class are capable under his direction of making sensible contributions regarding the above choices, he can involve them in the planning process.

A good teacher will allow a certain amount of feedback from the students during the planning and implementation of the curriculum. The information he acquires through this process will help him decide on the teaching strategy best suited to the interests and level of development of the students. Any curriculum planning which ignores the specific capabilities and characteristics of the students for whom it is planned will experience serious difficulties during the implementation stage. We can liken a teacher and his class to a football manager and his team. Just as the manager, if he wants to win a match, has to take into account the individual talents of his players, so too the teacher has to carefully consider all his students to successfully implement the curriculum.

In non-academic activities which are also part of the school curriculum, students can be much more involved in decision making, within the limits set down by the ministry and the school authorities. In Nigeria it has been the custom to have class monitors and school prefects helping extensively in the running of the school out of class hours. They help organise the school beginning with rising in the morning, cleaning the school compound, eating in the dining room, carrying out sports activities in the afternoons and, supervising study hours in the evening and ending with retiring to bed at night. Such responsibilities given to older students should, when conscientiously carried out, give them excellent training and experience for responsibility in their future places of work.

In conclusion it can be said that the consideration of students is of utmost importance in curriculum planning and implementation, and wherever possible the students should be involved in both processes.

EXERCISES

1. Discuss some of the definitions of curriculum and describe in your own words what you understand curriculum to mean.
2. Describe how the different forms of curriculum organisation discussed in this chapter have influenced curriculum design in Nigeria.
3. Discuss the teacher's role in implementing and influencing the curriculum.
4. How can the learner be involved in the planning and implementing of the curriculum?

ESSENTIAL READING

Taba, H. (1962) *Curriculum Development, Theory and Practice*, Harcourt Brace & World, New York.

SUPPLEMENTARY READING

Oliver, R. A. (1960) *Effective Teaching*, J. M. Kent & Sons (Canada) Ltd, Toronto.

Short, E. C. and Marconnit, G. D. (eds) (1968) *Contemporary Thought on the Public School Curriculum*, W. C. Brown, Iowa.

4

Traditional Time-tested Methods of Teaching

As a teacher you will find it necessary to use different methods of teaching to suit varying situations. In this and the following two chapters a fairly comprehensive description of teaching methods and techniques will be discussed to equip you to meet many, if not most of those situations.

There are some methods of teaching that have been used for many years and these we have decided to call Traditional Time-Tested Methods because they have stood the test of time. These methods can in certain situations be used very effectively by the skilled teacher of today, but it would be short-sighted to try to use them all the time.

These methods are:

1. The lecture
2. The discussion
3. The demonstration
4. The project
5. The study trip.

THE LECTURE METHOD

The lecture method, although considered by modern educators as traditional or out-dated, is probably still one of the most widely used procedures of teaching, especially in post-secondary institutions. Even secondary school teachers fall back on this method when they have had insufficient time to prepare their lessons. Often, beginning teachers resort to lecturing using portions of their own lecture notes gathered while they were students themselves. Despite the many criticisms regarding the lecture method, when carefully planned and skillfully delivered this method may in fact be pleasurable for the students, as well as achieving the desired teaching aims.

Nature and scope

Generally speaking, the lecture method is a process of delivering verbally a body of knowledge according to a pre-planned scheme. In the strictest sense, it is characterised by one-way communication. The teacher presents ideas or concepts, develops and evaluates them and summarises the main points at the end while students listen and take down notes. During the course of the lecture, students' questions are not normally encouraged and in cases where questions arise they are usually intended for clarification of facts and information and not for higher level discussion.

The lecture method has no place in the primary school and is not frequently used in secondary schools, especially in the lower forms. Nevertheless students in the upper forms of the secondary school should be given the experience of learning from lectures before proceeding to university, advanced teachers' college or the polytechnic where the lecture method is still the predominant approach to teaching. This should be accompanied by deliberate and conscious teaching of the skill of listening and the art of note-taking. This exposure to the lecture method in the final years of secondary schooling will surely prepare students for coping with the learning experiences they are likely to encounter when they go to post-secondary institutions.

When to use the lecture method in secondary schools

There are certain instances when the lecture method could be appropriately used in secondary schools. The following are justifications for its use at this level.

1. When introducing a new topic or unit

If the teacher's aim is to introduce a new topic or unit, a well organised overview in the form of a lecture may be advantageous. This will serve as an excellent opportunity for the teacher to develop students' familiarity with the subject as well as build appreciation of the values they will derive from its study.

2. *When presenting important materials not easily obtainable*
In secondary schools in Nigeria, good libraries are not always available. Materials like reference books, magazines and journals are frequently insufficient and outdated. Under these circumstances the teacher can gather important and relevant information for herself and deliver them to the students. She can then plan and organise her materials exactly the way she wants to present them. Students are saved from the frustrations resulting from searching for something difficult to locate.

3. *When supplementing textbook materials*
When supplementary materials are needed to enrich textbook materials, lectures can be very useful. Occasional supplementary lectures will make students realise that there are a vast number of things to be learned apart from what is in their textbooks. Sometimes awareness of one's ignorance can serve as a motivating force to learn.

4. *When developing interest and appreciation*
The lecture may serve as an effective means of arousing students' interest and appreciation. In the arts subjects, like literature for instance, the study of a poem, an essay, a play or a short story, will be better appreciated if it is preceded by a lecture revolving around the life of the author and the circumstances of its creation. In history, the lecture may be used to motivate students to a study of a particular era, by giving them an interesting historical background that would set them in the right emotional mood or frame of mind. In science, students will appreciate more the study of the Law of Flotation if they have an idea of how Archimedes came about his law (it is commonly believed that he discovered this law in the bath!!).

5. *When summarising important points after a unit of study*
When tying together the day-to-day lessons of a unit of

study, the lecture may be appropriate. A summary lecture could be organised where specific and seemingly isolated facts and information learned are related to each other to form a broader and more meaningful concept. As advocated by the Gestalt psychologists, in learning the whole is greater than the sum of all its parts. This implies that facts and information are meaningful only when taken in relation to the whole concept being taught.

6. When attempting to cover a lot of material in a short time
Using the lecture method just for the sake of covering more material in a shorter time may not be a very good justification for the use of this method in secondary schools. However in Nigeria, where the educational system is very much examination oriented, teachers sometimes have no choice but to try to finish all the units prescribed in the syllabus in any way possible. Towards the end of the school year when time is running out lectures may be the only means for the teacher to teach those topics still to be covered.

The technique of lecturing

Preparation. Just like any other approach to teaching, the lecture needs adequate and careful planning. It is important first to consider the objectives you would like realised. If the lecture is intended to arouse reactions or certain types of emotions, strong persuasive language may be necessary. In this case an outline of the main points to be treated may be more effective than the full written text. This will help ensure flexibility and spontaneity in the treatment of the topic, thus giving more life to what otherwise might have been a lengthy and boring verbal exposition. Often your style is hindered if a fully written lecture is in front of you, because the tendency is to follow closely what you had earlier written. Occasional spur-of-the-moment examples or remarks are effective in making the lecture more interesting.

Secondary school children have a relatively short attention span. They can only digest a few important points at a time. So in preparing lecture notes the teacher should limit his exposition to a few salient points.

It is important to prepare illustrative materials to accompany the lecture. Short demonstrations or other visual materials are effective means of helping facilitate students to understand. If illustrative devices are not used, try using verbal examples in the form of stories of people's experiences to enable students to form mental images. Words may easily be forgotten but mental pictures will long be remembered. As Callahan (1966) suggested, it is best to think of the lecture as encompassing a wide range of related methods and techniques, not just a continuous, uninterrupted unfolding of facts and ideas.

Design a systematic way of tying up the ideas presented. This entails drawing a plan for relating thoughts together to form a more meaningful concept.

Introduction. A good introduction is catchy and challenging. It should create an expectant mood in the students to get them to listen attentively. A short thought-provoking question could be used to get the lecture started. An anecdote or a story related to the topic could also be used, or a statement of the topic in the form of a problem might be effective. Sometimes a brief explanation of how you are going to treat the topic is sufficient to get the class ready.

If the lecture is aimed at developing a complex concept or idea the logical outline should be written on the board for the students to use as a guide in their attempt to listen and take down notes. If the material in the lecture is fairly straightforward the teacher can conceal his outline from the direct view of the students. This will add an element of sophistication to the teacher's style besides creating an impression of confidence and competence. As the lecture develops the main points can systematically be written on the board.

Presentation. The development of the topic should follow a logical order. It helps students if ideas or concepts are unfolded to them in a simple, easy to understand manner. The use of prepared illustrative materials at the appropriate time will make the lecture more dramatic and more meaningful. Repetition of concepts or ideas stated in different ways will help the teacher really drive home his points. A little humour here and there will also help ease the strain on students in their efforts to get as much out of your lecture as they can. The use of examples which are life-like could make theories and ideas more concrete, meaningful and will ensure better understanding. It is however essential not to use too many 'down-to-earth' examples to the neglect of the actual concept being presented. Students might well remember your examples while forgetting the concepts that prompted you to give the examples. Teachers marking examination scripts have complained that their students give them back their own stories and examples but fail to identify the related concepts upon which they were based.

Conclusion. Just as a good beginning is essential so also is a good ending. If you can get your students to think and discuss your lecture long after you have delivered it, you have made a good ending. If students as a result of your lecture are encouraged to search for more knowledge related to your topic you have achieved a desirable educational goal.

In Nigeria teachers very often summarise a lecture for students and give an outline summary on the board. Although this is one way of finishing up the lecture it has some drawbacks. When students know that the teacher will summarise the lecture for them they may not listen attentively during the lecture nor take down any notes of their own. How you as a teacher decide to wind-up a lecture will depend on the nature of the learners and the topic. At the end of the lecture the students should be able to see how the ideas you have presented are related to each other as a complete whole.

Suggestions for improving lecturing

1. The teacher's personality counts

Remember that in the lecture method of teaching you are the key person. All eyes are focused on you for a period of thirty-five to forty-five minutes. During this period your weaknesses and strengths can easily be noticed. Endeavour therefore to take care of your personal appearance, your manner of dressing, poise, mannerisms and so on. Even the way you speak is an expression of your personality. A well modulated voice, good diction, correct pronunciation and proper intonation are certainly essential ingredients of an effective lecturing technique. Facial expressions, gestures when used to emphasise points, are effective means of developing students' enthusiasm as well as of making the lecture alive.

A shrill or squeaky voice is irritating to the ears. A bellowing or rasping voice is equally annoying. A teacher with an unpleasant voice is therefore better advised to refrain from using the lecture method in its pure form, and should use other methods involving less talking but more student activities. A teacher who is slovenly dressed and untidy will have great difficulty in commanding the respect of his students. Remember that a teacher's personality is one of the most crucial factors affecting the total teaching-learning process.

2. Talk to your students

Learn to guide your eyes across the room attempting to look into the eyes of your students. Talk to your class, not at the ceiling, the table or the floor. This is an effective way of catching students' attention especially those whose minds tend to wander off to other things rather than the lecture.

3. Constantly check on students' understanding

Consciously observe students' reactions during the course of your lecture. Their behaviour may give indications as to whether you are being understood or not. Constant checking of the watch, yawning, forced coughing, unnecessary shifting of the feet or even blank stares may be signs that your students are not following your lectures or that they are bored. A good teacher is sensitive to students' reactions and is quick to think of ways to deal with them.

4. Adapt language to the level of students' understanding

Consideration should be given to the language level of the class. When lecturing to younger students, clear, simple and easy to understand language is essential. Terms needing explanation or elaboration should be adequately treated. High-sounding words may be impressive but they can result in misunderstanding and subsequent frustration on the part of the students.

Advantages of the lecture method

1. It has high inspirational and motivational value. It is therefore an effective method for creating interest and appreciation. If the objective however is to develop a skill another method should be used.

2. It supplements and enriches materials found in students' textbooks.
3. The teacher has complete control over the choice of knowledge the students learn. He can present exactly *what* he wants in the *way* he wants.
4. It results in economy of time and effort. Students' time and efforts are not wasted trying to discover things for themselves. In cases where the teacher has to cover everything specified in the syllabus before an external exam the lecture method is effective.
5. It can be used to teach large classes.

Disadvantages of the lecture method

1. It violates one of the principles of learning; that is, learning through active involvement as advocated by Bruner, Suchman, Austel and others (this is the reason why the lecture method should never be used in the primary school and only sparingly in the secondary school).
2. It reduces students to passive recipients of ideas and does not encourage the enquiring or creative mind. It could at worst produce students who are mere listeners and not thinkers.
3. It does not provide students with enough opportunities to practise their oral communication skills.
4. Giving lectures based directly on the textbook or readily available materials may be considered by the students as a waste of time as they can always read these things for themselves.
5. Students' understanding is rarely assessed during the lecture since they are not encouraged to participate or respond. During the lecture the teacher is limited in his judgement of their understanding.

THE DISCUSSION METHOD

Boardly speaking, when two or more people interact with each other verbally, we say that they are involved in a discussion. In the classroom discussions of one type or another often take place, sometimes deliberate and at others spontaneous. From this point of view, discussion is referred to as a technique within a method. It may occur at brief intervals during an informal lecture, a demonstration, or even during a laboratory lesson.

In this section, discussion is treated as an overall, step by step procedure of teaching a specific aspect of a subject or a course in order to achieve definite instructional goals. It is therefore considered as a pre-planned, organised, unique method by itself, and not as a part or element of another method.

The nature of the discussion method

This method covers classroom learning activities involving active and co-operative consideration of a problem or topic under study. It is characterised by increased involvement and active participation of members of the class. Unlike the lecture or the expository method where the teacher is the dominant person, in the discussion the teacher stays very much in the background. She poses the problem, initiates interaction, and allows students to pursue the discussion towards the attainment of the goal.

The interaction that goes on in a discussion group is illustrated in figure 4.1.

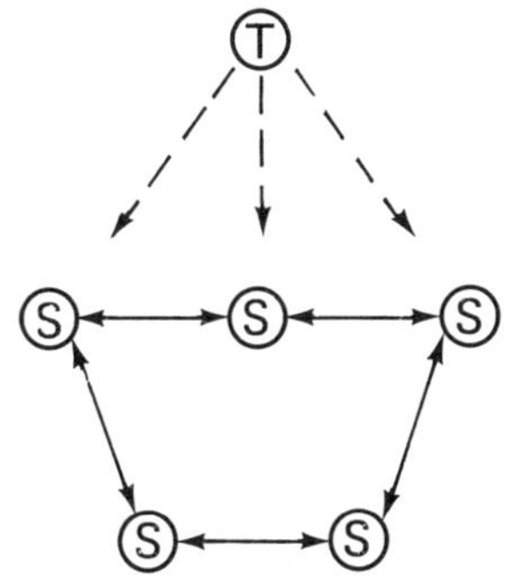

Figure 4.1

The unbroken lines with arrow-heads indicate a more or less maximum active verbal interaction among members of the group. This is the main feature which distinguishes this method from other teacher dominated procedures. The students carefully consider a topic, react to it, argue with one another, suggest solutions, evaluate alternatives and draw conclusions or generalisations. Thus they become creators rather than passive recipients of ideas. The broken lines indicate that the teacher, although an active participant, functions mainly as the initiator of interaction. From time to time he may clarify points to ensure that the discussion is proceeding in the desired direction.

The discussion method can be seen as a departure from the more traditional assign-study-recite approach to teaching where students are only required to reproduce what they have previously studied by giving the correct response when asked a question or when given the right cue.

Scope and limitations

The method has a wider application in arts and social science subjects, for example, Social Studies, Literature and History. However it can also be used in Science and Mathematics when the objective is to apply knowledge previously learned, and when there are relevant controversial issues. Thus this method is more appropriate when dealing with topics which are debateable, or problems with more than one possible solution.

Discussion is an effective means of developing the skill of utilising facts and information. This helps guard against knowledge becoming what A. N. Whitehead referred to as 'inert ideas', that is ideas which cannot be used to improve oneself or the society in general. In this method students learn not only to accumulate ideas, but also to dissect and evaluate them and find wider and more practical applications for them. As a consequence, better understanding is ensured making learning more meaningful and more lasting.

The degree of individual interaction in the discussion method increases as the group size decreases. This means that maximum student participation can be better achieved with smaller rather than larger groups in which every member can have a chance to express his or her views as well as to follow them up with supporting evidence. It is also easier for the teacher to get everyone involved if the number of participants is small, say between five and ten. When too many students are involved, between thirty and thirty-five, which is the normal class size in a secondary school in Nigeria, it is easy for the less able students to get lost or to withdraw.

It is probably better to use this method with older children who have already acquired the abilities necessary for intelligent discussion, for example, critical and evaluative thinking, listening and the ability to argue with supportive evidence. The teacher is the best judge as to whether the discussion is the most appropriate method in a given situation, bearing in mind the students' background and ability level.

Discussion procedure

Before deciding to use the discussion method, consider first the topic to be discussed. It could be a real problem or a hypothetical one. In either case, it should be an issue with more than one side to it, or a problem with no single clear-cut acceptable answer. In addition, the topic should be interesting, and interest stems mainly from familiarity with the subject. One cannot engage in a discussion on a subject one knows nothing about. Make sure therefore that the topic chosen is within the range of the students' experience as well as within their ability to discuss.

The subject should be not only interesting but also relevant to the lives of the students. Problems which do not concern them in one way or another may be regarded as a waste of time.

Discussion involves the intelligent exchange of ideas. It does not proceed in a hit-and-miss fashion. Participants should be able to present their views logically and support them as well, and the only way to ensure this is to give students adequate time to prepare themselves beforehand. They could do some preliminary readings on their own, and the teacher could suggest possible sources of information. He could even suggest possible ways of looking at the problem. The important thing is to get the students ready so that the discussion is not reduced to a pooling of nonsensical opinions.

Before actually beginning the discussion it is probably better to remind the participants of the rules of conduct to be observed. This includes talking only when given the floor, listening when someone is talking, respect for other members' points of view, and guarding against arguments turning into a personal conflict or fight. If there are no guidelines governing students' behaviour, your role becomes that of a traffic policeman trying to direct the flow of ideas or arguments, to avoid two or more people talking at the same time. You may not have problems getting some students to talk, but you may on the other hand have difficulty in getting others to stop talking.

Some discussion techniques

The discussion may take several forms depending on the objectives, class size and the ability of the students. The *whole class discussion* may be used when students have not had the training or experience in leading or conducting a discussion by themselves. Here the teacher becomes the leader of the discussion group, which in this case is the entire class of say thirty to thirty-five students. He poses the problem or the issue, initiates interaction, directs discussion among participants, ensures that the flow of ideas or arguments, proceeds towards the desired goal, and concludes the discussion by summarising the main points made. The success of this type of discussion depends to a large extent on the teacher's skilful handling of the interaction as well as the degree of students' readiness in terms of familiarity with the topic.

With more mature students, the *small group discussion* may be used. This involves dividing the class into smaller discussion groups and appointing a leader and recorder for each group. During the discussion session, the teacher goes from one group to another to assess their progress. He may help direct the discussion by asking leading questions. He may also lead the group back to the main issue if he observes that they are digressing from the topic. A time limit may be necessary in this type of discussion. This will encourage students to treat only important issues, and not to waste time arguing over unnecessary details. After the discussion, the recorder of each group reports to the class the summary of points for further discussion. The crucial factor that determines the success of this technique is the grouping.

Researchers working with discussion groups of four, six, eight and ten students found higher satisfaction and instructor grading. With increasing group size there is not only less time for each member to speak but there is also an increasing reluctance to participate. In larger groups the discussion also tends to be dominated by a few students.

In comparing groups of four students of similar personality traits to groups in which the students were different, it has been found that the heterogeneous groups produced superior solutions. Researchers suggest that heterogeneous groups are more likely to have a variety of alternatives proposed and that this permits inventive solutions.

In selecting members for each group, the teacher should consider the students in terms of their abilities, competencies and so on. It is obvious why only bright students, dull ones, or talkative ones should not be grouped together. Students with leadership potential can be distributed among the groups so that the discussion will progress at a reasonable speed. Otherwise, if a group consists of too many dull and shy students interaction will stop even before the discussion starts.

Another discussion technique that could be used is the *panel*. A panel of four or five selected students are each assigned to give a five minute talk about different aspects of the chosen topic. Suppose the issue is 'The Impact of Modern Technology on Society'. Each member of the panel presents a pre-prepared talk on any of the following aspects of technology: (a) its effects on the economy of the nation; (b) its effects on the way of life of the people; (c) its effects on the environment; (d) its effects on the educational system. While each speaker is delivering his or her piece, the rest of the class listens critically and jots down questions or points that they would like to support or refute. After the panel has concluded its presentation the discussion is opened on the floor (the members of the class not on the panel). Here, the teacher's role is to direct interaction towards constructive discussion. When everything is said and done, the class with the guidance of the teacher shares in summarising the main points and in drawing conclusions.

The discussion could also take the form of the usual debate, where two groups of speakers talk for or against the motion.

Sometimes it may be necessary for the teacher to modify the debate procedure to suit the situation.

Whatever type of discussion the teacher decides to use the following points are worth considering:

1. While the discussion is in progress make sure that every student is actively participating – sometimes the more talkative or able students tend to monopolise the discussion. In such cases you should be quick but subtle in directing the discussion to involve the less able ones.
2. Do not allow the discussion to digress into less productive side issues. If it does be alert to lead it back to the right path.
3. Limit the discussion to a few major facets of the topic. One cannot hope to achieve an in-depth treatment of a topic without limiting its scope.
4. Remember that the secondary schools and Grade II teachers' colleges have lessons which only last 35–45 minutes. The discussion should be so designed as to fit into the time available.
5. There are some students who will not be coherent in expressing their views. It may be necessary therefore to re-state what they say more clearly so that the rest of the group can understand what was said. The student can then be asked to confirm the clarification. Do not engage in this practice too often, however, as it does not encourage students to make an effort to express themselves in an understandable manner.
6. In the whole class discussion a periodic summary of what has been said is essential. This helps to evaluate the progress of the discussion as well as keep everybody up-to-date.

Advantages of the discussion method

1. It provides an excellent opportunity for students to practise their oral communication skills.
2. It gives students practice in critical and evaluative thinking and listening. This is often neglected by teachers.
3. Students seem to learn more readily from each other.

4. It helps students clarify their thinking – ideas get clearer when expressed orally.
5. It provides good practice for problem-solving.
6. It gives students training in the democratic processes.

Disadvantages of the discussion method

1. It does not easily lend itself to all types of subjects or topics. The choice of a suitable topic is the problem of the teacher.
2. It is difficult to achieve maximum interaction when the group is large.
3. It may give opportunities for brighter students to show off.
4. When a discussion leader is weak the discussion can result in unorganised unproductive activity.

THE DEMONSTRATION METHOD

Nature of the method

Demonstration has been described as an audio-visual explanation, emphasising the important points of a product, a process or an idea. It is basically an activity which combines telling, showing and doing for the benefit of an audience, be it a person or a group of persons. In teaching, the demonstration is generally used as a method but it is also frequently used in relation with other approaches to teaching as a special technique (Sund and Trowbridge, 1973). Thus in the *discovery approach* the teacher may demonstrate to his class the physical and chemical properties of several different metals after which the students are able to discover and formulate the concept of metal. In the *process approach* he may demonstrate the different process skills to be learned before giving the students exercises to practice them. Even in the laboratory the teacher shows students how to use a machine before letting them operate it on their own. Whether as a method or as a technique the demonstration can be very effective in the hands of a skilful and competent teacher in appropriate situations.

Although the emphasis in demonstration is learning by observing, it is often followed by doing. Thus, drills and practice exercises are frequently provided to enable students to perform the activity on their own or in groups. In any case, demonstration is a dramatic performance; the teacher or the demonstrator being the actor, the students the audience, and the materials and equipment the stage props.

Scope and limitations

The demonstration can probably find more applications in subjects involving skill learning, such as Physical Education, Vocational and Technical Education, and the sciences. For example, an Accounts teacher may demonstrate on the blackboard the procedure for preparing balance sheets. In Home Economics a teacher shows the steps to be followed in making a pattern and then laying it on the cloth, or she may demonstrate why one brand of food mixer is better than another. In Physical Education the teacher may demonstrate the breast stroke or frog kick in swimming. In Mathematics the teacher can demonstrate the addition of fractions, while in Science the teacher in the laboratory can demonstrate how to use the microscope. Although it may seem that this method is often used with material objects, one should not discount the fact that even abstract things like concepts, ideas and attitudes can be demonstrated.

Educators stress the values of discovery in learning and therefore regard other methods involving self-instruction and active manipulation as superior to demonstration. However there are occasions when it is necessary and appropriate to tell and show students what they have to learn. After all in real life we do not really discover things on our own all the time. There are things that we need to be told and shown.

The following are instances when demonstration is appropriate if not necessary.

1. When teaching a skill

In learning a skill, it is important that students learn the proper way of practising the skill right from the start. For example, when teaching swimming or typing a demonstration of the skills involved will provide a correct model of performance before any practice is carried out. It is true that students may learn skills on their own, but they may adopt a poor style or an incorrect technique if not taught, and it is difficult to modify a faulty skill which has become a habit.

2. When materials and equipment are insufficient
Very few schools can afford to provide enough instructional materials for individual or group study. This is especially true in subjects with laboratory periods where equipment is not only expensive but also difficult to procure. In such situations the teacher can set up a demonstration of an experiment while students observe, answer questions, record observations and formulate conclusions. In order to avoid students having accidents or damaging things like sewing machines, mixers or microscopes a demonstration and guided practice of how to operate them are necessary.

3. When experimenting with dangerous chemicals or solutions
In Chemistry and Physics for example, the use of high voltages or of dangerous chemicals like concentrated acids could be harmful to the students. While older students can after due warning be allowed to handle these things, with younger students it is advisable for the teacher to demonstrate experiments which require their use.

Techniques in preparing and performing a demonstration

To ensure an efficient and effective demonstration, the following should be carefully carried out.

1. Task analysis
It is necessary to determine and analyse first the objectives of the demonstration. This will serve as a guide in deciding which aspect of the demonstration to emphasise. If the objective is to develop a *skill*, the 'how' of the skill is probably the main emphasis. If it is to promote *attitude* then the emphasis would be the 'why' aspect. If it is to enable students to *formulate concepts* then a series of leading and thought provoking questions needs to be carefully prepared.

2. Preparation of explanatory materials
Since a demonstration is a dramatic performance, make sure

that all the materials needed are available and that every piece is exactly where you want it to be when you require it. It is most embarrassing and annoying to stop in the middle of the demonstration only to say, 'I'm sorry class, but I forgot to bring the weighing scale. Adamu, could you please go and fetch one for me from the store?' Interruptions such as this will reduce if not kill the interest of the students and once interest is lost it is difficult to regain it.

3. Rehearsal of the demonstration

It may be useful to give your demonstration a trial run, if possible with an audience which knows little or nothing about the subject. This will help you determine the clarity of your procedure and will also give you an idea as to whether you have planned too much or too little for the time allotted. In addition this is the best way to make sure that all the equipment is in working order.

4. Preparation of an outline

The outline is a subdivision of the whole demonstration into logical steps or stages. For younger children it is better to limit your outline to only a few steps, say four or five. With older students more complete outlines showing all the major steps can be designed. The outline can be shown to the students at the end of the demonstration when the teacher is summing up.

5. Preparation of the environment

Make sure that everyone can see and hear the demonstration. If materials are too small to be seen by students seated in the back rows, arrange for two or three students to go around with duplicates for close viewing. An enlarged diagram or illustration may also be useful in solving the problem of visibility. Another alternative is to organise the class into several small groups and then perform the demonstration to each group separately.

6. Decision on which type of demonstration to use

You may choose to do the demonstration yourself or ask one or two students to help you in the performance. You may also train one of your brightest students to perform the demonstration while you are explaining. Involving students can be very effective, especially if the one selected is well liked and respected by the rest of the class.

7. Preparation of written material
These may be in the form of a mimeographed handout or a written summary on the blackboard, and covered with a curtain. The back side of a large wall map would serve to hide the board. In any case written materials should not be given or shown before or during a demonstration, otherwise students might be reading your notes when they should be paying attention to what you are doing.

Written materials are useful because students rarely remember everything they see during a demonstration, and the provision of notes frees them from taking notes of their own and enables them to give all their attention to watching the demonstration.

Performing the demonstration

1. Establish the proper attitude
Get students ready and interested to attend to your demonstration. A properly and carefully stated problem which the demonstration will help solve may make a good start. A precise statement of the objectives of the demonstration is often sufficient to get students in the correct mood. Sometimes the way you organise your materials on your demonstration table will be enough to gain their interest and attention.

2. Keep the demonstration simple
Do not go into fine details which are not basic to the understanding of the demonstration. Bear in mind that students will have difficulty remembering too many points at a time. Keep your presentation so simple that even your less clever students will be able to follow.

3. Refrain from deviating from the main points
Try to stay on the right track all of the time. Be certain that the presentation is clear enough and postpone answering questions which might lead you to other points not so relevant to the understanding of the demonstration.

4. Pace the demonstration for dramatic effect
Do not take the demonstration at too fast a pace. If you go too quickly the students are likely to get confused. On the other hand if you go too slowly or drag out the demonstration the students are going to become bored and lose interest. By planning and rehearsing your demonstration you should be able to determine the optimum pace to achieve the effect you want.

5. Constantly check on students' understanding
As in other methods the teacher's sensitivity to students' reactions while he is demonstrating is very important. When symptoms of boredom or bewilderment become apparent be quick to do something about it. Students can be questioned to see if they understand what was just demonstrated.

6. Summarise and conclude the demonstration
The prepared written materials may be useful as a summary to the whole demonstration. As the teacher is winding up the demonstration students can also be involved in drawing up the summary.

Advantages of the demonstration method

In the hands of a resourceful, efficient and competent teacher the demonstration method of teaching can be very effective. Some of the advantages of the method are these:

1. It trains the students to be good observers.
2. It stimulates thinking and the formation of concepts and generalisations.
3. It has high interest value since it often involves the use of gadgets and equipment which may be new to the students.
4. It is economic in terms of time and money.
5. It is very effective as an introduction to skill learning.
6. It is most appropriate when teaching students how to operate a machine or some other piece of equipment.

Disadvantages of the demonstration method

1. It provides less opportunity for children to discover things or solve problems on their own.

2. Active participation is reduced as the children mainly act as observers.
3. When classes are big problems of audibility and visibility may arise.
4. It is difficult to evaluate thoroughly students' understanding during a demonstration.

THE PROJECT METHOD

The nature of the project method

The project has been defined as a unit of activity carried on by the learner in a natural and life-like manner and in a spirit of purpose to accomplish a definite, attractive and seemingly attainable goal. Although this definition was made a long time ago it still describes the main characteristics of the project as it is used today.

The project is essentially a learning unit, designed and conducted by students under the guidance of the teacher. Project goals are established by the students based on their own background experience, and they are encouraged by the teacher to work through study activities towards the attainment of those goals. The project differs from other traditional methods like the discussion and demonstration in that the student has much more autonomy in deciding what and how he or she is to learn. The project method also allows the student more freedom to investigate and gather data, and in some ways resembles more modern methods of teaching.

Scope and limitations

Projects can be undertaken in all subject areas in the curriculum but not necessarily all topics within a subject can be taught by means of the project method. Projects can be conducted by individuals or groups and they can be short or long. Short term projects last a few lessons, are easier to direct and control but they tend to achieve less. In long term projects which last for ten lessons or more, there is the opportunity to achieve more but students can lose their enthusiasm, become discouraged and lacking in ideas, and sometimes indisciplined. Group projects help students to work together and be creative. They also provide a natural mode of learning which is freed from the limits imposed by artificial subject area divisions.

Here are some examples of topics which could be studied using the project method:

Social studies. Writing a history of the local community. Writing an account of the development of the school.
English. Writing and staging a play for the school. Organising a school poetry competition.
Science. Studying ways of improving health in the school and local community. Surveying the different types of crops grown in an area near the school, the methods of farming, and other aspects of agriculture.
Home economics. Organising some classes in baby-care and child rearing for local mothers. Preparing an exhibition illustrating desirable nutritional and dietary practices for local schools.

Projects require materials and resources for the students, and the necessary expense is one of the disadvantages. Choosing a project that will interest all the students in the class at one time is also difficult. Some teachers argue that projects take too long to complete and are not justifiable in terms of the amount they actually teach. Scheduling a project can also present problems if a teacher has only one or two lessons per week with a class, as large blocks of time are really needed.

In spite of the arguments against the project method some teachers have used the method very effectively on occasions and beginning teachers are advised to bear it in mind when planning their teaching strategy.

Steps in the project method

1. Selecting the project

Before attempting to select a project it may be necessary to make the students aware of what a project is and what it entails, as they may not have taken part in one before. Ideally the project goals and objectives should be selected before the topic itself, but in practice the two are often considered together. A list of feasible project goals and topics can be drawn up by the class. Individuals or groups of students can then select their own projects or, if the class prefers, they can all work on a single project together. The teacher's function is to help the students select goals that are attainable and project topics that are practicable in view of the time and facilities available.

2. Planning the project

The educational value of this method depends upon the manner in which students are guided in assuming intelligent responsibility for their own learning activities. As far as possible the students themselves should make the plans to attain the project goals they have identified. To help them in their decisions the teacher should try to answer the following questions:

(i) What desirable skills, understandings, ideals and attitudes will the students acquire through the project which will contribute to their development?
(ii) Will the chosen project activities be suitable to the level of development of the students?
(iii) Will the outcomes or objectives of the project be in keeping with those of the course?
(iv) Will the learning experiences in the project be of sufficient scope and variety to hold the students' interest?
(v) Is the project the most effective method to use in order to achieve the identified objectives? How would it compare with other methods?
(vi) Are there adequate facilities and materials for the successful completion of the project?

Throughout the planning of the project the teacher should take a positive constructive attitude in stimulating and guiding pupil initiative.

3. Conducting the project

Students in the higher classes of secondary school may be able to progress with project work for some time without much direction or supervision, but younger students will need almost constant attention. Those who have never taken part in project work before are likely to be a little confused to begin with and may need special help from the teacher. The freedom accorded the students does not mean that they should be allowed to become over playful, frivolous or indisciplined. A relaxed attitude in the classroom is desirable but there should still be order. Students should be allowed to try things that the teacher knows may fail or not work out since problem solving is an aspect of learning. When very difficult problems are encountered committees of students can be formed to help solve them and the teacher can participate in their discussions. As the project progresses towards a conclusion the students should be advised to prepare their work for final presentation.

4. Evaluating the project

The evaluation of the effectiveness and value of a project is an on-going process conducted informally by the student himself while he is engaged in project activities. If he sees that some of his plans are not working out he should attempt to revise them or draw up better ones to achieve his goals. At the completion of the project the student and teacher should try to assess together the success of the project and consider what modifications might have been made to improve the end result. Were the resources and materials adequate? Was there sufficient time? Was the project worth the time and effort expended on it? These are some of the questions that need to be asked if future work is to be improved.

Advantages of the project method

1. It encourages creativity, freedom of expression, cooperation and initiative.
2. It applies Dewey's philosophy of learning by doing.
3. It gives experience in planning and organising.
4. It provides a natural approach to learning that is not confined by artificial subject area barriers.

Disadvantages of the project method

1. During project activities order and discipline are sometimes difficult to maintain.
2. There are sometimes problems in scheduling the project.

3. It is difficult to choose topics of interest to all students.
4. The expense, effort and time given to complete a project are sometimes not justifiable in terms of what is learned.

STUDY TRIPS

The nature of study trips

Study trips generally consist of planned organised visits to points of interest outside the classroom such as factories, universities, agricultural projects, museums and Houses of Representatives. Trips are often planned to places where the students will be able to see in practice or reality what they have studied in class. Concepts and generalisations which were difficult to formulate should become clearer once the students see working applications of those concepts. Study trips can be organised to broaden students' general knowledge but it should be quite clear that what they will learn from such trips will be educationally useful, and not just a waste of time and energy or simply an excuse to get out of regular classes.

The duration of a study trip will depend on the distance to be travelled to the place (or places) of interest, the purpose of the trip and the age level of the students. A study trip that is too brief is not worth all the preparation efforts, while one that lasts too long may excessively tire or even bore the students.

If the students are sufficiently mature they can be involved in planning and organising activities for the study trip. A list of questions to be answered or items to be observed by the members of the class can be drawn up. They can help arrange the class into pairs or groups to examine particular aspects of interest and to report on them at the conclusion of the trip.

Scope and limitations

Given a sufficient number of available places to visit, study trips can be organised in any subject area for any level of student. Nevertheless if the teacher wants her class to have a look around a nearby factory or company, then in the letter she writes to the management she should specify the age and area of interest of her students so that whoever is to guide the tour of the institution will know what to emphasise and what to leave out. If the place to be visited is a university the teacher can inform the authorities there ahead of time of the departments the students would like to see and the sort of questions they would like answered.

Study trips definitely enrich the school curriculum and when they are properly organised can help students develop a keen interest in a subject. When students can see industry applying the theories they have learned in class they can then better understand why they are learning those theories.

There are a number of drawbacks involved in the organisation of study trips which may explain why they are not frequently undertaken. If students are to travel out of the school to a place of interest there will almost certainly be transport costs involved. If a Principal allows one class to go on a study trip he may feel obliged to let the other classes take part in similar trips and this could end up being very expensive. Travelling in itself can be a risk. The time taken for a study trip is also considered by some teachers to be excessive in terms of the rewards it will reap. In addition such trips can require quite a lot of administrative work which is not usually welcomed by teachers who are already busy with other commitments.

Steps in the planning and organisation of a study trip

Step 1: Preparation

(a) *Preparing the class.* The first job of the teacher in preparing his class is to arouse their interest in the idea of a study trip to the chosen place or places. He can do this by telling them of some of the things they will see, how these will relate to what they have been studying and of what use the knowledge they gain will be to them in the future.

Once the students are committed to the idea of making the study trip they can be organised to gather background information on the place they are going to visit and the things they are likely to see. They can be helped to plan their activities, the questions they will ask and the information they should record. If the teacher thinks it advisable he can design a questionnaire for the students to complete during the trip.

Students going out together in a group must also be given certain rules of conduct to abide by, to ensure order, to avoid accidents and to prevent any unnecessary damage to property. Running across busy roads, operating machinery while unsupervised or tampering with equipment could result in students being injured or hurt and to prevent this they should be given strict instructions about how to behave before leaving the school. They can also be advised on how they should be dressed.

(b) *Administrative arrangements.* Before beginning to plan a study trip a teacher must have discussed the matter first with the school Principal. Only when approval has been given by the Principal should the teacher proceed to discuss the possibility of such a trip with his students. If the students in their turn appear interested a preliminary letter can be written to the company or institution in question to see if they will permit such a visit by the students and under what conditions. Not all institutions welcome student visits as they interrupt the regular work schedule. This is why it is important to obtain approval for such a visit before proceeding further with any administrative or class preparation. Once all requisite permissions and approvals have been obtained the teacher in a boarding school can go ahead and make transport and feeding plans with the co-operation of his students. If there are day students in his class or if the school is day-secondary, written permission for each student to make the study trip must be obtained from parents or relatives. Study trips organised on school days will result in students missing classes with several teachers. These teachers should be informed ahead of time that the students will be absent from their lessons because of the study trip. To fail to do so is not only discourteous, but may cause problems the next time such a trip is planned.

Step 2: Activities during the trip

The students' activities during a study trip will be governed by many factors, such as the nature of the place, the age of the students and the co-operation of the authorities. They will certainly be asked to observe a number of things and to listen to the person showing them round.

They may be given printed material or be advised to write notes on the things they see. Many factories provide visitors with free samples of their products and some will allow students to operate the simpler forms of equipment. If the teacher or some students possess cameras it is a good idea to take photographs of the class during the trip.

Step 3: Activities after the trip

(a) *Follow-up activities.* After a successful study trip the students should be asked to make a report on what they saw that they enjoyed most, what proved most (and least) interesting, and what they feel they have learned from it. If there is a sufficiently large number of aspects of interest to report on, the students can embark on a small project, preparing an exhibition on the class bulletin boards, displaying pictures and writing on what they saw and experienced. Their individual contributions can be used as a form of assessment of what they have learned, or if this is not possible the teacher could give the class some kind of test.

(b) *Evaluation of the study trip.* For his own records and for future reference a teacher should try to assess whether or not a study trip was successful and in what ways. It will be apparent during the trip if the students are enjoying themselves, and if they are not he should try to establish the reason. There may also be points of organisation and administration that the teacher feels need examining before embarking on any future trip of this type.

(c) *Culminating activities.* After a study trip there will be letters of thanks to be written to various people who made the trip possible. The teacher should try to involve the students in writing the letters. Not only will it be good training for them but it will also be more gratifying to those receiving the letters.

Advantages of the study trip

1. It provides a sound and concrete basis for conceptualisation.
2. It provides first hand learning experiences.

3. It makes learning more meaningful and lasting.
4. It gives an opportunity for improving social relationships among students and between students and teacher.

Disadvantages of the study trip

1. It can be very time consuming in terms of planning and organisation as well as in what is learned.
2. It can involve additional expenses.
3. Travelling can increase the risk of accidents.

EXERCISES

1. Justify the use of the lecture method in the secondary schools.
2. How can the lecture method be improved to achieve maximum desirable effects?
3. Compare and contrast between the lecture and discussion methods.
4. What are the things to be considered when preparing and performing a demonstration?
5. What are the educational values of field trips? What are its limitations?
6. Think of a project that you might want your students to undertake. Discuss what steps to take to ensure its success.

ESSENTIAL READING

Blount, N. S. and Klausmeir, H. J. (1968) *Teaching in Secondary Schools*, Harrap, London.

Bruner, J. S. (1960) *The Process of Education*, Harvard University Press, Cambridge, Mass.

Clark, L. H. and Starr, I. S. (1976) *Secondary Teaching School Methods*, Macmillan, New York.

Risk, Thomas M. (1958) *Principles and Practice in Secondary Schools*, American Book Company, New York.

Shipley, Morton C. *et al.* (1964) *A Synthesis of Teaching Methods*, McGraw-Hill, New York.

Sund, P. B. and Trowbridge, L. W. (1973) *Teaching Science by Inquiry in the Secondary School*, (2nd ed.), Charles E. Merrill, Columbus, Ohio.

SUPPLEMENTARY READING

Alcorn, M. D. *et al.* (1970) *Better Teaching in Secondary Schools*, Holt, Rinehart & Winston, New York.

Bossing, Nelson L. (1955) *Teaching in Secondary Schools*, Houghton Mifflin, Boston, Mass.

Callahan, Sterling G. (1966) *Successful Teaching in Secondary Schools*, Scott, Foresman, Chicago.

Douglass, H. R. and Mills, A. H. (1948) *Teaching in High School*, Ronald, New York.

Grambs, J. D., Carr, J. C. and Fitch, R. M. (1970) *Modern Methods in Secondary Education*, (3rd ed.), Holt, Rinehart & Winston, New York.

Highet, G. (1963) *The Art of Teaching*, Methuen, London.

Kilpatrick, W. H. (1925) *Foundations of Methods*, Macmillan, New York.

Lee, James M. (1963) *Principles and Methods of Secondary Schools*, McGraw-Hill, New York.

Oliver, R. A. (1960) *Effective Teaching*, J. M. Kent, Toronto.

Pinsent, A. (1941) *The Principles of Teaching Methods*, Harrap, London.

Yoakam, Gerald, A. and Simpson, R. G. (1948) *Modern Methods and Techniques of Teaching*, Macmillan, New York.

5

Newer Approaches to Teaching

INTRODUCTION

As Froebel once pointed out, 'to have found one fourth of the answer by his own effort is of more value and importance to the child than it is to half-hear and half understand it in the words of another'.

This chapter discusses the more modern approaches to teaching in which the emphasis is shifted from the teacher to the student. The learner is transformed from a passive receiver of knowledge into an active creator of the process in which he learns. The stress is placed not on learning facts, but rather on understanding the structure of the discipline and the way our knowledge is organised.

The chapter describes four approaches to teaching which are:

1. The process approach.
2. The discovery approach.
3. The inquiry/problem-solving approach.
4. The use of the laboratory and laboratory techniques in teaching.

In some respects the approaches overlap with each other. Thus the process approach could take place in the laboratory but does not need a laboratory always. When problem solving, discovery learning will often occur, but discovery can also occur outside of such a situation. We have chosen to differentiate between the approaches because there are differences in emphasis in each of them and the beginning teacher should be aware of these.

Although the newer approaches to teaching which emphasise

active involvement by the students in the learning experience are being used more and more, it would be a mistake to ignore expository methods completely. There is still a place for the use of expository methods of teaching in the classroom. It is up to the teacher to decide on the fine balance between the different methods or approaches which he feels will produce the best results.

THE PROCESS APPROACH

Nature of the method

This approach emphasises helping the students develop process skills through practice. Process skills are those skills we are called on to use in solving everyday problems and include observation, classification, inference, prediction and so on. Someone who is a poor observer of detail or who is not able to predict with some success the outcome of a series of events, is likely to find these limitations a handicap in later life. On the other hand, a person who can infer correctly, can formulate a hypothesis, or can interpret data correctly will find these skills an asset in whatever profession he takes up. The process skills which have been identified as being most useful and which can be acquired through practice are described below. They are arranged in hierarchical order and begin with the simpler processes and progressively the skills become more complex.

1. *Observation.* Whether a person plans to be an engineer, a doctor, lawyer, sociologist or an aircraft pilot, he needs to be able to observe the details of a situation, object, report or person. Careful observers in responsible positions can save lives and public funds and uphold justice whereas careless observers can cause the loss of all these.

2. *Measurement.* In adult life people are called upon to measure weights, distances, areas, volumes and time, not only in their professional activities but also in civilian and domestic situations. Tailors, technicians, architects, artists, cooks and people in many other forms of employment need to be able to measure accurately and without much difficulty.

3. *Classification.* Objects can be classified by means of shape, colour, size and by their similarities and differences.

People can be classified by their age, sex, race and they can be grouped according to whether they are short, tall, fat, thin, poor and so on. The ability to classify or group correctly requires careful observation of similarities or distinguishing characteristics.

4. *Communication.* It is possible to communicate with other people by talking, listening, writing, reading, drawing or by using facial or bodily gestures. It is important for young people to be able to communicate their needs, feelings, ideas or problems to others. Accurate encoding and decoding skills can be developed with practice.

5. *Using numbers.* Modern society demands that everyone be able to handle money which means that each individual has to be familiar with the use of numbers. Skill in addition, subtraction and division are so essential that all school curricula contain arithmetic or mathematics as a compulsory subject. Using numbers is a skill which can be taught outside the Mathematics lesson in Physics, Chemistry, Economics, Accounting and Home Economics.

6. *Using space–time relationships.* Objects, persons and places are positioned relative to each other in space. Terms like *behind, in front of, above* or *below, left* or *right*, are used to describe space relationships. Young children learn quite easily how to describe the position of something relative to themselves. For example they might say, 'that banana tree is on my right side', but they find it more difficult to describe the position of the same banana tree with reference to someone else.

Before and *after* are used to describe *time* relationships. In trying to describe a sequence of past or future events a clear understanding of time relationships is essential.

7. *Predicting.* If you examine a situation or make a series of observations, and then say with some certainty what the outcome will be, you are making a prediction. To make a valid prediction all the available evidence has to be carefully studied beforehand. Predictions are about events which will occur in the future and are made with more certainty than guesses.

8. *Inference.* To infer can mean to deduce, to imply or even to conclude. If after the posting of examination results on the College or Faculty notice-board we see someone walk-

ing away with a large smile of his face, we could infer that he has not only passed his exams but probably passed them well. When we infer we are deciding the cause of something. In this example we are inferring about the cause of someone's very obvious joy.

9. *Making operational definitions.* Sometimes situations arise which have no simple term by which they can be described. Among students it is common for a certain kind of jargon to be developed containing words which have some special meaning for the students but to an outsider they mean something entirely different or nothing at all. In Ahmadu Bello University the women's hostel has been referred to as the Golan Heights because of the struggles among the men to gain the attentions of the ladies who stay there and the tall nature of the buildings. Presumably someone thought there was a likeness to the situation in Israel some years ago when there was a struggle to conquer the hills of that name. In a sense the students have formulated an operational definition to describe the competition among the males over the female residents of Amina Hall. In more serious circumstances operational definitions are devised to describe a situation for which no formal definition exists at the time.

10. *Formulating models.* Teachers of all subjects are making increasingly extensive use of pictures, maps, flow charts, graphs and all types of visual materials in order to improve and facilitate learning in their students. It is now generally believed that two or three dimensional models of objects, situations or related events make understanding these things easier and more permanent than verbal descriptions. Concrete models help towards the formation of mental models and concepts, and these are more readily retained by the memory.

11. *Interpreting data.* In Social Studies, Politics, Mathematics and the sciences, data can be collected during an investigation or project which needs to be interpreted. This may involve taking averages, percentages, drawing graphs, and then coming to some conclusions. The accurate interpretation of data requires skill and this is something that can be developed with practice in students and adults. In fact the development of this skill can be a life-long process.

12. *Controlling variables.* Farmers who attempt to grow food crops like vegetables, potatoes, yams, and rice usually

try to repeat year by year the farming techniques which they have found to be the most successful. They try to ensure that planting is carried out at around the same time and that there is an optimum amount of fertiliser in the soil. In other words they try to control the variables that affect plant growth. Housewives who discover a soup recipe that their families enjoy will continue to use the same quantities of ingredients each time they make that particular soup. In any manufacturing process, from making top quality steel to tranquilisers there are numerous variables that have to be controlled if the same type and quality of product is required.

13. *Formulating hypotheses.* If the Principal of a college observes that his students do consistently badly in public examinations, he might infer that:

1. The students do not study hard enough.
2. The public examinations are too difficult.
3. The students in the College are not properly prepared for the examinations by their teachers.

These generalised inferences based on a series of observations are called *hypotheses*. To test which hypothesis is most correct would require an investigation involving further observations. This could result in a revision or the formulation of a completely new hypothesis. Hypotheses are intelligent guesses as to the causes or outcomes, based on some initial observations.

14. *Experimenting.* In industry attempts are continually being made to produce better aircraft, more economical cars, improved fabrics and more effective drugs. Agriculturalists are trying to devise methods for increasing crop production while economists are trying to find new ways of fighting inflation. In every field of human endeavour experiments are being carried out to improve man's living conditions. Experimenting is a process skill which embraces *all* the process skills and a competent experimenter must be proficient at all of them.

Teaching technique using the process approach

Preparing the lesson

In planning the lesson the teacher first has to identify the process skill or skills he wants the students to develop and the level of success he wishes the students to attain. Activities then need to be designed in which the students can engage, either individually or in groups, and for which there is an adequate supply of materials. Behavioural objectives can be stated in such a way that they specify the level of skill attainment that the teacher wants from the students by the end of the lesson.

Suggested steps in the lesson

1. *Introduction.* The teacher can begin by introducing the process skills he wants the students to practise. He can motivate them by telling a story, anecdote or even a joke which illustrates the importance of the skills he is introducing. The students are shown the materials that they are going to use and are given instructions about what to observe or how to manipulate the things they are to be given.

2. *Process skill activities.* How the teacher arranges the students for working purposes depends very much on the type of activities that they are going to perform and on the number of materials available. It is better for the students to work in small groups or in pairs so that they are all physically and mentally involved. If the students are learning to be better observers by looking at the parts of a flower or cockroach, then they should have at least one specimen between two. If they are learning to infer from a series of pictures what caused a certain event to happen then the students could work in groups of three or four. Whatever activities the students engage in the teacher will in most cases have to guide them by asking appropriate questions and making suggestions. During the lesson the teacher should be able to evaluate the students' progress as he moves about the class pointing out things and directing the students' efforts. Since the more gifted children are likely to complete successfully whatever assignment they have been given ahead of the others it is a good idea for the teacher to have additional problems and materials available for such students. After they have all completed the assigned activities all the students can be given new problems or situations in which they can apply what they have learned. Their performance will help the teacher evaluate further their process skill attainment.

3. *Concluding the lesson.* The teacher can summarise the main findings of the lesson by means of a brief discussion with the whole class. For example, questions like, 'What were the differences that you noticed between substances A, B and C?', or 'From the data you were given what was the percentage success of students in the State at the WAEC Biology exam in 1980?', can initiate discussion and emphasise the correct answers.

If the activities have helped the students to form a concept or generalisation then this can be reinforced at the end of the lesson.

Scope and limitations

The process approach to teaching was originally designed for use in primary schools and in the lower levels of post-primary institutions. It is very effective when applied to the study of science but it can also be used in general and integrated study courses which do not possess artificial subject area barriers. It presupposes no subject area content but rather that, through the continual practice of observation, classification, inference and so on, the students will be induced to form concepts and generalisations which are the basis of knowledge. The Nigerian Primary Education Improvement Programme (Science) adopts a predominantly process oriented approach and has achieved some measure of success in attaining its objectives.

Whilst the process approach might easily be adopted for use in the lower classes of the post-primary school where the curriculum is divided into discrete subject areas, and certain process skills are stressed in one area but not so much in another, it might be more difficult to use this approach.

Advantages of the process approach

1. It develops skills in children which can later be used in the study of any discipline.
2. Subject area content can become outdated as discoveries are made and new information is acquired, but process skills will always be useful and valuable to the individual.

3. Since the approach is predominantly practical in nature, students tend to be interested, to learn rapidly and as they become proficient in the practice of process skills they gain self-confidence.
4. Expertise in process skills is likely to enhance concept formation. Skills cannot be learned in a void – there has to be some substance or information on which to operate. For example, in learning how to measure there have to be things to measure. While measuring concepts of the metre, kilogram, cubic-centimetre and so on will be formed.

Disadvantages of the process approach

1. Only a few programmes exist which emphasise the process approach since it is a fairly recent innovation.
2. The approach requires a lot of imagination on the part of the teacher in thinking up activities in which the students can practise process skills.
3. The approach would seem to be more suited to science oriented studies rather than those which are arts oriented.

Lesson plan to demonstrate the process approach

SUBJECT: Integrated Science
TOPIC: Measurement of Speed
CLASS LEVEL: Form 2 (Age 12–13 years)
TIME: One hour twenty minutes (double period)
OBJECTIVES: By the end of the lesson the children should be able to:

1. Measure the time to travel 100 metres to the nearest one second.
2. Communicate their results by means of a straight line graph.
3. Use the numbers of metres and seconds to calculate speed in metres/seconds.

LESSON MATERIALS: Four or more time-measuring devices (stop clocks or wrist watches), graph paper and note books to record data.

PROCEDURE:

Teacher's activities	**Students' activities and responses**
1. Introduction The teacher introduces the students to the concept of speed as a function of time and distance by asking questions like: 'Who is the fastest runner in the class? How long does it take you to run a hundred metres? How far is it from Lagos to Ibadan? How fast do taxis travel? How long does it take them from Lagos to Ibadan?'	The students respond by raising their hands before being called upon to speak. 'Please Sir, I am the fastest runner.' 'Ojo can run the hundred metres in fifteen seconds.' 'It is a hundred miles from Lagos to Ibadan and taxis take three hours.'
Some of the students will give answers in miles instead of kilometres and the teacher should help them convert such answers.	
He goes on to ask the students why they should be interested in *how fast* or at what *speed* something travels.	The students will respond in various ways: 'Because we want to know when we will arrive.'
The teacher outlines the plan of the day's lesson: 'Today we are going to go out on the athletics field to measure how far you can run or walk.'	'I will come first and beat everyone Sir.' 'Felix will come last because he is fat.'

Teacher's activities	**Students' activities and responses**
2. *Development of the Lesson* The teacher demonstrates how to use a stop-clock and then divides the class into groups so that they can practise timing.	The students practise with the clocks and are shown how to use them properly.
Some students are appointed to measure time while others are selected to record results, to run and to walk.	Groups of students are posted at the 25, 50, 75 and 100m. marks on the track. Others are timed walking and running as they pass each of these marks.
The teacher and children return to the class and the results are recorded on the blackboard.	The children record all the results in their notebooks according to the format given by the teacher.
The teacher asks questions based on the results. 'Who was the fastest runner? The slowest runner? The slowest walker? The fastest walker? How can we calculate their speed in metres per second?'	The students study the results on the board and answer the teacher's questions as well as asking some of their own.
Generalisation The teacher explains, if students cannot tell him, that: $$\text{Speed} = \frac{\text{Distance (run or walked)}}{\text{Time (to run or walk)}}$$	

Teacher's activities	**Students' activities and responses**
Application The teacher calculates the speeds of two or three students, over a stated distance, on the blackboard, while allowing for questions, until he is confident that the students understand the method.	The students practise the calculations as the teacher has shown them, and ask questions.
Evaluation From his observations during the lesson and from the students' questions and answers the teacher will have some idea of how much has been learned in terms of skill in measuring and calculating (using numbers). Further evaluation will be possible when the students submit their assignments.	*Assignment* The students are asked to complete the calculations.

THE DISCOVERY APPROACH

Nature of the approach

1. What is discovery?
Discovery has been defined in different ways by Bruner, Wittrock and Cronbach. Sund and Trowbridge take the view that discovery occurs when an individual is involved mainly in using his mental processes to mediate (discover) some concept or principle. If we accept this definition then discovery is the mental assimilation by which the individual grasps a *concept* or *principle* resulting from physical and mental activity.

In your preparation as teachers you may have come across study material which you found very difficult to understand clearly. For days you may have read around the topic, talked to your lecturers and classmates, but to no avail. Then after some lapse of time you have had a chat with someone or you found a new book which you have never read before and suddenly everything became clear to you. What to you was before very muddled and confused became crystal clear. You had *discovered* the concept or principle that eluded you before. In such situations scientists have been known to shout 'Eureka!' (meaning I have found it or understand it).

2. *What are concepts?*

Psychologists believe that concepts are vitally involved in thought processes. An understanding of concepts leads to the formulation of principles and generalisations which make for efficiency in solving problems.

Throughout every conscious minute of every day we are bombarded by sense perceptions of the infinite variety of objects and processes that surround us. The brain, instead of reacting to every individual event tends to categorise or group what is perceived. If we hear a particular sound we might say, 'that is a car passing', because we have previously formed a concept of the sound of a car engine. If we see a particular type of animal we might say to ourselves 'dog' because we have a concept of the class of animals which we call *dogs*. All empirically based knowledge is learned through the senses. The beginning of knowledge is the perception of a phenomenon in nature.

What is a percept and how are percepts related to concepts? A child who eats pounded yam, omelette, rice, fish and meat learns after some time to group all things he eats under the heading *food*. Each of these perceived types of food is a *percept*, in other words yam is a percept, fish is a percept and so on. The collective term for them in the context of eating leads to the formation of the concept of food in the child's mind.

There are many different types of concepts. Some are related to classes of concrete objects such as table, chair, lorry and metal. There are others which refer to on-going processes, for example growth, ageing, socialisation and learning. Others again show how objects, persons or events are related in time or space, for example: above, below, before and after.

A person's conceptual view never ceases to change as he

or she matures and gains in experience. Concepts are modified and revised to take into account new information the individual has assimilated. As Cronbach (1966) said; 'The depth of understanding, the range of application of a concept, and the precision with which it is learned can grow for years after the definition is learned.' This growth can be likened to an ever widening spiral, narrow at the bottom and broad at the top. Thus a secondary school student's conception of a human cell is likely to contain some elements of misconception, more so than a biochemist who has spent many years researching on cells. In a similar way a farmer will have a different and probably less accurate conception of *democracy* than a lecturer in political science, because a farmer has had less opportunity to formulate a concept based on a deep understanding of democracy.

3. What are generalisations or principles?

Generalisations or principles are statements based on observations of the environment which describe the normal course of events. Sometimes these generalisations or principles have to be revised or modified in the light of new evidence or because circumstances have changed. These are some examples of generalisations or principles:

Water is necessary for life.
In humans and animals, diet affects growth.
Metals give up electrons in chemical reactions.
Carefully controlled crop rotation increases yield.
In any business income affects growth.
War is a major world problem.

Before we can fully understand a principle we have to have a clear understanding of the concepts which are involved in such a principle. If we take for example the statement 'Diet affects growth', which is a generally accepted principle among nutrition experts, then a complete understanding of this principle demands very clear concepts of what is meant by diet, affects, and growth. Discovery learning leads first to an understanding of concepts and after this to a discovery of generalisations, principles and even laws related to these concepts. Discovery by its definition implies *induction*, because the learner proceeds from specific examples (percepts) to concepts, and from concepts to a generalisation or principle. Many of the other methods of teaching which are mentioned in this book will also lead to the formation of concepts, principles and generalisations in the learners. The difference between this approach and those is largely one of emphasis. In other methods of teaching concept formation is not the primary objective while in discovery learning it is the main purpose.

Teaching technique using the discovery approach

The teaching technique will very much depend on whether it is a concept or generalisation that is to be taught. In the lower levels of secondary school it is more usual to concentrate on the teaching of concepts and simple principles. For example, take the statement, 'Water is necessary for life in plants and animals'. The teacher would first ensure that the students have a chance to form concepts by studying *water, living* and *non-living things, plants* and *animals*, before leading the students to form the generalisation.

Technique of teaching concepts

These are some suggested instructional steps in the teaching of concepts. The first two steps are part of the teacher's preparation.

Step 1: Describe the performance expected of the student after he has learned the concept.

After learning any concept the student should be able to recognise new examples of that concept. Suppose during a Chemistry lesson students are shown numerous examples of metals and by means of observation and experimentation they establish a set of criteria by which metals can be identified. In so doing they will have formed a concept of what is meant by a metal. They are then presented with some further examples of metals and non-metals to establish whether or not the concept *metal* has been correctly formulated in their minds.

Step 2: Reduce the number of simpler concepts (attributes) needed for a thorough understanding of a complex concept.

In the former example students were to be taught the

chemist's conception of a metal. A number of simpler concepts or attributes need to be learned before the student can begin to formulate a concept of a metal. For example metals (1) are good *conductors* of *heat* and electricity, (2) *react* with *acids* to form *salts*, (3) are *electron donors*. For the formation of a correct concept of a metal there are at least eight attributes or associated concepts which the student must understand first. The teacher's function is to reduce the number of attributes involved in the learning of a complex concept. This may involve leaving some of them out and only stressing those which are most important.

Step 3: Provide the students with useful verbal mediators.

This step concerns the initial behaviour of the students. It has been shown in research studies (Wittrock, Keisler and Stern, 1974) that if the concept to be learned is named or labelled, it facilitates the formulation of the concept in the students' minds. Thus if the teacher wants to teach the concept *mammal*, it is more effective if the students are told at the beginning that the examples they are being shown represent different types of mammals, than to say, 'this is a dog, horse, rabbit'. Children who are taught when the concept is named or labelled (when a verbal mediator is provided) are better able to recognise new examples of the concept than those who were given no verbal mediator.

Step 4: Provide positive and negative examples of the concept.

In trying to teach students concepts the teacher should use both positive and negative examples, as this has been found to be more effective than using examples of only one kind. A positive example of a concept is one which contains the attributes of the concept while a negative example is one that does not contain one or more of the attributes. Positive examples of the concept *food* are egg, beef, yam, cassava, banana; while rose, albisia, vulture, petrol, soap are negative examples.

The number of positive and negative examples that the teacher uses will depend to some extent on the time available for teaching. Gagné suggests that the teacher uses enough positive examples to represent the range of the concept he is teaching. The number of negative examples presented ultimately depends on the teacher but in general all negative examples of the attributes that usually confuse the students should be presented.

Step 5: Present examples in close succession or simultaneously.

As the teacher shows the children positive and negative examples of the concept, many, if not all, of them should be visible to the students at one time. This lessens the load on their memories and makes for better continuity. As the students respond to the examples being shown to them the teacher should provide immediate reinforcement by indicating to them whether they are right or wrong. The type of reinforcement will depend on the judgement of the teacher but generally it should be to encourage the students.

Step 6: Assess the learning of the students.

In this part of the lesson the teacher carries out the planned evaluation as outlined in Step 1. The students are presented with new positive examples of the concept(s) they have learned and also some negative examples. Correct responses are reinforced by appropriate verbal or auditory feedback to the student. The value of assessment of concept learning at this point is mainly for the teacher, who is able to find out to what degree he has obtained his lesson objectives.

An illustration of concept teaching

Mr Eze wished to teach his students the concept *journalist*. He began his lesson with these words: 'Today I want to teach you about a person who is a journalist. By the end of the lesson you should be able to identify whether or not the person in each of the examples is a journalist.' (Step 1.)

Mr Eze had analysed the concept (Step 2) and had decided that it had three attributes, namely *profession, report,* and *news*. Each attribute had its own value: for profession it was membership of a group and full time employment; for report it was a written account, possibly with accompanying photographs, for a journal, magazine or newspaper; for news it was current affairs of interest to the general public.

He ensured the necessary verbal association (Step 3) by writing the word JOURNALIST on the blackboard in big bold letters and asked the students to pronounce it several times which they did enthusiastically.

Mr Eze presented positive and negative examples of the

concept (Step 4) by writing sentences on the blackboard. He completed the first four examples before asking the class to respond (Step 5). His examples were of this type:

> Mr King travels up and down the country taking photographs and writing reports for Drum magazine. 'Is Mr King a journalist?'
> Professor Ayodele has written many books. 'Is he a journalist?'
> Mrs Ojo wrote to a newspaper to complain about the water shortage in the town. 'Is she a journalist?'
> Mr Nuru wrote about the 12th African Cup of Nations Football Competition for the New Nigerian. 'Is he a journalist?'

As Mr Eze went through his examples he gave encouragement by saying, 'Very good, well done,' for correct responses. Incorrect answers were treated in this way, 'No that is not correct. You are wrong.' After numerous positive and negative examples, when the class seemed to have grasped the concept of Journalist, Mr Eze wrote two new sentences on the blackboard beneath those already there (Step 6). When asked whether the people represented in the sentences were journalists all the class answered correctly in unison showing the teacher that they had understood the concept.

The teaching of principles

The teaching of principles is an extension of the method of teaching concepts which has already been described in some detail. Only the headings of suggested steps in the method will be indicated here.

Step 1: Describe the expected performance of the student after he has learned the principle.

Step 2: Identify the concepts or principles that the students must recall in order to learn the new principle.

Step 3: Help the students recall and revise the concepts involved in the principle.

Step 4: Help the students combine the concepts in the correct order in deriving the principle.

Step 5: Give the students extensive practice with enough

examples of the principle and reinforce their responses.

Step 6: Provide new examples of the principle in an attempt to evaluate the students' learning of the principle.

Scope and limitations

The discovery approach has been strongly advocated by Jerome Bruner. His approach to teaching is summarised in the following statement (Bruner, 1961):

> To instruct someone in a discipline is not a matter of getting him to commit results to mind. Rather, it is to teach him to participate in the process that makes possible the establishment of knowledge. We teach a subject not to produce little living libraries on the subject, but rather to get a student to think mathematically for himself, to consider matters as an historian does, to take part in the process of knowledge getting. Knowing is a process, not a product.

The way the term discovery has been interpreted in this chapter makes the approach applicable to virtually all areas of teaching. In the next section of this chapter we will be looking at the Inquiry/Problem-Solving approach which incorporates discovery as one of its elements, and is a natural extension of the discovery approach. While inquiry and problem-solving are better suited to the higher classes of the secondary school, the discovery approach is suited to all levels. The types of activities the students will be involved in will vary from topic to topic and with the age and ability of the children. The amount of guidance the students receive from the teacher will also vary, but it should never be excessive. As A. N. Whitehead (1929) said:

> From the very beginning of his education the child should experience the joy of discovery. The discovery which he has to make is that general ideas give an understanding of that stream of events which pours through his life, which is his life.

Some educationists, by contrast are very critical of the discovery approach. They maintain that it is virtually impossible for the student to discover for himself any substantial part of the wisdom of his culture. The extent to which you as a teacher use the discovery approach in your teaching will very much depend on the time and materials available to you.

Advantages of the discovery approach

1. It provides for understanding as opposed to rote learning.
2. The students are actively engaged in the process of acquiring knowledge instead of being passive listeners.
3. Students are taught concepts or principles which are more easily remember than isolated facts.
4. Students are more interested in and remember better things they have found out for themselves.

Disadvantages of the discovery approach

1. The discovery approach is time consuming.
2. The discovery approach requires a lot of materials to be effective.
3. With the vast expanse of knowledge ever growing it is not possible for the student to discover all of the laws and principles for himself.

THE INQUIRY/PROBLEM-SOLVING APPROACH

In this approach to teaching the students inquire into a problem with a view to finding some answers or reasons why the problem exists. In this book the inquiry and problem-solving approaches to teaching are considered to be equivalent to each other and to be built on discovery. Inquiry and problem solving go further than discovery, although a student must use all of his discovery capabilities and many more in this approach. Some examples of problems that the students might formulate for themselves are 'what causes rain?' or 'the rising cost of living'.

Much of the current interest in inquiry and problem-solving

teaching can be traced back to the work of John Dewey. He maintained that the learner should develop the intellectual tact and sensitivity to solve problems by inquiring constantly in the classroom (Dewey, 1933). An inquiry-oriented teaching strategy must provide an opportunity for the learners to identify and clarify a purpose for inquiry; formulate a hypothesis; test the hypothesis by collecting data; draw conclusions; apply the conclusions in new situations to new data; and develop meaningful generalisations.

Using inquiry in the classroom does not mean leading the learners towards conclusions already clear to both student and teacher alike. What is important, even central, to inquiry is that the students use *accepted* methods in collecting data so that they gain some insight into the situation or problem that actually exists in their own classroom, laboratory or environment. From this experience they should see that statements about phenomena are based on more than guesses or casual observation; they are rather the result of rigorous investigation. In addition the students will be given an appreciation of the scientific method of acquiring knowledge. As a result of the inquiry and problem-solving method a student may discover a concept or principle or he may widen his understanding of both.

Three main types of inquiry/problem-solving have been identified. They are Guided Inquiry, Free Inquiry and Modified Free Inquiry.

Guided inquiry

If students have not had any experience in learning through inquiry, their initial lessons should be considerably structured. First the problem itself is posed by the teacher. Then in order to assist the students the teacher might break down the problem into simpler questions to be answered and may even give advice about the steps which the students take to answer these questions. When the students have had some experience in the inquiry method the teacher will give less and less guidance in order to let the students formulate their own questions to solve the problem being investigated. The amount of of guidance given in any situation will depend on the grade level of the students, the problem and the teacher. In any event the students must come to an understanding of and a solution to the problem at the end of the time allowed for inquiry.

Free inquiry

Free inquiry occurs when students themselves formulate the problem to be solved, devise methods and techniques to solve the problem, carry out an investigation and come to a conclusion. Free inquiry is suited to more intellectually gifted children with a minimum amount of guidance from the teacher. In a large class of thirty or more students it is doubtful whether more than a handful of the children would profit from this approach.

Modified free inquiry

Modified free inquiry falls between guided inquiry and free inquiry. Generally speaking the teacher provides the problem. The students are then encouraged to attack the problem on their own or in groups. The teacher acts as a resource person giving only enough assistance so that they do not become frustrated with what appears to be a lack of progress. Without telling the students what steps to take the teacher rather asks appropriate questions, which are more hints than directions, to help the students move forward in the investigation.

Scope and limitations

Merwin (1976) maintains that research related to the method of inquiry is neither conclusive enough nor convincing enough to warrant its universal adoption. However he goes on to say that the successful outcomes of the inquiry method as recorded in several research reports cannot be ignored. The success or failure of the method, he maintains, will very much depend on the competence, enthusiasm and confidence of the teacher.

Inquiry and problem-solving methods will have some use in the lower classes of the secondary school under the guidance of an experienced teacher. In the higher classes (four and five) where there is a more concerted effort to prepare for forthcoming examinations, selected topics can be treated using this method with limited guidance from the teacher. It will probably not be possible to use the method in every situation as the school syllabuses in Nigeria are quite extensive and the inquiry approach is somewhat time consuming.

Cox and Messiales (1966) maintain that students learn just as many facts and tend to be more interested, enthusiastic and to display a sense of relevance when taught using the inquiry approach as compared with more expository methods.

Each teacher has his own style of teaching which he tends to modify as he gains in experience until he develops a system of teaching which seems to achieve results. The inquiry or problem-solving approach might fit very conveniently into the system developed by one teacher but might be unsuitable for another. Nevertheless students have to be taught to *think* and *find out* for themselves, if not always at least sometimes, and the inquiry/problem-solving approach is the ideal way to help them do this.

Advantages of the inquiry/problem-solving approach

1. It tends to generate enthusiasm and interest in the students.
2. Since the students find things out for themselves they remember them better.
3. Some researchers maintain that the approach enhances critical thinking and skills of scientific investigation.

Disadvantages of the inquiry/problem-solving approach

1. It is time consuming.
2. It may not be possible to use it in all situations.
3. Some researchers maintain that it is more suitable for intuitive and creative children.

Example of an inquiry/problem-solving approach lesson

CLASS LEVEL: Secondary Three or Four
If the class has not been exposed to problem-solving and inquiry teaching earlier the teacher can begin the series of lessons with a teacher-directed discussion. He can first state the problem and then involve the students in formulating questions about it.

Step 1: The teacher introduces the problem

TEACHER 'The problem I want us to investigate over the new few weeks is *the rising cost of living*. Now what do we mean by the rising cost of living?'

STUDENTS 'We mean that things are becoming more expensive.'
'Cars cost more than before.'
'Gari is 60 kobo per mudu.'

TEACHER 'Yes, food and cars and things like that continue to cost more every year. Let's list all the important things that we know have increased in price over the past few years.'

STUDENTS 'All foodstuffs have increased in price.'
'Clothing materials and textiles.'
'All forms of transport like taxis and buses have increased in price.'

TEACHER 'How do you think we could find out *by how much* prices have increased each year over the past three years?'

STUDENTS 'We could ask local traders, our parents and older people in the town or villages.'

TEACHER 'Yes, one way to find out about the changing cost of important things would be to question people. At the end of this lesson I will ask a group of students to draw up a list of questions on the changing cost of important items each year over the past three years.'

'Now what do you think are the *causes* of the rising cost of living? *Why* have prices increased? What are the reasons?'

STUDENTS 'Because wages and salaries have increased.'
'Traders want bigger profits.'
'People are becoming more materialistic.'
'Transport costs more because petrol costs more.'

TEACHER 'Good, you have mentioned some of the causes that are responsible for the rising cost of living. I will be asking another group in the class to design some questions to ask people like teachers, traders, and people in the town, the *causes* of rising prices, in order of importance. You will also be able to find information from the newspapers and magazines.

How do you think the rising cost of living has affected people? What are the consequences of increased prices?'

STUDENTS 'Poor people have become poorer.'

'Some people still have plenty of money.'

'Wages have not increased by the same amount as prices.'

TEACHER 'What do you think can be done to *prevent* these prices from rising and causing hardship to people?'

STUDENTS 'The government should do something.'

'Wages should be increased more.'

'No Sir, if we increase wages again prices will increase.'

'There should be a price-control board.'

'The price-control board did not work before.'

TEACHER 'Well in order to find some answers to the questions we have raised this morning we will divide the class up into three groups. Each group will elect its own group leader and secretary.

Group 1 will investigate the increase in prices of important items over the past three years.

Group 2 will investigate the causes behind the increasing cost of living.

Group 3 will investigate the consequences of the rising cost of living and will also suggest some remedies to prevent people from suffering because of inflation.'

The teacher takes the class to a place where he can select the groups and the students in each group can elect their leaders and secretaries. In the lessons that follow the teacher will advise and assist each group in the formulation of questions and the collection of data.

If the students have to go out of the school the permission of the principal will be required. Once the data has been collected the teacher may have to suggest ways in which it can be analysed and displayed. The students can use tables, graphs and bar charts for instance, as well as calculate averages, percentage increases per annum and so on. A display can be made on the class notice-boards for the whole class to see, and other classes and their teachers can be invited to view it.

THE USE OF THE LABORATORY AND LABORATORY TECHNIQUES IN TEACHING

Nature of the method

Although laboratories and laboratory techniques of teaching have long been associated with science teaching, the beneficial and lasting effect of learning that has taken place in laboratory situations has led to the technique being adapted and used in other areas of study as well as science.

This broader interpretation of the laboratory method has been defined as, 'a teaching procedure dealing with first hand experiences regarding materials or facts obtained from investigation or experimentation. It is experimentation, observation or application by individuals or small groups dealing with actual material. Essentially it is the experimental method enlarged and expounded.' (Lardizabel et al. 1978)

In physical and health education the use of apparatus and materials on the sportsfield is a form of laboratory teaching. For the mathematicians and social scientists the mathematics and social studies rooms are their respective laboratories where they can work with and store materials useful to them in their areas of study. In some cases the local environment can be considered to be an extension of the laboratory because it can be used in practical ways to gain experience. In the teaching of language as well as literature and drama, language laboratories utilising cassettes and tape recorders have been found to be very effective.

Brandwein and Schwab (1962) point out that one of the general features of laboratory teaching is that it 'erases the artificial distinction between classroom and laboratory, between mind and hand'.

One of the false assumptions made in training teachers has been that anyone can teach in a laboratory or use laboratory techniques in teaching. It is one thing to have a laboratory but it is another thing to know how to use it effectively. The new teacher, when attempting to run a laboratory class for the first time, finds, all too often, that he just does not know where to begin, and the investigation he had planned turns out to be a complete failure. Learning in laboratory type situations probably depends more upon the teacher than on the elaborateness or sophistication of the equipment.

Schorling and Batchelder (1973) maintain:

> Schoolwork will be more interesting and meaningful if the class period is used for work and the classroom takes the form of a workshop in which laboratory type techniques are employed. In general, a good laboratory lesson may be described as one in which (1) the work is individual and the pupil or small group of pupils is at work on a problem; (2) the teacher serves as a consultant doing a great deal of work at the pupil's elbow; and (3) the student lives through certain experiences and emerges with one or more concepts or principles.

From the above statement it is apparent that the laboratory provides the ideal setting for skill development, discovery learning, inquiry and problem-solving activities, all of which have been discussed earlier in this chapter and examples of these approaches with lesson plans have been outlined.

Teaching technique

The way in which the teacher will utilise the laboratory or laboratory technique (and these are many) will very much depend on what he plans to achieve. However, there are some general steps which the beginning teacher can use as a guide. Risk (1965) identifies three steps in the teaching procedure:

Step 1: Introduction
Step 2: Work period
Step 3: Culminating activities

Introductory step

The preparation of the laboratory exercise is extremely important and is demanding on the teacher's time and energy. Preparation time can often be longer than the laboratory period itself. Once the teacher has decided what he wants the students to investigate all the relevant materials should be prepared the day before the class is due to take place. Beginning teachers are advised to try out the investigative exercise before the students attempt it, if it is the type of exercise for which an answer is readily found. In this way the snags and steps which can go wrong will reveal themselves.

If the students are not familiar with the type of investigation, skill learning, or problem to be solved, the teacher will have to give them some orientation at the beginning of the class. He can do this by discussing what is to be done in the lesson, or provide guide sheets giving directions about the investigation. If the students lack interest or enthusiasm the teacher should try to generate these by pointing out the usefulness of the exercise to be undertaken. Exercises which are pure repetitions of experiments for which the answers are known should not be carried out too frequently. Laboratory work should as much as possible lead theory lessons rather than lag behind them.

Work period

This is the period when the students, either individually or in groups, investigate the identified problem or inquire into a situation in practical ways. The nature of the problem will determine the length of the work period. Students can work on different problems, on the same problem or even on different aspects of the same problem. What is important is that each individual is actively involved in experimenting, critical thinking, planning and searching for an answer. The more capable students are likely to come up with answers to their problems before the other members of the class. They can be given other tasks to work on to keep them usefully busy while the less able students catch up. During the work period the teacher will have to direct, supervise and give hints to the students so that the investigation keeps progressing. As data is gathered it must be recorded in an organised fashion so that it can be presented later in the form of a report. Students not accustomed to writing such reports may need additional guidance and directions from the teacher.

Culminating activities

As the practical side of the investigation nears completion the students may need to discuss their findings in groups or with the teacher. They should be guided to draw some conclusions from the data they have gathered. In the process of writing up their results further unanswered questions may arise and these can serve as the basis of further laboratory work.

In this period of the laboratory experience the teacher should attempt to assess what the students have learned from the exercise. What skills have they developed, what knowledge have they gathered which they did not fully grasp before? In terms of time and effort the teacher might also try to assess whether the laboratory exercise was worthwhile and interesting for the students, so that he can better plan future laboratory work.

Advantages of the laboratory method

1. It trains students in research methods.
2. Students learn better and retain knowledge longer when they are practically involved in the knowledge acquiring process.
3. Because the students are actively involved they tend to be more interested.

Disadvantages of the laboratory method

1. It is more time consuming and requires a generous supply of materials and equipment.
2. It requires careful planning and a lot of time for preparation on the part of the teacher.
3. The student cannot learn about everything through practical experience.

EXERCISES

1. Outline the main features of the process approach to teaching, and describe five process skills that can be developed by students. What are the main advantages and disadvantages of this approach? Draw up a lesson plan on a topic of your choice to illustrate how the process approach can be used in the lower classes of secondary schools or Grade II teacher training colleges.

2. Describe what you understand discovery learning to mean and explain the terms *percept, concept,* and *principle* in this context. By way of a lesson plan illustrate how you would teach a concept or principle to a class, following the steps outlined in this chapter.
3. Briefly describe what you understand by guided inquiry, free inquiry and modified free inquiry. Select a topic and outline the main steps you would lead the students to follow in a guided inquiry lesson or series of lessons.
4. What features do the approaches described in this chapter have in common? Can you describe the finer points which distinguish between the approaches? What makes these approaches differ from more traditional forms of teaching?

ESSENTIAL READING

Jegede, O. J. and Brown, D. P. (1980) *Primary Science Teaching*, Macmillan, Lagos.

Risk, Thomas M. (1965) *Principles and Practice of Teaching in Secondary Schools*, (3rd ed.), Eurasia Publishing House, New Delhi.

Sund, Robert B. and Trowbridge, L. W. (1973) *Teaching Science by Inquiry in the Secondary School*, (2nd ed.), Charles E. Merrill, Columbus, Ohio.

SUPPLEMENTARY READING

Beyer, Barry K. (1971) *Inquiry in the Social Studies: A Strategy for Teaching*, Charles E. Merrill, Columbus, Ohio.

Brandwein, Paul F. and Schwab, Joseph, J. (1962) *The Teaching of Science as Inquiry*, Harvard University Press, Cambridge, Mass.

Bruner, Jerome S. (1961) The act of discovery, *Harvard Educational Review*, 31 (1), 21–32.

Commission on Science Education of the American Association for the Advancement of Science (1965) *Science – A Process Approach Commentary for Teachers*, (3rd experimental ed.), American Association for the Advancement of Science, Washington D.C.

Cronbach, L. J. (1963) *Educational Psychology*, Harcourt Brace Jovanovich, New York.

Cronbach, L. J. (1966) The Logic of Experiments on Discovery, in *Learning by Discovery* (eds L. S. Shulman and E. R. Keisler), Rand McNally, Chicago.

Cox, Benjamin C. and Messiales, Byron (1966) *Inquiry in the Social Studies*, McGraw-Hill, New York.

De Cecco, John P. and Crawford, William R. (1974) *The Psychology of Learning and Instruction* (2nd ed.), Prentice Hall, Englewood Cliffs, N.J.

Dewey, John (1933) *How We Think*, D. C. Heath, Boston.

Gagné, R. *et al.* (1965) *The Psychological Bases of Science – A Process Approach*, American Association for the Advancement of Science, Washington D.C.

Institute of Education, Ahmadu Bello University (1975) *Primary Science Teachers' Book I*, Longman (Nigeria) Ltd, Lagos.

Lancaster, Otis E. (1974) *Effective Teaching and Learning*, Gordon Breach, New York.

Lardizabal, A. S. *et al.* (1978) *Principles and Methods of Teaching*, (2nd ed.), Alemar-Phoenix, Manila, Philippines.

McKeachie, Wilbert J. (1969) *Teaching Tips – A Guide for the Beginning College Teacher*, D. C. Heath, Boston, Mass.

Merwin, Will. C. (1976) The inquiry method, in *Handbook on Contemporary Education*, (ed. Steve E. Goodman), R. R. Bowker, New York, pp. 388–91.

Schorling, and Bethelder, H. (1973) Using laboratory techniques, in *Instructional Planning in the Secondary School* (ed. Anne R. Crayles), David McKay, New York.

Whitehead, A. N. (1929) *The Aims of Education*, Williams & Norgate, London.

Wittrock, M. C. (1966) The learning by discovery hypothesis, in *Learning by Discovery*, (eds L. S. Shulman and E. R. Keisler), Rand McNally, Chicago, pp. 33–76.

Whittrock, M. C., Keisler, E. and Stern, C. (1964) Verbal cues in concept identification, *Journal of Educational Psychology*, 55, pp. 195–200.

6

Improving Specific Teaching Techniques

INTRODUCTION

While method is the overall procedure used to teach a particular lesson, technique is the art or skill of performance. You may be using the discussion method but the way you ask questions to trigger off participation is your own technique. You may use the method of discovery but the way you make your students apply or practise what they have learned is your own technique. Technique is, therefore, the way you handle the different aspects or phases of your instructional method or procedure.

There are some important activities in the classroom that are almost always used in everyday lessons. These are review, drill, practice, assignment and questioning. Because they are always used, they are often taken for granted and no deliberate effort is made to prepare for them. We fail to realise that the success of the teaching-learning process depends to a considerable extent on how well we perform these activities. This chapter discusses the nature and scope as well as the advantages and disadvantages of these different activities. It also offers some valuable pointers which should help you develop effective techniques.

DRILL AND PRACTICE

Not everything in a lesson is retained no matter how vivid and exciting the learning experiences. Often students may appear to be understanding and even enjoying the lesson while it is in progress but, unfortunately, they have difficulty recalling or producing exactly the response you would have expected or wished them to learn. There is therefore a need to provide activities that ensure that important things are learned and committed to memory for ready recall and used whenever necessary. The three most commonly used techniques are drill, practice and review.

Many modern day educationists consider drill and practice as one and the same technique. Others not only consider them the same but feel that drill in the strict sense of the word should be discouraged, and that all activities involving repetition are better referred to as practice. The authors of this book hold the belief that drill, even in its strictest sense, is an invaluable technique in achieving certain specific instructional objectives and has a special place in the total teaching-learning process. Because of the great similarity between drill and practice, especially in the overall procedure, as well as in the conditions surrounding their effective use, they will be treated together.

Nature of drill and practice

These are both techniques which are carried out after the initial teaching and learning have taken place. They are not used to teach, but rather to reinforce, supplement, fix, or add to what has already been learned. Furthermore, they both employ a substantial amount of repetition of some sort and of varying intensity.

The difference between drill and practice is largely a difference in emphasis. In the drill, the emphasis is on repetition for the purpose of memorising important facts, and making automatic the use of simple motor skills. In practice, the emphasis is not on mere memorisation but for the application or intelligent use or manipulation of facts, and for the acquisition of an ability to the point of accuracy or perfection. While drill implies an unthinking repetition of mental or motor responses, practice implies a more meaningful and purposeful varied repetition. You therefore drill your students on the table of multiplication, but you give them practice in solving mathematical problems; you drill them in spelling, but you give them practice in letter writing; you drill them in passing the ball in soccer, but you give them practice in attacking the goal. In other words, you drill students on some specific details needing attention, but you practise them on their performance of the whole skill or an ability.

Scope and limitations

In most, if not all, subjects there are certain facts and abilities that must simply be developed and therefore attacked directly. These facts and abilities are usually determined by the teacher at the beginning of the school year. She carefully takes note of the important mental and physical (motor) skills that need to be learned thoroughly, memorised, or made automatic. Some of the materials chosen may be better attacked using the drill, while others may be more appropriate as practice materials.

The following are specific situations when the drill is probably the most appropriate technique to use.

1. When memorising important facts, such as basic formulae, quotients, symbols such as those used in set theories, names, dates, places, vocabularies, spelling, etc.
2. When memorising verbatim definitions, laws, theories, principles or rules.
3. When making important mental or motor skills automatic such as correct pronunciation in French, grammar, conversion of units (miles to kilometres, yards to metres, etc.), spiking the ball in volley ball, place kicking in football, etc.
4. When developing and fixing a habit, such as passing papers or other materials to the monitor or the teacher, without standing; putting away materials or equipment in their proper places after using them; or waiting to be recognised before talking.

The following are specific situations when practice may be more appropriate than drill.

1. When specific facts and skills drilled need to be applied in more meaningful situations, such as essay writing using vocabularies learned; problem solving using the different specific mathematical symbols and formulae mastered.

2. When learned abilities need to be polished or refined to perfection, such as outlining in literature, oral or interpretative reading, swimming, typing, performing simple experiments in chemistry or physics, etc.

As with other techniques or methods, the use of drill or practice in teaching and learning has some limitations. In the first place, not all aspects of the lesson are appropriate for drilling or for practice. There is, therefore, the problem of choosing or identifying those parts that need to be drilled or practised.

In the second place, not all students have the same need for drill or practice. Some students may need fewer sessions in some areas, while others may need more. This is why educators as well as psychologists strongly suggest that exercises provided for drilling or practice must be organised towards individualised or independent activity.

In the third place, because of the very nature of repetition, drill and practice exercises must be highly motivating, otherwise they may become boring or monotonous, thus causing misbehaviour.

Lastly, drill and practice are not most effective in teaching understanding and developing attitudes and appreciations. They are therefore often branded as rote learning, which connotes memorising without really understanding.

Techniques of drill and practice

Generally speaking, the techniques of drill and practice follow the same procedure. Probably the most obvious difference is that in drill the repetition exercise is more intense, brief and snappy, and the pressure on the students more demanding. The goal in drill is to make students respond automatically once the cue is given and leave them little time to think.

Let us then assume that the initial understanding of the material has already been developed. The following suggested steps may be used for the drill or practice exercise.

1. Identifying materials for the drill or practice

This involves focusing students' attention on the specific skill or set of facts for drilling or practice. This may also include a brief statement of the value of the exercise for future learning. In other words, a bit of convincing on the need for the drill or practice may help in developing students' concentration.

2. Providing the model for the drill or practice

Here the pattern to be imitated or followed is demonstrated by the teacher. The material may either be verbal, as in the case of memorising, or non-verbal, as in the case of physical skill. It is very important at this point to emphasise that the model for performance be correct or accurate. The tricky parts should also be highlighted or accentuated.

3. Initial practice or drill

In this step, students are given the chance to explore or to gain a feel of the material for the drill or practice. They can try out their skills on their own and may even ask questions about them. Initial repetition may start as a whole class activity and is usually closely guided by the teacher. If a motor skill is being drilled or practised, then each step should be accompanied by verbal instruction. This initial repetitive exercise continues until every student knows exactly what he is expected to and is aware of the level of performance he is supposed to attain. Remember that early practice is largely diagnostic in nature, and therefore accuracy should be emphasised before speed.

4. Varied practice

This step demands that teachers be imaginative or creative, because this involves devising various drill or practice exercises. The more varied the exercises are, the more interesting the drill or practice will become.

5. Individual exercise

All types of group drill or practice exercises should be replaced with individualised activities. These days, various drill or practice exercises are available in the form of workbooks or manuals. They can also be found in most of the standard textbooks used in schools.

Improving the techniques

For more efficient drill or practice techniques, the following suggestions or points are worth considering.

(1) Learning is more efficient if students have adequate prior understanding of the materials for the drill or practice. For example, before memorising the whole multiplication table, students should already have had a thorough understanding of the operations involved in multiplication and, probably, division also. They should have already learned the significance of some important dates and places in history before they memorise them. Thus practice or drill is not reduced to mere parroting or rote learning.

(2) Practice is more meaningful when done by wholes rather than by parts. When practising skills that are closely knit together or skills that are not too complicated and difficult, one needs to perform the skill in its entirety and not in bits. However, if the skills are complicated and the parts are loosely organised, part-whole practice is more effective. In other words, specific parts needing concentrated attention will be practised first before the whole set of skills is performed (Clark and Starr, 1976).

For instance, when a poem to be learned is short, memorising it by wholes is usually more efficient. Each line can then be seen as part of a meaningful whole, the learning becomes a complete unit and the repetition more interesting. However, if the poem is too long, it can be divided into smaller but still meaningful parts before being taken as a whole.

(3) Practice should not be too far removed from the conditions under which it is normally carried out. In other words, repetition is best done in context. One good example is the Teaching Practice Exercise which is a requirement for graduation in all teacher training programmes. During the exercise, student teachers are given the opportunity to try out methods and techniques learned in almost the same situation as that they will find themselves in when they finally go out on their own. All problems that they may encounter will then be similar to if not the same as those that may well arise in their future classrooms.

Practice, therefore, should be done in as real a setting as possible. You can only perfect your style in swimming in the pool, your driving with a real car on a real road, or your typing with a real typewriter. Simulating situations for practice has its own merits, but practising in context has some important real and lasting values.

(4) Practice is more effective when it is distributed over a period of time with rather frequent breaks than when it is concentrated in long continuous sessions. This implies that practice sessions should be kept relatively short and interspersed with rest periods. Since motivation and effort can be sustained at a high level only for a short time before the student begins to feel tired, the shortness of the practice period and the rest periods in between will give him the chance to renew his concentration and interest. This prevents him from developing incorrect habits or responses from practising when he is tired. This will also give him the chance to forget his mistakes before proceeding to the next session (Clark and Starr, 1976).

(5) Drill and practice should always be done under some pressure. The pressure in the drill should be more intense than in the practice exercise. The pressure, though, should not be too demanding or impossible to cope with, but just enough to encourage pupils to work harder towards perfection or towards the attainment of the maximum level of performance.

(6) Be quick to correct mistakes as soon as they are spotted. If you leave them too long, you will have difficulty in correcting them especially if they have already been mastered.

(7) More attention should be given to weak spots. If students are observed to be having difficulty in some parts of the activity, repetition on those particular parts should be intensified.

(8) As soon as practicable, practice should be given to applying what has been drilled. This will help convince students of the significance of drilling and also help justify the time and effort they spent on the exercise.

(9) Always work towards individualising practice or drill to meet the particular needs of individual students.

(10) As the skills become more and more fixed or perfect, practice or drill periods should become shorter, and the intervals longer. When sessions go on for a long time, the material becomes stale and boring. An alert teacher should

be quick to recognise when practice or drill should be stopped.

Advantages of drill and practice

The following advantages could be said to apply to both drill and practice especially when they are properly conducted, and appropriately timed and spaced.

1. Drill and practice are probably the most effective techniques for extending associations and skills. Although they are not used to teach, they are certainly invaluable in increasing understanding of what has already been learned.
2. They are efficient in refining or polishing skills and abilities that have been learned. After all, it is a popular belief that practice makes perfect.
3. They provide the basic foundation on which higher level cognitive skills are built.
4. They are necessary for correcting and improving specific parts or aspects of a skill or ability simply because they utilise a substantial amount of repetition.
5. They reinforce retention, and to some psychologists they are efficient techniques for developing one's general ability to memorise, an important factor of intelligence.

Disadvantages of drill and practice

Drill and practice have the following disadvantages only if they are not handled properly.

1. Drill and practice tend to become boring or monotonous unless the purpose is clear and accepted, and the motivation is high.
2. Because of the very nature of repetition, high motivation may be difficult to develop and alertness and concentration hard to sustain. Thus, it may breed misbehaviour in class.
3. Both drill and practice may degenerate into mere rote learning, especially when initial understanding is not adequately developed.

4. Much time may be wasted if materials for drilling will never really be needed, or if the setting is without meaning to students.

THE REVIEW TECHNIQUE

Nature of the review technique

Review, like the drill and practice, employs a substantial amount of repetition and recall. However, drill and practice exercises are concerned with repetition for the sake of memorising or rendering a response automatic and accurate. Review, although it serves to assist in achieving these goals, aims to do much more.

Review implies taking a new look, or renewing an old view in order to deepen understanding of relationships and associations previously studied. It is an enlightening process, frequently not everything is grasped when it is first taught. A second study will help clarify any misconceptions, extend and deepen understandings, and may also serve to develop new insights.

Like practice and drill, review is carried out after the initial learning and it assumes a certain amount of understanding. It may occur incidentally during a lesson as well as in special review sessions. Unlike drill and practice, where exercises are most useful if individualised, review is more effective as a group activity. It is, therefore, better organised as a co-operative enterprise.

When to use review

Review accomplishes the same end as drill and practice, but its main purpose is to extend associations or broaden understanding previously learned. As mentioned earlier, review may be done anytime during the class activities, or during a separate or special time reserved for it. The following are probably the most common and may be the most appropriate times for conducting a review.

(1) *At the beginning of the class period.* Most teachers begin each day's lesson with a short review of the previous day's lesson. This is useful in reinforcing what has been learned and also in assisting students to see materials of instruction in

their proper sequence. Normally students attend several different subjects in a single day, and the most probable thing that occupies their minds before they start with your period is the lesson that they have just finished. A brief reminder of what was taken the day before would help connect the past lesson with the new one, thus providing an excellent opportunity to develop an appropriate apperceptive basis for the day's lesson.

(2) *At the end of the lesson.* A short review after a lesson could serve to summarise the important points taken. It also serves to tie together loose ends to ensure better organisation of students' thoughts.

(3) *At the end of the week, month, or after each term.* This provides an excellent opportunity to reorganise or regroup students' learning, thus giving it more meaning, clarity and significance. It serves to make students see the different aspects of a course or subject in their proper perspective.

(4) *Before examinations.* It is a common practice among teachers to prepare their students for examinations by giving them review lessons. Many modern educators feel, however, that if this is the sole or major purpose of the review it may degenerate into a mere device for passing exams. But to most students this is the most important justification for the exercise, and therefore it is not surprising if, during these times, they are highly motivated to attend your class and to listen intently to every word you have to say. This high motivation gives you an excellent opportunity to achieve many of the more desirable purposes of the review, particularly clarifying relationships or associations, placing proper emphasis on important points and assuring mastery of the most significant concepts in the unit or course.

In any case, review can be used whenever loose ends need to be tied together and students' thinking needs to be reorganised or reassembled. Through the review, you can make learning more permanent; tie concepts or ideas together; and connect the past, present and future learning.

Review techniques

There are several ways of conducting a review. The following are some of the most commonly used techniques.

1. The socialised review

This is one of the most widely used and sometimes, if not often, it is overworked to the point of defeating the real purpose of the exercise. However, if carefully planned and properly conducted, it certainly can help achieve desired ends.

In this type of review a student is designated to ask a question on the topic or unit and then call on another to answer. The student who gives the correct answer then asks the next question and calls on somebody else for the reply. This process continues until all aspects of the materials for review are covered or until everybody has had the chance to participate. While the questioning process is going on, the teacher usually acts as the moderator, whose primary role is to keep the 'ball rolling', as well as clarifying points or giving extended explanations. Whenever a misconception is detected he is quick to correct it. He also sees to it that all students are actively participating.

Sometimes, for variety, a sort of competition is introduced. The class is divided into two teams, and questions coming from one team are thrown to any of the members of the other team. One point is given to the team asking the question for every wrong answer given by the opposing team. One problem that may arise is that either team may take advantage of the situation by calling on the dull members to answer questions in their effort to get more points. The effect of this on the slow learners who are unable to answer the questions may be damaging.

2. Written review tests

This type of review not only serves to motivate students but also provides a basis for diagnosis. Here students are given short written tests concerning the topic under revision. These tests are evaluated not for marking, but for identifying students' weaknesses. Usually students are made to check their own papers in order to make them aware of where they went wrong. Correct answers to all questions are normally given by the teacher, or are decided upon by the whole class. They may be opened for discussion if the need arises, giving the teacher an excellent opportunity for teaching again or clarifying misunderstandings. Thus, although the test itself is an individual affair, the marking or checking of the papers becomes a co-operative or a socialised activity.

3. Oral review quizzes

This type requires students to answer oral questions prepared in advance by the teacher. In this situation, only one student at a time is directly involved. While a student is being questioned, the others may be nervously waiting for their turn, or anxiously wondering what question will hit them. There is therefore the possibility that verbatim recitation will be mistaken as real learning, when in reality students are only memorising things without fully understanding them. Suggestions to improve questioning techniques, are discussed in the next section on the Technique of Questioning.

In conclusion, no matter what technique is used, a good review lesson should be such that it stimulates reorganisation of thoughts, provides a new view of past learning, thus broadening understanding and appreciations, and serves to guide students to see the different aspects of a unit of study in their proper sequence and perspective. It should also furnish a basis for diagnosing the weaknesses and strengths of the students.

It is important to emphasise here that review procedures should be closely related to testing procedures. There is nothing more frustrating to students than having to review certain aspects of the course or topic and being tested on the others. To give a review on one thing and a test on another is certainly a sure way of making enemies out of your students, or making them feel they were cheated.

Advantages of review

1. Review is an effective technique in teaching understanding and appreciation.
2. It is efficient in co-ordinating or relating facts or materials learned for better understanding.
3. It leads students to see the different parts of the unit or course in their proper sequence and perspective.
4. It could be used to diagnose students' weaknesses, especially regarding lessons already taught and supposedly learned.

5. It is useful in making learning more meaningful and hence more lasting.
6. When conducted before the examination period, it helps develop a feeling of confidence on the part of the students.
7. It helps facilitate transfer of learning from one situation to other related situations.
8. It provides an excellent opportunity for re-teaching or for clarifying misconceptions.

Disadvantages of review

When overworked, the review may have the following disadvantages.

1. It may degenerate into a mere device for passing examinations, thus defeating the other more important goals of the review.
2. Verbatim recitation during the oral test review may be mistaken for true learning, when it may only be repetition without real understanding.
3. The use of competition may prove to be disadvantageous to slow learners, as well as offering a good opportunity for the more clever ones to show off, which is not desirable.
4. It may cause frustration among students, especially if the examination questions are not related to or of the same level as the review questions.

THE TECHNIQUE OF QUESTIONING

Introduction

Questioning is probably one of the most versatile and the most readily available techniques in the hands of the teacher. With skilful handling, it can accomplish a host of important instructional goals. Although questioning can be used frequently, it should not be overdone, especially in a single class period. One of the authors had the unfortunate experience of observing a class where the whole period was spent on asking and answering questions. The lesson started off well, but the teacher went on asking question after question, sometimes without any apparent reason, until some students became restless and started looking miserable. Remember, an overdose of anything, however good it may be, can be dangerous.

With the change of emphasis in our educational goals, from mere acquisition of facts and information to development of reflective thinking and intelligent manipulation of materials, the technique of questioning has become more challenging for the teacher. Fortunately, this technique can be developed, improved and perfected given enough time and sufficient practice. An awareness of the different purposes of questioning, the types of questions, the characteristics of good questions, and ways of improving the technique is probably a good start for any teacher, especially the inexperienced teacher, in his effort to master the art of questioning.

Purposes of questioning

In the past the main purpose of questioning was to find out whether or not students had prepared their lessons. Although this is still acceptable today, with the change of emphasis in the curriculum of our schools questioning is now used for several more important reasons. A close look at the various materials available on the uses and purposes of questions in teaching and learning, revealed five important general uses or purposes. They are (1) for teaching (as in the so-called socratic method); (2) for drilling or practising; (3) for guidance or leading; (4) for stimulating or motivating; and (5) for evaluating.

A more specific and probably one of the most comprehensive list of these uses is given by Clark and Starr (1976). Examine the list and see if you can place the items under each of the general uses mentioned above.

Uses of questions

1. To find out something one did not know
2. To find out whether someone knows something
3. To develop the ability to think
4. To motivate pupil learning
5. To provide drill or practice
6. To help pupils organise materials

7. To help pupils interpret materials
8. To emphasise important points
9. To show relationships such as cause and effect
10. To discover pupil interest
11. To develop appreciation
12. To provide review
13. To give practice in expression
14. To reveal mental processes
15. To show agreement or disagreement
16. To establish rapport with pupils
17. To diagnose
18. To evaluate
19. To obtain the attention of wandering minds

Types of questions

Questions can be conveniently grouped into two general types. All questions involving mere recall of facts and information, as well as questions requiring only either a 'yes' or a 'no' answer, are referred to as *factual questions*. Questions requiring reflective thinking, or application and intelligent manipulation of learned materials, are called *thought questions.*

Although educationists generally agree that teachers should emphasise the development of students' ability in critical thinking rather than in the mere accumulation of facts, researches conducted for many years have revealed that teachers' questions are more of the factual than the thought type.

This may be because factual questions are much easier to formulate and evaluate. It is of course true that these questions have their own merits because mastery of information provides the basis for higher order mental processes. However, these questions should be immediately replaced or followed up with questions that cause students to think or to apply information. Obviously, these are the more superior type of questions. The following are examples of both kinds of questions:

Factual questions

1. When did the Nigerian civil war end?
2. What are the three major tribes in Nigeria?

3. What is the boiling point of water in degrees centigrade?
4. What is meant by adjective?
5. What is the formula used for finding the circumference of the circle?

Thought questions

1. If the Ministry of Education increases the grant to schools from ₦100 to ₦200 per student per annum, what is the percentage increase per student?
2. Differentiate between factual questions and thought questions.
3. How would you deal with questions intended to challenge your ideas?

Characteristics of good questions

Generally speaking, the best questions are usually those which were carefully thought of in advance. Specifically, good questions possess the following characteristics. They should be:

(1) *Clear, brief, concise and direct.* They should ask something that is definite, in simple, clear and straightforward language. They are therefore, free from any ambiguity that may be caused by complex and confusing construction or by the use of vocabularies beyond the level of understanding of the students. Double-barrelled questions or tricky questions should therefore be avoided.

(2) *Thought provoking.* Questions that require students to think are challenging and therefore superior to questions that call for repetition of facts. Good questions are those which encourage students to manipulate or apply knowledge learned, rather than those only requiring either 'yes' or 'no' answers, or single-word responses. Words, such as why, how, explain, describe, compare and justify, when used to begin a question often tend to encourage thinking on the part of students, as well as triggering a higher level discussion. In addition, such questions do not give much opportunity for students to guess the right answer, or bluff their way out.

(3) *Suited to the age, abilities and interests of the pupils to whom it is addressed.* Questions intended for more advanced

students should be more challenging than those for the slower ones. It is not wise to formulate a question and call a student whom you know very well cannot answer it. This practice can do more damage than good, especially to the slow learners. The vocabulary used as well as the construction of the question should be within the level of understanding of the students. To students there are no more difficult questions than those they could not understand.

Improving the techniques of questioning

It is a common belief among teachers, that the effectiveness of teaching can be measured to a considerable extent by the teacher's ability to ask the right question, at the right time, in the right way. Although questions are widely used in almost every phase of the instructional process, there are still a good number of teachers who are guilty of mis-using or over-using this technique. For instance, there are those who have no idea as to what constitutes a good question. There are also those who do not even have any purpose in mind for asking the question they ask. Still there are others who ask questions which they themselves cannot answer. Most often, the beginning teachers and the lazy ones are the usual culprits. The new graduates tend to pitch their questions to the level of abstraction that they were used to while in college, and the lazy ones do not have the dedication or commitment to their profession to bother about the outcome of their behaviour. Fortunately, the technique of questioning can be developed and improved. With practice and time, any teacher conscious of the conditions for effective questioning will certainly become proficient.

The most widely accepted procedure for asking questions that has proved very satisfactory to teachers, consists of the following ordered steps:

1. State the question.
2. Pause: allow time for students to consider the question and think about the answer.
3. Call on the name of the student.
4. Listen to the answer.
5. Comment on or evaluate the answer.

In this procedure everyone has the chance to consider the question before anyone tries to answer it. Because nobody knows who is going to be called, this technique helps to keep the students alert, thus discouraging inattention.

There are certain situations where calling on the student first before asking the question may be desirable. One such situation is when calling on a shy or a slow student. This way he is given time to prepare himself for the question. Another situation is when calling on an inattentive student. By so doing, unnecessary embarrassment on the part of the student is avoided, because he does not have to ask for the question to be repeated. In addition, this is one way of waking up or jolting students who may be daydreaming.

With this general procedure in mind, the following guidelines for the improvement of the techniques of questioning should be considered.

(1) All key or important questions should be prepared in advance. These are the questions that you cannot afford to forget and, in order not to miss them, it may be good practice to include them in your lesson plan.

(2) Questions should be asked in a natural, friendly and conversational manner. Students tend to feel nervous if you sound like an interrogator or a commander in chief of an army. Questions should be asked in an atmosphere of informality, but without sacrificing order and discipline.

(3) Questions should be addressed to the whole class, but most often should be formulated with a definite group or individual in mind. This ensures that the right questions are designated to the right student or group of students. The slow learners need to feel successful to bolster their morale, and therefore, should be able to give correct answers to questions asked of them. They may not be able to answer every single question, but at least they should not have too much problem with some, if not most, of them. For the brighter students, questions should be more difficult and challenging.

(4) Refrain from repeating questions unless there is a legitimate reason for doing so. Unnecessary repetition encourages inattention on the part of the students. If they are certain that you will ask the question twice or three times anyway, they surely will not listen to the question the first

time you ask it. However, if they realise that questions are usually asked just once, then they will make every effort to listen and understand them.

(5) Questions should be fairly equally distributed among members of the class. Many teachers have the tendency to concentrate their attention on the more clever students to the neglect of the less clever ones. This situation may be challenging for the bright students, and satisfying for the teacher, but it may be depressing for the slower ones.

Handling students' answers

Teachers will find the following tips for handling students' answers properly useful.

(1) Insist that students answer in complete thought units as well as in good English. This should provide them with opportunities to practice their oral expression.

(2) Accept all genuine answers sincerely. However, only correct ones should be approved. If the answer is partly correct and partly wrong, then acknowledge that portion that is correct and point out or comment on the wrong part. Do not ignore any wrong answer given. If you do so, students might mistake them to be the right answer.

(3) Students should not be made to feel afraid to make mistakes, but they should not be encouraged to guess or to bluff. Insulting, reprimanding or mocking students because of wrong answers will discourage them from trying, especially when they are not very sure of the accuracy of their responses.

(4) If a student seems not to be answering to the best of his ability, follow-up questions may push him to try and do better. Usually, he will sense that you mean business, and that he is not 'getting off the hook' that easily.

(5) Refrain from repeating or re-phrasing students' answers, except for purposes of emphasis or clarification of points. The habit of re-stating the correct answer for the benefit of the whole class tends to encourage inattention.

(6) Answering in unison as a class should not be allowed too often or for too long. This may help enliven the class, or encourage the shy ones to participate, but these apparent advantages are outweighed by some inherent disadvantages. These are: (1) it discourages students from thinking; (2) it

gives an excellent opportunity for the lazy child to do nothing or to do something else; and (3) it gives the teacher no opportunity to evaluate an individual student's progress.

(7) If the question elicits blank stares, bewildered looks or bowed heads, then the question needs to be reconsidered. The best thing to do is back-track a little and ask questions that may provide additional background for the original question. In addition, it may be broken down into component parts, each part being answered one at a time, until the original question is fully understood.

Handling students' questions

Some teachers, especially the insecure ones, feel offended, threatened or challenged every time students ask questions. However, you should be pleased if your students start firing questions at you, no matter what their reasons are. This gives an indication that they are reacting and, therefore, are actively involved. In addition, the questions students raise give you insight into their thinking which will guide you in planning and organising future learning activities for them.

The following are some of the most important points to consider in dealing with students' questions.

(1) Students should be encouraged to ask questions. The questions they ask can be a good demonstration of their intelligence, evidence that could be of great help to the teacher in his attempt to know individual students better.

(2) All sincere questions should be handled with appropriate consideration no matter how silly they may be. Questions that may seem stupid or trivial to you may be genuinely important to the student who asked them.

(3) When students start questioning authority, they are best answered using logic and reason, coupled with much patience and tact. After all, as the teacher you are supposed to be in good if not complete control of the situation to be able to prove your point.

(4) When a student starts asking questions just to show off or to prove to his classmates or even to you that he is smart, his questions are best thrown back to him tactfully. Usually, he gets the point.

(5) Sometimes, it is best to turn a question to the whole class for discussion.

(6) If you do not know the answer to a question, it is best to admit your inability rather than be caught lying or bluffing. You can always promise to give the correct answer as soon as you have done your research.

THE ASSIGNMENT

Introduction

One of the complaints teachers make about their students is about their negative attitude towards extra work and their tardiness in completing and submitting the work. Some teachers would not hesitate to say that there is nothing one can do about the situation because students 'nowadays' are just plain lazy. However, if we took a closer look at the kind of assignments we give and how we give them, we might change our minds about blaming students and start doing something about the assignments we give.

Creating good assignments is not an easy task, especially for a beginning teacher. This section, therefore, offers some pointers on how to make good assignments. The values and requisites of a well planned assignment are also discussed.

Nature and functions of assignments

The assignment is that part of the lesson that tells students what to do after school hours and is related to what they have already done or what they still have to do in class. It is a set of tasks or a specific task which students are expected to complete in a given time. It may be a project, a series of problems to be solved, some questions to be answered, a chapter to be read and summarised, a story to be outlined, or a review of past lessons.

Assignments could be given to individual students or to groups depending on the type and the time available to students to complete the tasks. Simple and smaller units of work may be given to individuals and larger units to groups.

Individual assignments may be the ideal, but not only are they time consuming, but they also require a genius of a teacher to be able to cater for individual needs, interests, abilities and experiential background when giving assignments. In fact, under the present system, it is almost impossible to differentiate the tasks of about forty to fifty individual students per class of say, three to four different streams.

Group assignments may be for smaller groups or for the entire class. The assignments given to small groups are tailor-made to suit the needs, capabilities and interests of each member of the group. Hence, once the problem of grouping (deciding who should work together) is settled, planning assignments for each group would not be that difficult. The class assignment involves giving the same piece of work to everyone in the whole class. This type has been criticised since it does not provide for individual differences. However, it is still the most widely used in our classrooms.

Assignments may be given daily either as a follow-up activity after the development of a lesson, or as a preparatory exercise to help build the apperceptive basis for new lessons. They can also be given on a long-term basis; larger units of work can be assigned for completing over a longer period. Often projects such as staging a drama, putting up a school display, making a scrapbook, or structuring a bulletin board are given as long-term assignments.

Educational research has shown the superiority of giving fewer assignments covering larger units of study over numerous small isolated ones. This implies the desirability of providing more small group assignments where each member can perform an individual task while recognising that his work is very closely tied with the other members'. He is fully aware of the ultimate goal to which his particular contribution is directed.

When carefully planned and properly given, the assignment can perform the following functions.

(1) *To serve as a follow-up activity to what has already been learned in the classroom.* The class period is often too short for students to apply or to practise what they have learned. In such a situation, the assignment provides an excellent opportunity for reinforcing previously learned skill or knowledge. For example, after teaching the operations involved in adding unlike fractions, a series of problems applying the concept learned can be given for students to solve in their homes, in the hostels, or during the prep period. This type of assignment will surely offer the practice necessary for retention and mastery.

(2) *To prepare students for the next day's lesson.* Assignments can be designed to give students background information and knowledge about the lessons yet to come. This can help establish the apperceptive basis for new learning experiences, as well as develop the proper attitude among the students.

(3) *To provide direction and guidance for independent study.* Very few secondary school students are able to develop the skill of studying on their own. When given an assignment without specific instructions as to what they are expected to do, they become lost and bewildered. Assignments can provide a direct and deliberate means of teaching students the skill of independent study. This includes being able to pick out important points in whatever they are reading or listening to; summarise a chapter, selection, story or a unit; outline important concepts, facts, or events; use various sources of knowledge and information; and many others. Given enough practice, students will be able to learn effectively on their own, without having to rely on their teacher's direction all the time, a skill which will be of tremendous help to them long after they have left school.

(4) *To develop a positive attitude towards extra work, and good study habits.* Stimulating and challenging assignments help create a favourable attitude towards learning activities inside and outside the classroom. Students usually take pride in their work and each task successfully completed is regarded by them as an accomplishment. Consequently, they are motivated to do better in each succeeding assignment.

(5) *To provide an excellent means for developing the other higher order mental processes.* One of the criticisms of our educational system today is that most of the normal classroom activities are directed towards the mere acquisition of facts and information. There is no provision for the development of thinking and reasoning abilities. In this regard, the assignment can offer an excellent opportunity for teachers to give students activities that call for the use of judgement and reasoning. It can become an important vehicle for challenging students to think creatively, logically and critically.

Techniques of giving assignments

Much of the failure or reluctance of students to complete

assigned tasks may be attributed to badly conceived assignments. The following are some useful pointers that should help you improve your technique.

1. Assignments should be clear and definite

The extent to which a student will work hard on a given assignment will depend on how well she understands what she is expected to do. Assignments should therefore be explained fully and explicitly, in simple and easy to understand language. Sufficient instructions should be given along with guide questions and definite sources of information and advice on how they may be obtained. How many times did you have to postpone doing an assignment just because you were not really sure about what to do? How many times have you wished that your lecturers would tell you more about the essays they wanted you to write for them?

2. Assignments should be closely related to the lessons under study

They should grow out of past or present lessons, and should fit logically and consistently with other learning activities. Assignments that are unconnected with what the students are doing in class may be regarded by them as irrelevant and therefore a waste of time. Hence they should be made aware of the value as well as the purpose of the task they are being asked to do. Many of our young students many not be able to see beyond 'what is', and it may be difficult for them to understand the values of some of the things we assign them to do. However, we do not even have to go further than making them realise that their assignments are closely tied up with what they are actually studying in class.

3. Assignments should be adapted to students' capabilities

It is essential that students' readiness to complete the work assigned to them be assessed. If the assignment is too simple and easy, they will not be encouraged to do it. If it is too difficult, they will either get bored or frustrated, or they will get somebody else to do it for them.

4. Whenever possible, differentiate assignments to suit individual differences in your class

Do not lose sight of the fact that you have forty to fifty

different individuals in your class with varying interests, abilities, needs and backgrounds. To differentiate assignments may not be easy, but it certainly is worth considering.

5. Assignments should be interesting and stimulating
They should not be so easy or so difficult as to bore or frustrate the students. Interesting and stimulating assignments are those which challenge students to engage in creative and reflective thinking. Thus activities that call for judgement, reasoning or evaluating should be used in assignments.

6. Enough time should be allotted for the giving of assignments
There is no one best time for giving assignments. They can be given at any time during the class period: at the beginning, while the lesson is in progress, or at the end. It is not uncommon for teachers to give the assignment hurriedly before the bell rings. Very often you will hear a teacher say, 'Read Chapter Two of your textbook for tomorrow', or, 'Write an essay on democracy for Monday'. Assignments such as these which are given carelessly and haphazardly, will stand a greater chance of not being completed because they are easily forgotten. It is therefore, important to remember that sufficient time should be allowed for thorough explanation of the assignment as well as for students' questions regarding the task.

6. Consider the time available to students to complete assigned tasks
Remember that your students live in varying circumstances. In a day secondary school for instance, children have to go back to their homes after classes everyday. Children of the affluent families are not bothered by household chores which the less fortunate ones have to contend with, and they may have all the time they need for their assignment. In addition, brighter students may need less time than the average or dull ones to complete their work. It should not be forgotten, too, that it is not only your assignment that your students have to do. They have other subjects and other teachers who may require them to perform important tasks.

7. Evaluate assignments promptly
Making students aware of the progress they are making is one way of motivating them do more work. Hence, every task given should be collected, assessed, and quickly returned for students' evaluation of their own work. Failure to evaluate and return assignments is a sure way of encouraging children to do careless work or even not to do work at all.

EXERCISES

1. What are the differences and similarities between drill and practice?
2. How does review differ from drill and practice?
3. How should questions be asked so that the teacher gets the response he wants?
4. Give four chief characteristics of a good question. Explain each briefly.
5. What do you think are some of the undesirable practices of teachers in asking questions? Explain why you consider them undesirable.
6. Why do students ask questions? How would you handle students' questions?

ESSENTIAL READING

Callahan, Sterling G. (1966) *Successful Teaching in Secondary Schools*, Scott, Foresman, Chicago.

Grambs, J. D., Carr, J. C., and Fitch, R. M. (1970) *Modern Methods in Secondary Education*, (3rd ed.), Holt, Rinehart & Winston, New York.

Oliver, R. A. (1960) *Effective Teaching*, J. M. Kent, Toronto.

Risk, Thomas M. (1958) *Principles and Practice of Teaching in Secondary Schools*, American Book Company, New York.

Shipley, Morton C. *et al.* (1964) *A Synthesis of Teaching Methods*, McGraw-Hill, New York.

SUPPLEMENTARY READING

Alcorn, Marvin D. *et al.* (1970) *Better Teaching in Secondary Schools*, Holt, Rinehart & Winston, New York.

Bossing, Nelson L. (1955) *Teaching in Secondary Schools*, Houghton Mifflin, Boston, Mass.

Burton, William H. (1962) *The Guidance of Learning Activities*, (3rd ed.), Appleton-Century-Crafts, New York.

Highet, G. (1963) *The Art of Teaching*, Methuen, London.

Pinsent, A. (1941) *The Principles of Teaching Methods*, Harrap, London.

Yoakam, Gerald A. and Simpson, Robert G. (1948) *Modern Methods and Techniques of Teaching*, Macmillan, New York.

7

Organising Instruction

INTRODUCTION

As in any human endeavour that aims for a successful outcome, planning in teaching is absolutely essential. At the beginning of the school year a teacher has to think ahead and map out what she plans to do with each of the classes she is going to teach. She has to consider the *objectives* she wants to achieve, based on the *syllabus* that she has to follow. She has to think about the facilities and materials available for teaching, the ability and background of her students and the design of her *scheme of work*. While deciding on her scheme she will have to work out her *unit plans* and subsequently her *lesson plans*.

In section one of this chapter the terms syllabus, scheme of work and objectives are clarified. In sections three, four and six the terms unit plan and lesson plan are discussed and examples of each are provided.

1. CLARIFICATION OF TERMS

The syllabus

In Nigeria a syllabus consists of a description of what subject matter or content is to be taught in each of the disciplines (Mathematics, Home Economics, History and so on). A syllabus lists only what is to be taught but not how it is to be taught. The syllabi for the higher classes of secondary schools are at present drawn up by the West African Examinations Council and are contained in a booklet regularly published. In some states the WAEC syllabuses are reproduced by the Ministries of Education and are sent to the various school principals. A new teacher arriving at a school should be able to obtain copies of the syllabi for the subjects he is going to teach from the principal or head of each subject department.

The subjects taught in the lower forms of secondary schools (forms 1 and 2) have syllabi usually prepared by the State Ministry of Education. For Grade II teacher training colleges the Federal Ministry of Education prepared syllabi in 1974 and these are currently being used by teachers in most subject areas. In addition, Institutes of Education of the different universities have in the past prepared syllabi for Grade II subjects taught in neighbouring states.

The scheme of work

A scheme of work is more detailed than a syllabus and not only does it contain what is to be taught but it also describes how the teaching should take place. It will advise on what text-books to use, what exercises are to be completed, what activities the students should engage in and the number and type of materials needed. A scheme of work is an essential part of any teacher's equipment. With one you may be very successful in teaching but without one you can certainly never be.

A scheme of work would be very difficult for a beginning teacher to design, as it needs years of experience in teaching to prepare one successfully. If the Ministry of Education does not provide a scheme of work for the teachers in the state then heads of departments should take on the responsibility of helping beginning teachers in their departments. If, as is sometimes the case, the beginning teacher does not have a department head nor a scheme of work from the Ministry to work with then he should consult the principal and senior members of the staff to get assistance in preparing a scheme.

In section two of this chapter you will find some advice on how to prepare a scheme of work that might be useful to you.

Aims, goals, purposes and objectives

There has been considerable confusion over the use of these

words as applied to education. In this book we consider the words aims, goals and purposes to mean the same thing. They refer to very general and long-term outcomes of the educational process as a whole. Objectives, on the other hand, are much more specific and narrow. Nations, states and schools draw up aims, purposes or goals. The individual teacher draws up objectives for his courses, unit plans and lessons. The educational goals as stated in the Federal Republic of Nigeria National Policy on Education (1977) are the building of:

1. A free and democratic society.
2. A just and egalitarian society.
3. A united, strong and self reliant nation.
4. A great and dynamic economy.
5. A land of bright and full opportunities for all its citizens.

As can be seen, these aims, goals, or purposes are very general in nature and they are not really a great help to the teacher in framing his courses. Nevertheless the teacher should be aware of the nation's overall goals in the educational process so that he can better appreciate how his efforts contribute to those goals. The average teacher has little or no involvement in the drawing up of the nation's or state's educational goals and, since these are usually studied in philosophy of education courses, we will not spend any more time on them here.

What does involve the teacher to a much greater extent are objectives for the courses, units and lessons that he is going to teach. In the following sections two, three and four of this chapter you will find examples of objectives written for year courses, units and lesson plans. One thing is common to all these objectives, namely that they are all written in terms of desirable outcomes of student behaviour.

2. PLANNING A SCHEME OF WORK FOR A COURSE

In planning a scheme of work the teacher will have to take into account the national and state educational goals, the special goals of the school, the school facilities, the syllabus, the age and ability of the students, the materials available for instruction, the size of the class and the time available for teaching. A scheme of work is never satisfactory the first time it is designed, so as a beginning teacher you can be expected to modify your scheme as the school year progresses. Even experienced teachers change their schemes of work to improve them and to take into account changing conditions.

Deciding on course objectives

In Nigeria teachers do not often follow a class as they progress from form 1 to form 5. Sometimes they are given a class to teach that they have not taught before and they may end up only teaching that class for the one year. If it is not a first year class, the teacher will have to find out what the class was taught the year before. In our experience it is useless and ill-advised to talk to the whole class to try to ascertain what they have covered. The teacher should try to get hold of the class records and talk to the former class teacher. The form monitor can also be asked to show his exercise books to give the teacher further information.

Once the teacher has ascertained the level of attainment of the students or the place they have reached, he can begin to plan his objectives for the year. His objectives will be linked to the content of what he decides to teach. Course objectives can be general but they should be attainable. They are best stated in terms of changed student attitudes, behaviours and skills. These are typical examples of course objectives:

By the end of the course the students should:

1. Be able to identify the following parts of speech:

The noun	The preposition
The pronoun	The conjunction
The adjective	The interjection
The verb	

2. Be able to write examples of sentences in which there is agreement between the subject and the verb, the pronoun and the antecedent.
3. Have read and developed an appreciation for the novel *Things Fall Apart*.

If the teacher decides to teach his course for the year in the form of units, his course objectives can be a broader summary of the objectives for all the units. In drawing up his objectives the teacher does not have to list every possible outcome of his teaching. The list of objectives should not be longer than the description of the content that the teacher plans to teach.

Sequencing topics

Since teachers are provided with a syllabus for the subject and form they are about to teach, the problem is not so much *what* to teach but *when* to teach it, and *how*. The sequence of topics and teaching strategy have to be decided on by the individual teacher.

The sequence of topics should be logical and generally the easier topics are best treated earlier. The students' knowledge should be built up systematically, so that when they have to tackle more complex ideas they already have a sufficient foundation. Thus students studying a language cannot be expected to write compositions in that language until they have sufficient grasp of the nouns, verbs, and adjectives, and adverbs as well as practice in sentence construction. Chemistry students cannot be expected to learn chemical formulae until they have studied atoms, molecules and forms of chemical bonding.

Many textbooks used in Nigerian post-primary institutions have been based on the WAEC or Grade II syllabus. These books also treat topics, for the most part, in a logical sequence. Beginning teachers who find it difficult to organise their teaching properly can follow the order of the textbook, providing their students with additional information when the textbook seems to be lacking.

How much time to spend on topics

In Nigeria the average school year consists of thirty-six weeks. Inevitably the first week of each term is spent organising the school and in settling down. The last week of each term is often lost with tidying up, packing and waiting for teachers to mark end-of-term exams. Other days are used up throughout the year in the form of national and local holidays, speech days and so on. The amount of teaching time left for the teacher is unlikely to be more than thirty weeks and it may be somewhat less. It is important to keep this in mind when trying to decide how much time to spend on each topic in your scheme of work.

Keep a certain amount of flexibility in your plan so that you are not rushing or moving too slowly in an attempt to finish a topic on a particular day. It sometimes helps students if they have an idea of approximately how many weeks they will be spending on a particular topic. Those who like to read on their own can then plan their study hours.

In planning your course you do not have to cover the entire syllabus. Some less important or marginal topics can be left out, if there is insufficient time. Rushing the teaching usually results in little or no learning. As Clark and Starr (1976) point out, 'It is better to teach more by attempting less than to attempt more and teach nothing.'

3. THE UNIT PLAN

What is a unit?

A unit is a planned sequence of learning activities or lessons covering a period of several weeks and centred around some major concept, theme or topic. It is a way of organising subject matter so as to make for more individualised instruction, student planning and student responsibility for their own learning. In a unit some of the activities are basic and are required of all the students but others are optional.

All lessons can be taught in units. In order to preserve the idea behind the unit method of teaching the teacher needs a generous supply of materials and planning time in order to ensure maximum participation by the students. A unit has four basic phases:

1. The introductory phase
2. The laboratory phase
3. The sharing of experience phase
4. The evaluating phase

How to plan a unit

The manner in which a unit is planned and carried out is best illustrated by an example. Let us take as a Social Studies topic, 'Neighbouring African Countries', which could follow on from a study of Nigeria itself. The countries that can be included in the topic are all those that share their borders with Nigeria and some others that are geographically close. The selection of a topic is the *first step* in planning. It is important that the topic is interesting for the students and one about which they can be at least a little enthusiastic.

The *second step* in planning is for the teacher to choose the objectives that he hopes to achieve in the unit. (Some educationists maintain that choosing the objectives should be the first step in planning but in practice it is easier for the teacher to choose a topic first followed by the objectives.) The objectives will include skills, understanding, attitudes and appreciation to be acquired by the students. Objectives can be clarified by first drawing up a rationale or set of reasons why the teacher feels that a study of the unit would be valuable to the students.

A study of the unit 'Neighbouring African Countries' should improve the students' knowledge of the countries studied and enable them to view these in relation to Nigeria. The life-style, standard of living, religious affiliation and economic development of the countries can be compared and ways of improving co-operation between these nations can be suggested. The teacher could draw up objectives like these:

By the end of the unit the students:

1. Will know at least five features of Nigeria's neighbouring countries.
2. Will be able to apply knowledge and understanding by making three suggestions to improve co-operation between the countries.
3. Will be able to analyse and hence correctly evaluate their standard of living by comparing the countries studied.
4. Will have developed additional skills in carrying out research and should be able to apply these skills in studying other countries.

Notice that these objectives are stated in terms of intended student behaviour. They are called *behavioural objectives* and the next chapter will treat these in more detail.

The *third step* in planning a unit is the selection and organisation of the activities and materials needed for the laboratory phase. For this chosen topic the teacher will need Social Studies and Geography books that describe West Africa. In addition magazines like *Time, Newsweek, Africa, Drum* and *Trust* and newspapers will provide the students with useful articles and photographs. The students will be divided into groups and each group will study one country. They could be required to provide and display the following information:

(a) A map of the country showing the major cities or towns.
(b) The name of the Head of State (with a photograph if possible).
(c) A coloured drawing of the flag of the country.
(d) Information on – population, main tribes and languages, type of government, practised religions, crops grown, climate, main exports, industries, per capita income, number of universities, design of traditional dress, name of colonising power, date of independence, special features of ports, forms of transportation and so on, trade relationship and forms of co-operation with Nigeria.

The teacher can prepare a study and activity guide for each of the lessons in the unit in which he suggests what to read, where to find materials and when to perform certain tasks. The teacher should also plan to encourage students to provide additional ideas for activities during the introductory and laboratory phases of the unit.

The teacher will have to plan how the students will share their experiences with each other. In the topic chosen each group could make a display illustrating their main findings on the country they have studied. Each group could give a short talk to familiarise the rest of the class with what they have discovered. A final display of all the materials can be held in the classroom and even students from other classes can be invited to see them.

Finally, in the *fourth step* the teacher should plan how to evaluate the children's learning, interest and skill development at the end of the unit. The tests the teacher constructs will incorporate the objectives stated at the beginning of the unit.

4. LESSON PLANNING

This element of planning is probably the most important of them all, and unfortunately it is often neglected, even by young and inexperienced teachers. If a teacher does not know *what* or *how* she is going to teach on entering the classroom she is really asking for a miracle if she expects anything valuable to come of the lesson. Making lesson plans is time-consuming and it does mean that at the end of each day the beginning teacher must expect to spend an hour or more planning her lessons for the days ahead. Even though it requires an effort to make such lesson plans the teacher who does so will find it well worth while. Students are very perceptive and soon discover those teachers who prepare their lessons and those who do not.

The lesson plan format

There are many types and formats of lesson plans. In chapter five there is an example of a *detailed* lesson plan which spells out everything that the teacher plans to say and do, and the expected responses and actions of the students. Detailed lesson plans are necessary for the beginning teacher but as she gains in experience such plans can become briefer. Whatever format a lesson plan takes it should adequately describe the following:

The objectives
The topic or subject matter
The lesson materials
The lesson procedure
  Introduction
  Development of the lesson
  Generalisation
  Application
  Conclusion
Student Evaluation
Student assignment

Preparing the lesson plan

In the lesson plan the objectives are simply and briefly listed. In the next chapter advice is given on how to formulate objectives. We give here a few hints on how to select your objectives.

(i) Selecting the objectives

When preparing a lesson the first thing to do is to decide what things you want the students to learn from it. These are called the lesson objectives. In selecting objectives the teacher should keep certain criteria in mind.

Objectives may be percepts, concepts, generalisations, skills, attitudes or generalisations. Objectives should be very specific so that the teacher can directly aim at their attainment in the students. Lesson objectives should as often as possible be stated in terms of desirable changes in student behaviour. Objectives should be feasible. They should be attainable by all of the students within the lesson. Objectives should be relevant, worthwhile and useful. If students ask 'Why do we have to learn this?', the teacher should have a ready answer demonstrating the worth of what is being studied.

(ii) Selecting the topic or subject matter

The subject matter you choose is directly related to the objectives you have decided upon. If you have made a carefully planned scheme of work the selection of subject matter will be much easier. Inexperienced teachers will find it difficult to know how much to attempt in a lesson of forty minutes. Some will attempt to teach too much and end up by rushing while others will finish their teaching fifteen or twenty minutes before the end of the lesson and are at a loss as to how to fill up the remaining time. With a few months of practice you should be able to judge how far you will be able to go in a lesson with the class in question. If you finish ahead of time you can review, give the students more skill practice or even give an introduction to the topic of the next lesson to follow the one you have just taught.

(iii) Selecting lesson activities

The activities you decide on for a lesson will depend on the objectives and subject matter you have chosen. The activities should be directly aimed at achieving the objectives or else left out. Undirected activity will lead to chaos and little or no learning. Some initial activities to arouse the students' interest can be included even if these are not directly aimed at achieving the objectives. All lesson activities should be suited to the students' abilities and allowances should be made for individual differences. Sufficient time and materials should be available for the activities to be successfully completed.

If the students have several things to do in sequence, the time that will be taken on each should be estimated in minutes.

(iv) Selecting lesson materials

In the lesson plan the materials to be used and their number can be indicated in the form of a list. Here are some hints on selecting some appropriate materials.

When selecting objectives and a topic for the lesson, the teacher has to bear in mind what materials are available to him. If he has recently arrived at a school, one of the first things he should do is to survey the materials that can be made available to him in his area of specialisation. It is pointless planning a lesson involving the use of the microscope if you have not first checked the laboratory to see if the school possesses any microscopes. In a recent survey carried out by ABU science education students it was revealed that some post-primary schools had laboratories with little or no equipment, while a few schools had equipment but no laboratories. Never take things for granted when it comes to lesson materials. Check first to see that what you want is available and in sufficient quantity.

(v) Selecting the procedure

Chapters four and five will help you familiarise yourself with the various methods that can be used in teaching. Here we are concerned with how you summarise your planned method in a written lesson plan. You need only to write brief notes on how you plan introducing and developing the lesson, generalising, applying the concept or principle that has been learned, and concluding.

In the introduction of the lesson plan there should be a few words describing how the teacher plans to introduce the lesson and arouse the students' interest in the lesson. It should be remembered that the average schoolteacher in Nigeria has four or five lessons every day. It is very difficult for the teacher to remember how he planned to introduce each lesson if nothing is written down on paper.

In the plan there should be a line or two describing how the teacher plans each step in the development of the lesson. In the generalisation part of the plan the teacher should write down the generalisation, concept or principle that he plans to teach and briefly state how he hopes to get the students to arrive at the concept or principle. In the application stage he should describe how students will apply the concept or principle learned. A few words should also be made in the plan to describe how the teacher will sum up the main points of the lesson.

(vi) Evaluation

In many cases evaluation is something that is continually going on during the lesson. It is also good to have some exercise in evaluation towards the end of the lesson. In the evaluation stage of the lesson plan the teacher can briefly list the things he plans to do, the questions he is going to ask or the problems he is going to pose to test the students' knowledge.

(vii) Assignment

In some subjects like Mathematics and English many teachers give assignments every day because stress is laid on these two subjects. Even if you are not teaching either of these subjects it is good to give assignments regularly. In the lesson plan you should briefly describe the assignment by indicating the page number of the book where it can be found and the title of the essay or map that you want the students to complete.

5. WHEN TO ABANDON YOUR LESSON PLAN

Generally speaking a teacher should stick to his lesson plan but occasions do arise when he can legitimately abandon what he planned to teach. If he is teaching a group for the first time, or if he has not taught them for very long, he may find that they have insufficient background to follow what he had planned. This will be manifested by blank looks on the students' faces and a certain restlessness and fidgeting in the class. His class seems to be lost! Obviously the teacher has taken for granted some key piece of knowledge which his students do not have. In such a situation the teacher should forget his lesson plan for the moment and go back to fill in whatever is missing in his students' knowledge.

Another occasion when a teacher can leave aside his lesson plan, at least temporarily, is when a very important local or national event is obviously preoccupying the minds of his students. When this occurs the teacher can talk about or discuss the event with them for some time until they have settled their minds. He can then gently lead them back to the topic of the lesson he planned to teach.

Students' questions can give rise to situations that seem to indicate to the teacher that a change of approach or a digression is needed. In circumstances like these the teacher can sometimes follow his instincts and modify his approach or provide a digression. A bored class can be livened up by means of an unplanned story or joke, after which the teacher can go back to his planned lesson and continue where he left off.

If a planned lesson is obviously not working, either because the students are tired, as they usually are towards the end of the day, or because the teacher is himself too tired, then a change of plan is indicated. In some parts of Nigeria at around 1 p.m. to 2 p.m. it can become very hot and humid, and students' minds do not seem to function so well in such heat as they do in the cool of the early morning. If you or your students do not seem to be able to concentrate under such conditions it is probably better to give them some writing or reading to do. Practical classes in laboratories or Home Economics can be conducted late in the school day but classes like Mathematics should always be scheduled in the early morning.

6. AN EXAMPLE OF A LESSON PLAN

General information
FORM LEVEL: 2
SUBJECT: Integrated Science
CLASS SIZE: 36 students

Objectives
By the end of the lesson the students should:

1. Know that magnets are made of iron and that other materials do not possess noticeable magnetic properties.
2. Know that the north pole of a magnet seeks the magnetic north and that the south pole seeks magnetic south.
3. Know that similar poles of magnets *repel* each other while dissimilar poles *attract* each other.
4. Be able to apply their knowledge to determine which is the north and which the south pole of an unmarked magnet.
5. Be able to apply their knowledge to determine whether an object is magnetic.

Materials
Blackboard and coloured chalk, 18 sets of magnets (2), a compass, a candle, biro, cotton, a stick of wood. Some pieces of aluminium, cutlery, nails and some unmarked magnets.

Procedure
Introduction. The teacher introduces materials and asks students if they know what they are and what they are used for. Explains use of *magnets* to determine direction, in radios, television, stereos, amplifiers and loudspeakers (4 minutes).

Development of lesson. 1. The teacher distributes materials and asks the following questions while directing the students towards the correct responses.

(a) How many magnets do you have?
(b) Which materials are magnets and which are not?

2. The teacher asks students to suspend magnets from the centre using cotton, and asks the following questions:

(a) What do you notice about the direction the magnet finally faces? How does this compare with the needle of the compass?
(b) What shall we call the end of the magnet facing geographic north and that facing south?

He guides the students towards the correct responses (5 minutes).

Generalisation. The teacher instructs the students to place the north poles of the two magnets so that they face each other, and to note what happens. He then tells them to repeat the experiment using the south poles. He then asks them what happened. He guides the students towards the generalisation that similar poles repel each other while dissimilar poles attract (4 minutes).

Application. The teacher passes around pieces of aluminium cutlery, some unmarked magnets and some nails to each group and asks the questions:

(a) Which materials are magnetic?
(b) Is the nail a strong magnet – could it be made into a stronger magnet?
(c) What are the magnet and the nail made of?
(d) Which end of the magnet [unmarked] is a north pole and which a south?
(5 minutes)

Conclusion. The teacher summarises the main generalisations of the lesson on the blackboard which the students copy in their exercise books (4 minutes).

Evaluation

Part of the informal evaluation of the students' learning will have been carried out during the lesson itself. As an overall evaluation the teacher can ask students to write down answers to four or five questions on a piece of paper at the end of the lesson, or at the beginning of the next lesson.

Assignment
The students can be asked to review the main points of the lesson for a short test on the following day (if the test is not given at the end of the lesson) or to read on for the next few pages in the Integrated Science textbook.

EXERCISES

1. How can one distinguish between an objective and a goal, aim or purpose?
2. Describe the four steps in the planning of a unit.
3. Describe the seven aspects that need to be considered in drawing up a lesson plan.
4. List the essential elements that any lesson plan should adequately describe.

ESSENTIAL READING

Callahan, J. F. and Clark, L. H. (1977) *Teaching in the Secondary School*, Macmillan, New York.

SUPPLEMENTARY READING

Clark, L. H. and Starr, I. S., (1976) *Secondary School Teaching Methods*, Macmillan, New York.
Davies, I. K. (1976) *Objectives in Curriculum Design*, McGraw-Hill, Maidenhead.

8

Formulating Behavioural Objectives

INTRODUCTION

For a curriculum or course it is usual to draw up aims and goals which it is hoped the students will achieve by the end of the period of instruction. In any unit or lesson a teacher must have an even clearer and more precise idea of what he plans to achieve through instruction in terms of changed student behaviour. In other words, it is necessary for the teacher to clarify his unit or lesson objectives and he can best do this by writing them down.

In the past, teachers have tended to state their objectives in terms of their own activities. For example:

1. The teacher will explain what was meant by indirect rule in Nigeria under the colonial administration.
2. The teacher will demonstrate combustion to the class.
3. The teacher will clearly illustrate examples of pronouns to the class.
4. The teacher will draw a diagram of a cockroach and point out its main features.

What is lacking in all of these statements is any direct mention of the students. What are they doing while the teacher is explaining, demonstrating or drawing? The implication is that they are somewhat passively listening, watching or drawing. Objectives stated in such a way that there is no mention of the ultimate behaviour expected of the students (or if it is mentioned there is no statement on how it will be measured) are called *non-behavioural objectives*.

WHAT ARE BEHAVIOURAL OBJECTIVES?

Modern thinking favours stating objectives in terms of *measurable student terminal behaviour.* In other words the teacher should plan and state in his objectives what specific measurable student learning or changes in student behaviour will take place as a result of instruction. Objectives stated in this fashion are called behavioural objectives.

Behavioural objectives are very specific. Aims or goals for courses which last for some length of time are usually general, and general aims can be broken down into more specific behavioural objectives covering the units or lessons of the course. General aims are expressed in such terms as, 'the students will understand, appreciate, enjoy, know', which in themselves are not directly measurable. We cannot measure what a student knows or understands unless we ask him to write down, recall or apply what he has learned. An example of a general aim or goal is: 'The students will be able to understand the difference between common and proper nouns, adjectives and adverbs, by the end of the term.'

Behavioural objectives make use of verbs like recite, identify, pick out, apply, add and subtract, write down, deduce and so on. An example of a behavioural objective is: 'By the end of the lesson the students will be able to correctly pick out and write down lists of the common and proper nouns, adverbs and adjectives, from an appropriate passage.'

In the behavioural objective the students' performance is immediately measurable in that he has a definite task to achieve, in this case: picking out and writing down lists.

Here are some examples of aims and behavioural objectives. Try to identify those which are aims and those which are behavioural objectives.

1. The students will be able to correctly write down the formulae of the ten chemical compounds mentioned in the chapter they are studying.
2. The students will learn to appreciate poetry.
3. The students will learn the main physical and chemical properties of metals.
4. The students will be able to express correctly, twenty numbers of 4 or more digits to 3 significant figures.

5. The students will be able to correctly identify the main parts of a flower, using a specimen from the school garden.
6. The students will develop an understanding of the concept of speed.
7. The students will be able to identify and tell the teacher the nouns, verbs, adjectives and adverbs in a given passage in the English language.

HOW TO STATE BEHAVIOURAL OBJECTIVES

The essential difference between behavioural and non-behavioural objectives is the statement in a behavioural objective of the terminal behaviour expected of the student at the end of the lesson or unit, and an explanation of how this will be measured. Here are two examples which should help pin-point the difference between a behavioural and non-behavioural objective.

A behavioural objective: By the end of the lesson the students will be able to correctly calculate the areas of circles, using the circle radii and π, in nine out of ten cases.

A non-behavioural objective: The students will learn how to calculate the areas of circles.

There are some educationists who maintain that apart from stating the terminal behaviour expected of the student and how this will be measured, two other additional criteria should also be mentioned.

According to Mager (1975) there are four essential parts to any behavioural objective. Each should state:

(i) Who will perform the behaviour (in most cases this is the student).
(ii) The measurable student terminal behaviour; some observable and therefore measurable behaviour that the students will be able to perform at the end of the period of instruction.
(iii) The standard of performance expected of the students.
(iv) The conditions under which learning will take place.

Behavioural objectives are best stated in a form which

covers all these four criteria. In the case of the behavioural objective given in the example above, (i) is the students themselves, (ii) is the students being able to calculate the areas of circles, (iii) is their being able to calculate correctly in nine out of ten cases, (iv) are the time limit (by the end of the lesson) and the use of the radii and π.

Here are two additional examples of behavioural objectives containing the four essential parts:

> By the end of the laboratory exercise the students will be able to correctly measure the focal length of any of the given concave mirrors with 1 cm accuracy.

> At the end of the lesson the students will be able to name the State capitals and main sources of revenue of each of the nineteen states in Nigeria with not more than two mistakes.

Although it has been said that behavioural objectives are the most useful and possibly desirable form of objectives, nevertheless they are difficult and time-consuming to construct and there are educationists who do not consider them always suitable. For a teacher who has four or five lessons every day it might not be possible to formulate behavioural objectives for every lesson.

In spite of the disadvantages of behavioural objectives using them would seem to be an improvement on past practice, and until some better form of planning presents itself, teachers are recommended to use them when possible.

Advantages of behavioural objectives

1. They can serve as guides for teachers and curriculum developers who are involved in designing courses.
2. They can force teachers to come down to earth and be realistic, making them plan in specific terms objectives that are attainable by most of the students.
3. When objectives are stated in a behavioural form it makes it easier to judge the success or failure of a lesson.
4. When lessons have been conducted using behavioural objectives it is easy to set tests and examinations, questions being set that are based on the objectives.

Disadvantages of behavioural objectives

1. Some educators doubt that all that is contained in a learning experience can be expressed in the form of behavioural objectives. What about unintended but desirable effects?
2. Innovations and creativity in teaching might be hampered and restricted by too early a demand for isolating and identifying objectives. Behavioural objectives might make a teacher too rigid in sticking to his lesson plan when unplanned spontaneous activities or experiences would, if followed, result in useful incidental learning

COGNITIVE, AFFECTIVE AND PSYCHOMOTOR DOMAINS

Behavioural objectives can be classified according to Bloom (1956) as belonging to the cognitive, affective and psychomotor domains. In this book we will only attempt a brief explanation of what is meant by these terms, as they are normally treated in more depth in the later years of most education degree courses and this book is primarily directed to first year degree and ATC students.

The *cognitive* domain deals exclusively with the mind and mental activities or skills. At the lower level of the domain are the knowing and understanding skills of *knowledge* and *comprehension*. Knowledge of facts does not mean that those facts are understood. Hence the simplest cognitive skill is knowledge, and comprehension is above it. As a person increases in understanding he becomes able to apply and analyse the knowledge acquired using the cognitive skills of *application* and *analysis*. At the highest level of the domain are the skills of *synthesis* and *evaluation*. As each succeeding mental skill level is attained, with reference to specific concepts or generalisations, it is implied that all the preceeding levels are contained in the higher level. Thus if someone is able to apply what he has learned he must have had the requisite knowledge and comprehension. If he is able to evaluate the knowledge he has acquired then he can see its value with reference to other facts, concepts or generalisations apart from knowing, comprehending, and being able to apply, analyse and synthesise that knowledge.

It is fairly true to say that in the past teachers concentrated on imparting facts or knowledge to the students, developing some level of understanding but little ability to analyse, synthesise and evaluate the knowledge so acquired. Little emphasis was placed in examinations on testing the higher cognitive levels, more was placed on the recall of facts and their simple application. This situation is now recognised by the universities and bodies like the WAEC, and efforts are being made to correct the balance. Classroom teachers should now make efforts to set more objectives for the higher levels of the cognitive domain and plan their end of term and year examinations to test these cognitive skills.

The *affective* domain, according to Bloom, concerns the emotional aspect of a persons make-up. This influences his attitudes, interests, appreciation and values. The *psychomotor* domain deals with reflex, visual, tactile, and auditory skills in discriminating, and physical abilities.

It is now recognised that there is a need to set objectives with reference to the affective and psychomotor domains. The development of proper attitudes, interests and values in students is extremely important as is the development of physical skills. As the Federal Republic of Nigeria National Policy on Education (1977) states:

> The national educational aims and objectives to which the philosophy is linked are therefore:
> 1. The inculcation of national consciousness and national unity.
> 2. The inculcation of the right type of values and attitudes for the survival of the individual and the Nigerian society.
> 3. The training of the mind in the understanding of the world around.
> 4. The acquisition of appropriate skills, abilities and competencies both mental and physical as equipment for the individual to live in and contribute to the development of his society.

To help the reader understand better how to set objectives in each of the three domains here are some examples.

Two examples of cognitive domain objectives

By the end of the unit on the calculation of areas of different shapes the students will successfully apply their knowledge to the calculation of the areas of a football field, running track and floor plan of a house, given relevant dimensions.

By the end of the unit on the study of nutrition the students will be able to design four balanced diets from a list of appropriate foodstuffs.

Two examples of affective domain objectives

By the end of the unit the students will be able to select from a series of twenty sentences the five which most represent expressions of good citizenship.

From a description of five persons' living habits the students will be able to recognise the two with the most acceptable and the two with the least acceptable types of behaviour according to established values of the society.

Examples of psychomotor domain objectives

By the end of the laboratory unit the students should be able to:
(a) operate a bunsen burner
(b) boil water in a test tube
(c) pour liquids from acid and base bottles into test tubes
(d) place solids in test tubes using a spatula
without any mishap or accident.

By the end of the unit the business education students will be able to phrase and correctly type a well-constructed letter to the local bank manager asking for a loan to set up a small business.

CONCLUSION

In this chapter you have been introduced to behavioural objectives. The chapter is brief and should be regarded only as an introduction. Behavioural objectives definitely should have a place in the planning strategy of the teacher. Ideally they are best employed the majority of the time but because of preparation time constraints on classroom teachers it may not be possible for them to be used always. When they are used they are likely to make your teaching more effective.

EXERCISES

1. What is the difference between an aim or goal and a behavioural objective?
2. Construct 3 behavioural objectives, containing the four essential elements described by Mager, and discuss them in the class with your colleagues and lecturer.
3. Discuss the advantages and disadvantages of behavioural objectives.

ESSENTIAL READING

Bloom, B. S. (ed.) (1956) *Taxonomy of Educational Objectives: The Classification of Educational Goals. Handbook 1: Cognitive Domain*, McKay, New York.

Federal Ministry of Information (1977) *Federal Republic of Nigeria National Policy on Education*, Information Printing Division, Lagos.

Mager, R. F. (1975) *Preparing Instructional Objectives*, (2nd ed.), Fearon, San Francisco, Calif.

9

Classroom Management and Discipline

MANAGEMENT

The meaning and importance of classroom management

Classroom management involves the organisation of certain non-academic tasks which are essential for effective teaching. It consists of checking class attendance, keeping a record of class progress, controlling students' conduct and activities, manipulating instructional materials, the improvement of classroom working conditions and the elimination of any distractions which may arise. A teacher who has good classroom management skills will find it easier to establish and maintain class discipline.

Class attendance and student records

In Nigerian secondary schools it is the function of the form master to check the attendance register before the first lesson of the day. Teachers who are not form-masters should also keep some form of attendance record for their lessons as some students can cut classes and return to the hostel during the day. An efficient and time-saving method of checking attendance is for students to keep the same seating positions in the class for each lesson. The teacher will then find it easy to mark down the students who are absent, and this is usually quicker than marking down those who are present.

In boarding schools it is relatively simple to find out from the form-master the reason why a student is absent. In day schools students who have been absent should be required to bring a letter from their parents or relatives which specifies the reason for this absence. Such letters can be filed in the school office for future reference.

Students who are frequent latecomers should be cautioned by teachers and if the behaviour continues be reported to the form-master or vice-principal.

Two other important aspects of classroom management for the beginning teacher are: (i) keeping the students' record of work book up to date, and (ii) recording student assignment and test marks. Each class has a record book, usually kept in the staff room, in which each teacher writes down what he has taught, the students' activities and assignments, at the end of each week. It is important to keep this record up to date in case a change of teachers takes place in the middle of the school term or year, or a teacher becomes sick for a prolonged period. With such a record on hand the substitute teacher will know what has been covered and where to begin.

The consistent recording of student marks for class tests and assignments is a task that the beginning teacher has to learn. At the beginning of the school year, as soon as he knows the classes he has been given to teach, he should take the time to write down all the students' names, class by class in a mark book. As marks are entered it will soon become apparent which students are and are not applying themselves, and the teacher can take appropriate action.

Handling instructional materials

All teachers are regularly involved in distributing and collecting exercise books or test papers in the classroom, and unless a system is developed for these operations a lot of time can be wasted. The collection of exercise books should be brisk and efficient, the teacher noting mentally or in writing those who do *not* submit their work and their reasons for so doing. As a teacher returns corrected work he can draw the attention of the class to the most common mistakes they have made. It is not advisable at such times to pick out individuals who have done badly and ridicule them in front of the rest of the class. Occasionally the class monitor can be asked to assist the teacher in collecting or returning written work, but as a general rule it is better for the teacher to do this job himself.

As part of their teaching strategy many teachers find it

necessary to provide supplementary materials or notes for the students in addition to the information in the textbook. When notes or diagrams are written or drawn on the board *during* the lesson, a lot of teaching time is wasted. If the school administration will allow it, notes and diagrams should be duplicated on a machine and each student given a copy. Alternatively, in boarding schools, the teacher can instruct a student to write the notes neatly on the blackboard before the evening prep period so that the others can copy.

Another important aspect of classroom management to which the teacher should give his attention is the physical condition of the students' text and exercise books. If these are incomplete or falling apart the students will not be encouraged to perform well. Usually a textbook lasts up to three years after which it needs to be replaced. It is up to the subject teacher to inform the school administration if new books are needed. It is also his responsibility to make sure that the students have an adequate supply of pencils, pens and drawing materials. When exercise books have been filled up by the students, they are usually eligible for a new one from the school store. In many schools it is the class teacher's job to sign the old exercise book as proof that the student needs a new one. A beginning teacher should try to find out about the school customs with regard to all aspects affecting teaching as soon as possible after arriving at a school.

In most classrooms there are bulletin boards and lots of empty wall space for charts, diagrams, notes and other forms of visual materials. A teacher should endeavour to make use of such facilities as frequently as possible, otherwise he will be neglecting an important dimension in the management of learning.

Handling classroom activities

It is very important to get a lesson started quickly. In Nigeria the system requires the teacher to move from one class to another while the students normally remain where they are, and hence the teacher has to move quickly at the end of a lesson to be in time for the next. On entering a class he should ensure that the students pack away in their desks all the books from the former class and take out only those they will need for the present one. He should then get the class settled down quickly and begin the lesson without wasting time. If the blackboard often needs cleaning when the new teacher enters the class he should appoint someone to be responsible for it so that it is ready for use on arrival. Chalk is normally kept by the monitor in each class and so does not present a problem.

Once a lesson is in progress a teacher should encourage students both to ask and to answer questions. In order to avoid more than one student talking at one time he will have to operate a system such as the raising of hands by those who want to speak. The same system can be used in lessons when students are writing or working problems. Those who are having difficulties can raise their hands to attract the teacher's attention as he moves round the class to help them.

Teachers who have specialist rooms like science laboratories and Social Studies workships, where they can conduct many if not all of their lessons, have a distinct advantage over teachers always on the move from one classroom to another. Teachers working in specialist rooms are there before the students. They can arrange relevant materials for the lesson ahead of time. Diagrams and wall charts can be posted on bulletin boards or the walls of the room without inconveniencing other teachers. The teacher can decide on the seating arrangement for the students, putting the troublesome ones where he wants them within easy reach. He can also make the room pleasant and attractive to work in by arranging the furniture and equipment the way he wants.

Regulating physical conditions

The average teacher is not able to control the temperature or lighting conditions of the rooms he teaches in since school buildings are in most cases constructed according to specifications supplied by the Ministry of Education. If desks, chairs, globes, fans, lights or windows are broken or missing, however, the teacher should report the matter to the form master or to the school administration. Classrooms are usually cleaned by students before teaching starts in the morning and it is important that this is done thoroughly and in time. Students working in a clean and tidy environment tend to be neat and organised in their written work. The form-master has a special responsibility for his own classroom and it is his responsibility to make the room as attractive and conducive to working in as conditions will permit. He should ensure that the room is tidy, that there is always chalk, that the board erasers are functioning and that the bulletin boards are used in the proper fashion.

DISCIPLINE

What is discipline?

Discipline, like education, is very difficult to define. We know an educated man when we meet one but to say exactly what it is that makes him educated is difficult. In a similar way we recognise a man as disciplined but again to define what makes him the way he is is not easy.

One thing a teacher believes he can recognise, either in his own class or in that of another teacher, is discipline or its absence. Unfortunately many teachers have a false idea of what discipline really means. If a class is making any kind of noise they believe the class is being unruly and that the teacher involved therefore has no discipline. In truth this may not be the case at all. Silence, as we will later explain, does not necessarily mean the presence of discipline. Students who are terrorised by their teacher by the fear of a severe beating are not learning discipline, rather they are learning survival.

The word discipline is apparently derived from the word disciple, meaning a follower or student of an accepted leader. In early civilisation discipline implied teaching or helping people to grow or achieve. Later it became associated with blind conformity (Hoover, 1968). One thing is certain, discipline has many shades of meaning. To the army sergeant it means one thing while to a pastor it means quite another.

To the teacher the aim of good discipline should be to help the individual adjust to the personal and social forces of his experiences. The student has to adjust to the existing culture and institutions within which he participates. A reasonable degree of co-operation, conformity and consistency of behaviour on his part is expected. Discipline seeks to educate towards self discipline, that indispensable foundation of character. At the very core of education is the triangle of discipline from without, self discipline and the sustaining force of courage from within.

The problem of discipline today consists mainly of helping the young people develop disciplined and acceptable inner controls.

Why is discipline necessary?

It is generally recognised that doing what one dislikes is a necessity in life and hence it should also follow that discipline of various sorts is an inherent part of succeeding in anything. In history great men were all disciplined, struggling against apparently insuperable odds until they overcame them. Discipline teaches the following:

1. Respect for authority

In any democracy laws must be obeyed by the vast majority of the people or the result is chaos and anarchy. In a successful business the president or chairman has to be able to issue directives that will be followed by the employees. If the clerks and typists have no respect for authority and only do those things that they feel like doing there will be no progress, and the business will collapse. Teachers have to respect and obey their principals, and principals for their part have to follow orders issued by the Ministry of Education. Ministry officials in their turn are subject to the Federal Government. In all walks of life people have to respect authority. Even presidents are not wholly autonomous. They too have to listen to their advisers before coming to important decisions.

2. Co-operative effort

In any community venture that aims to achieve anything worthwhile, whether in digging irrigation ditches or in collective farming, close co-operation among those involved is of utmost necessity if time, energy and money are to be used effectively and efficiently. One of the teacher's basic aims should be to instil a spirit of co-operation in his students. If they can be taught to co-operate not only with the teacher but also with each other, learning will proceed at a much faster pace. By putting the needs of the group before their own they will be practising self discipline.

3. The need for organisation

Planning is an essential prerequisite for any programme of activities, and this implies organisation and order. University or college students have to organise their reading habits in order to complete their assignments on time as well as to revise for examinations. They cannot afford to read at random.

Organisation is a form of discipline, and secondary school students need to see its value. This they can do by observing the way in which their teacher organises the sequence of learning experiences and activities in their class.

4. Respect for others

Every individual has to realise that other people have as much right to happiness and fulfilment as they do. Stealing from, fighting or obstructing others while they pursue their rightful goals is in direct contradiction of the spirit of the Nigerian Philosophy of Education which advocates 'respect for the worth and dignity of the individual' (National Policy of Education, 1977).

The teacher in his handling of discussions and other class activities can foster mutual respect among his students.

5. The need to do the unpleasant

In every profession and walk of life there are times when day to day work becomes a routine. There are also occasions when you are asked to do disagreeable things as part of your job which, if you had the choice, would be avoided. When you pursue any goal or objective these periods of unpleasantness always seem to occur and cannot be avoided. The undisciplined person gives up in the face of difficulties of this kind. It is very important for students in school to learn that they cannot only do what pleases them at a particular time. Doing the unpleasant and sticking to a plan when things become boring or disagreeable are essential factors in any project that is to achieve success.

6. Examples of indisciplined behaviour

In order to understand better why discipline is necessary, let us consider some examples of indiscipline in students that the Nigerian teacher is likely to encounter in the school classroom.

1. Insolence
2. Continued disturbance in class
3. Failure to complete assignments satisfactorily
4. General apathy
5. Fighting with other students
6. Cheating in examinations
7. Damage to school books and property

In boarding schools other additional types of indisciplined behaviour may also occur outside the classroom. For example:

1. Neglect of school duties
2. Failure to obey school prefects and duty teachers
3. Leave the school premises without permission
4. Untidy habits in dress
5. Misbehaviour in the dining hall
6. Stealing the belongings of others

Clearly, the types of behaviour listed above cannot be allowed to go unchecked or the school will become a battlefield rather than an institution of learning. In the next section we will try to understand what causes some of these disciplinary problems.

What causes indiscipline?

The causes of indiscipline in secondary school students can be conveniently grouped under four main headings.

(i) Teacher-caused misbehaviour

Student misbehaviour in the classroom can on occasions be caused by the teacher himself. If the teacher does not properly plan his lessons with clear objectives and adequately motivate his students they may become bored and listless, showing little or no enthusiasm for what is being taught. A teacher should endeavour to show his students why a particular topic is being taught and how it will be useful to them. His treatment of topics should be interesting and lively, with plenty of opportunities for the students to be actively involved in the learning process. A lack of variety in teaching methods can result in the lessons becoming a monotonous grind and under such circumstances misbehaviour is likely to occur.

In addition to paying attention to the way he teaches, the teacher should ensure that he comes to class on time, dresses smartly and treats his students with firmness but respect. Rude, arrogant, unsympathetic and sarcastic teachers are most likely to have discipline problems. They should avoid having favourites and be consistent in the sorts of behaviour they expect from the students. Invariably, if students feel that teachers do not like them, they for their part do not like the teachers.

(ii) School-caused misbehaviour

Sometimes the misbehaviour of students can be attributed to the school itself. One of the most common reasons students in boarding schools give for rebelling is the food. Either there is not enough or the quality is poor, or both. With the ever rising cost in the price of food, and given that Ministries of Education are themselves on a tight budget, principals of schools sometimes find it extremely difficult to make the money allocated for food last until the end of the school year. Principals have been known to use the money allocated for other things to pay the food bill, in order to avoid a student disturbance. Even if students do not actively rebel or complain about food, if they are not given enough to eat it can make them apathetic and unco-operative in class.

Other school-based causes of misbehaviour may be a result of overcrowding in the hostels and classrooms as well as a shortage of teachers. With the ever increasing demand for secondary education, schools are sometimes required to take in more students than they really have room for. This in itself can lead to student unrest and if in addition classrooms are sometimes left unsupervised because of the shortage of teachers, then discipline problems result.

(iii) Student-caused misbehaviour

Misbehaviour among students, apart from being caused by those things already mentioned, can also result from their own rather confused mental and emotional state, and from an excess of physical energy.

Students in the lower classes of secondary boarding schools

can suffer emotional upset if they are away from their parents and relatives for the first time, causing them to become withdrawn and unco-operative. Young students also find sitting in a classroom for long hours every day an extremely difficult task since they are naturally energetic and playful. They usually run anywhere and everywhere once they get out of class; this is not because they want to break school rules deliberately, but because they feel the physical need to burn up some energy.

Adolescents suffer from emotional problems of a different sort. Major physical and emotional changes are taking place in their bodies, giving them the physique of adults while their minds are still childlike. They can be expected to behave in an erratic fashion, moody one minute and exuberant the next. Unless the teacher is aware of the inner confusion these students feel he may misinterpret their actions and take offence when none was meant.

Students generally need to be accepted by their peer group as well as by their teacher. They are very competitive and will sometimes study very hard to obtain recognition. If they cannot succeed academically, they may try to be outstanding in sports or in other ways. Some students who do not seem to be very good at anything may misbehave in order to gain attention.

(iv) Misbehaviour due to the curriculum

The curriculum comprises all the learning programmes and other extra-curricular activities in which the students are involved in the school and can itself be the cause of some discipline problems.

If the content of the subjects which the students are supposed to learn is out of date, irrelevant, or of little interest as well as being unrelated to their culture or future needs, they are likely to become apathetic. If the materials for teaching are so inadequate that lessons tend to become note-taking sessions or lectures, the students will soon be bored and restless. Attempting to teach science without adequate laboratories or equipment can so frustrate students that they will end up dropping the subject.

The way in which lessons are arranged in the school timetable can also be a source of problems. As all teachers in

Nigeria are aware, after 1 p.m. in the afternoon it often becomes extremely hot and humid, or hot and dry. If it is difficult for the teacher to teach under such conditions, it is even more difficult for the students to think clearly and listen attentively. It is better to schedule laboratory and workshop classes at such times where the students can move around and engage in activities. A mathematics lesson scheduled after 1 p.m. is almost certainly doomed to failure and may even result in a failure verging on despair.

How to approach disciplinary problems

Earlier in this chapter some types of indisciplined behaviour were listed and four main causes of indiscipline in the school were described. This section discusses how to deal with disciplinary problems as they occur with reference to: (a) immediate discipline problems, (b) how and when to punish students, (c) preventing future discipline problems.

(a) Immediate discipline problems

Faced with an immediate disciplinary problem, the teacher has to do something. The student does not expect to be let off or to go free without some comment or reprimand, unless of course there is a good reason or excuse for the misbehaviour. What specific action the teacher takes will ultimately depend on the nature and gravity of the offence. In general, however, we have found from our experience in Nigerian schools that the following types of immediate action have proved satisfactory for:

(1) A very minor offence. The student is cautioned or given a verbal reprimand or a sharp look, or the teacher snaps his fingers in his direction. Examples of minor offences are: talking out of turn, frequent laughing or giggling, coming late for class, failing to do an assignment properly, untidiness in dress, running in the dining hall.

(2) An offence that is not too serious. The student is given a verbal reprimand and is instructed to meet the teacher outside the staff room at break-time. Examples of offences are: continuous disturbance, continuous failure to pay attention or to complete assignments, insolence, minor damage to

textbooks or school furniture, a scuffle with another student, cheating in a weekly test.

(3) A serious offence. The student is sternly reprimanded and is told to meet the teacher outside the office of the principal, vice-principal or school guidance-counsellor. Examples of offences are: insulting behaviour to the teacher, considerable damage to school property, stealing or immoral conduct, obvious cheating in a formal end of year examination.

The advantage of the types of action suggested in (2) and (3) above is that the teacher is given time to reflect on how he will deal with the student. Also the student is given a cooling off period to consider what he has done and his excuse for behaving the way he did, and to possibly gain the courage to apologise. When a student is no longer in front of his classmates he or she may behave in a much more reasonable fashion. The teacher will have the opportunity to discuss privately the reasons for the student's misbehaviour, motivate him or her to do better in future or, in the last resort, decide on a suitable form of punishment.

The majority of students respond to a sincere and genuine discussion with their teacher, especially if the teacher uses positive as opposed to negative forms of reinforcement to motivate them. If it is clearly pointed out to the student how and why his misbehaviour is harming him personally, as well as threatening his future success, he is likely to attempt to improve.

It is not recommended that students be asked to stand outside the classroom or be made to kneel on the floor near the blackboard when they misbehave. Not only will such students miss the important remaining points of the lesson but they may also distract the other members of the class. Physical forms of punishment by classroom teachers are not recommended. If corporal punishment is permitted in the schools in your state it is better for the principal or his representative to decide how and when this form of punishment should be used. As much as possible a teacher should avoid the use of sarcasm, threats, nagging, shouting and heated arguments with students, especially in front of other members of the class. Such behaviour is more likely to undermine rather than strengthen his authority.

On rare occasions a teacher may find that a particular

student continues to misbehave in spite of repeated attempts by the teacher to make him change his or her ways. In such situations the teacher should try to find out whether other teachers have the same problems with this student. By talking to other more experienced members of staff, the teacher may find out how they cope with this particular student and so learn to handle him better himself. If a student misbehaves, no matter who the teacher is, then the guidance-counsellor, vice-principal or principal should be consulted.

In most boarding schools each teacher is expected to be 'on duty' one or two days each month, when he or she supervises meals, prep-time and lights-out in the hostels as well as attending to those students who become ill. On these occasions the teacher has to write a report listing down the important events of the day. A duty teacher may encounter some minor disciplinary problems which he or she can deal with without too much difficulty. Serious infringements of school rules, however, should be written down in the duty report book, which is checked by the principal or vice-principal every day. Leaving the school premises during the day or night without permission, stealing and fighting are generally considered serious enough to be reported in the duty book with accompanying names. In a coeducational boarding school sexual misbehaviour involving male and female students or any outsider should also be reported. Failure to do so could result in more serious problems at a later date.

We would like to include here a note of caution, especially to the young male graduate teaching in a school where there are girl students. Undue familiarity between a teacher and a student is a very serious offence and can lead to profound consequences as well as undermining the discipline of the school. It is the duty of the teacher to ensure that such relationships do not develop and with self discipline on his part it should not be difficult to defuse what could otherwise become a dangerous situation.

(b) How and when to punish students

On occasions the teacher may feel it necessary to punish because even after talking and reasoning with a student there seems to be no noticeable attempt at improvement in his or her behaviour.

If the cause of the problem is unsatisfactory written work or assignments, probably the best form of punishment that will help the student improve is to insist that the written work be repeated until it is up to standard. If it is a question of not being able to work maths problems correctly, it may be that the student needs extra tuition as well as further examples to work in order to understand. As much as possible written work which is given as a form of punishment should not be such that it results in the student developing an intense dislike for the subject. 'Writing lines', which usually consists of one sentence repeated hundreds of times, is not recommended as a form of punishment.

It is fairly common practice in Nigerian boarding schools to give students punishment by making them perform a period of manual labour cutting grass, cleaning rooms or helping tidy up the school premises. This practice may in some cases be useful in achieving the desired objectives, but the student should not be asked to carry out these tasks during teaching time. If a student is already poor academically it will only make the situation worse if he or she misses more lessons. The period for carrying out punishments should be such that the student misses either free time or something else he or she likes. Many schools have a recreation/sports period from 5 p.m. to 6 p.m. every day and this period can be effectively used for the type of punishment outlined above, as can Saturday mornings and afternoons. If a school has outing days when students are allowed to visit the town or another school for a sports event, these can be cancelled in the case of those who misbehave.

The objective of punishment is to make the students stop their undesirable behaviour, and this they will do if properly motivated or if they tire of the punishments which result after misbehaviour. The teacher has to decide carefully on the right amount of punishment. Too much will result in antagonism while too little will effect no desirable change in behaviour.

In the last resort the teacher can appeal to the principal when a student stubbornly refuses to behave. The principal has the power, after proper consultation, to suspend a student from the school. The ultimate punishment for extremely serious misbehaviour is expulsion from the school, but the approval of a committee comprising members from the State Ministry of Education is usually required before this step is undertaken.

(c) Preventing future discipline problems

Some teacher have very few discipline problems. They relate well with their students, they are well organised and what they teach they make interesting and challenging. Other teachers seem forever to suffer from conflicts with either a few or many of those they teach. The modern approach to discipline, and the one we are adopting in this book, is that students can practise self discipline and be well behaved most of the time if the teacher adopts the right approach. Our experience teaches that it is only rarely necessary to punish students, but that sometimes they do need guidance and advice to sort out their behavioural problems.

The beginning teacher should find the practice of the following principles helpful in establishing discipline in his classes.

Principles of effective and constructive discipline

1. Lessons should be introduced in such a way that a receptive mood is developed in the learners.
2. The teacher should take advantage of the students' present motives and interests and make lesson materials seem useful and worthwhile.
3. Lessons should not drag or become dreary and boring but move along at a reasonable pace with students and teacher actively involved in the learning experience.
4. A teacher with a sense of humour who does not take himself too seriously is more likely to succeed in establishing discipline.
5. If a teacher likes his students and treats them in a firm but respectful manner, his students will be inclined to like and co-operate with him.
6. The teacher should stress order, courtesy, co-operation and self control in the classroom, as opposed to repression.
7. The teacher should appreciate that lectures and demonstrations require quiet attentiveness on the part of the

students while in laboratory and workshop classes a certain amount of subdued talking is permissible without being a threat to order.

8. Student assignments should be relevant, related to what was studied in class, neither too easy nor too difficult, challenging and interesting, but most important they should be marked by the teacher otherwise students may neglect them and hence cause the teacher a problem.

EXERCISES

1. Briefly discuss four classroom management responsibilities of the teacher.
2. Describe three student qualities that school discipline should teach.
3. How can the teacher be a cause of indiscipline in students?
4. Give three examples of student indiscipline and describe how you would attempt to deal with each.

ESSENTIAL READING

Risk, T. M. (1968) *Principles and Practices of Teaching in Secondary Schools*, (4th ed.), American Book Company, New York.

SUPPLEMENTARY READING

Hoover, K. H. (1968) *Learning and Teaching in the Secondary School*, (2nd ed.), Allyn & Bacon, Boston.

10

Instructional Materials in Teaching

INTRODUCTION

Teachers are often accused of 'over-verbalisation'. By this we mean the excessive use of words to convey meanings. Unfortunately, some of us do love to hear the sound of our voices, so much so that we often forget to consider whether or not our students are really understanding and enjoying whatever we are saying. The problem is that we tend to talk too much without really saying anything. We also tend to 'talk at' our students instead of tending to 'talk with' them. Thus we keep on talking regardless of students' non-verbal signals that they are bored or even completely lost.

Because of the development of modern technology, teachers no longer have to rely solely on words to make their meanings clear. There is a great variety of materials around that can be used to make our meanings more vivid and more interesting. These materials are often referred to as *instructional aids* or *devices* in as much as they are used to supplement or complement the teacher's tasks. They vary from very simple and inexpensive ones such as the chalkboard, flat pictures, diagrams, illustrations and maps, to more complicated and expensive ones like the television, movie projectors, slides and filmstrip projectors.

The mere use of these materials however, does not guarantee effective communication, nor effective teaching. It is their careful selection and skilful handling by the teacher that renders them useful in facilitating learning. It is therefore important for teachers, especially at the beginning, to become familiar with the various types of instructional materials as well as the values that can be derived from their proper use.

It is also necessary for teachers to have a working knowledge of the criteria to be used in selecting and evaluating them and the principles underlying their effective use.

TYPES OF INSTRUCTIONAL MATERIALS

Below is a list of available instructional materials. Although this list is not exhaustive, it should help the teacher in his choice of appropriate materials for different occasions.

I. VISUAL MATERIALS
- A. Three dimensional materials
  - a. Objects
  - b. Models
  - c. Specimens
- B. Printed materials
  - a. Textbooks
  - b. Workbooks
  - c. Programmed instructional materials
- C. Chalkboards
- D. Flannel or felt boards
- E. Bulletin boards
- F. Still pictures
  - a. Non-projected
    - 1. photographs
    - 2. illustrations
  - b. Projected
    - 1. slides
    - 2. filmstrips
    - 3. overhead projections
    - 4. opaque projections
- G. Graphics
  - a. Charts
  - b. Graphs
  - c. Maps and globes
  - d. Posters
  - e. Diagrams

II. AUDIO AIDS
- A. Radio
- B. Record players
- C. Tape recorders

III. AUDIO-VISUAL AIDS
A. Motion pictures
B. Television
IV. COMMUNITY RESOURCES

Visual materials

Three dimensional materials (objects, models and specimens)
Objects are real things. A table, pencil, jars, cooking utensils, are examples of objects. *Specimens* are objects which are representative of a group or a class of similar objects. Examples of specimens are flowers, leaves, fish, frogs, insects and many others. Specimens could also be a part of an object such as the wing of a butterfly, the head of a grasshopper, the bark of a tree and others.

Since objects and specimens are real things they provide direct first-hand experiences which are necessary for concept formation. Students can see, touch, smell or even taste them, hence giving them a richer and more meaningful understanding of the things being learned.

However, if the real thing is not available, too large to take to the class, or too small for the naked eye to see, or too dangerous for the students to manipulate, the use of models is very advantageous. A *model* is a recognisable representation of a real thing. It may be a reduced or enlarged reproduction but it is made into a size convenient for detailed study. Some parts are sometimes removed or de-emphasised so that the essential elements can be studied more readily. Somc models are made to show the interior views of things which are normally covered or invisible. The more useful models are those which can be taken apart and put together again: examples are, the skeletal system of man, the parts of the human eye, and motors of machines.

For the effective use of objects, specimens and models, the following suggestions are worth considering.

1. Make sure that everybody can see the object, specimen or model being presented. It is, however, a mistake to pass around a sample and then continue with the explanation while the students are busy examining it. Students will then concentrate on the sample not on the explanation.

2. Teachers should help students understand not only the object or specimen being studied but also its natural setting.
3. When using models, students should be made to realise the actual size of the real object being represented. This prevents any misconception that students may form as a result of the necessary enlargement or reduction in size.
4. Models are more effective when used in combination with other instructional materials such as illustrations, diagrams, films or even the real objects themselves.
5. Plan for student participation. They should be given the opportunity to handle and examine the material being studied. They should also be encouraged to ask questions and be critical in their examination.

Printed materials

A large proportion of the instructional materials found in most schools are printed. The reason is not that they are considered to be the most effective, but that they are the most accessible and easy to use. The textbook, for instance, is already waiting for you when you first arrive in your new school. Stocks of duplicated materials accumulated over the years and left by your predecessors may even be handed to you for you to use or dispose of. Normally, too, the library has some magazines and journals which, though not very up to date, can be useful not only to teachers but to students as well.

Because printed materials will continue to dominate the array of materials in our schools for more years to come, teachers should know and understand certain fundamental facts about them. Generally speaking, there are two broad categories of printed materials that are being used in the classrooms: the textbook and the supplementary reading materials (Callahan, 1966).

The textbook

The textbook is the one required book that is used by the entire class in studying a particular subject. This does not imply that all learning activities should be geared towards teaching the contents of the book, or that it should form the sole basis for organising the day to day teaching. Instead, it should be regarded only as one of the several useful materials that will aid us in making our lessons more exciting and more interesting. If well written, textbooks have the following advantages.

(1) *They save valuable time for teachers.* Most textbooks are prepared to cover a stated syllabus. A review of the chapter organisations of different textbooks available will be of great assistance to the teacher in determining what units or topics to include in his subject as well as the best or the most logical sequence they should follow. Furthermore, textbooks include a list of suggested activities, recommended readings and review questions which the reader can use or modify to suit his needs.

(2) *They provide the necessary basic knowledge of a particular subject.* A good textbook contains most of the facts and information one need know about a subject presented in a well organised and logical fashion. By mastering the textbook alone, students will obtain the fundamental knowledge necessary to learn a particular subject.

(3) *They provide a common experience for the whole class.* Students are often required to use the same textbook for a particular subject. Hence, they share the same experience from reading it which is essential in promoting a more intelligent class or small group discussion and other similar activities involving co-operative endeavour.

(4) *They are readily available.* Students can always refer back to the textbook to review or verify points. Derek Rowntree (1974) said about the permanency of the textbook, 'At least . . you can make it stay still while you chew over a point; you can go back to the beginning and start again, see the whole shape of the argument in black and white, and and above all, re-read it whenever you like .'

(5) *They ensure continuity of learning in case a class has a change of teacher.* A new teacher has only to ask the class what chapters they have already covered and he will have an idea where to begin his work.

Choosing the right textbook

Teachers, especially the new ones, rarely have a hand in the selection of textbooks for use in their subjects. Nevertheless, they should be able to spot a good textbook when they see one. They should also know how to judge the strengths and the weaknesses of those which are already selected for them.

With enough experience, you should be able to tell a good book at a glance. Things to look out for include the price, quality of paper used, durability of the binding, size of prints and number of illustrative materials such as photographs, charts, diagrams and drawings. Other things to take note of are the original date of publication, the number of editions already made of the book and whether or not the editions were revised. Several editions may mean that the book is widely used and therefore may be good, but if no revisions were made of the later editions, it might suggest that the book is out-dated.

More important than the external appearance of the book is its structure and content. It should be attractive and easy to read. Materials presented should suggest evidence of careful planning and logical organisation. The range of vocabulary used should be appropriate to the level of students for whom the book was intended. In addition, the illustrations should be accurate and within the students' level of understanding. It has been found that colour adds to the attractiveness of a book and makes it more appealing especially to younger readers.

There are many good textbooks on the market if only we know where to look for them. Apart from the information given by colleagues in the field, representatives from different educational publishing firms who visit the schools every year would certainly be very glad to show you what they have to offer by way of textbooks. You could even request inspection copies which you can keep free of charge. How do you think some teachers can afford to collect books for their own private libraries? Furthermore, exhibitions where various firms are invited to display their wares are being arranged from time to time by various institutions. The Department of Library Science of the Faculty of Education, ABU, Zaria for instance, organises such exhibitions every year which are open to anybody interested.

Textbooks, no matter how good they are, will not yield the desired maximum results if they are not properly put to use. The following are some useful pointers on how to use them effectively.

(1) The textbook should not be regarded as the course or the subject. There are a host of other interesting learning experiences that could supplement the content of the book.

(2) The use of the textbook to the exclusion of other instructional materials is not a sound practice. Plan to use the textbook along with other teaching aids to make the subject more concrete and more meaningful.

(3) The textbook is not the only good source of knowledge. Enrich it by introducing additional relevant reading materials.

(4) No textbook, not even the best, is self sufficient. It may contain the basic knowledge, but it is in the power of the teacher to make the written words come alive through further elaborations or explanations, as well as relating the content to other relevant areas of knowledge.

(5) Teach students how to use the textbook effectively. Practice should be given on how to use the table of contents, index, glossary (if any) and footnotes. In addition, they should be taught how to read and interpret graphs, charts, diagrams and other illustrative materials, and to evaluate and discriminate as they read.

(6) Make sure that students are reading the textbook consistently and well. Organise class discussions or small group discussions on important concepts contained in the book. This will enable you to determine how much the students understand what they read.

(7) Feel free to rearrange the topics in the textbook if it suits your needs. Remember, however, that some students prefer to follow the chapters in the order in which they are presented in the book. To reorganise the sequence may confuse or disturb them. Hence, limit 'juggling' of topics or chapters to the minimum.

(8) Do not skip or omit topics from the textbook unnecessarily. Students may feel that they have missed something if you do.

Chalkboards

Of all forms of media, the commonest and most readily available form is the chalkboard. The term chalkboard is now used instead of the conventional term blackboard since chalkboards now come in different colours. The most popular colour but not the most common in Nigeria is green because it is easier on the eyes and it makes the room look more cheerful. In addition, green makes a pleasant contrast with while and yellow chalks which are the most commonly available types.

The chalkboard is a versatile device: its use can be adapted to any kind of subject and to various types of situations. No special talent is necessary to be able to use it. Because the chalkboard is so common, teachers tend to forget to make maximum use of it and yet, when it is not there, they find it difficult to teach. It is unfortunate that very little instruction is being given to would-be teachers during their pre-service education on the proper utilization of the chalkboard.

Like other instructional materials, effective use of the chalkboard lies in the professional and skilful handling by the teacher. The following are some suggestions for using the chalkboard effectively.

(1) Always keep the chalkboard clean. Periodic washing with cloth and water will help. Use downward strokes when erasing. They give a better result. It is a matter of courtesy and consideration always to erase the board after each class for the next teacher. If you do not feel like doing it, let your class monitor do it for you.

(2) Don't clutter your chalkboard with unnecessary materials. Keep your handwriting neat and legible. Bold and firm strokes suggest self-confidence and skilfulness. Remember that board writing is one skill that students will readily observe, therefore we might as well be good at it.

(3) Make sure that everybody can see the board. The best way to check for visibility is to view the materials written on the board from the back and both sides of the room.

(4) Do not cover the materials on the board with your body. When presenting the material it may be necessary to step to one side so as not to block the view of certain students. A long stick to use as a pointer is desirable. Do not be tempted to use the stick on misbehaving students, though.

(5) Use underlining, encircling or framing to focus attention on important materials. The use of coloured chalks not only catches attention but also makes the material more interesting.

(6) If possible, complicated drawings, diagrams, charts

or graphs should be done before the class begins. This helps to prevent time wasting and student misbehaviour as a result of boredom from waiting for you to finish. However, if the chalkboard is being used by several other teachers in a day portable boards are very handy.

(7) When you need to talk while writing, make sure that you talk to the class and not to the chalkboard.

(8) It is a bad practice to erase or make corrections with your fingers or hand. The oil from your hand might cause the chalk to smear. Besides, it is a sign of untidiness.

(9) If you intend to use a particular map, diagram or geometric figure several times, it may be useful to make a ready outline which you can trace whenever needed. For example, an outline of the map of Nigeria can be constructed out of thin plywood or hardboard. The outline, which is called a *template*, could then be held firmly against the chalkboard and traced on the outside.

Another method is the punched pattern or the perforated outline. First the map or the diagram is drawn on a large sheet of paper. Holes two inches apart are then punched along the lines drawn. When the paper with the perforated outline is held against the board and a 'chalky' eraser is rubbed over it, a chalk-dust outline is left on the board which can be easily traced to make the desired drawing.

Flannel boards

The flannel board works on the idea that rough surfaces when pressed against each other will stick together. To construct your own flannel board, secure either plywood or hardboard and cut it to the required dimensions. Although a large flannel board is desirable, it should be such that it can easily be carried from one place to another. Cover one side with flannel or felt, stretching it tightly as you pin it on the other side of the board with drawing pins. If flannel is not available, an old blanket tacked very tightly will do the trick.

Materials for use on the flannel board can be cut out from magazines or they could be drawn by you. If numbers are required, old large calendars can be used. By backing these materials with flannel, sandpaper, inkblotters, sponges or sacking, they will all adhere readily to flannel or felt. Pictures and drawings can be glued on the backing and, when dry, cut around the outline with a pair of scissors. If you want to be economical and do a quick job as well, strips of the chosen backing glued at the back of the drawings or pictures should be sufficient.

Using the flannel board

The flannel board, if used properly, provides a unique and dramatic medium for presenting ideas and facts in the classroom. It is a flexible piece of equipment with endless applications in the hands of a creative and resourceful teacher. With younger children, for instance, the flannel board can be used to tell stories with the aid of cut out pictures or drawings. With older children, it can be used to teach reading and to build vocabulary. You can even put a picture on the flannel board and ask one student to tell a story about it. This is an excellent opportunity for children to practise the use of their imagination as well as their oral language ability.

In Mathematics fractions, geometric figures and mathematical principles involving set theories can be introduced with the use of cut out figures, numbers and other symbols. In Geography children can build up maps in stages by gradually filling an outline map with the names of the different states and their capital cities. Symbols for crops, ethnic groups and industries may also be added for each state.

For a more effective use of the flannel board the following suggestions are worth noting:

1. Plan and rehearse your flannel board presentation. Decide where each picture should be placed on the board and when.
2. Keep your presentation simple. Do not clutter the board with too many materials that are not essential for the understanding of the story or explanation.
3. Make sure that the board is *securely* placed where everybody can see it. Sometimes accidents happen and the board might fall on somebody's head!
4. Always draw the attention of the students to the flannel board presentation not to yourself. Stand on one side so as not to block the view of some students.
5. Before starting the presentation arrange all materials exactly in the order you want them to be and place them within easy reach.

6. When placing materials on the board, a downward stroke accompanied by firm pressure from the hand will result in better adhesion.
7. It may be advisable to tilt the board slightly backwards. This also helps the adhesion of the materials.
8. Test the backing of each material to make sure that they stick to the board. There is nothing more embarrassing than having to pick up your materials all over the floor in the middle of your presentation. Students have their own sense of humour. It is more likely that they will laugh at your misfortune rather than sympathise with you.
9. Remember that the materials can be easily blown down by the wind coming from the door, window or the electric fan. Be sure to place your board away from any possible source of sudden strong winds.

Bulletin boards

A bulletin board is a display or exhibit medium more commonly known to most people, including teachers, as the notice board. The term notice board probably came about because most of the teachers in the past have failed to realise the teaching potential of the bulletin board. To them it is merely a space on the wall to display instructions, new rules and regulations, current news and other similar notices. However, there is now a growing interest in the use of this board, regardless of what it is called, as a teaching aid that can help enrich and facilitate instruction and student learning. More and more teachers now are using the bulletin board for purposes such as these:

1. To supplement textbook materials thus enriching students' learning experiences.
2. To arouse students' interest in a particular subject or topic so that they are motivated to do further study or research.
3. To initiate a new topic or unit by displaying materials that will provide background information or a bird's eye view of the whole unit.
4. To summarise or culminate a unit of study by displaying materials that would help students organise their

thoughts and knowledge, and draw conclusions or generalisations.

5. To display the work of students either individually or in a group. This will encourage students to do better because they know that other students will be viewing the board.
6. To display relevant current news, or ideas designed to stimulate students to think, evaluate and criticise.
7. To serve as a point of reference for developing a lesson or for using other audio-visual aids.

Most classrooms are equipped with at least one bulletin board. Although few teachers have much control over its size and location, these are crucial to its effectiveness. The bulletin board should be placed at the eye level of the students who would be viewing it. There is no hard and fast rule as to the best size but it should be as large as the area allows. Moreover, it should be in the part of the room which is well lighted and out of the line of traffic.

There are, however, still quite a number of classrooms, especially at the primary level, which do not have bulletin boards. Under these circumstances the walls would probably serve the purpose. Sellotape could then be used to stick the materials for display without spoiling the wall in the process.

For a more effective bulletin board display the following additional pointers should be considered:

1. Keep the display simple. Do not clutter your board with too many unnecessary materials.
2. Change the display materials frequently. Do not leave them on the board to turn yellow because of age.
3. When arranging materials, remember that balance is important. Sometimes an informal balance is more interesting than the formal one.
4. Materials mounted on a coloured background add to the attractiveness of the display.
5. There should be only one central theme for each bulletin board display. Too many ideas presented may confuse rather than clarify the intended message.
6. Try to involve the viewers by including questions in the display.
7. The theme or the title and other captions should be

bold and large enough to be seen some distance away.

8. Use commercial letterings, stencils, or cut-outs if your freehand lettering is not good.
9. Keep bulletin board display materials used in the past such as pictures, articles, and letterings, for future use.
10. From time to time involve students in constructing bulletin board displays. This helps in developing creativity as well as co-operation.

Still pictures

Still pictures, as the name implies, refers to pictures that are motionless as opposed to the moving pictures of the television and movies or cinema. They are often regarded as a form of 'universal language' in that they are understood everywhere. Thus you do not need to be able to read or speak a certain language in order to interpret the message a picture conveys. This does not deny the fact that an individual's interpretation of pictures depends to a large extent on his or her background as well as his or her past experience on the subject.

Still pictures may be grouped into two general types: the non-projected and the projected. Photographs, pictures cut out from magazines, newspapers and old calendars, and illustrations from textbooks would fall under the first group, while pictures on slides, filmstrips, opaque and overhead projections would fall under the latter.

Non-projected still pictures

The non-projected pictures are the most widely used and most readily available. They are easy to prepare and cost very little. This is why teachers as well as those who are still in training are well advised to collect and preserve pictures for future use. Because they are so plentiful, teachers fail to think of them as instructional aids. They fail to realise the values that can be derived from them if they are put to proper use. Non-projected still pictures in the classroom have the following advantages.

(1) They assist in clarifying meanings because they provide dramatic realism that words alone cannot portray.

(2) They help overcome the limits of time and space. Past events as well as faraway places can be studied more meaningfully.

(3) Through photography events too quick for the human eye to observe can be captured and preserved for detailed study. Tiny things can be enlarged and large ones can be reduced, which makes in-depth study possible and convenient.

(4) They are flexible. A teacher can use them in any manner she wants. She can vary the speed or her technique of presentation in accordance with her purpose as well as the ability of her students. For instance, younger children will certainly enjoy the creative experience of just colouring, cutting and pasting pictures. Children in the upper grades could be asked to tell stories about a picture shown. This will not only help develop their imagination but will also provide them with opportunities to practise their oral language skills. For the older students, pictures can provide a means of correcting misunderstanding and also a means of enriching knowledge and information acquired from words, printed or oral.

Projected still pictures

Projected still pictures have the same advantage as the non-projected ones. However, they have the added advantage of compelling attention because of the light caused by the projected pictures in a darkened room. Furthermore, they make it possible for large groups to study individual pictures for as long as necessary. Thus the teacher is saved the trouble of having to hand round a small picture for individual students to examine.

Although in some ways projected still pictures are more advantageous than the non-projected ones, they are more expensive and more difficult to use. They also require electricity and this is not always available in most rural schools. Even in places where electricity is available, the power supply is often unpredictable or irregular. In addition, very few schools have the facilities for darkening classrooms for projections.

The most commonly used still picture projectors in the classrooms are the filmstrip, slide, opaque and overhead projectors. A *filmstrip* is a strip of 35 mm film which carries a series of transparent positive still pictures usually called frames. Typically it contains from twenty to fifty frames of either black and white or coloured pictures. A *slide* is a single picture on transparent film mounted for use in a slide projector. The most common commercially prepared slides for use in the classrooms are 5 cm x 5 cm in size, in black and white or colour. For beginning teachers filmstrips are relatively easier to use because the sequence of the pictures has been pre-arranged by the producers. Both filmstrip and slide projectors require only moderate darkening of the room, which makes projections possible in any room at any time of the day.

The *opaque projector* does not need pictures in transparencies for projection. It can project non-transparent materials such as illustrations from books, photographs, and other printed materials on to a screen without the processing necessary for the transparencies of the filmstrip or slide projectors. Although this projector is less expensive because the materials for projection need no special preparation, it may present more problems because it needs to work in a completely darkened room.

The *overhead projector* works in a similar manner to the opaque projector. However, instead of using materials directly from books and magazines, it requires the material to be transferred to a transparent sheet of cellophane or acetate. In addition, the overhead projector throws the image over the shoulder or over the head of the person manipulating it so that the picture is projected on the screen behind her. The advantage of overhead projection over the opaque projection is that it can be used in a lighted room. The teacher can also face the class and talk to the students as she refers to the materials on the screen to illustrate her points.

For a more effective use of still pictures, whether projected or non-projected, the following suggestions may be worth considering.

(1) Pictures should be appropriate to the level of understanding of the intended viewers. The way pupils read pictures usually depends on their age, knowledge and experience. Studies have shown that every child undergoes three stages of picture reading development: (i) the ability to see and identify by name familiar objects in a picture, (ii) the ability to describe the object seen, (iii) the ability to interpret and draw inferences.

When children in the lower grades are shown a picture they

will simply name the objects they can see. As they get a little older they not only name the objects but they also describe them as well. By the time they reach the third stage, they begin to realise that a picture tells a story or a message. It is therefore necessary that pictures chosen are suitable for the stage of picture reading development the children are in and assist them to pass from one stage to another.

(2) Do not attempt to show too many pictures in one lesson because they might confuse rather than clarify meanings. Remember that to study a good picture takes time. Therefore a few but carefully selected and properly used pictures are more effective than several haphazardly chosen and carelessly used ones.

(3) Make sure that pictures are large enough to be seen by everybody in the room. Otherwise, arrange for individual or small group study to follow class presentation.

(4) Prepare yourself to use the picture. Carefully study the details, the people, objects, background and so on. Decide to which portion of the picture you will draw students' attention. Plan exactly what you want the students to do with it.

(5) Pictures cut out from magazines or newspapers are more attractive and can be handled better if they are mounted on hardboard. Mounted pictures can also be easily preserved for longer use.

(6) Preview filmstrips or slide sets to make sure that they are suitable for your own specific purpose. It is not always wise to rely on the brochures or reviews that accompany them. They are often better than the materials themselves.

(7) Still pictures cannot accomplish much by themselves. They should be introduced to the students so that they can see how they fit into the other learning activities. Whenever possible, students should be encouraged to participate actively in the presentation.

Graphic materials

Graphics have been defined as materials which communicate facts and ideas clearly and succinctly through the combination of drawings, words and pictures. They are generally used to present facts and information in a condensed form. To be able to understand and appreciate them, students will need sufficient background knowledge about the subject being presented. They are therefore best used to summarise or review lessons rather than to introduce them. The most commonly used graphic materials in the classroom are graphs, charts, diagrams and posters.

Graphs. Graphs are visual representations of data involving numbers. They show relationships between sets of numerical data in a summarised form. A table representing the amount of rainfall in Zaria for the past ten years may contain all the valuable information, but a graph of the same data will show at a glance which years had the highest and the least amount of rainfall. It will also show very quickly relationships as well as trends in the data. Look at table 10.1 and figure 10.1; which one is easier to read or interpret?

Table 10.1 *Rainfall in Zaria 1970–80*

Year	*Rainfall in millimetres*
1970	948
1971	885
1972	907
1973	974
1974	1115
1975	989
1976	1196
1977	947
1978	1149
1979	1194
1980	1029

For graphs to be effective for teaching purposes, they must be simple. They should present only a limited number of concepts at a time. If there are many variables to be compared, it is more effective to present relationships in a series of simple graphs instead of showing them all in one graph. Approximate amounts are better used to express values rather than exact figures.

Line graphs are used to show relationships between two sets of data. They are the most convenient and the most effective when much numerical data is to be plotted or when

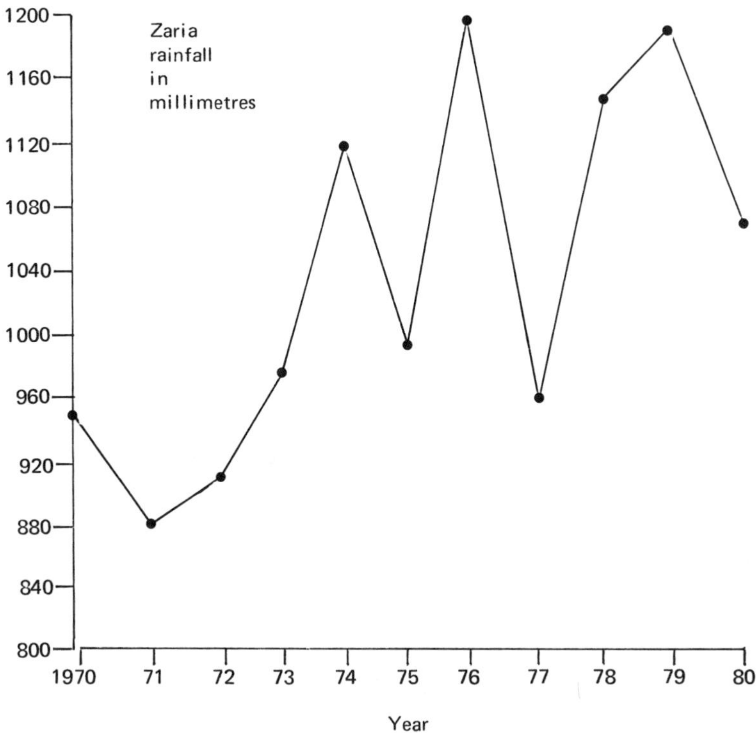

Figure 10.1 *Zaria rainfall in millimetres*

the data is continuous. Figure 10.2 is an example of a line graph.

Bar graphs (see figure 10.3) are used when not more than eight figures are to be compared. Each of the series of numerical or statistical data is represented by either vertical or horizontal bars of the same width. The length of the bars represents the value of each group of data which is sometimes expressed in percentages. To make the bar graph interesting colours are sometimes used. Of all the different types of graphs, the bar graph is the easiest to read and to construct.

The *pie or circle graph* makes use of a circle (the usual shape of a pie) divided into segments to represent the relationship of parts to a whole. Each segment is expressed in percentage or in fraction form and the whole circle always represents the whole amount. In Home Economics, for instance, the pie graph (figure 10.3) is particularly useful

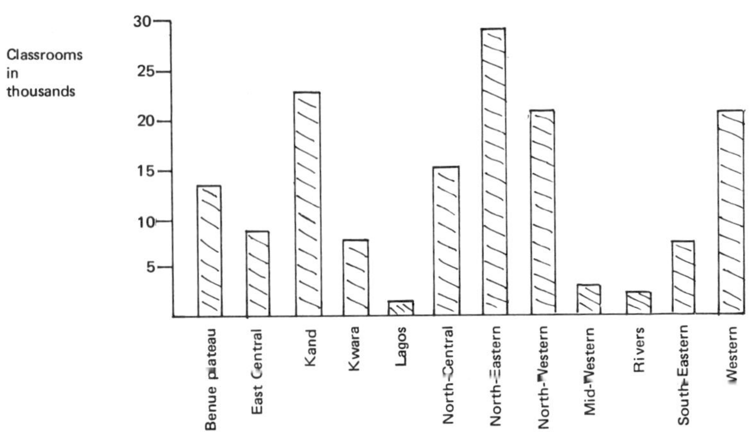

Figure 10.2 *1975 estimates for construction of classrooms for universal primary education in Nigeria*

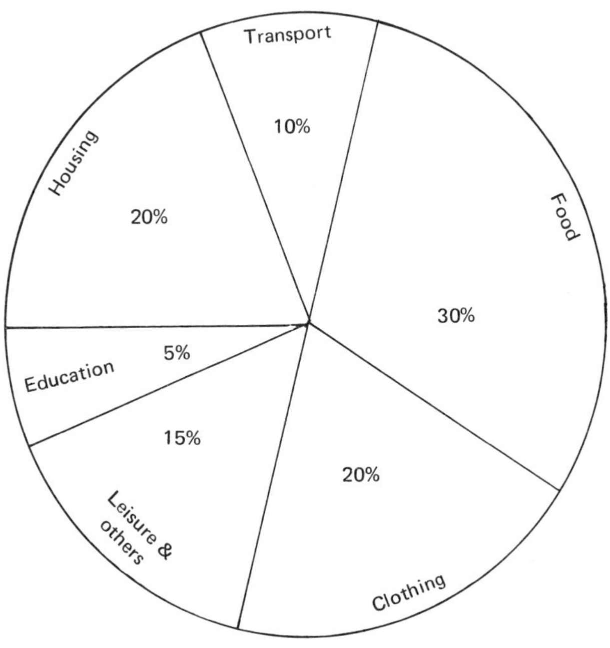

Figure 10.3 *The monthly expenditure of a typical Nigerian family*

in showing how a typical average Nigerian family spends its monthly income.

Pictorial graphs use pictorial symbols to represent values. The quantities of the pictorial symbols are indicated by the number of symbols drawn and not their size. Thus, as the amount being plotted gets larger, the number of pictorial symbols increases (see figure 10.4).

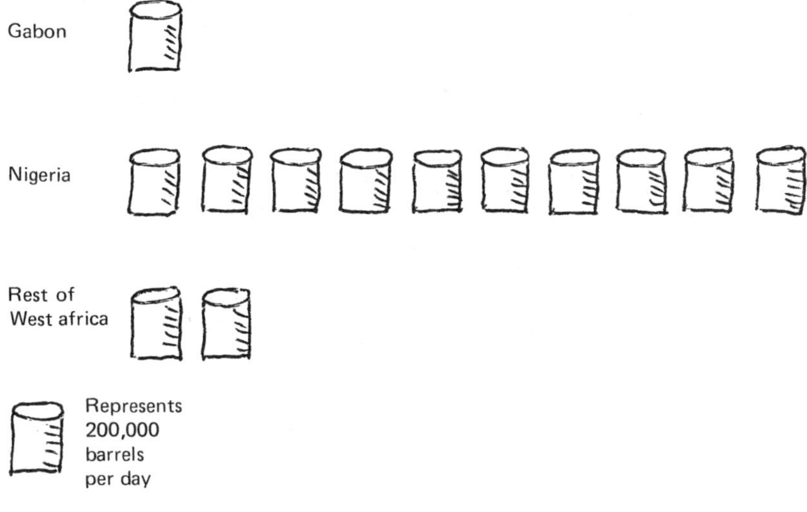

Figure 10.4 *West African oil: output per day in 1981*

Diagrams. Diagrams are sketchy visual representations of interrelationships of facts and ideas, general patterns or essential features of a process, an object or an area. Of all the different types of graphic materials, diagrams are the most abstract because they include only the key elements essential for intelligent interpretation. This implies that adequate prior knowledge and experience of the subject is necessary before diagrams can be understood and appreciated. To understand the way in which blood flows through the heart (see figure 10.5), students would first have to have an understanding of the heart itself. In some cases the diagrams can be used to summarise or review rather than to introduce or present new lessons. Furthermore, they are better used along with other audio-visual materials to make them more effective and more meaningful.

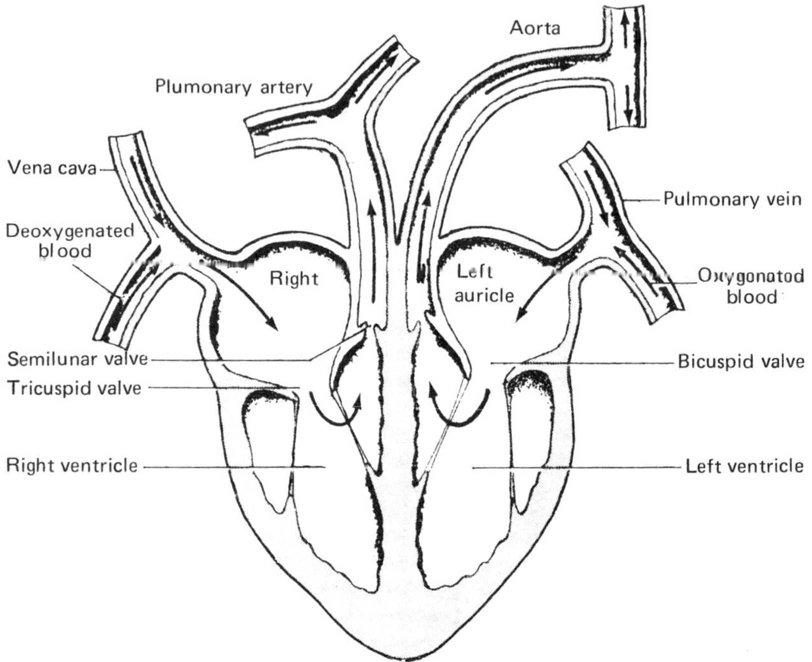

Figure 10.5 *The heart and associated blood vessels – vertical sections*

Posters. A poster is a visual combination of bold design, colour and message which is intended to catch and hold the attention of the passer-by long enough to implant a significant idea in his or her mind (Wittich and Schuller, 1962). From this definition the following characteristics of posters may be identified:

(a) They attract attention.
(b) They have the power to convey a message very quickly.
(c) They use very brief captions often using strong, moving and sometimes shocking language.

Posters are used in schools largely for announcing important school or community events, such as a school drama, an art exhibition, or even a football match. They are also used for reminding students of certain things like, maintaining the values of a good posture at all times, brushing one's teeth regularly, and looking left and right before crossing the street. They are used for promoting such campaigns as a drive for cleanliness and beautification of the school compound or student council elections.

As a teaching aid, posters can be used to provide an appropriate learning atmosphere. For instance, when studying diseases posters relating to the prevention of malaria, common colds and similar other illnesses could be displayed in different parts of the room in order to get students in the proper frame of mind. Sometimes, making students design and construct their own posters will provide them with opportunities for expressing their own views and ideas, apart from providing a satisfying creative experience.

Maps and Globes. It is universally accepted that maps and globes are significant materials in the teaching of Social Studies, History, Geography, Mathematics, Science and even Languages. Their value lies in their ability to give an almost accurate visual representation of the earth's surface, which makes the study of large and remote areas in a more concrete and meaningful way possible.

Maps are visual scaled representations on a flat surface of the land and water masses of the earth or some portion of it. For use in the schools, four types of flat maps can be identified.

(a) Physical-political maps: showing political boundaries such as states or nations, as well as outlines of land areas like mountains, deserts, rivers, and other bodies of water.
(b) Relief maps: indicating through a system of colouring the inequalities in elevations of the earth's surface.
(c) Pictorial maps: using pictures, drawings and other symbols to show things like population, ethnic groups, crops or products.
(d) Outline maps: giving bare outlines which can be developed by students as they go along their lessons.

Although maps are not generally as accurate as globes, they are useful for detailed study and for viewing the whole earth at one time. They also enable students to understand, compare and contrast political units, land masses and water bodies, as well as furnishing information about area, directions, size, shapes and distances.

Globes are spherical representations of the earth's surface. They are more accurate than maps because they represent the true shape of the earth. Moreover, they show correct distances and directions as well as exact locations and areas true to scale at any point. In addition, globes can (as maps cannot) be very useful in developing such concepts as the shape of the earth and its relationship with other heavenly bodies, longitudes and latitudes, time relation and distance, and comparative sizes of nations and continents.

Appropriate maps and globes for teaching in the lower classes should be simple, large and coloured. Just as with other types of graphic materials, students should understand first the symbols used before they could read maps and globes intelligently.

Audio aids

A large portion of classroom learning experience involves listening: listening to lectures, discussions, explanations and comments. It has therefore become necessary to include such audio aids as the radio, tape recorder and record player. Unlike television, filmstrip, slide, opaque and overhead projectors, these audio aids do not require a regular NEPA supply of electric power, but they can be operated using dry cell batteries which are readily available in the market. They can be carried and used anywhere, anytime even in villages where there is no electricity supply.

Radio

The radio has been found to be a valuable tool in teaching students how to listen effectively. It provides them with opportunities to develop the ability to listen critically and with discrimination, a skill which they increasingly need as they go up the educational ladder.

One of the significant values of the radio in the classroom is that radio programmes enrich curriculum materials for learning. Often radio broadcasts such as on the spot coverage of an important event, or the speech of a prominent person, can supplement older materials in textbooks, thereby giving an air of freshness and news to the subject being studied.

Listening to radio broadcasts also provides a pleasant variation from normal classroom work. Because radio in teaching is something new, it has a high interest and motivational value. Its novelty sets the class in an expectant mood which helps ensure concentrated attention – the key to effective listening. Radio is also valuable because it stimulates the imagination. While the class listens to the words and sound effects, each student forms his or her own mental pictures of the subject.

In Nigeria, school radio broadcasting is probably still in its infancy. Every teacher should therefore endeavour to get hold of the list of programmes as well as the timetable for the broadcast, and try to find ways of using them to enrich their teaching. Brochures are also available upon request, which provide descriptions of the different programmes and extra information that may be needed while listening, as well as suggestions on how to prepare students for effective learning.

The record player and tape recorder

Recordings, whether on disc or on tape, have the same educational values as the radio. However, unlike the radio, they can be used whenever the teacher chooses. Radio programmes are broadcast at the time people in the radio stations set. Therefore if you want your class to listen to a certain programme you have to make necessary adjustments in your own class timetable in order to fit it in where you want it to be. In short, the radio controls you, while the record player and tape recorder are controlled by you. You can play the recorded material over and over if necessary and at exactly the time you need it. One added advantage of tape recordings over radio broadcasts and disc recordings is that a teacher can make his own recordings and play them back on the same machine. This allows him to change or erase unwanted portions or to edit by cutting and splicing.

Tape recorders can be used effectively in so many ways. They can be used to individualise instruction. This is especially useful for slow learners, because they can be listening to tapes on their own without holding back the rest of the class. They can also be used to record the news on television or radio, as well as other contemporary sounds like the noise of machines in a factory, the noises animals make in a farm, the humming of the bees, and other similar sounds for future instructional purposes. Furthermore, they can be used effectively in teaching shorthand and typing. A shorthand teacher who teaches several streams of a particular form for instance, can pre-record his material for dictation to ensure that all streams will receive the same rate of dictation. A typewriting teacher can record music and have students type to its rhythm.

In addition to these instructional possibilities of the tape recorder, the teacher can also use it to improve his own speaking ability. Listening to your own voice on the tape will often surprise, if not shock, you. However startling your voice may be, the tape recorder helps you become aware of how you really sound to your students. It will perhaps make you realise just how often you use a particular word or expression, and also whether you talk clearly and distinctly.

If they are to benefit from audio aids, students should be adequately prepared. The room should be free from distracting noises from outside, and if possible a 'DO NOT DISTURB' note should be pinned on the door. For better assimilation, sufficient background information should be given about the subject on the tape. Explanations of different words may also be necessary for better understanding. One important reminder is for you to listen with your students, do not leave them to listen on their own, so that you can mark notebooks or do other things. It is also often desirable to write on the board important ideas or phrases which could be discussed further after the listening session. This is useful in teaching students how to be discriminating and critical listeners.

Audio-visual aids

Educational research indicates that students remember only 10 per cent of what they read, about 20 per cent of what they hear and about 50 per cent of what they hear and see. Retention increases as the student gets more involved in the learning process. Two instructional devices which appeal to both sight and to hearing are now becoming invaluable teaching aids. These are the sound motion picture and television.

Films

The film offers all the advantages of projected still pictures, but it has the added advantage of being able to portray motion.

It is therefore an excellent device in promoting learning when movement is necessary for understanding. In addition it has the capability of re-creating the past, as well as bringing distant places to the classroom. Like other newer instructional media, the film generates students' interest. They often regard the film as fun and entertainment, and so movie time is often looked forward to.

Because of the high cost of the motion picture projector and films, very few schools actually use this device in teaching. However, most universities and advanced teachers' colleges possess projectors as well as collections of educational films which can be borrowed on a short term basis. Embassies and consular offices of different countries also have films that might be of interest to teachers of Social Studies and Languages.

For students to gain maximum benefit, films should be appropriate to their level of understanding. The best way to judge the suitability of a film is to preview it. After all, you are the best judge of the capabilities and background of your own class. Suggestions from others or descriptions given in the reviews are not always the best guide for selecting films.

Before showing a chosen film, it is often necessary to make students aware of your purpose for showing it. Problems or questions which the film hopes to solve or answer should be made clear to them. Whenever possible, specific questions to be answered after viewing should be written on the board and explained thoroughly. It is generally accepted that note-taking while viewing should not be encouraged. If students try to take notes in a dark room, their attention is divided between watching the film and writing; they miss more than they gain.

There are films that use some camera tricks that might distort students' concepts about certain things. For example, if time-lapse photography is used, students should be made aware of the actual time involved in each stage; whether shortened or prolonged. A teacher once related an incident that happened after he showed his class IV pupils a film on insects that carry diseases. In the film a close-up of a fly was shown followed by a series of diseases that it can carry. Because the fly was magnified to occupy almost the entire screen, one pupil said, 'Anyway, we don't have to worry about our flies here. They are not that big.'

It is important after viewing to discuss the film with the class. Questions raised before the film showing should be answered and comments or other relevant and related questions from students encouraged. These follow-up activities will help ensure that students understand and learn from the experience.

Television

Of the newer instructional aids, television is probably the most recent. Two types of telecast can be identified: (1) open-circuit, and (2) closed-circuit. The former is the usual telecast tuned in by homeviewers, while the latter is not telecast in the conventional way, rather the signals are sent out over wires to specially equipped receivers. In open-circuit television, programmes are usually commercially sponsored and are purposely produced for public viewing. In closed-circuit television, programmes are specifically designed for classroom instructional purposes and are therefore of interest only to educators and students.

At present, even in the more developed countries like the USA, the UK and other European countries, not all colleges or secondary schools are making use of closed-circuit television. This is because of the expense involved in its installation as well as its maintenance.

The advantages of television viewing have long been the subject of educational research. Results show that television has the same values as the film. In addition, it has the power to bring into the classrooms many important events at exactly the moment they are taking place. Nevertheless, television has some disadvantages; some of the more important are these:

1. Students tend to become passive.
2. The teaching-learning process becomes too impersonal.
3. Scheduling is a problem.
4. It does not provide for individual differences.
5. Schools may not be able to afford to buy sets because they are expensive.
6. Reception presents a problem, especially in remote areas.

Community resources

Teachers should not forget that the surrounding community has a rich reservoir of instructional materials. All but the remote communities have some community institutions, business and industrial firms, and other places of interest that are not readily available in the classrooms or the school compound. Trips to these places will surely provide students with valuable first-hand experience of the realities of their social and physical environment. There is a fuller discussion of the field trip in chapter four.

The most important resource of a community is its people. Even the smallest village will have individuals who possess special knowledge and skills which are of significance and interest to students. Such people, when invited to schools to help in the process of educating the younger members of the community, are called *resource persons*. Among those who might be invited are the village heads, politicians, businessmen, crafstmen, clergymen, doctors, nurses, law-enforcement officers, foreigners, and many others.

When inviting a resource person, it is necessary for the teacher or the student committee in charge of the invitation to make sure that:

1. The resource person knows exactly what he is to talk about and the purpose of his talk.
2. The resource person has the special knowledge or skill required to achieve desired objectives.
3. The resource person knows how much time he is expected to spend for his talk. (This ensures that he does not engage in too much side-talk that may not be relevant.)
4. The students are fully prepared for the talk. They should know what to expect and be ready to ask questions.
5. Time is allotted for an open-discussion of the talk where students ask questions or give comments.
6. A formal 'thank you' letter is sent to the resource person.

THE VALUES OF INSTRUCTIONAL MATERIALS

The educational values of instructional materials are enormous. It is however important that the teacher is aware of the most important contributions they can offer to facilitate learning. They include the following.

1. They promote meaningful communication, hence effective learning.
2. They ensure better retention, thus make learning more permanent.
3. They provide direct or first-hand experience with the realities of the social and physical environment.
4. They help overcome the limitations of the classroom, by making the inaccessible accessible. This is especially true of films, filmstrips, slides and the like.
5. They provide a common experience upon which other learnings can be developed.
6. They stimulate and motivate students to learn.
7. They help develop interests in other areas of learning.
8. They encourage active participation, especially if students are allowed to manipulate materials used.

SELECTING INSTRUCTIONAL MATERIALS FOR TEACHING

For the beginning teacher, choosing the most appropriate material for specific teaching purposes would probably present a problem. In this connection the following basic criteria are worth considering.

Suitability or appropriateness for the intended purpose
No one type of material is appropriate for all kinds of learning. Some are more useful in teaching a skill, presenting facts, showing relationships, or changing behaviours or attitudes. Others are more effective in giving background information or in summarising a unit of work. The teacher therefore should select materials that would best aid him in achieving his objectives. In other words, only materials that would help serve instructional purposes should be used.

Suitability for the intended learners
Materials are effective only when they are understood and appreciated by the students using them. Unfortunately, most of the commercially available instructional materials, although attractive, are not always suitable for specific users. The teacher should therefore review, preview, or examine these materials to determine whether or not they are within the students' level of understanding as well as within the range of their experiential background. Moreover, teachers might find it more profitable in terms of goal achievement to make their own materials for instruction, such as charts, graphs, diagrams, and even maps.

Physical qualities
This includes such qualities as attractiveness, ease of handling and authenticity. Effective materials are capable of attracting attention. Simplicity, colour, novelty and, sometimes, familiarity add to the attractiveness of materials, especially the visual ones. In addition to attractiveness, materials should be easy to handle in the case of visual materials and easy to operate in the case of machines or equipment. Many projectors and recorders are now available in easily portable forms. If materials become too complicated to manipulate, it is better to consider whether or not they are worth the trouble. Materials should be accurate and authentic. In other words, they should provide a true picture of the things being represented or shown. Thus it is essential that the information being presented is up to date as well as truthful.

Other factors to consider in selecting materials are the cost and time involved. Cheap materials are not always the best. The same may be said about the more expensive ones. Materials should therefore be within the limits of the school budget. They should be reasonable in cost without really sacrificing the other desirable qualities.

The regular class period usually lasts only for forty-five minutes. However, some audio-visual experiences may need more than a class period, and so ways and means of extending the time without necessarily disrupting other teachers' plans should be considered. In any case, when you are selecting any type of material, the fundamental question you should ask yourself is, 'Is it worth the money and time involved to use this or that type of material?'

USING INSTRUCTIONAL MATERIALS

Instructional materials by themselves cannot do much to improve or promote learning. Their value lies in the professional skill of the teacher in using or handling them. For a more effective use of instructional materials, the following fundamental steps must be considered.

Prepare yourself
Familiarise yourself with the materials that you intend to use. This will enable you to decide exactly when and how materials should be presented. It will also enable you to plan what questions to ask the students and what follow-up activities might be appropriate. In addition you will be able to determine which part of the audio-visual experience needs emphasising or extended elaboration.

Prepare the materials
All materials to be used should be arranged and positioned in such a way that they come in handy at the exact time you want to use them. All equipment and machines should be tested for proper functioning and set ready for use with just a click of a button or a knob. The idea is not to waste time arranging the sequence of pictures or threading a movie projector in front of the class since this may generate impatience and consequently misbehaviour. The delay might be enough to kill the dramatic impact with which materials must be presented, if they are to catch the concentrated attention of the students.

Prepare the environment
This involves making sure that the environment is conducive to the audio-visual experience planned. If motion pictures, slides or filmstrips are to be used, the room should be properly darkened in order to improve visibility. If audio aids are used, the room should be as free from distracting noises as

possible. The important thing is that students can see clearly and hear distinctly what is being said and done.

Prepare the students

For students to gain maximum benefit, they should have sufficient background information about the subject under study. This is especially true of materials such as films, filmstrips, slides, radio and television. It is often necessary to stress what important things they can learn from the experience, and identify what problems the material hopes to solve or shed light on. Students should also be told what they are expected to do while and after using the material.

Use of the material

All materials used should be properly and adequately introduced. Students should be made aware of your purpose for using them and how they fit into the subject being studied. The presentation should be accompanied with the necessary explanations, comments, or demonstrations. This implies that you as the teacher should have prepared yourself thoroughly for their use.

When using technical equipment like projectors, make sure that the pictures are well focused and the sound audible. If pictures or three-dimensional materials are used, they should be held so that they can be viewed properly from all parts of the room. In short, materials should be used in the most professional way possible in order to get the desired effect.

Evaluate the materials

Some fundamental questions that you should ask yourself after using an instructional material are: (1) Did it help achieve my purpose? (2) Did my students understand and appreciate, or were they bewildered or confused? (3) What portion of the audio-visual experience needs improvement in future? (4) Was it worth the time and energy I spent to prepare and use it?

EXERCISES

1. Discuss briefly the philosophy behind the effective use of instructional materials in teaching?
2. What are the instructional materials that are commonly used by teachers in the secondary schools? How can each be used effectively in the classroom?
3. What are the advantages of using projected materials in teaching? What are the limitations surrounding their use in schools here in Nigeria?
4. What community resources can you possibly use in teaching your own subject area? What values can students derive from them?
5. What are the principles underlying the effective use of graphic materials in teaching?
6. What guidelines should you consider when selecting materials for instruction with your class? Explain each briefly.

ESSENTIAL READING

Callahan, Sterling G. (1966) *Successful Teaching in Secondary Schools*, Scott, Foresman, Chicago.

Dale, Edgar (1954) *Audio-Visual Methods in Teaching*, Holt, Rinehart & Winston, New York.

Kinder, James S. (1965) *Using Audio-Visual Materials in Education*, American Book Company, New York.

Wittich, W. A. and Schuller, C. F. (1962) *Audio-Visual Materials: Their Nature and Use*, Harper, New York.

SUPPLEMENTARY READING

Brown, James W. (1973) *Audio-Visual Instruction: Technology, Media and Methods*, McGraw-Hill, New York.

Clark, L. H. and Starr, I. S. (1959) *Secondary School Teaching Methods*, Macmillan, New York.

Kent, Graeme (1969) *Blackboard to Computer: Guide to Educational Aids*, Cox & Wyman, London.

Lee, James M. (1963) *Principles and Methods of Secondary Schools*, McGraw-Hill, New York.

Rowntree, Derek (1974) *Educational Technology in Curriculum Development*, Harper & Row, London.

11

Evaluating Instruction

WHAT IS EVALUATION?

Evaluation in the context of education is a process used to obtain information from testing, from direct observations of behaviour, from essays and from other devices to assess a student's overall progress towards some predetermined goals or objectives. It includes both a qualitative and a quantitative description and involves a *value judgement* of overall student behaviour.

Evaluation and measurement are not the same, although evaluation involves measurement. If we assess a student's knowledge and understanding in a subject by means of an objective or essay type test, that is measurement. If the teacher puts a *value* on the student's work, talents, attitudes and other characteristics of behaviour that is evaluation. Evaluation should in part involve testing that is non-subjective on the part of the teacher, otherwise it is likely to be erratic and unreliable.

WHY EVALUATE?

Evaluation has many purposes. It can be used in the following eight ways.

1. Evaluation as a basis for school marks or grades by teachers
Educational systems require that teachers occasionally submit marks or grades for students. These marks or grades can be arrived at through formal examinations, regular tests, assignments, laboratory reports, observational data or combinations of these.

2. Evaluation as a means of informing parents
Students' parents want, and have a right to know, how their children are progressing in school. Student evaluation is the most important way of providing them with this information.

3. Evaluation for promotion to a higher class
Student evaluation is sometimes used to determine whether a student has made enough progress to be promoted to a higher class or form in the school.

4. Evaluation for student motivation
Success in tests and examinations as well as sports and other school activities can give great encouragement to students. Similarly, failure to do well can make students work harder or strive to do better. Teachers should try to give their students feedback on the evaluation of all aspects of their learning and behaviour so that both those who do well and those who do not will be motivated to improve on their performance.

5. Evaluation for guidance and counselling purposes
All students need to be advised to help them solve their own personal problems, whether academic or emotional. The two types of problems are indeed often connected. Successful students tend to enjoy school more than those who are not so successful. It is generally those who appear to be failures, as indicated by the evaluation of the teaching staff, who need the most attention and it is to them that the class teacher must direct herself.

6. Evaluation to assess the effectiveness of the teaching strategy
If a teacher does not in some way assess the students' improved knowledge, understanding and higher cognitive skills as well as their attitudes and psychomotor abilities, she will not be able to evaluate the success or otherwise of the teaching strategy she has employed. A high failure rate in a course is more often due to poor teaching than to the lack of intelligence of the students.

7. Evaluation for employment purposes
Not all students who pass through post-primary schools will proceed to universities or other institutions of higher learning. Some students may decide to join a company or business. Employers normally require information on potential employees with reference to academic ability, attitude to work, moral character, personality and so on. Hence the necessity for the teachers to evaluate nearly all aspects of the students' performance while they attend the school.

8. Evaluation for university and college entrance
Universities and colleges often require evaluation reports from schools on applicants. These reports might be in the form of mock-WAEC results or character references. Such reports should neither under-rate nor exaggerate but should be honest assessments of the candidates' worth.

WHAT TO EVALUATE

For the organised teacher who has worked with well planned units or lessons and clearly stated behavioural objectives, the question of what to evaluate is not too difficult to answer. However, it is our experience that even such teachers, not to mention those who are less organised, do find it hard sometimes to decide what aspects of their students' knowledge and behaviour to evaluate.

As we stated earlier in chapter eight and also at the beginning of this chapter, all aspects in the behavioural, affective and psychomotor domains should be assessed in the overall evaluation process. The national objectives for Nigeria, clearly stated in the National Policy on Education (1977) maintain that, 'attitudes, values, physical skills and abilities are important for the students as well as cognitive skills'. Hence, in deciding what to evaluate, the teacher should take all areas of student progress into account. Clearly it would be unfair on the students to test them on things which they have not been encouraged to learn or to master, so the teacher should consider all these aspects in his course and lesson planning.

HOW TO EVALUATE

There are many different ways of testing and evaluating students' progress in school, but before considering any particular type of test the reader should first understand the following terms:

Validity: The validity of a test instrument is the extent to which it measures what it is supposed to measure.
Reliability: The reliability of a test instrument is the extent to which it measures accurately and consistently.
Objectivity: A test is objective if the scoring of it is not affected by the personality of the scorer (in most cases the teacher).
Usability: If a test possesses usability it should be relatively easy to administer and score and not too expensive in terms of materials needed.

The different methods of evaluating students in this chapter will be classified under three general headings:

1. Teacher made tests
2. Other evaluation devices
3. Continuous evaluation or assessment

Teacher made tests

The essay test

Advantages. This type of test is helpful in measuring the students' ability to organise, interpret, evaluate and apply knowledge. It helps the teacher assess the students' ability to summarise, outline and see relationships and trends. It also tests the students' ability in fluency and clarity of expression.

Disadvantages. The test has limited validity since there is no one correct answer and many other factors only indirectly related to the topic are likely to be included in an answer. Handwriting and neatness also tend to affect the essay score. The test has low reliability because of its dependence on the opinions as well as the physical and mental conditions of the scorer. Scoring may also be influenced by the teacher's knowledge of the students' previous work. In other words, scoring lacks objectivity.

Precautions in test construction. The teacher should construct the questions carefully so that they very clearly indicate the areas to be discussed. The sentences in each question must be logically constructed and follow on from one another. There should be sufficient questions on each test so that the students will not run out of things to say. If equal marks are being awarded for each essay the questions should be of equal difficulty and demand answers of approximately equal length.

Scoring. Before sitting essay type tests, students should be given a resume of the marking scheme. They should be told how many marks will be awarded for content, style and organisation of material. Allowance should be made and marks also reserved for additional pertinent points and creativity. In the marking of essay tests the same essay should be marked at one time on all the scripts, to ensure better uniformity of standards. It is also better for the marker to grade the scripts in several stages, if there are many, to avoid fatigue. A tired marker can be over severe on the essays he marks.

The objective test

The common characteristic of all types of objective tests is that there is only *one* correct answer to a question, unlike the essay type answer in which there are shades of right and wrong. There are many types of objective tests and it is not possible to discuss them all in a book of this nature. The four most commonly used objective tests are:

1. True/false
2. Completion
3. Multiple choice
4. Matching

1. *True/false.* This is a typical test of this type.

Below are a number of examples of mathematical statements, some of which are true and others false. If you believe a statement to be true, exactly as it is stated, encircle T; if not encircle F. Do not guess.

$4900 = 70$	T	F
$0.01 = 0.001$	T	F
$x^4 = x^3$	T	F
$y^6 = y^3$	T	F

The *advantages* of true/false items are that they are easy to construct and the teacher, by using such tests, is able to sample a wide area of what he has taught. This type of test is very useful in testing beliefs, attitudes and superstitions. The biggest *disadvantage* of this type of test is that the students tend to guess the answers, and in so doing they have a fifty percent chance, statistically speaking, of guessing correctly. As a *precaution in test construction*, the teacher should use at least ten to twenty test items and the number of true and false items should be about the same. Statements which are negative, long or ambiguous should be avoided. It is quite simple to *score* such tests if a master-key score is used. Usually one mark is given for a correct response and zero for an incorrect response.

2. *Completion.* The example below is a good illustration of this type.

Each statement below has a number or word missing. Fill in the blank spaces with the correct missing number or word.

1. The first President of Nigeria was __________ .
2. The capital of Niger State is __________ .
3. Yola is the capital in the State of __________ .

The *advantages* are that test items in completion tests can establish who, when, what, where and how many, in any chosen event. Test items are easy to construct and the correct answers are difficult to guess. The *disadvantages* are that completion test items are inconvenient to score and tend to emphasise rote responses. Scoring can become subjective. The teacher should take the following *precautions in test construction.* Only key words should be omitted from the blank spaces and as much as possible only direct questions should be used. The blank lines should all be about the same length whether the missing word is long or short. Blank spaces should be kept near the ends of the statements and the tester should avoid having too many. *Scoring* tends to be inconvenient, especially when students give answers which are plausible but not expected. Some credit should be given in such cases.

3. *Multiple choice.* These are standard multiple choice questions.

For each of the questions or statements below encircle the

letter of the item which best answers, or completes, the question or statement.

1. If $x + 7 + 2x = 14$, x equals:
   (a) 70
   (b) 21
   (c) 7
   (d) 3
2. If a cuboid is 7 cm high, 20 cm long and 5 cm wide, its volume is:
   (a) 7 cu cm
   (b) 70 cu cm
   (c) 700 cu cm
   (d) 70 cm

The *advantages* of multiple choice questions are that they can be used in all subject areas. They are easy to administer and to score. The *disadvantage* is that good test items are difficult to construct and test scores tend to be inflated due to a twenty-five percent chance (on four alternatives) of guessing the right answer. As a *precaution in test construction*, at least four choices of response should be provided for each item and, apart from the correct response, the other three should be reasonably close to being correct. The relative position of the correct response should not be the same in all the items. The *scoring* is fairly simple and can be completed rapidly if a master-key of the correct responses is prepared. Usually one mark is given for a correct response and zero for one that is incorrect.

4. *Matching items.* This example is typical.

In the left-hand column below is a series of words and each word can be associated with only one word in the right-hand column. Fill in the blank space for each word on the left, the letter of the word on the right with which it is most closely associated.

_____ 1. anopheles mosquito	a.	bubonic plague
_____ 2. rat	b.	malaria
_____ 3. tsetse fly	c.	yellow fever
	d.	sleeping sickness
	e.	hepatitis

The *advantage* of this type of test is that it can provide information on who, what, when and where. It is difficult to guess the answers correctly and each test item can provide useful information on what the student knows about several topics. The *disadvantage* is that it is difficult to construct the test items which consist of only single words or very brief phrases. As a *precaution in test construction*, there should not be more than ten pairs of words to match. In one of the columns there should be more words than in the other so that after matching has been completed some words remain. This reduces student guessing. There should not be more than one correct match for each word. Words in both columns should be labelled in alphabetical or numerical order. *Scoring* is fairly simple once the correct answer key has been designed.

Oral tests

Apart from the more formal tests, the teacher can make use of oral tests or quizzes in the classroom to assess students' learning. Most teachers use the questioning technique in their lessons and the quiz is simply an extension of this technique. The art of questioning is discussed in some depth in chapter six and the reader is advised to refer to that chapter for information on how to frame good questions for use in the classroom.

Laboratory type tests

In many subjects in the Nigerian curriculum, students are required to develop practical or physical skills as part of the course and as a complement to and an extension of their theoretical knowledge. In Home Economics students have to be able to cook and sew and not just know about these things. In Physical and Health Education students not only have to study soccer, volleyball and athletics but they are also expected to possess some expertise in playing such sports. In vocational subjects and the sciences, students have to exhibit certain skills in the handling and manipulation of and laboratory equipment, while the agriculturalist should be able to grow crops on the farm successfully in addition to knowing how they should be grown in theory.

It is clear, then, that there is a need for a laboratory type test in which the teacher attempts to assess the students' physical and practical skills either directly or as part of an exercise which can only be successfully completed if the students possess a modicum of such skills.

It is difficult to advise on the design of laboratory type tests because they will vary according to the subject and skills that are being assessed. However, it is essential that teachers remember to take into account the practice of psychomotor skills and plan their evaluation strategy accordingly.

Other evaluation devices

In the previous section the various ways of testing and measuring a student's behaviour in the cognitive, affective and psychomotor domains were discussed. Apart from testing there are at least three other ways in which the evaluation process can be made more complete and these involve the use of:

1. Assignments
2. Observation of in class and out of class behaviour
3. Individual discussions with students.

Assignments

In Nigerian secondary schools and Grade II colleges at which students are boarders, there is usually a prep period of about two to three hours each evening. During this time senior students or prefects supervise the other students while they read or work on their assignments in classrooms or study halls. The assignment is part of the way of life of the Nigerian student, and the way in which assignments are completed is a measure of his seriousness and application to his studies. Sometimes students swop notes on assignments, so the fact that a mathematics problem is correctly answered does not necessarily mean that the student arrived at that answer on his own. In day secondary schools where assignments are also given, students have the opportunity to consult parents and friends, so that assignments submitted cannot be considered to be solely a result of their own efforts. Nevertheless, the assignment is valuable, not only to the student but also to the teacher in his or her attempts to evaluate a student's overall behaviour. Students who conscientiously hand in satisfactorily completed assignments throughout the year of study, and yet do not perform so well in the end of year examinations, should be given a positive evaluation. They are obviously doing their best. Students who neglect their assignments and yet still perform well in examinations are clearly clever but lacking in seriousness about their studies, and they should be so told. If they do not correct themselves in school it is possible that when they reach the university they will fail.

Chapter six discusses the giving of assignments at greater length as a learning technique. It can be seen from what has been said here that the submission or otherwise of assignments can tell the teacher a lot about his or her students' attitudes.

In class and out of class behaviour

The average Nigerian teacher, apart from his teaching duties in the classroom, has other responsibilities around the school out of class hours. Every teacher has certain days in each month when he is said to be on duty. This means that he has to supervise meals, evening prep and ensure that students go to bed at the correct time. Other duties might include the organising of evening games, the coaching of a team, running student debates, school plays or the supervision of the infirmary or school farm. Apart from being in close contact with the students he teaches in the classroom, the teacher is also able to observe the same students in out of class activities. In attempting to evaluate a student's overall behaviour the unbiased observant teacher thus has sufficient opportunities to form a fairly accurate opinion.

The way in which a student interacts with others can provide valuable information concerning his or her talents, character, attitude, personality and values. The observation of such interaction both in and out of class is an important part of any reliable evaluation.

Personal discussions with individual students

In situations where a teacher is involved teaching between one and two hundred students in the course of a week, it is not possible to get to know them all individually. Occasions do arise, however, when a teacher is able to know a few of her students personally and in some depth. A private discussion with a student whether planned or not can provide the teacher with useful background information enabling her better to evaluate the student's behaviour and progress. Students sometimes have problems which they are reluctant to reveal and which can seriously hamper their efforts.

We had such an experience with a student who had not revealed his very bad eyesight to anyone. At the beginning of the school year the boy was told to sit at the back of the class because he was so tall. There he sat for a whole term without being able to read what was on the blackboard. He felt ashamed to tell anyone of his problem as he thought he would be ridiculed. Needless to say, his teachers believed him to be intellectually poor because whenever he was asked a question about something that was written on the board he was speechless. In a chance conversation one evening the student reluctantly admitted that he was very short-sighted. He was subsequently moved to the front of the class near a window. By the end of the school year he was placed near the top of his class in the examinations.

If a particular student is doing badly in your class and you think he has a problem which is preventing him from performing better, a private conversation with him may reveal the cause of his poor academic performance, enable him to improve, and lead to a more correct evaluation of his ability and potential.

Continuous evaluation or assessment

It was felt that mention should be made at some point in this chapter of continuous evaluation or assessment, to emphasise that student evaluation is something that should be continually on-going throughout the school year, and not something that happens only at the end.

A father who is attempting to train his child has to be correcting and encouraging his child almost daily if he wants him to learn and appreciate the proper way to behave. So it is with the teacher and his students. He should provide feedback to his students on a regular basis concerning their performance. Tests should be given once or twice every two weeks, and the students informed of the results, their errors being discussed with them. Frequent observations of their general behaviour, attitudes, and skill development should also be reported to the students so that they have a chance to improve. In the universities 40 percent of a student's marks towards his final grade come from continuous evaluation and only 60 per cent from the final examination. Such a system encourages students to work continuously during the year and rewards them for doing so.

REPORTING EVALUATION

Once a student's progress has been evaluated by the teachers, copies of the results of that evaluation have to be passed on to the students and their parents. It is customary to use a written report form containing all the relevant information for this purpose. Before discussing some of the different types of report forms that exist in different parts of the world, it would seem useful at this point to consider the system of evaluation reporting that is being currently used in Nigeria.

The situation in Nigeria

In Nigerian post-primary institutions teachers are frequently called upon for student marks or grades. It is the custom to have two or three sets of formal examinations each year and in the fifth year teachers have to provide mock-WAEC results as predictors of the students' performances at the formal WAEC exam.

Student reports in all subject areas are usually provided for students and their parents once each year. The format of such reports varies slightly from one state to another, but generally speaking they resemble the format shown in figure 11.1.

In order to assist the beginning teacher a few general points of explanation will be made as to how the different portions of this report form should be completed.

1. The subject mark or grade

In some schools, teachers record the mark attained in the end of year exam in the report form. Others include a continuous

Figure 11.1

Student Report
State Ministry of Education
Name of College
Address

Student's Name ________________________ Year/Term __________

Form _____________ Student's Age ________ yrs ______ months

Subject Mark Grade Comments

Overall Position in Class ______________________________

Form Master's Comments ______________________________

____

____

Principal's Comments ______________________________

____

____

Principal's
Signature ____________________

Form Master's
Signature ____________________

assessment mark, which takes into account the student's assignments and class tests during the year, in the final grade. Since some teachers are more lenient than others, a high mark may not mean that the student was one of the best in the class. For this reason some teachers also state the position of the student in the class in their subject.

2. Comments of the subject teacher

Sometimes the comments of the subject teacher are more valuable than the mark or grade awarded. For example a comment like, 'Has worked hard and made good progress. Co-operative and well behaved,' can do a lot to encourage the student and is very informative to the parents about his or her general attitude and behaviour. Unfortunately, because there is usually a big rush at the end of the school year with hundreds of examination scripts to mark and an equal number of reports to fill in, teachers do not always have the time to write more than a perfunctory, 'Good', 'Satisfactory' or 'Poor' on a school report. As a beginning teacher try to write meaningful and helpful comments in end of year reports. You owe it to your students and their parents. Remember that if most of your students do badly in your course it probably means that your teaching strategy was faulty and is in need of revision.

3. Comments of the form master

Usually it is the form master or mistress who best knows the students in his or her class, both regarding academic and all round performance. The form teacher conducts the role-call in the mornings and is responsible for the cleanliness of the classroom, as well as the welfare and behaviour of students in the class. A form teacher should not be biased in undeservably favouring some students more than others. All students should feel that they can approach the form teacher if they have problems of any sort.

An objective form teacher is in an ideal position to provide the most useful evaluation of the students in the class. He should make maximum use of the space he has available to him on the school report form.

4. The principal's comments

The principal's comments are usually brief and supportive of what the form master has already written. It is very difficult for principals to know all their students individually and unless the students have excelled or behaved very badly they may not know much about them.

The majority of post-primary institutions in Nigeria are boarding although more and more day secondary schools are being introduced in the different states. When the parent of a child in a far off boarding school receives a school report he has no knowledge of the teachers who recorded the grades and wrote the comments. Should the parent want to discuss anything with the staff or principal of the school it might mean travelling hundreds of miles to do so. Whatever the advantages of boarding schools, there is no doubt that communications between teachers and parents are far more limited than they are in day secondary schools. In a day school where the parents of unco-operative or lazy students are living in the immediate vicintity, meetings can be arranged at short notice at any time during the term to discuss the students' problems. Parent-teacher associations can be very active in day schools and fruitful relationships between parents and teachers can be established which will only benefit the students. In boarding schools the responsibility for educating the child is left, perhaps unjustly, solely with the teachers, whereas in day schools it becomes a joint venture with the parents. This is a much more desirable state of affairs and is certainly one of the reasons for introducing more day secondary schools in Nigeria.

Alternative suggestions for improving reporting

In the previous section the system of reporting evaluation as it exists in Nigeria was discussed. From what was mentioned in earlier portions of this chapter it should now be apparent that there are certain drawbacks with that system of reporting.

1. Giving formal written reports to students and parents once only at the end of the school year is considered too infrequent. Students in post-primary boarding schools in Nigeria travel home on at least three occasions during the school

year. The way students are performing should be reported early so that parents can use their unique influence on them, if necessary, to help them improve. At the end of the school year it is too late for any effective remedial action to be taken. Students at day secondary schools in Nigeria live at home, or with relatives, and to provide only one written report per annum on such students is, we believe, insufficient. We suggest that termly reports at the end of the first and second terms be provided even though they are not as detailed as that for the end of the school year. A briefer form such as that shown in figure 11.2 could be used.

Figure 11.2 *End of term report*

Name of School

Name of Student ____________________ Date __________

Form __________________

Subject	Grade	Teacher's Signature

Form Master's Comment ______________________________

____

______________________________ Signature ____________

Parent's Signature __________________________________

Figure 11.3 *End of year school report*

SUBJECT NAME	*ACADEMIC PERFORMANCE*						*Teachers' comments on Academic Performance*
	Continuous Assessment		*Exam mark*		*Overall*		
	Mark	*Grade*	*Mark*	*Grade*	*Mark*	*Grade*	

Form Master's Comments ______________________________

____

Principal's Comment ______________________________

Principal's Signature ____________________ Form Master's Signature ____________________

Figure 11.4 *Report on student attributes**

STUDENT ATTRIBUTES	VG**	G	A	P	VP
1. Utilisation of abilities					
2. Attitude to work					
3. Acceptance of responsibilities					
4. Politeness and consideration of others					
5. Leadership qualities					
6. Ability to obey orders					
7. Involvement in extra-curricular activities					
8. Personality qualities					
9. Respect for school property					
10. Future potential					

* This form can either be included on the same side of the paper as the other part of the end of year report, or be printed on the other side of the same sheet. By ticking in the appropriate column the teacher will be able to indicate far more about the student than he would be able to in the small space of the present end of year report.

Grades awarded will represent the class teacher's observations in consultation with other teachers.

**VG = Very Good, G = Good, A = Average, P = Poor, VP = Very Poor

2. The yearly report format presently used in Nigeria tends to concentrate on only academic performance, and teachers completing reports rarely comment on the development of attitudes and values in students. There is in fact no requirement obligating the teacher to write more than one or two words on a student's performance.

In addition, in reporting the students' academic results there is no separation of the continuous assessment component from that of the formal examination. An alternative end of year report format is suggested and is shown in figure 11.3.

EXERCISES

1. Briefly explain how educational measurement and evaluation differ.
2. Give four good reasons why it is necessary to evaluate a student's performance in school.
3. Apart from student academic achievement, name three other factors that should also be evaluated.
4. Construct two examples of test items for each of the following types of objective tests:
   (a) True/false
   (b) Completion
   (c) Multiple choice
   (d) Matching
5. What suggestions can you make for improving evaluation reporting in Nigeria?

ESSENTIAL READING

Blount, N. S. and Klausmeier, H. J. (1968) *Teaching in the Secondary School*, (3rd ed.), Harper & Row, New York.

Callahan, J. F. and Clark, L. H. (1977) *Teaching in the Secondary School*, Macmillan, New York.

Clark, L. H. and Starr I. S. (1976) *Secondary School Teaching Methods*, (3rd ed.), Macmillan, New York.

SUPPLEMENTARY READING

Grambs, J. D., Carr J. C. and Fitch, R. M. (1970) *Modern Methods in Secondary Education*, (3rd ed.), Holt, Rinehart & Winston.

Oliva, P. F. (1967) *The Secondary School Today*, World, New York.

12

Some Innovations in Educational Practices

INTRODUCTION

So much is going on in the field of education around the world, especially in the more developed countries. Changes are taking place very rapidly in areas such as teacher training, methodology, curriculum organisation and evaluation. Some of these newer practices are becoming widely accepted because of their proven values, while others are still in their experimental or trial stages. Although some of these new trends may take some time to affect the educational system in Nigeria, we deemed it necessary for teachers to have at least an idea of the recent developments taking place in their chosen profession.

This section provides a brief discussion of some selected innovations in education. These innovations are: programmed instruction, team teaching, microteaching, simulations and interaction analysis. The discussion describes the nature and scope of each and identifies their advantages and disadvantages or limitations, if any. An attempt is also made to suggest possibilities for adopting them in our schools taking into consideration the limitations in our resources.

PROGRAMMED INSTRUCTION

During the past two decades, this has been one of the most discussed ideas in education. The interesting thing about this type of instruction is that there is nothing really new in principle; it is based on the old psychological learning principle of conditioning.

The term programmed instruction refers to a procedure of self-instruction, utilising an instructional sequence in which the material to be learned is presented in a series of small steps, arranged in gradual progression from simple to higher levels of complexity. In each step, the learner is required to make an active response which is reinforced by the immediate confirmation of right answers or correction of wrong answers. The idea is for new concepts or skills to be mastered first before other new ones are introduced. In working through the material, the learner is aided by cues, hints and suggestions, as well as by frequent repetition of key terms and concepts.

Types of programmed instructional device

The process by which programmers or planners arrive at the material for use in programmed instruction is called *programming* and the resulting product is called *programmed instructional material* (Alcorn, 1970). This material is presented in two basic forms: the *teaching machine* and the *programmed textbook*.

A teaching machine is a mechanical device designed to present the material to the learner, provide immediate correction of her wrong responses, and test her on her mastery of the content of the material. The description below given by Christine and Christine (1971) is not only amusing but quite clear and informative.

> Teaching machine hardware is available as little boxes which look like adding machines advancing rolls of paper one click at a time. Other teaching machines appear like tiny slide projectors designed to advance rolls of films one click at a time. Some teaching machines consist of round sheets of paper which fit, record-like, on a platform covered by a lid which exposes only a small portion of the paper disc one click at a time . . . the most expensive teaching machine is a typewriter electrically connected to a program director either as simple as the mechanism on a mechanical music box, or as complex as an electronic computer. Whether music box or computer, the function of the hardware is to move the instructional program one click at a

time . . . In programmed learning *what* is being advanced one click at a time is more important than the machinery doing the clicking.

The programmed textbook presents the material in the form of a specially prepared book. To use this device, the learner is required to go through the three stages of a learning experience all at the same time: presentation, response and reinforcement. Obviously, of the two devices, the programmed textbook would probably be less expensive and less complicated to learn to use. Besides, the teaching machine is just a device for presenting programmed materials, and hence it is the excellence of the programme that determines its value. It is important to recognise that it is not the machine but the programme that does the teaching.

Types of programmes

There are several types of programming that are being used, but it is possible to divide most existing programmes into three major groups: linear programmes, adaptive or branching programmes and adjunct programmes.

Linear programming was popularised by Skinner, while the adaptive or branching programming was created by Norman Crowder. Sidney Pressey was not so sure of the value of both linear and adaptive, so he introduced the adjunct programmes to accompany conventional textbooks.

In linear programmes, the subject matter or the material is broken down into small steps called *frames*. Each frame is made so simple that the student does not find the work too difficult. In this type of programme, all students in a class work through an identical fixed sequence of frames. The sequence is said to be linear because there is only one line or path for all students to follow. The student reads a frame, makes a response, compares it with the correct response provided by the author, proceeds to the next frame, and then repeats the process until she completes the programme. Most linear programmes use the *constructed response* or the *fill-in response* type. This means that the student may be required to write down an answer in the form of a direct response to a question, or she may be required to fill in a blank space to complete an answer.

The following example of a linear programme is a portion of the *Student Guide with Programmed Units for Hilgard and Atkinson's Introduction to Psychology*, prepared by Teevan and Jandron (1967).

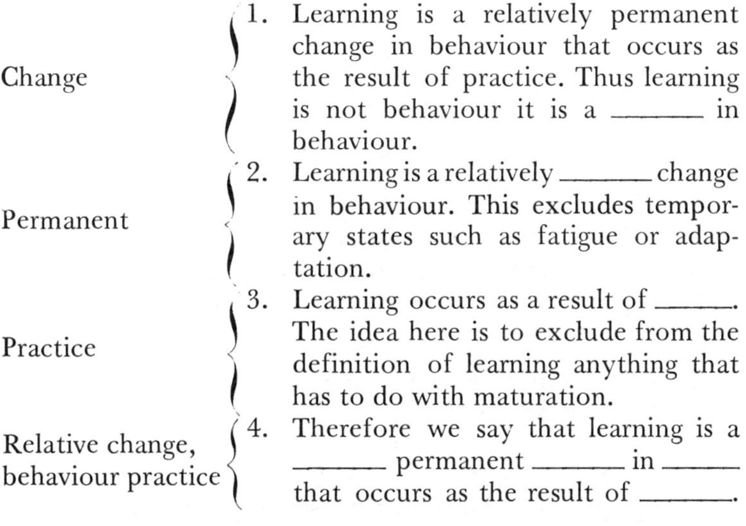

Change	1. Learning is a relatively permanent change in behaviour that occurs as the result of practice. Thus learning is not behaviour it is a ______ in behaviour.
Permanent	2. Learning is a relatively ______ change in behaviour. This excludes temporary states such as fatigue or adaptation.
Practice	3. Learning occurs as a result of ______. The idea here is to exclude from the definition of learning anything that has to do with maturation.
Relative change, behaviour practice	4. Therefore we say that learning is a ______ permanent ______ in ______ that occurs as the result of ______.

In the adaptive programme, the sequence of frames seen by a student is determined by her answer to the question asked. Each student reads a lengthier frame, and chooses an answer from a list of alternatives. If her choice is correct, she goes on to the next main-track frame. If not, she is directed to go to another frame and receives appropriate instructions or explanations depending upon the type of errors revealed by her choice. After this remedial frame, she is sent back to the original frame to try again. Eventually she will be able to work through in her own unique way at her own rate or pace. Sometimes, adaptive programmes are called branching programmes, which means that the student is 'branched' to the next frame depending on her response to the last frame. Hence, adaptive or branching programmes are those in which the selection of a particular alternative causes a programme to adapt to the response, by either sending the learner to the next frame if her answer is correct or sending her to a remedial frame, if her answer is wrong, for further explanation.

Below is an example of an adaptive or branching programme as given by Christine and Christine (1971).

FRAME 1

Any discussion of astronomy involves the use of measurements of great distances. The nautical mile (1 mile = 6000 feet) is a possible measurement unit in discussion of the solar system, but for distances beyond the solar system the unit of measure must be expanded to the:

1. light year (go to frame 3)
2. sidereal day (go to frame 2)

FRAME 2

You came from frame 1.
Your answer, sidereal day, is incorrect.

The unit of measure for distances beyond the solar system is the *light year*. Sidereal day is a measure of time.

Now return to frame 1.

FRAME 3

You came from frame 1.
Your answer, light year, is correct.

The light year is used for measuring distances so great as to be incomprehensible by any normal experience. The distance in miles, of one light year is calculated by multiplying the speed of light (186,000 miles per second), times the number of seconds in a minute (60), times the number of minutes in an hour (60), times the number of hours in a day (24), times the average number of days in a year (365). The multiplication of the five factors yields a distance of 5,865,696,000,000 miles which is the light year equivalent in miles.

For discussions such as this it is convenient to round the figure and say that a light year is equal to six trillion miles. It is even more convenient to use 'exponent shorthand' and express the 6,000,000,000,000 figure as:

1. 6×10^{12} (go to frame 5)
2. 6×10^{13} (go to frame 4)

In the adjunct programme, the student first reads a conventional textbook chapter, then proceeds to answer the set of questions based on the content. She then goes back to the text and re-studies those parts suggested by the questions she missed.

Although there have been several attempts to establish the superiority of each type, most of the empirical studies done failed to show any consistent advantage of one over the other. Most of the recent programmes are combinations of the three types. They are basically linear with multiple choice questions and lengthy passages, incorporated whenever appropriate.

Advantages of programmed instruction

Proponents of programmed instruction, especially the earlier ones, claimed the following advantages of programmed learning.

1. It allows students to progress at their own pace. Everyone in class works through the same programme in his own unique way with equal success. Of course the brighter students will finish first but the duller ones will surely complete the programme in exactly the same way, even if it takes them longer to do it.
2. It enables students to participate actively at all times, which encourages them to assume increased responsibility for their own learning.
3. The constant reinforcement from the machines or programmed textbooks provides high incentives. It gives students satisfaction to be able to know immediately how they are progressing. This knowledge of results then serves as a motivating force for them to continue pushing forward until they reach the end.
4. More content is covered in a given period of time and is covered better than by conventional methods of teaching.
5. It causes no scheduling problems. Programmed instructional materials are completely at the service of the teacher. He controls their use in the classroom; they do not control him.
6. Expensive machines are not necessary. Improvised devices, and programmed textbooks are equally satisfactory.

7. In effect, instruction is individualised. It is equivalent to having individual tutors for each student.
8. It is believed that it is highly effective in teaching factual content and in language teaching.

Disadvantages of programmed instruction

Not all believed in the promises offered by programmed instruction especially because many of the claimed advantages were not backed up by empirical evidence. In addition, although some of the advantages are worthwhile, they may not be unique to programmed learning. A skilled and dedicated teacher may be able to accomplish whatever teaching machines can, by using various instructional aids, providing opportunities for each of his students to proceed at his own pace where appropriate, and by carefully organising learning experiences such that the subject matter gradually unfolds to them. Some of the major criticisms of programmed instruction are summarised below.

1. There are usually no dramatic highlights in typical programmed learning. The student just keeps on going through virtually the same process, programme after programme. Programmed instruction therefore may generate boredom among the students, especially if the programmes are long (Dale, 1954).
2. Programmed instruction is limited only to materials where there are right answers. It cannot ask questions that call for original but equally correct answers, nor questions that require elaborate answers (Morse and Wingo, 1962).
3. Because of the cost of teaching machines, certain educators consider them to be impractical. This is probably more true in Nigeria and other developing nations where schools do not get enough funds to procure needed instructional devices let alone teaching machines (Hough and Revsin, 1963).
4. Struggling companies mass-produced unreliable teaching machines and programmed texts which were not tested and validated (Thiagarajan, 1977).

Trends in programmed instruction

Today educators in the Western world have come to the consensus that programmed instruction is not after all the cure-all of the ills of education. Teaching machines and programmed materials are here to stay, but they are better regarded as another useful device that a good teacher can use to enrich students' learning experiences. They will never replace the teacher, but they will surely complement and supplement his tasks.

The present trend in programmed instruction is towards more programmes being used in industrial training as well as in teaching handicapped individuals. In academic circles, programmed instructional materials are becoming a major feature of the new concept of individualised instruction. In classrooms, more and more programmed materials are being used in informal situations as part of the more traditional or conventional teaching procedures.

Although programmed instruction as such was regarded as a failure some years after its inception, many of the newer innovations that followed were either outgrowths or derivations of programmed learning. In short, most of the effective elements were not totally ignored: they were quickly absorbed into the main streams of educational practice (Thiagarajan, 1977). For example, the concept of behavioural objectives – which is becoming a constant subject for educational research – was an offshoot of Mager's book *Preparing Objectives for Programmed Instruction*. The new idea of Educational Technology which is gradually replacing the old Audio-Visual Education is another derivative of the programmed instruction movement.

SIMULATIONS

One of the innovative practices which are now being considered by some universities and teacher training colleges in Nigeria is simulation. To simulate means to imitate. However, broadly speaking, it means much more. Simulations are models of real things and situations. They are attempts to replicate reality in a highly modified fashion such that it becomes more accessible and better understood. This means that unimportant, impractical and expensive parts are omitted or modified while essential aspects are emphasised. Thus, students who are learning under simulated situations have more control over the learning process. Simulations have been found effective in providing on the spot training to students in various fields. For example, machines simulating the cockpits of big aeroplanes are used to train pilots before they are allowed to fly a real plane. City and highway traffic are simulated so that student drivers can be exposed to as many problematic situations as possible, instead of allowing them to drive on the roads looking for real problems to tackle. Difficult situations are simulated to train soldiers in the skills necessary for survival in time of war. In this section, simulation will be discussed as a specific approach to the training of would-be teachers.

Simulations in teacher training

In teacher training, simulations have been found valuable in cases where the teaching practice exercise presents problems such as difficulty in scheduling and excessive cost. It has also been found useful in providing student teachers with a more relaxed setting to practise certain skills without the pressures of the real classroom.

In the United States, for instance, the University of Tennessee used simulation exercises to prepare student teachers for two weeks before they are sent out to their respective co-operating schools. To provide students with opportunities to deal with problematic situations, a series of simulation exercises which made use of films, filmstrips and cumulative records of students was developed and used. Each student teacher assumed the role of a beginning fifth-grade teacher in Longacre School. To give them an introduction to the town and the school system, a filmstrip with accompanying narration by the superintendent of schools was shown. This was followed by a more detailed orientation to the community, the school, the faculty and the educational programme by the principal. Each prospective teacher was given all the materials that a new teacher would normally be given, such as a faculty handbook, curriculum handbook, an audio-visual catalogue and the cumulative records of thirty-one pupils. Equipped with the necessary information and materials, the student teachers were presented with thirty problems selected as significant to teaching from the Perceived Problems Inventory. Some problems were presented in films, others as written incidents. In each incident the trainee teacher is frequently asked what he would do if faced with the same situation.

One example of the problems presented is a film concerning facing a class for the first time. The scene is a class reading silently. All of a sudden a boy yawns loudly, stands up to sharpen his pencil making a great display of it. As he goes back to his seat, he slams shut another boy's book, who shouts, 'Cut it out'. The voice of the teacher on the film is heard asking the offender to get back to his work. Then the boy starts to hum a tune and the teacher tells him to stop and asks him if he has finished his work. The film ends at this point. After viewing the film, student teachers are required to: (a) define the problem, (b) identify contributing factors, (c) locate information to be found in the materials which have been handed out to them, (d) give some alternative actions which the teacher might have taken, (e) suggest more desirable action the teacher should have taken, and (f) give some implementing decisions (Cruickshank, 1966).

Students who participated in this simulation exercise reported that they were able to cope with teaching problems more satisfactorily and preferred to have the simulated experience before they actually went out to the field. It was believed that the series of simulation exercises allowed the student teachers to encounter problematic situations in a more relaxed manner than would have been the case in the real classroom setting. It was also reckoned that these simulations helped students develop their ability to identify problems, locate information and apply them to a given situation, and to think of alternative courses of action to solve problems.

Another simple example of simulation as a device for training future teachers is microteaching which is discussed fully later in this chapter.

Advantages of simulation

When properly planned and carefully executed, simulations have the following advantages:

1. They provide valuable first-hand experience or training in skills and procedures that are not easily acquired from reading or attending lectures.
2. They simplify the teaching process, thus cutting the cost when real things and situations are used.
3. They minimise the risks that accompany practice with real things and in real situations. This is especially relevant to teaching practice where mistakes may have lasting damaging effects on the pupils as well as on the student teacher's self esteem.
4. Simulations permit the creation of specific learning situations as and when desired.
5. The learner has greater control over the learning process. He can make decisions and become aware of the consequences without actually suffering the consequences had the decisions been made in reality.
6. Consequences can also be simulated such that the learner may be able to rectify his mistakes or even try the whole experience again.

MICROTEACHING

Nature and scope

Like simulation techniques, microteaching is a fairly recent innovation in training future teachers. It is a process which aims primarily to teach students specific teaching skills or teaching behaviours by requiring them to practise on a small group of students or their peers. The philosophy behind this technique probably lies in the assumption that teaching consists of specific skills which can be learned individually. Thus, microteaching can be used to teach techniques such as, asking different kinds and levels of questions, using specific instructional material, encouraging participation, conducting reviews, conducting drills, responding to silence or non-verbal signs, initiating a unit and the like. This does not imply, however, that complete fragmentation in the study of teaching is possible but that some is desirable. After all the real test for good teaching comes when you actually meet your own class in a real classroom.

A typical microteaching process follows the following sequence:

1. A specific teaching skill or behaviour is identified.
2. The student teacher plans a short lesson (called the microlesson) of about five to twenty minutes which aims to achieve a very specific objective.
3. The student teacher teaches the lesson to about five pupils, if available, and if not to his peers. During this time his performance is observed and recorded by his supervisor and his fellow student teachers. Sometimes audiotape is used but videotape if available is more advantageous.
4. The microlesson is immediately reviewed and analysed. If tapes were made, they are viewed by the student teacher, the supervisor and others involved. Major difficulties and weaknesses are pointed out and discussed and suggestions for change are made.
5. Suggestions to improve technique are noted by the student teacher with a view to re-teaching the lesson.
6. Student teacher re-teaches the lesson attempting to improve his performance in the light of the changes previously suggested. Sometimes re-teaching may not be necessary.

Although microteaching is now rapidly finding its way to various teacher training institutions, especially in the more developed countries, there are still those who question the desirability or the 'ethics' of getting pupils to 'practise on', since their learning is not really the major concern of the microlesson. They argue that microteaching is a teacher centred not a child centred technique, hence all attention is focused on the teacher's teaching behaviour. Whether the children learn or not is not the most crucial point.

However, since the pupils involved in microteaching are usually volunteers or peers and not captive guinea-pigs presented to the student teacher during the usual teaching practice exercise, the question of ethics does not really arise.

Besides, microteaching was really intended to precede and enhance the field teaching exercise not to replace them.

Another valid point supporting microteaching techniques is that they are always done in the presence of a supervisor and, therefore, the materials and the method used are not without the supervisor's sanction. Furthermore, the ultimate goal of microteaching is to prepare our future teachers better, which is after all the real concern of teacher education.

Advantages of microteaching

As a necessary part of the training of teachers, microteaching has so many advantages that all other criticisms may be considered negligible. For instance, research has revealed that the apprehensions usually felt by student teachers concerning their first classroom teaching experience are drastically reduced. There is, therefore, the assurance of minimum risk for both student teacher and pupils. The chances of teacher embarrassment due to some possible mistakes or misjudgements, with the resultant student mistrust and misbehaviour, are greatly minimised. Bruce Shore (1976) stated this advantage succinctly when he said:

> By providing simplified teaching settings, microteaching can provide a low-threat environment for experimenting with new ideas. It can allow for some discovery learning in teacher preparation . . . a good example of the idea of learning how to learn, of giving students at all levels techniques with which they can learn on their own.

As a summary, the following are other additional advantages of microteaching as found by Allen and Ryan (1969):

1. Even though the complexities of real teaching are drastically reduced, it is nevertheless real teaching.
2. It allows student teachers to focus practice on certain teaching skills or the accomplishment of certain tasks.
3. It provides opportunities for numerous practice, immediate correction of mistakes, and a wide range of experiences.
4. It has the advantage of being able to offer feedback

immediately after the microlesson. The student will then have several sources of feedback to help him gain more insight into his teaching behaviour.

TEAM TEACHING

One of the most recent and most discussed innovations in the area of curriculum organisation is *team teaching*. Although the principles involved are not exactly new, the identification and recognition of team teaching as a distinct pattern or approach of organisation is quite recent. A review of the various descriptions of team teaching reveals that the approach is a departure from the more traditional 'one-teacher/one-class' or 'one-teacher per subject' set-up commonly practised in most schools in Nigeria. The major purpose of team teaching is to improve the quality of instruction by utilising the school staff as efficiently and economically as possible.

Broadly speaking, team teaching is an approach in which two or more teachers share the responsibility of teaching a large group of students through co-operative planning, putting the plan into effect and evaluating its effectiveness. It is based on the idea that each teacher has his own area of specialisation, preference, or strength with reference to subject-matter content, teaching ability or techniques, which can be best utilised for a larger group of students rather than for one class of only thirty-five to forty-five.

A review of the different variations of team teaching as practised in the USA and Europe reveals the following common features:

1. The team consists of two or more teachers.
2. Large groups of 150 students or more are taught at the same time. Sometimes several sections, streams or arms at a particular class level are combined into one big group.
3. The team leader or chairman is usually the most qualified or most experienced member of the team. Sometimes, a team has no leader, but each member assumes leadership depending upon his involvement in the large group instruction.
4. Various instructional materials and devices are exten-

sively used, especially those which are suitable for large group presentations.

5. Other non-professional personnel to do clerical as well as other routine jobs such as checking attendance, collecting and distributing materials, marking examination scripts and the like are hired as members of a team. Most often student teachers are utilised for this purpose.

General patterns of team teaching

There are several approaches to organising team teaching. Examples of these will not be treated in this book, primarily because most of them may not easily find application in Nigerian schools. For further reading on variations in team teaching the attention of the reader is drawn to the list of books on the topic included at the end of this chapter.

For our own purposes, however, four general approaches to team teaching organisation are briefly described below.

1. A number of teachers teaching the same subject, say Mathematics or Science, team up to teach a large group. Often several sections or streams of the same class level are combined and all teachers teaching them in a particular subject will form the teaching team. This is found to be particularly advantageous in science where there are specialised areas and very few teachers can claim to be expert in all of them. In this pattern, each teacher is allowed to develop further, and become an expert on certain units or topics in the subject.

2. The same team as above can be organised, but this time teacher specialisation is not on content but on specific techniques or methods. Thus, a member who is regarded as skilful in handling large audiences may be given the task of giving large group presentations, while one who is effective in small group inter-action may be given the responsibility to organise and conduct group discussions or recitations. In this pattern, classes are organised to suit the techniques or methods employed.

3. Another team of teachers may be assigned to handle one class each separately for the teaching of the same subject. Whenever the need arises, these different groups are combined and given instruction by the team. Teacher specialisation may either be on subject matter content or technique. This pattern

then has the classroom as the basic unit, but periodically several streams are combined for special instructions.

4. Another pattern uses the large group as the basis of organisation. A team of teachers is put in charge of the whole large class. From time to time, it is subdivided into smaller groups for special lessons or techniques.

When organising team teaching, it is important to bear in mind that it is more than the pattern of organisation that guarantees success. As Dean and Witherspoon (1962) said:

> The heart of the concept of team teaching lies not in details of structure and organisation but more on the essential spirit of co-operative planning, constant collaboration, close unity, unrestrained communication, and sincere sharing.

Advantages of team teaching

Much has been written about team teaching and its values in improving teaching and learning. Below are some of the most important advantages of team teaching claimed by its advocates:

1. Team teaching provides an opportunity for teachers to work on a common goal through close association and co-operative planning.
2. The expertise or specialised skills of teachers can be used to benefit more students. Thus students are exposed to good teaching at all times.
3. Members of the team learn from each other. They have the chance to observe experts or specialists perform at their best, and hence they are encouraged to do better work.
4. When non-professionals are employed to assist the team, the regular teachers are given more time to plan, prepare and evaluate instruction as well as engage in other professional tasks such as curriculum evaluation, revision and the like.
5. Teachers are allowed to develop further or master their own specialisation whether content or technique. Each can then utilise his or her strengths to advantage and avoid embarrassment in weaknesses.

6. Because instruction is the product of the co-operative efforts of a team of teachers (experts) working together on a common task towards a common goal, the quality of instruction is greatly improved.
7. It allows for economical and efficient use of school staff. A team of three instead of six, for example, could take charge of a group of, say, two hundred and fifty students, so that the budget for hiring three more regular teachers could be used to employ non-professional aides.
8. Students benefit from contact with different teachers of different points of view and different personalities.

Team teaching in schools

Despite the many advantages of team teaching, its proper organisation and its subsequent success may be difficult to achieve. Four major factors may be identified as possible sources of difficulties in adopting team teaching in our schools.

1. The teacher factor

At present, most teachers have no real working knowledge of the concept. Therefore any attempt to sell the idea to them could be a very taxing job. Even if they accept the idea, they have not been trained to engage in co-operative planning, instruction and evaluation. In addition, they lack training in the use of methods and techniques for large group instruction as well as in group dynamics.

One of the more serious problems that may hinder successful operation of team teaching is the problem of staff relationships. Any group is bound to have members of varying personalities. It is therefore likely that personality clashes may arise and, when they arise, related tasks are difficult to carry out to the satisfaction of all members. As a result of personality differences, several possible situations may occur which could affect the effective functioning of the team. They include the following:

(a) Some members may want to dominate the team making others feel left out or 'bossed around'.

(b) An assigned or chosen team leader may become power conscious and think that his colleagues are his 'men' to do jobs for him.
(c) Other members may not be contented to be members only.
(d) If no remuneration is attached to leadership roles, very few teachers would willingly accept leadership responsibilities.
(e) A hard working member may be regarded as a threat because he embarrasses the lazy and nonchalant ones.
(f) Some teachers may not like to be observed by their peers while teaching for fear of being criticised behind their backs.

2. The student factor

Team teaching usually involves relatively larger groups. Thus relationships among students tend to become too distant. This impersonality of big groups may make some students feel lost and insecure. Students often need to feel they belong and, therefore, they may be confused with the constant changing of rooms and teachers. Furthermore, some students may need a consistent person to relate to and identify with in order to feel confident.

3. The time factor

Under the present system, it is often difficult to find a common convenient free time for team members to meet in order to plan and evaluate their work. Besides, very few teachers are prepared to stay even one minute later than the regular school closing time, their reason being that they have families needing their attention, or that they have other important commitments. Furthermore, scheduling classes for purposes of team teaching may not be easy, especially if it involves large numbers of students with differing timetables.

4. The financial factor

Team teaching would mean additional big rooms and special aids suitable for large group instruction such as public address systems and large wall charts. It also means hiring a number of non-professional aides to assist the various teams. All these require additional money which, under the present circumstances many schools may not have.

Though it may seem difficult to introduce team teaching in our schools, it does not necessarily mean that we should abandon the idea altogether. With careful planning and sincere co-operative efforts on the part of the teachers it may well provide some solutions to problems existing in our schools at present, especially that of lack of experts in fields like the sciences and Mathematics.

INTERACTION ANALYSIS

There is now a growing interest among educators to analyse what is actually going on in our classrooms. Approaches to methods of observing and recording on-going events during a lesson have been developed and are now being used by many schools in the West. In Nigeria, these approaches are slowly being considered and finding applications in the universities and some teacher training colleges for the purpose of improving classroom instruction, as well as helping future teachers acquire the necessary professional skills for effective beginning teaching.

Interaction analysis is one approach to the study of classroom events. It refers to one of the numerous methods developed to 'describe in a systematic way, the frequency and type of spontaneous interactions that occur between teachers and students' (Cohen and Manion, 1977). One such method, the Flanders System (Flanders, 1970), has gained wide acceptance and has had wide applications in teacher education. This system uses a ten-section category to describe the on-going activities in the classroom. The Flanders Interaction Analysis Categorization System is reproduced in figure 12.1.

Briefly, the Flanders system involves the following procedure:

(1) *Preparation.* Before the actual observation and recording session, the student (observer) is trained to observe and record accurately what is going on in the classroom using the ten categories. His training is done using videotapes as well as actual classroom situations and his training continues

Figure 12.1 *The Flanders system of categories for interaction analysis*

Teacher talk	*Indirect influence*	1.*	ACCEPTS FEELING: accepts and clarifies the feeling tone of the students in a non-threatening manner. Feelings may be positive or negative. Predicting or recalling feelings are included.
		2.*	PRAISES OR ENCOURAGES: praises or encourages student action or behaviour. Jokes that release tension, not at the expense of another individual, nodding head or saying, 'um hm?' or 'go on' are included.
		3.*	ACCEPTS OR USES IDEAS OF STUDENT: clarifying, building, or developing ideas suggested by a student. As a teacher brings more of his ideas into play, shift to category five.
		4.*	ASKS QUESTIONS: asking a question about content or procedure with the student that a student answers.
	Direct influence	5.*	LECTURING: giving facts or opinions about content or procedure; expressing his own ideas, asking rhetorical questions.
		6.*	GIVING DIRECTIONS: directions, commands, or orders to which a student is expected to comply.
		7.*	CRITICIZING OR JUSTIFYING AUTHORITY: statements intended to change student behaviour from non-acceptable to acceptable pattern; bawling someone out; stating why the teacher is doing what he is doing; extreme self-reference.
Student talk		8.*	STUDENT TALK-RESPONSE: a student makes a predictable response to teacher. Teacher initiates the contact or solicits student statement and sets limits to what the student says.
		9.*	STUDENT TALK-INITIATION: talk by students which they initiate. Unpredictable statements in response to teacher. Shift from 8 to 9 as student introduces own ideas.
		10.*	SILENCE OR CONFUSION: pauses, short periods of silence and periods of confusion in which communication cannot be understood by the observer.

* There is *no* scale implied by these numbers. Each number is classificatory; it designates a particular kind of communication event. To write these numbers down during observation is to enumerate, not to judge a position on a scale.

Source: Amidon, E. J. and Flanders, N. A. (1963) *The Role of the Teacher in the Classroom*, P. S. Amidon, Minneapolis, Ma.

until he reaches an acceptable level of reliability by comparison with recordings made by other observers.

(2) *Actual observation and recording.* After several practice sessions the observer should be able to record accurately the on-going classroom activities by jotting down the numbers corresponding to the different categories as they occur without necessarily referring to the explanatory notes. The category numbers representing classroom activities are recorded every three seconds for about twenty to twenty-five minutes. Christine and Christine (1971) have given a detailed description of how to use Flanders Interaction Analysis Categorization System.

(3) *Analysis of coded materials.* After recording the classroom events, coded materials are analysed and discussed with the view of improving classroom interaction.

Advantages of interaction analysis

Interaction analysis has several advantages. First, this system is widely used, and is a reliable technique which is quick and easy to learn. Second, it enables the observer to describe objectively and in detail the sequence of events in the classroom. Thus, teachers are able to discuss the act of teaching in more specific terms. Third, interaction analysis enables the prospective teacher to gain insight into his weaknesses and strengths in relation to his tasks. Fourth, it provides a means of examining objectively how closely the intended instructional methods or techniques match what is really going on in the classroom.

EXERCISES

1. Develop a rationale for the adaptation of microteaching in the teacher training colleges in Nigeria.
2. What are the factors affecting the successful operation of team teaching in the primary schools and secondary schools in Nigeria? Explain each briefly.
3. How can simulation be used in classroom teaching?
4. What are the advantages of programmed learning? What are its limitations?

ESSENTIAL READING

Flanders, N. A. (1970) *Analysing Teacher Behaviour, Reading,* Addison-Wesley.

Morse, W. C. and Wingo, M. G. (1962) *Psychology and Teaching* (2nd ed.), Scott, Foresman, Chicago.

SUPPLEMENTARY READING

Alcorn, Marvin D. (1970) *Better Teaching in Secondary Schools*, Holt, Rinehart & Winston, New York.

Allen, D. and Ryan, K. (1969) *Microteaching: Readings*, Addison-Wesley, Reading, Mass.

Brown, G. A. (1975) *Microteaching*, Methuen, London.

Christine, C. T. and Christine, D. V. (1971) *Practical Guide to Curriculum and Instruction*, Parker, New York.

Cohen, L. and Manion, L. (1977) *A Guide to Teaching Practice*, Methuen, London.

Cruickshank, D. R. (1966) Simulations: new direction in teacher education, *Phi Delta Kappan*, 48: 23–24.

Dale, Edgar (1954) *Audio-Visual Methods in Teaching*, Holt, Rinehart & Winston, New York.

Dean, S. E. and Witherspoon, C. F. (1962) Team teaching in the elementary school, *Education Briefs*, no. 38, Washington, D.C., US Office of Education.

De Cecco, J. P. (1974) *The Psychology of Learning and Instruction*, (2nd ed.), Prentice Hall, Englewoods Cliffs, N.J.

Gregory, T. B. (1972) *Encounters with Teaching: A Microteaching Manual*, Prentice Hall, Englewood Cliffs, N.J.

Haddan, E. E. (1970) *Evolving Education*, Macmillan, New York.

Hough, J. B. and Revsin, B. (1963) Programmed instruction at the college level: a study of several factors influencing learning, *Phi Delta Kappan*, 44: 290.

Mager, R. F. (1962) *Preparing Objectives for Programmed Instruction*, Fearon, San Francisco, Calif.

O'Keefe, R. A. (1967) Effective programming for the classroom, in *Montessori for the Disadvantaged*, (ed. R. C. Oren), Putnam, New York.

Shore, B. M. (1976) Microteaching, in *Handbook in Contemporary Education* (ed. Steven E. Goodman), Bowker, New York.

Teevan, R. C. and Landron, E. L. (1967) *Student Guide with Programmed Units for Hilgard and Atkinson's Introduction to Psychology*, (4th ed.), Harcourt, Brace & World, New York.

Thiagarajan, S. (1976) Programmed Instruction, in *Handbook in Contemporary Education*, (ed. Steven E. Goodman), Bowker, New York.